THE CODA ALLIANCE

Michael Brady

A DELL BOOK

Published by
Dell Publishing Co., Inc.
1 Dag Hammarskjold Plaza
New York, New York 10017

Dell ® TM 681510, Dell Publishing Co., Inc.

ISBN: 0-440-11415-2

Printed in the United States of America
First printing—July 1981

A MYSTERIOUS OATH . . .
A TERRIBLE PURPOSE . . .

On a signal each of the six stepped forward and was handed two objects—the old SS dagger with the words "Blood and Honor" engraved on the hilt, and a 9 mm automatic. Last in line came Karl Bauer. Kraske handed him the dagger. "Unsheath it," he commanded.

Bauer obeyed.

"Hold it by the blade in your right hand, hilt upwards, and repeat after me, 'I, Karl Bauer, pledge my blood and my life to the cause of Group 666.' "

Bauer repeated the oath of allegiance.

"Kiss the blade," Kraske ordered.

Bauer pressed the cold steel to his lips.

"Now listen to me," Kraske said. "The oath will not be consummated until you have killed with the dagger in the name of the Fatherland."

THE CODA ALLIANCE

PREFACE

Washington, D.C.

The warm sun of a June afternoon shone down on the packed crowds in the gardens of the White House.

Dignitaries from all over the world had gathered to watch the ceremonial presentation of the Presidential Medal for Freedom—the highest award that could be given to a civilian for services to the country, the nation's security, and the cause of freedom—to an unknown man David Maxwell.

As the Marine Corps Band played while waiting for the President's arrival, all eyes were fixed on this man, standing apart in front of the presentation rostrum, a beautiful woman by his side.

David Maxwell stood tall and erect, his short, blond hair blowing lightly in the summer breeze. But those close enough saw the drawn and haggard lines that marked his face, and they wondered what nightmare of suffering could so affect a man.

The band stopped as the President arrived and mounted the rostrum. For several minutes the President stood in silence, looking at the man in front of him. And in that silence the people gathered for the ceremony detected a special private tribute being paid by the head of a great nation to the unknown man.

The President began his address. Although he talked of great courage and self-sacrifice for country and for freedom, he spoke quietly and with care, avoiding the rhetoric and clichés common to such occasions—another tribute to the unknown man.

But David Maxwell was not listening to the carefully chosen words of his President. His mind was in torment, tortured by the recollection of horrendous events: the loss of his loved ones; insane murder and treachery: the terror of a world on the brink of nuclear war.

The knowledge that his part in these events had led him to commit acts of indescribable brutality. And in so doing to betray those values he believed in most passionately—the sanctity of life; the dignity of man.

Could a man who had committed such acts be honored?

Did the ends *ever* justify the means?

He looked down at his hands and shuddered. Perspiration formed on his brow as he recalled the shattered flesh, the agonized screams, and the breaking bones. Could such hands ever be fit to touch another human being?

As if reading his thoughts, the woman beside him moved her hand to cover his and squeezed it gently. She smiled up at him, her eyes filled with compassion. She understood.

The President finished his address, leaving his audience moved by the sincerity and depth of feeling he had expressed. But they were curiously silent for a moment, aware of the fact that he had framed his praise only in generalities. No specifics.

The man named David Maxwell and the reason for honoring him were still unknown.

And they did *not* understand.

David Maxwell walked forward to receive the Presidential Medal of Freedom. Standing to one side of the President's rostrum, he saw, was the uniformed figure of the Joint Chief of Staff, and once again he was reminded of the tragedy of General Wade Horton. . . .

PROLOGUE

Naples, Italy

In the plush Vesuvietta nightclub a swarthy tenor cupped the microphone with his hands and began to sing a melodious Neapolitan ballad. The kind of poignant song that brings virgins to the beds of ardent young lovers and tears to the eyes of old men.

On the dance floor U.S. Army Brigadier John Sangford, a staff officer at NATO's southern headquarters in Naples, put his arms around his wife Alice and pulled her close. They danced with the easy familiarity of a happily married couple.

"I'm worried about leaving Jean alone with the general," the brigadier's wife said and leaned back from her husband's embrace to glance anxiously toward the table where General Wade Horton sat with Jean Caulfield.

"Don't be silly, Alice. Jean can take care of herself. What do you think's going to happen? The general's going to rape her under the table?"

"That's not what I mean, and you know it." Alice frowned up at her husband.

"I've no idea what you mean," the brigadier answered with honest good humor.

Alice was silent. The truth was that she didn't

know exactly what she meant. When her husband had told her General Horton's wife had died after a long illness, she had agreed it would be a kindly act to have him stay with them for a few days in Naples. The warm Italian sun would be a welcome break from the somber cold of Brunssum in Holland where the general was stationed.

Now she wasn't so sure about their decision to invite him.

"There's something strange about the general," she said echoing her thoughts and looking up at her husband. "I can't put my finger on it, but it's there just the same."

Brigadier Sangford groaned. His wife was being her usual, enchantingly vague, intuitive self. He loved her for it, but there were times when it was downright impossible to tune in to her wavelength. "Strange?" he queried.

"Yes. Tell me what you actually know about him? As a person, I mean."

The brigadier hesitated. How could he explain someone like General Wade Horton to a woman—to anyone! The youngest man to make four star general since World War II and presently deputy commander of NATO forces in Central Europe. A man for whom the army was more than a career: it was his religion. He was a solitary man. Apart from formal military occasions he never socialized. No one really got to know him. But they did respect him. The general was a one hundred percent professional soldier and a brilliant strategist.

"We were friends at West Point. I served under him in Korea and Vietnam, and then, as you know, I was on his staff in Holland before we came to Naples. I guess I know him as well as any man. He's a fine soldier, and I respect him."

Alice snorted. "Just like a man. You respect him, but really you don't know a thing about him. What about his family . . . children?"

Again the brigadier hesitated. The general *had* a son. But "had" was the operative word. There had been a time when his son was the only personal subject the general would talk about. He had been inordinately proud of him, and with good reason. At one time it looked as if the boy was going to repeat the general's own meteoric rise in the army. And then about two years ago he had vanished. Vanished. There was no other word for it. The general had ceased to talk about his son, completely. And the brigadier had not met anyone who even knew if the boy was still in the army. He had disappeared from sight . . . and it seemed, from the general's life.

But this was one subject the brigadier was not going to discuss with his wife. The general would be with them for another six days. Alice wouldn't be able to resist probing him about his son (if she knew he had one).

"He has no children," the brigadier lied.

Alice read the lie. "John," she looked at him reproachfully.

"Alice!" The brigadier stopped dancing and held his wife at arm's length. "There's a tenor up there singing his heart out about love. The way only an Italian can. Just about every woman around has gone weak at the knees, while we argue about a goddam general!"

A soft smile spread over Alice's face as she moved inside her husband's outstretched arms, and, draping her own arms around his neck, she pressed her body against his. "Yes, silly isn't it," she said. "And I do so love to feel weak at the knees."

While the brigadier and his wife danced in silence, Jean Caulfield was staring at General Horton, her face flushed with anger. Her husband was away on exercises with the Sixth Fleet. She had welcomed Alice's invitation to be the general's escort. It would make a welcome break. Now she regretted her decision.

The instant they had met she had decided she didn't like the general, with his short-cropped gray hair, unblinking, hard brown eyes, and the deep-etched lines down each cheek following the lines of his jaw.

A hard nut of a man. Impenetrable.

But it was his crushing, formal politeness which had confirmed her dislike. She had tried to get through to him on every possible level—personal talk, little girl talk, sexy woman talk—but her every attempt to be sociable had been met by a few well-chosen words, courteous in their meaning but deadening in their effect.

Like a period to end her sentences; to foreclose on her, to shut her out.

Jean Caulfield had very quickly come to the conclusion that the general didn't give a damn about her, her conversation—or anything else going on around him.

Until—and this was why she was now staring at him with increasing anger—until the woman with the long black hair had come in and sat a couple of tables away.

The bastard! Jean Caulfield cursed to herself. He spends all evening ignoring me, and now he's acting as though I don't exist at all!

With relief she saw the brigadier and his wife returning from the dance floor. The general addressed the brigadier before he could sit down. "Could I have a word with you in private, John?"

"Of course, Wade. I'm sure the ladies will excuse us for a moment," the brigadier said and joined the general who had moved a few feet away from the table.

"You see that woman, two tables behind me. Black hair, sitting with the young fellow in the light check suit?"

The brigadier stepped to one side and looked past the general. "The one with the low-cut gown, bare shoulders?"

The general nodded. "Do you happen to know who she is?"

"Sure I do but—"

"I'd like to meet her." It was an order.

The brigadier frowned, then shifted on his feet, uncomfortable. "I don't think she's exactly the kind of woman you'd like to be seen with."

"Why not?" the general's eyes narrowed.

"She has something of a record around here, if you know what I mean. Name's Frau Gensert. Elizabeth Gensert."

Something flickered in the general's eyes. "German?" The question came out like an accusation.

"Yeah. Apparently she was married to some wealthy

industrialist. The guy died and left her with nothing but money and time to indulge her considerable sexual appetite. The guy she is with now is a navy lieutenant. He should know better. . . . No, sir, I don't think Frau Gensert is someone you'd want to be seen with at all."

"Let me worry about that, John. Introduce us."

The brigadier looked uneasily toward his wife who was watching with open curiosity. "Look, Wade . . . If you want, I can fix you up with something a whole lot more discreet than–"

"Forget it. I want to meet her."

The brigadier saw the look in the general's eyes and with another quick glance at his wife, led the way to the nearby table. "Frau Gensert . . . Lieutenant . . . General Horton. The general is spending a few days down here with my wife and me."

Frau Gensert raised her wide, dark blue eyes and looked at the general. For an instant the corners of her mouth twitched, then she switched on a brilliant smile. "A pleasure to meet you, general."

The lieutenant was on his feet, his face flushed with anger and embarrassment. Jesus! A four star general pulling rank over an easy lay like Frau Gensert!

"Would you join us at our table?" the brigadier said trying to make the best of the situation.

"I think Frau Gensert would like to dance," the general said evenly.

"Why, of course, general, I'd love to." She rose to take the general's outstretched arm.

General Wade Horton danced holding Elizabeth Gensert a good six inches from him. He scrutinized her face, not speaking for several minutes. He guessed she was in her late thirties. *That fitted.* Her black hair didn't. But there was a certain freshness to the tone of her skin that went with blond hair. *Blond hair would fit.* But it had all happened fourteen years ago. It was hard to tell.

"Why the inspection, General?" Frau Gensert smiled at him pleasantly.

"Because you're a very beautiful woman."

"That's flattering."

"Not in the least. It's the truth, Frau Gensert."

"You're very direct, General."

"You know Naples well, Frau Gensert?"

"I should. I've been here two years."

Her voice fitted.

"Where exactly?"

"That's a very leading question," she smiled archly.

"It's not exactly a military secret."

Frau Gensert threw back her head and laughed. A soft, husky laugh from the back of her throat.

The laugh fitted.

"And how long have *you* been in Naples, General?"

"About twelve hours."

"And already you've heard the gossip about me."

"Is it true?"

"Most of it . . . Some exaggeration. You know how people are."

The general smiled. "I like that," he said. "At least you're honest about it."

"Then suppose you be honest with me. You broke every rule in the book busting in on me and the lieutenant the way you did. What do you want?"

"You."

"That's *honest.*"

"I'll spell it out. I'm here for a week. I don't know anybody except the brigadier and his wife. They're both charming but . . ."

"But you'd like a little excitement."

"A lot of excitement. I'll pick you up at ten tomorrow morning, and we'll take it from there. Do we have a deal?"

Elizabeth Gensert laughed the same husky laugh. "How can I refuse? Your directness is more seductive than your flattery. Ten o'clock tomorrow. The Villa Consetti, on the Via di Pasilippo . . . Now get me back to that lieutenant before he walks out on me. I don't like to sleep alone."

Had Jean Caulfield overheard this conversation, she would not have believed it. But the general was a good actor. He'd been acting for the last two years of his life. Acting as though he wanted to be alive when all he wanted was to kill himself. But that was the one thing he could not do. In the simple philosophy of the general, suicide was the coward's way out. And to take his own life would be to disgrace the army. The army he loved; the way he loved his father until . . .

The general returned to the brigadier's table and sat in silence, his hands clenched tightly at his sides. He heard nothing of the stilted conversation which filled the gap until they could leave the nightclub without their departure being too pointedly linked to his inexplicable behavior.

The general was thinking about Frau Gensert. She had almost certainly been acting too.

Because she wouldn't know if he had recognized her for sure.

But she wouldn't be at the villa in the morning.

The SSD—the East German Intelligence Service—would see to that; they would get her out just as fast as they could.

The general would not be at the villa in the morning either.

He would be there later that night.

Because he knew how to identify her beyond all doubt.

And then he would kill her—before she could get away.

If he was right; if she *was* Elfrieda Horton.

The supposedly dead wife of his dead son.

He could not kill himself; but he could kill the woman who had caused his son to betray his country and ultimately hang himself in his cell.

Vengeance he *could* have. And with it, perhaps, some release from his mental agony. *Some* sanity.

The general felt a hand on his shoulder. It was the brigadier. They were getting ready to leave.

The general rose to his feet, unclenched his hands, and felt the warm stickiness in them. The palms were running with blood where his nails had dug deep into the flesh.

He had felt nothing.

No physical pain could penetrate the pain of his tortured mind.

Naples, Italy

General Wade Horton crouched patiently behind the bushes in the garden of the Villa Consetti, waiting for Frau Gensert to return.

After leaving the nightclub he had excused himself; he wished to take some exercise before retiring to bed; he would make his own way back to his host's residence.

The brigadier and his wife had not believed him. The brigadier had taken him to one side and suggested a suitable brothel. The general had thanked him and said good night.

Now, in the garden of the villa, the general peered at the luminous dial of his watch. Three minutes past one. Frau Gensert would be back soon and alone. He knew that. The navy lieutenant was going to be a disappointed man, for she was not going to share her bed that night. Frau Gensert had other things to do, urgent arrangements to make.

She would want to be a long, long way from her villa by ten o'clock that morning.

The general heard the sound of a car turning sharply off the road and up the long curved drive to the front of the villa. For a brief second, brilliant headlights swept across the white walls of the villa before the car stopped abruptly by the porch, the crunch of the tires sending little clouds of white dust floating through the piercing lights.

Hurriedly Frau Gensert got out of the taxi. The general moved swiftly from his hiding place and along the wall of the villa. By the time she had paid the driver and climbed the steps to the door, he was standing behind her at the bottom of the steps.

"Good evening, Frau Gensert," he called quietly.

He heard the sharp intake of breath as she turned. "Who is that?"

"General Horton . . . remember?"

"What do you want?" Her voice was controlled but heavy with apprehension.

"I happened to be walking this way taking the night air. I saw you drive up and thought it would be a nice idea to drop in for a nightcap."

He started up the steps. He knew she didn't believe him, but it didn't matter.

Not if it was really she.

She had to invite him in—to play for time, to figure out what to do.

"Come on in, General," she said.

"What will it be?" she asked as he sat down on one of the gold-embroidered settees in the luxurious living room.

"Scotch and soda."

She went to the bar and poured the drinks. Scotch and soda for him; a large brandy for herself. She placed the glasses on the low table in front of him, withdrawing her hand quickly to hide the tremble; then sat on the facing sofa.

The general sipped his drink and looked at her appreciatively. "You know what I find so attractive about you?" he said.

"My immoral reputation." She forced a smile.

He returned the smile. "You remind me of someone I once knew."

"Oh," she raised her eyebrows. "A compliment?"

The general raised his eyes, looking at nothing, as if lost in memory. "It was a long time ago, but I can still see her now, standing in front of an old stone church in a village near Wiesbaden. She was wearing a long, flowing white lace wedding gown, and the bright sunlight filtering through her golden hair made a sort of halo effect. She was quite the most beautiful creature I've ever seen. You know . . ." he lowered his eyes to look at her, "at that moment I think I loved her almost as much as I loved my son."

"Your son?"

"Yes, my son was the bridegroom. He was stationed at Wiesbaden with the American army. That's where he met his wife. She was German."

Frau Gensert was watching him, hardly breathing, the brandy glass cupped between her hands, the base of the stem pressed firmly against the thigh of her crossed leg.

"I only saw her once more after the day of their wedding. She was killed a few months later in an automobile accident on the Autobahn between Frankfurt and Wiesbaden. A head-on collision with a gasoline tanker." He smiled bitterly. "She was burned beyond recognition."

The general looked intently into her dark blue eyes. "You remind me of that beautiful woman." He drained his glass and held it toward her.

She rose quickly and, taking his glass, walked thoughtfully to the bar. Perhaps he *didn't* know who she was. Maybe it was simply some sexual hang-up about his dead son's wife. It was possible: it wouldn't be the first time she had met men who lusted after their young daughters-in-law . . . and their daughters! Why else would he be talking to her the way he was? If he *knew,* he would have confronted her with it. Challenged her.

She had to play for time.

Until the morning.

"I'm deeply touched I remind you of such a lovely woman," she said placing the refilled glasses on the table. For a moment she stood erect in front of him; then, bending forward, she rested her hands on the back of the settee, one on each side of his head. Slowly she lowered her head and pressed her lips to his. A long, insistent kiss of tender sensuousness. The general raised his hands and cupped the soft breasts which hung firm and free inside her loose-fitting dress.

"Bring the glasses," she whispered and led the way to a door at the far end of the room.

A large four-poster bed obscured a large portion of the thick carpet. Full-length mirrors ran down the walls on each side of the bed, and fixed to the underside of the red canopy over the bed was another mirror.

She smiled at him, the kind of smile that went with the room. He wondered how many men had seen that same smile.

In that room and others.

Like the room in the little chalet near Wiesbaden where his son had spent his honeymoon with his German bride.

He was watching her as she turned the blue silk bedcover down, and for an instant his face became contorted with hatred. She turned and caught the look as it died. "Relax, general, we've got all night.

Make yourself at home while I freshen up." She nodded to the bed, then went into the adjoining bathroom.

The general stood motionless, listening to the sound of the shower from the bathroom.

The sound of the shower stopped.

A minute later she came in, wearing nothing. She stood at the door a teasing smile on her lips.

The general caught his breath. Christ! She really was beautiful.

"You're still dressed, General. That's not very flattering. A woman likes to think a man is just a little bit impatient."

With a provocative smile she moved to lie on her back on the bed and began massaging her breasts.

"It would be nicer if you took your clothes off," she said. She ran the tip of her tongue around the lips of her open mouth.

The general moved to the side of the bed and looked down on her in silence. Her skin was flawless, smooth and white as alabaster.

"Turn over," he said softly.

She gave a puzzled frown.

He repeated it, harshly this time. "I said, 'Turn over.' "

She gave a slight shrug and turned to lie on her stomach.

His eyes went to her soft, round buttocks and to a spot about three inches up from the base of her spine and an inch to the left. The birthmark was a symmetrical diamond shape, the length of each of the four facets being about half an inch. He had seen this almost perfect geometrical mark fourteen years ago, a few months after his son's marriage. He had visited the boy and his wife, and they had gone swimming in a lake surrounded by rocks. He had leaned forward to help his son's wife climb out of the cold water, up over a large, flat rock jutting into the lake. As he pulled her up, she was bent double, and her bikini had slipped down her buttocks. That was when he had seen the mark before.

It belonged to Elfrieda Horton.

The supposedly dead wife of his dead son.

Now he knew!

Beyond all possible doubt.

Now he was going to kill her.

But first he must find the answer to the question which had tormented him for so long.

How had it happened?

How had she turned *his* son into a traitor!

For two years, ever since his son had been convicted of spying for the Soviets, since his son had hanged himself in his cell, the general had lived in a hell of torment. All his adult life he had loved his country and his army with a passion few men could understand. He had taught his son this same love. And then his son had betrayed his country—had betrayed *him.*

Because of this woman!

Why?

"*Elfrieda.*" His voice was sharp as he spoke the name, and he saw the muscles of her back suddenly contract as if struck by a whiplash. She turned her head to look at him, and her eyes were full of foreboding. "So you *do* know," she said in a whisper.

He stabbed the birthmark with his finger. "This . . . I saw it that time we went swimming at the lake. Remember?"

"Such a small thing." She smiled faintly.

"My son's death was not such a small thing," the general hissed between clenched teeth. "How did you do it, Elfrieda? How did you turn him into a traitor?"

She looked into his wild eyes. "I can tell you nothing," she said.

"*Tell me!*" the general yelled and crashed the back of his hand to the side of her face.

A trickle of blood came from the corner of her mouth, and she swallowed. "I *dare* not tell you anything, General. Far more is at stake then you could ever imagine. Wait until the morning, I beg you."

"Wait. For what?"

"I have never worked for the Soviets, I swear it, but I cannot prove it now. Only three men alive know the truth about your son. One is a general in American military intelligence. He is in Rome, but you can contact him in the morning. One of the others is the President of your country. Does *that* tell you how big this thing is?"

"It tells me how big a liar you are. My son's trial was kept secret, but military intelligence *had* to tell me something. *You* recruited my son to work for the Soviets. They told me!"

"They lied. They had to."

"Liar!" The general was astride her now, and his savage blows rocked her head from side to side on the pillow, the blood flying from her mouth with every blow. "Tell me the truth before I kill you," he yelled.

And with the increasing power of every blow and the madness in his eyes, she knew he meant it. *This man was going to kill her.* Before she lost consciousness she got the words out "Stop . . . yes . . . I will tell you."

She sat up slowly and wiped the blood from her battered face with the sheet. "Would you pass my cigarettes and lighter, please, General."

She lit a cigarette between her swollen lips, inhaled deeply, pulled the sheet up over her nakedness, then spoke: "Your son was *not* guilty of espionage," she said simply. "Nor did he hang himself. He was murdered."

The general stared at her, dumbfounded. He had expected lies, excuses, pleading . . . but not this!

"I come from East Germany, General," she went on quietly. "That's where I learned to hate the Ivans, the Russians. To make a long story short, I became the lover of a senior Russian officer in the KGB. I convinced him I was a dedicated Communist and eventually persuaded him to have me trained as an agent for the SSD. As you know the SSD work under the direct control of the Russian KGB. After my training I was sent to West Germany."

The general was watching her intently now, searching her face for the slightest trace of duplicity. He saw none.

"I went straight to the Americans and offered my services as a double agent, to work against communism. After a long interrogation I was accepted by your military intelligence services."

"My son?" the general said, his voice low and hoarse. "What has this to do with my son?"

She looked at him for a long moment, then said, "Everything. You see, American military intelligence had long-term plans for your son. The first step was to get the SSD interested in him. So I pretended I had met him by accident and six months later reported to my SSD controller that he had fallen in love with me and wanted us to marry. The SSD fell for it. They instructed me to marry him so I could trap him into an act that could ruin his military career, and then use this to blackmail him to work for them. The trap worked (naturally—your son and I made sure it did). The details do not matter. You can check them out tomorrow with the general from military intelligence in Rome."

She leaned across the bed and stubbed her cigarette out in the ashtray on the bedside table, then took a fresh one and lit it. Momentarily the sound of a motor scooter roaring homeward down the hill past the villa broke the heavy stillness in the room.

"Once they had your son, the SSD wanted me out of the way. They're smart. They don't take unnecessary chances. They didn't want me to know how they were using him. Anything could happen to me. I might even develop undesirable loyalties to the West, particularly if I returned to America with your son. That sort of thing happens, and the SSD knows it. So I disappeared—the automobile accident was faked.

"For years," she went on, "your son passed information to the Russians under instructions from military intelligence. Some of it was accurate—enough to fool the Russians. But among it was fake information which totally misled them about vital areas of NATO's defense plans. Then military intelligence had him transferred to the staff of the Joint Strategic Planning System at Omaha, Nebraska. For two years he carried on his work for the SSD, only by that time he was fooling them about the strategic defense of America itself."

She rose to her knees, the sheet falling from her, and leaned, hands on thighs, toward the general, who was still sitting on the edge of the bed. Very quietly she said, "Then your son was given his last assignment . . . the assignment which led to his death. A senior naval officer at Norfolk, Virginia, had a nervous breakdown. A massive attack of the male menopause maybe. He started to play around in a big way. Women, gambling, drink . . . the lot. He got heavily into debt, and the KGB moved in like he was a gift from the gods. For a quick hundred thousand dollars he sold the Russians information about the Sosus submarine detection system. I don't have to tell you what that meant."

The general knew what it meant. America was years ahead of the Russians in this vital area of strategic defense. The Russians had made it a priority target for their espionage apparatus. He gave an impatient nod of his head. "Yes, I know the importance of Sosus."

"We were lucky. The naval officer confessed a few days after collecting his money. Guilt. He wasn't a professional agent, just a man who had fallen apart inside. But at all costs the Russians had to be tricked into believing they had wasted their money, that the information they had got was useless. Fortunately, Sosus involves some of the most sophisticated technology in the world. Some of it technology the Russians didn't even have. So the information was not a straightforward blueprint the Russians could work from. But it was enough to indicate the path their research would have to follow to catch up with us. Navy experts reckoned it would take them four, maybe five years to do this."

She paused and reached for another cigarette. She wondered if the general had any idea of what was coming. And how would he react to the final, terrible truth—a truth so obscene it could unhinge anyone's mind.

She continued speaking quickly. "Military intelligence sent your son to naval headquarters in Norfolk as a liaison officer. He pretended to the Russians he had found out that the naval officer had been a plant. That his menopausal aberrations had been bait for the KGB; that the information he had given them had been phony, to lead them down a blind research alley. And to make sure the Russians really *did* go down a blind alley, he gave them new information which *was* fake."

She drew on her cigarette nervously. "But that wasn't enough. The Russians had to be *convinced*—beyond any shadow of doubt—that your son's information was the real McCoy. So military intelligence made a deal with him. They would pretend they had discovered he was working for the Russians and had given them Sosus information. He would be put on trial, found guilty, and given a life sentence. They promised to release him after a couple of years and to set him up with a new identity and a new life. Only—" she broke off, biting her lip.

"Only what?" the general demanded, his eyes boring into hers.

"Your son didn't understand the ruthlessness of the men he worked for." She took a deep breath. "The fact was, General, military intelligence had no intention of releasing your son. Inevitably the KGB would have found out—they watch for things like that. But they couldn't keep him imprisoned indefinitely. When he realized he wasn't going to be released, God knows what he might have done. So, they killed him. . . . They had intended it from the beginning."

The general was looking at her in stunned disbelief. "You expect me to believe *that*? My son killed—*murdered*—by his own army!"

"You wanted the truth, General. Now you have it. I'm sorry I had to tell you."

"You're lying." The general was shaking his head. "There is no way you could know any of this. You've had no contact with my son since your phony death."

"I know, but after my 'death' I took on a new identity and carried on working as a double agent. I was told about your son's conviction and suicide by my SSD controller. I was congratulated for having laid the foundation for such an espionage coup. But I just couldn't believe he had *actually* turned against his country." She hesitated for a moment, then continued very quietly, "You see, General, during the short time I was with him, I *did* fall in love with him. A love without any future, I know. But there are some feelings we cannot control."

There was a silence, and the general saw the clouding in her eyes which was the beginning of tears.

She spoke on hurriedly. "Eventually it preyed on my mind so much I contacted military intelligence in Washington. I threatened to reveal to the SSD that your son had been a double agent unless they convinced me he was really guilty. They tried every trick in the book to convince me, but I didn't believe them. I knew them too well. In the end they had to tell me the truth. I was sickened to my soul. I wanted to get out of the whole espionage business. To just disappear. But they persuaded me that the coincidence would arouse Russian suspicion about your son. I realized they were right and your son would have died for nothing. So I agreed to stay working as a double agent for five years. That's what I'm doing here in Naples—'milking' NATO officers for information about the Sixth Fleet for the SSD." She gave a tired smile. "From time to time I give them harmless information, enough to keep them happy."

"And military intelligence trust you? With what you know!" The general laughed again, but there was a false note to it. He did not want to believe her. The implications were too horrendous. But her story had a terrifying ring of truth: too elaborate to have been made up without warning; told with too much conviction.

She smiled wearily. "They have to. I've lodged a letter with a firm of German lawyers containing complete details of your son's activities. If they don't receive a certain message known only to me and them, each and every month, they are under instructions to send it to the SSD."

There was a long silence before the general spoke

very quietly, his voice ominous. "You mean that in the final analysis you have put your life before the security of your country? You could die suddenly and accidentally, and that letter would be sent."

"*Your* country, General," she spat back at him, her eyes flashing with anger. "I've served your country with my body and my soul—for twenty years. *Isn't that enough!* Without that letter, I'd be dead now. Like your son . . . *murdered*!"

For a long, long moment the general remained transfixed, no longer able to doubt the truth of what she had told him. Then suddenly he was filled with a calmness. A calmness he had not known for a long time. Now he knew; *his son had not betrayed his country*. He had been betrayed *by* his country . . . by his army!

Betrayed. The word echoed through the general's head, reaching down to the deepest recesses of his mind.

Suddenly a blinding, jagged whiteness exploded inside his head bringing a searing pain of intolerable agony, and he cried out, clutching his head. Again and again the pain shot through, tearing at his skull like the eruption of volcanic forces seeking to escape from the pressures which contained them. And with the pains, his head was filled with a piercing cacophony of demonic sound. He let out a last, long desperate cry of agony and then was silent, the pains gone as abruptly as they had come, and he was calm again.

But General Wade Horton was no longer a sane man. The betrayal of his son had unleashed savage forces suppressed in his subconscious since his childhood.

And now these forces demanded vengeance against the army that had murdered his son.

The general looked at the terrified woman lying on the bed in front of him with empty eyes. She no longer mattered to him, but she could be used. Stretching out his arms he took her throat in his hands and squeezed. And, for an instant, as the life drained from her, his eyes gleamed with a manic hatred as between his crushing hands he saw the face of his father!

Slowly he lowered her head onto the blood-splattered pillows. Then, moving quickly, he took a set of clean sheets and pillowcases from the linen closet.

He stripped the bed and laid her naked body on top of one of the dirty sheets he had spread on the floor. Then he forced her knees up against her breasts and pushed her head forward and down so her body would occupy the smallest space possible. He dropped the remaining dirty linen on top of her, then walked quickly to the walnut desk in the living room. With his handkerchief wrapped around his hand, he opened the top center drawer and found a pad of writing paper. He tore off a sheet, and, taking his gold pen, he carefully printed:

GENERAL WADE HORTON
DEPUTY COMMANDER
ALLIED FORCES CENTRAL EUROPE

In a kitchen drawer he found a ball of string, cut off a three-foot length, then threaded it through a hole he pierced with his pen an inch from the top of the sheet of paper.

Back in the bedroom he lifted the dead woman's head and passed one end of the piece of string around her neck. He knotted the string firmly at her throat, with the piece of paper hanging over her breasts like a label.

He made up the bed with the fresh linen, then cleaned his prints from the cigarette pack and lighter. Next he went to the bathroom and wiped the faucet.

On the hall table he found her car keys and made his way to the garage through the storeroom next to the kitchen. He opened the trunk of the Mercedes coupe, unlocked the driver's door, and got in. He inserted the key in the ignition, turned it, and peered at the gas gauge. Half full. Plenty.

Returning to the living room he picked up the two glasses, washed them in the kitchen, then, holding them with his handkerchief, replaced them in the rack behind the bar.

For a moment he stood perfectly still, thinking, his mind absolutely clear. He had missed nothing.

He switched off the lights with his elbow and returned to the bedroom. Elfrieda was still there, lying on the sheet in a neat ball the way he had left her, the label around her neck. He gathered the four corners of the sheet and tied them firmly together in a knot. Then grasping the knot with both hands he swung the bundle over his shoulders.

In the garage he dumped the bundle in the trunk of the car and locked it. Sliding into the driver's seat, he turned the ignition, and the engine purred to life.

Twenty minutes later he came to a stop in a deserted street on the outskirts of the city. On his right was a wall and on the other side of the wall the garden of an imposing residence.

He got out, opened the trunk, and grasped hold of the bundle that was the dead Elfrieda. Checking to make sure that the street was still clear, he carried the bundle to the wall, raised it above his head, and toppled it over into the garden. He heard the soft thud as it fell onto the loose soil of a flower bed.

A flower bed in the garden of the Russian Consulate.

ONE

•

Frankfurt, Germany

Five hundred miles to the north of Naples, Barbara Maxwell stood in a bar in Frankfurt looking for a seat.

A little under five feet four inches tall, with short, fair hair and an elfin face, she looked frail and vulnerable among the roistering crowd filling the bar. The appearance was deceptive. Barbara Maxwell had more than her share of the quiet determination and toughness of mind which so much characterized the talented Maxwell family.

Through the smoke-filled room she saw a vacant chair at a small table next to a door at the far end of the bar. She made her way to it, edging between the jammed tables, and sat down.

Unzipping her black leather shoulder bag, she reached for a pack of Marlboros. She cursed as she saw the letters she had forgotten to post to her father and her brother, David, in California.

She lit a cigarette and for a few moments was lost in thought. It was funny about her and David. Although he was eight years older than she—or perhaps because of this age gap—there was a special fondness between them which she treasured.

Not that she understood him. Nobody did, she guessed. Like his father, he was a brilliant physicist. The youngest project director ever to work on the development of nuclear energy by laser fusion at the Lawrence Livermore Laboratory in California.

But why, Barbara wondered, as she looked around at the revellers filling the bar, did David have so little social life. He was successful, not exactly short of money, and undeniably handsome. Yet his way of living was almost monastic. When he wasn't working, he was reading–philosophy mainly.

Not that he was a complete recluse. Every few weeks he would take off for Los Angeles or San Francisco and spend a few days with her or in the welcoming company and beds of any number of women who were more than eager to see him.

She had asked him about it, of course. And the answer was always the same. "I'm just a crank," he'd reply. And then he'd give her the diffident smile which had been a part of him for as long as she could remember.

This wasn't much of an explanation, but she had to settle for it. Which was frustrating because digging to find out what made people tick was her business. She had majored in psychology at Berkeley and was now working on her thesis: "The Psychology of Urban Terrorists."

Barbara stubbed out her cigarette and looked around. She had chosen this bar because it had been a favorite haunt of the Baader-Meinhof terrorists and their successors.

She reached down into her bag for another cigarette and, as she raised her head, caught the eye of an elegantly dressed blonde sitting two tables away. The woman looked at Barbara for a second, registered her unmistakably American casual clothes, then returned her gaze to keep watch on the six men sitting at a table on the other side of the bar.

One of them, in particular, appeared to hold her attention. He was young and wearing an expensive mohair coat with a wide belt. He was drinking—too much. A glass of Schnapps followed by a gulp of dark beer, followed by another Schnapps—too many Schnapps. Every few seconds his eyes flickered to the entrance of the bar at the top of a flight of stairs.

The door opened, and two men started to walk down slowly, their eyes alert, methodically scrutinizing the occupants of the bar.

Barbara caught the quick assessing look the elegant blonde gave the two men as they continued their descent. Then, very casually, she rose and walked to the door behind Barbara. As it opened, a draft of cold air struck Barbara; then it was closed, and the woman was gone.

Barbara's eyes returned to the two men who had reached the bottom of the stairs.

Suddenly the man in the mohair coat leaped to his feet and hurtled across the bar, sending people, tables, chairs, and glasses crashing to the floor.

What followed happened very quickly. The man reached the door behind Barbara and flung it open. Then he turned, grabbed her with powerful arms, and thrust her through the door into a long corridor with a stone floor and gray-tiled walls. At the far end, one bare bulb in the ceiling dimly illuminated a flight of stone steps.

"Run," the man commanded harshly in German.

Barbara hesitated, turned, and saw the dull metallic blue of the gun in his hand. She felt the sudden pain as he thrust it into her back. She stumbled forward and ran, their footsteps echoing in the hollowness of the corridor.

A few yards from the stone steps the man pulled her tightly to him and swiveled her around to face back down the corridor. A figure about to enter the corridor was clearly visible.

The man holding Barbara fired, and the sound of the shot reverberated in the corridor with a deafening, stunning force. The door was slammed.

Barbara was filled with terror as she realized she was being used as a human shield.

Once more the gun jabbed her viciously. Without further command she scrambled desperately up the steps. At the top the man opened the door and stepped out cautiously, holding Barbara in front of him.

Quickly he peered in either direction. Then, without a word, he released his grip. Barbara's knees crumpled, and she toppled to the ground. She raised her head and in the moonlight saw the man running toward a parked car down the deserted back street. He made all of ten feet. . . .

A crack like a whiplash in the night came from behind Barbara. The man flung his arms in the air, teetered forward a few steps, then slumped to the ground.

Barbara got to her feet, her legs like jelly, and turned. Standing immediately behind her was the elegant blonde. Gripped in her hands was a gun. A few seconds previously it had been pointing at the head of the dead man. Now it was pointing at the center of Barbara's forehead.

She met the woman's eyes, and her heart stopped. At that instant a decision was made. For life or death: her own.

There was no going back. "Come with me," the woman spoke in English with a heavy German accent. "Move!" the woman pointed up the street with the gun. "In front of me. Run!"

Barbara ran. She reached a parked car. A black Mercedes 450SL. "Stop. . . . Get in the back."

Barbara opened the door and got in. The blonde followed, and the car shot down the narrow street and turned into a main highway.

A man was at the wheel. He didn't speak.

The car glided through the late night traffic. The sidewalks were crowded with people making their way home from theaters, restaurants, and bars. All very normal; very civilized.

But the thoughts of the blonde woman beside Barbara were elsewhere. She had to get rid of this American. Discreetly. She needed somewhere to hold her until arrangements could be made to dispose of her body. Gartmann would know where. Gartmann could arrange to get rid of her body—Gartmann was a hundred miles away in Bonn! The woman leaned forward and whispered to the driver.

The car glided to a stop by a phone booth. The woman made a call, returned to the car, and whispered to the driver again. Twenty minutes later the car came to a stop outside an old apartment block by the river.

The blonde ordered Barbara out, and the car pulled away.

The apartment was dirty, with dust on everything and sparsely furnished. But it was adequate. Nobody ever stayed there very long. The blonde indicated for Barbara to sit on a threadbare settee, then rummaged in a cupboard against the wall. She found what she was looking for. A bottle of Schnapps. She had guessed right. There would be Schnapps in an apartment like this. To keep out the cold and steady the nerves. She raised the bottle to her lips, took a deep swallow, and lowered the bottle, looking at Barbara.

It was a pity, she thought. If the woman had been German, she would have killed her in the street at the back of the bar. But it was different with an American. When the police found the body of the man, they would soon discover he had consorted with known Marxist terrorists, and they wouldn't mind too much about him being dead. In fact, they wouldn't mind at all. But if an American woman had been found dead as well, they would have felt it their duty to find out who had done this terrible thing.

She wouldn't like that. Gartmann wouldn't like it either. And Gartmann had a lot of friends. The whole goddamn SSD! Not that she minded his political affiliations. But she did care about her arrangement with him. In return for her body and various political services she performed for him, she had a luxury apartment, a high-powered Mercedes, all the clothes she wanted, and only a little less than two hundred thousand marks in three bank accounts.

The trouble with this arrangement was that if it

was terminated, her life was likely to be terminated also. It was that kind of business. She knew too much. Not that she was about to terminate it. But she had a feeling Gartmann might.

Behind her hard eyes, the elegant blonde named Renate Schultze was frightened. Very frightened. She took another gulp of Schnapps.

"What are you going to do with me?" Barbara asked, unnerved by the woman's silence.

Renate ignored the question and pointed to Barbara's shoulder bag. "Give it to me," she said.

Barbara passed the bag, and Renate took out the passport. "Barbara Maxwell," she read aloud without looking up. Then after a pause she asked, "What are you doing in Germany?"

She had been expecting the question and considering how to answer it. It was a reasonable assumption that this woman was a terrorist. And from her study of such people she already knew they liked to talk about themselves, to justify what they were doing. Perhaps if this woman were kept talking long enough —and drinking—she might get careless about where she put the gun she was still holding.

"Studying terrorists," Barbara said evenly.

Renate was in the act of gulping from the bottle again. "What!" she spluttered, jerking the bottle from her mouth. "*Studying* terrorists. What the hell for? I can tell you all anyone needs to know in two minutes flat. A bunch of useless bourgeois shit! That's all they are. Christ! I should know."

And she did know.

She had told Gartmann it was a waste of time trying to organize the terrorists into an effective force to disrupt German society. But Gartmann was a brainless dolt. Even the fact his father was a member of the East German politburo wouldn't be enough to protect him from his own stupidity. He needed her.

She took another gulp of Schnapps, and her fear of Gartmann turned to anger.

Wasn't it enough for him that the brothel she operated in Bonn ran like clockwork? So maybe she was skimming money from it at the same time. That didn't hurt anybody. Certainly it didn't hurt Gartmann. The SSD were pleased with him. He'd just been promoted to major. Because of *her*!

But now Gartmann wanted to ease her out, feet first. She knew it: all the signs were there. The biggest sign of all was the new prostitute at the brothel. The English bitch, Judy Sinclair. And while she, Renate, was running around with an adolescent bunch of hoodlums trying to turn them into competent terrorists, all that English whore was doing was lying on her back—thinking of England, no doubt. No, Judy Sinclair would be doing more than that. Gartmann really liked her and with someone as sexually satiated as he, that took real expertise. The bitch!

Suddenly the resentment, anger and fear spewed out, and she glared at Barbara. "You really want to know about German terrorists? I'll tell you. They're good for talking about, writing about, and they're good for the media. Apart from that they're useless shit. So mentally screwed up they don't know what they are doing half the time. The spoiled children of the rich. They live it up. Luxury apartments, fast cars—all the benefits of capitalism they claim to despise. If the police weren't so incompetent, there wouldn't be any terrorists in Germany. Everyone knows that. The Federal Criminal Bureau are a bunch of comedians. . . . A bad German joke."

Barbara was watching and listening intently. The woman wasn't talking like a terrorist although she obviously had connections with them. So who *was* she? She was waiting for something. What?

And why was she drinking so much?

Renate Schultze raised the bottle to her mouth again, then began to pace up and down. She turned to look at Barbara, her eyes blazing. "Take that man —that *boy*!—who grabbed you in the bar. He was one of your brave bourgeois revolutionaries. When he saw the two plainclothes policemen coming down the stairs, he panicked. I knew he would!"

Renate Schultze fell into a sullen silence.

"So you killed him," Barbara said quietly.

The woman looked at her absently. "Of course. If the police had caught him, he would have talked his head off."

"And what about me?" Barbara asked, her voice tight with the realization of just how perilous her position was.

"I'm not worried about you," Renate replied. It was a lie. She was worried. Gartmann wasn't going to like it when he found out the full extent of the mess. Two people killed and one of them an American. She hadn't told him much on the telephone—only the few cryptic sentences necessary to inform him she had an urgent disposal problem. But Gartmann was going to want details. The girl might have important connections. Precautions might have to be taken. She needed more information.

Renate Schultze frowned, picked up Barbara's shoulder bag, and emptied the contents onto the table. Her hands darted first to the airmail letter Barbara had forgotten to post to her father. She ripped it open and began to read.

Barbara watched intently and, from the look in the woman's eyes, saw that some sudden and totally unexpected thought was forming in her mind.

For an instant a look of triumph flitted across the woman's face before she lowered the letter and looked up at Barbara between narrowed eyes.

"So your father worked at Los Alamos on atomic weapons."

"Yes, but he's retired now." In her letter Barbara had referred to her father's life at Los Alamos where he had worked with almost frenzied energy, driven by the belief that only by maintaining nuclear superiority over Russia could the West be kept safe. She had said how she hoped he was happy taking things easy now and enjoying his retirement.

"Has your father any political connections?"

"No, not especially. A few congressmen, people at the defense department. People connected with his work. No one important." Without understanding why, Barbara felt uneasy at the woman's line of questioning.

"No one at the White House—people like that?"

"No."

"The rest of your family . . . brothers . . . sisters?"

"A brother. He's—"

A sharp rap came from the wooden door of the apartment. Renate slipped the letter and envelope into her pocket and dropped to her knees in front of

Barbara. She spoke in an urgent whisper. "Listen to me. There's a man at the door who's been sent to kill you. I'm going to stop him . . . if I can. Sit down and keep absolutely still. If you make a scene, there will be nothing I can do. He'll kill you. Understand?"

Barbara nodded, but she understood nothing.

Gun in hand, Renate moved swiftly to let the man in. He was no more than five feet six inches tall and weighed a good hundred and ninety pounds. Both his hands were deep in the pockets of a light brown topcoat which hung from his huge shoulders like a tent. A bull of a man with dark, glittering eyes set in a heavy pockmarked face. On his head was a small narrow-rimmed hat with two shiny green feathers stuck in one side. He had the air of a comic, a funny man; he wasn't.

Renate drew him to a corner of the room well away from Barbara. "It's off," she said in a low voice. "The girl must not be killed."

"Oh?" He blinked once.

"She's valuable. We need her."

"We?"

"Gartmann."

The man released his grip on the silencer in his pocket and raised his hand to scratch the side of his face. The other hand remained where it was—wrapped around the butt of a 9 mm automatic. "I know of no such change in plans. Gartmann spoke to me personally and ordered me to dispose of the girl with maximum efficient speed," he said.

"I know. I asked him to arrange it. But something new has come up. It's essential we keep her alive."

"Gartmann says so?"

"He doesn't know about it yet."

"Oh!" The man raised his eyebrows a fraction of an inch. "Then suppose we telephone him and tell him about his change in plans."

"That's not necessary. I have all the authority to make such decisions."

"Perhaps. But you have no authority to give me orders. The telephone . . ."

Renate shrugged. "Very well." She had played for all the time she could. To think how she was going to explain to Gartmann about her plans for the girl *and her father* on the telephone.

It was an audacious plan, and she knew it. A long shot. But she knew if she had enough time to work on Gartmann, she could persuade him to go along with it. And that in time he would come to believe it was *his* plan and *his* brilliant idea.

But how could she do it in one telephone conversation?

She *had* to.

To convince Gartmann he needed her—not her body, but her brains.

That he could not afford to terminate his arrangement with her!

She dialed and listened to the muffled buzz of the phone in Gartmann's apartment in Bonn. There was no answer, and it took her about twenty seconds to guess why. Gartmann would be out dining . . . with Judy Sinclair, a bottle of 1971 Neirsteiner Rehbach in an ice bucket beside the table and a fat smile of anticipation on his face. She let the phone ring another thirty seconds.

"There's no answer," she said and moved quickly to stand facing him, her back to Barbara.

"That's a shame," the man said. He took both hands out of his pockets and began to screw the silencer onto the automatic. He was a professional killer. It was a low risk occupation—provided you knew your job and followed orders. Provided you didn't listen to blondes who breathed Schnapps all over you.

He pushed Renate aside and stepped toward Barbara. One step only. Far enough to bring the side of his head to the right position. Renate pivoted on her hips and swung the butt of her gun. It caught him behind his left ear. He crumpled to his knees and fell flat on his face, without saying a word, even a moan.

TWO

Bonn, West Germany

Bruno Gartmann stood in front of the full-length mirror and adjusted his white silk tie. A piece of thread on the lapel of his dark blue suit caught his eyes. He flicked it off with the finger of a well-manicured hand, then leaned closer to the mirror and preened his thick but orderly black mustache. He smoothed a few strands of graying hair which had strayed out of place on the left side of his head and stood back.

Two months past his fiftieth birthday, he was, he thought, still a fine figure of a man. A bit on the stout side perhaps, but he was tall enough to carry it. If anything, it added to the impression of his being a man of substance. A man to be reckoned with, a product of the German economic miracle. All of which he was; he ran the most exclusive brothel in Bonn, the capital of West Germany and the hub of diplomatic activity in Western Europe.

His services were much sought after. His establishment catered to (indeed encouraged and developed) the most bizarre sexual proclivities of his clients. It was his proud boast that, given sufficient warning "to make the necessary arrangements, you understand," there was no requirement of a valued client he could not meet. All this was known—and much appreciated—by the diplomatic community of Bonn. It was yet another example of German efficiency.

What was not known was that Gartmann was a major in the East German intelligence service; the brothel, a simple and subtle operation conceived by Moscow—an exclusive establishment to attract the high and mighty and cultivate the sophistication of their sexual tastes. The very exclusivity, even respectability, of a "Gartmann-Nacht" tempted men who would not normally have considered visiting a brothel. And there, in expert hands, they would be introduced to experiences not found in their marital beds, or even in their fantasies.

These men, their sexuality corrupted, became easy targets for the "swallows," the professional seducers for the SSD. The precise details of their sexual desires were recorded in its archives in East Berlin. From there the information was fed to swallows in a dozen major cities throughout Europe. And when these men traveled, as men of power do, the swallows would be waiting for them. An apparently chance meeting, a quiet knock on a hotel bedroom door, a quick word from a hotel clerk—whatever the method of contact, the bait would be offered, sometimes subtly, sometimes explicitly, but always the same; their secret sexual depravity.

Then came the photographs from hidden cameras in the apartments of the swallows, followed by blackmail. Information was asked for and given. Documents dealing with the most sensitive political issues found their way from the vaults of a dozen foreign embassies and the German Chancellory to the political analysts of the SSD. The analysts studied, weighed, and refined the information, collated it with information from other sources, and produced their political poisons to be injected and leaked back to the West. A tip-off to a highly respected newspaper from a "usually reliable source"; the unexpected arrival on an ambassador's desk of the secret instructions issued to the ambassador of another country by his government; whispered words in the corridors of the parliaments of Europe and the American Congress. Nation was set against nation; negotiations collapsed; grand designs died at conception, and mutual trust was replaced by reciprocal suspicion among the nations of the West.

But there were no hidden cameras in the brothel in Bonn. Bonn must be above suspicion. Men of the highest political principle did not succumb to blackmail. They put loyalty to their countries above the preservation of their careers. They exposed the source of their blackmail. A swallow would be lost. Swallows were expendable, and there was nothing to link them with Bonn.

Bonn remained unsuspected. A training ground for depravity: its graduates, candidates for treason.

Bruno Gartmann put the final touches to his appearance, then turned from the mirror and addressed the woman sprawled on her back on the large bed across the room. "How do I look, eh?" He pulled himself to his full height, a smug smile on his face.

"Absolutely fabulous, darling," she drawled lazily with the unmistakable accent of the English upper crust.

Gartmann's eyes roved lasciviously over her body; the long, elegant legs, her incredible twenty-inch waist around which his hands met when he grasped her really hard, and the firmness of her full, protruding breasts.

"And I make love like a bull of a man, eh?"

"A whole herd of bulls, darling."

"A herd!" Gartmann bellowed with a laugh. "You think so, eh?" Then he gestured expansively around the expensively appointed room. "How do you like your new apartment?"

Judy Sinclair sucked at her full lower lip and gave a shrug. "It's quite nice, I suppose."

Gartmann's face clouded. Whore! What made her think her pussy was so special. If she wasn't careful, she could damn well go back to work with the other girls in the brothel. Then his eyes went back to her sensuous body and the high pubic mound between her legs, and he felt the urge to upend her and hump the ass off her. Christ, he'd paid enough for it, hadn't he?

He gave her a sullen stare and went out, slamming the door behind him.

Judy Sinclair swung her long legs to the edge of the bed and sat up, a quiet smile on her face. She understood men like Gartmann: make them good and mad, and they were all the more eager to screw you. It was the only way they knew how to get back at you. They didn't like women, not even a little bit.

Gartmann walked the two blocks to the brothel and entered his office. Frau Brusche, his trusted, well-paid, and somewhat elderly secretary was waiting for him.

"Renate Schultze has called twice already this morning," Frau Brusche announced. "I said I didn't know where you were." She gave Gartmann a confiding look.

Gartmann grunted. "Very correct of you, Frau Brusche. Thank you."

"And Professor Cramer called to say he wants to meet you at ten o'clock."

"Oh!" Gartmann's eyebrows shot up. "Thank you, Frau Brusche, that will be all." He sat back with a frown as Frau Brusche left the room. What could Cramer want, he wondered. Then he scowled. Cramer was a supercilious little shit—always theorising. He had no idea what it was like to be a field operator.

He pushed up the cuff of his shirt and looked at his watch. Nine-twenty. He would have to leave in ten minutes to reach his customary meeting place with Cramer in the *Kottenforst* southwest of the city.

The scowl left his face as his mind was drawn back to Judy Sinclair. God! What a body. And that cool, detached upper-class face. Screwing her was like raping the whole English aristocracy. Irresistible.

He felt the stirring between his legs. Rape wasn't exactly the word. She might look distant and untouchable but, God! she knew how to use her body. When she said she "simply adored fucking," she meant it!

But half an hour later, as Gartmann pulled off the road on the edge of the *Kottenforst* and got out of the car, the attractions of Judy Sinclair's body had been replaced in his thoughts by the apprehension he always felt before his meetings with Professor Cramer.

With his round, jovial face and the ever-present twinkle in his blue eyes, the professor was well liked by the students at the university where he lectured in social history. But Gartmann knew him in a very different role: he was head of the whole SSD network for the Bonn district. A man to be feared. A summons by Cramer could mean many things, some of them unpleasant in the extreme.

Gartmann hurried forward as he saw Cramer standing under the large horse chestnut tree, their appointed meeting place.

There was no twinkle in Cramer's eyes as he accepted Gartmann's extended hand before speaking with a clipped coldness his students would not have recognized. "Moscow has decided to withdraw all support from German left-wing terrorists. Not only have they proved totally incompetent, but their indiscriminate acts of violence and decadent life-style have alienated even the proletariat."

Gartmann looked at Cramer with guarded eyes, trying to conceal his fear and dislike.

There was a long silence while Cramer regarded Gartmann speculatively; then momentarily he pursed his lips like a shriveled apple before continuing. "Tell me, comrade, what do you know about the activities of the neo-Nazi movements?"

Gartmann shrugged. "A bunch of geriatrics hankering after the past glories of Hitler's Third Reich. They are of no importance. Most of them will be dead soon enough anyway."

"You are wrong, comrade. And if you spent less time sampling your merchandise in the brothel and took the trouble to look around, you would know it." There was no serious reproof in Cramer's voice.

Gartmann was an intellectual buffoon; a maggot who thrived in the rotten cheese of capitalism. *But,* an effective maggot if properly used.

"There is a new breed of neo-Nazis," he continued. "Young university students who care nothing for *Hitler's* Germany. All they know is that under the Nazis people had something greater than themselves to believe in. Something to make the blood run faster in their veins. Excitement. *Commitment.* You know what Goebbels said? He said, 'It doesn't matter what you believe; what matters is *that you believe.*' He was right. People cannot live in a spiritual vacuum. They will give themselves, their money, even their lives to any crazy cult that seems to offer them spiritual purpose. They are hungry for commitment. *You*—comrade—are going to feed that hunger."

Gartmann frowned, not certain he understood. "Help the neo-Nazis?" he said hesitantly. "What good can that do us?"

"The forward defenses of America are in Europe—NATO. The linchpin of these defenses, American forces, and their nuclear weapons. If we loosen this linchpin, remove it even, Europe will be defenseless. We will be free to concentrate on the final destruction of America itself."

"But the connection between neo-Nazis and American forces . . . ?"

For an instant there was a twinkle in Cramer's eyes; not of warmth, more like the jagged glint from the razor-sharp edge of a piece of broken glass. "The connection? *Direct,*" he snapped. "The neo-Nazis are fanatical nationalists. Above all they want to unite East and West Germany. They do not accept—will *never* accept—the division of their country. To them, all German governments since the war have been groveling lapdogs of the Americans. They believe it is the Americans who have stopped their country from building the armed forces and developing the nuclear weapons necessary to unite their country by force. They hate the Americans because American foreign policy has legitimized the division of their country."

"Then they are mad, that's all I can say." Gartmann shrugged heavily.

"If that is *all* you can say, comrade, then you are a fool." Cramer made no attempt to keep the contempt from his voice or the sneer from his face. "They *are* mad, and the mass of the German people know it, but that is irrelevant. What matters is that they are fanatics. They have found their spiritual purpose for living, a commitment, a faith for which they will willingly die. We will help them. We will organize them, and then we will unleash them against the Americans here in Germany—servicemen, their families, even tourists will be their targets. A reign of terror using every possible means—submachine guns, grenades, bombs, rocket launchers. Now do you understand . . . comrade?"

Gartmann lowered his eyes, feeling (as he always did with Cramer), like a schoolboy being reprimanded for his slowness of mind. But he *did* understand. The American Congress and administration would be in confusion. Relations between the American and German governments soured beyond repair. Above all, the American people would be outraged that their servicemen and families were being killed by the very people they were helping to defend. The surge of pressure to withdraw their troops from Germany might be irresistible.

"Yes, I understand." Gartmann's eyes were full of resentment as he raised them to meet Cramer's.

"Good. Then you will also appreciate that there must not be the slightest possibility of our connection with the neo-Nazis being discovered."

Gartmann bit his lip. "Of course. I am not a fool."

An almost imperceptible pause and the faintest flicker of a smile preceded Cramer's reply. "The only link between us and the neo-Nazis will be the one man we select to organize and lead them. A man prepared to die rather than allow the connection to be discovered. Have you such a man?"

"Yes," Gartmann answered. "His name is Günther Kraske."

"Tell me about him. Everything," Cramer said.

In the Bonn suburb of Bad Godesberg a black BMW stopped at one end of a tree-lined street. Although it was spring and the weather mild, the man who emerged from the car was wearing a long, black leather coat. He was tall, well built, with short-cut black hair, and as he began to walk down the street, he was whistling between his teeth. He appeared to know where he was going, but his stride was unhurried. From time to time, as he passed one of the expensive houses spaced far apart and set well back from the road, he would glance at it through a gate or over a hedge. Whether or not he was interested in what he saw was impossible to tell, for there was a blank indifference about his light blue eyes, a cold arrogant wall of nothingness.

Halfway down the left side of the street he looked at his watch, stopped, took out a cigarette, lit it, then proceeded even more slowly, the cigarette jutting from between his teeth.

He came to a solid oak gate set in a high wall which obscured the house behind it. Taking the cigarette from his teeth, he dropped it onto the paving stone and ground it out methodically with his heel; then grasping the wrought iron catch, he opened the gate, stepped through, and shut it behind him.

The garden in front of the house was large and well cared for. He left the path leading to the door, walked across the lawn, and, skirting a round bed of budding roses, reached the side of the house. He was whistling again as he made his way to the rear of the house where he stood to one side of some French windows, shielded from the view of neighboring houses by a large, heavily leaved shrub.

He remained where he was for almost a minute, rocking gently on the balls of his feet. Then, looking at his watch again, he waited for the second hand to come to exactly ten o'clock. He pressed his head against the wall and peered through the window.

Inside the room a door opened. A plumpish woman with well-coiffured blond hair entered. She was in her mid-thirties and was wearing a tight black satin skirt and a white silk blouse with long sleeves. Around her waist was a crimson sash.

The woman moved to stand in front of a long, ornate mirror and, raising her hands to her breasts, began gently to knead them. After a few minutes she removed her blouse, reached behind her back, and unhooked her brassiere, releasing her bulbous breasts.

For an instant she cupped her breasts in her hands and, turning to face the window, began to massage them slowly with her palms while gently stroking her nipples with forefingers and thumbs.

The urgency of her movements increased as she rocked from side to side on her heels, pressing her thighs together.

The man at the window took a roll of wide adhesive tape from his pocket, tore off a six-inch strip, and stuck one end of it to the back collar of his leather coat. Reaching into his other pocket he pulled out two short lengths of nylon rope and a flat metal disk.

Grasping one breast in her hands, the woman began to suck feverishly at the nipple. Then her hands dropped and, pulling up her skirt, she worked on each side of her pelvis with the outstretched fingers of each hand, at first slowly, then with rapid, jerking movements.

The man took three steps forward, inserted the metal disk between the French windows, and released the lock.

Flinging one window open, he burst into the room.

The woman let out a scream as her arms flew to cover her breasts. "What do you want?" she yelled her eyes wide with terror.

The man advanced toward her, his face expressionless. With a scream the woman dashed for the door, but before she reached it, he had grabbed her around the waist with one arm. With the other he tore the piece of tape from his collar and clamped it over her mouth. As she tried to tear off the gag, the man grabbed her by the wrists and dragged her, kicking and writhing, to a high-backed, cushioned chair with wooden armrests. Flinging her into the chair, he thrust his knee against her stomach and, forcing her down, tied first one, then the other of her wrists to the armrests.

He stood back for a moment while she looked up at him with wild eyes. Then slowly he undressed, placing his clothes neatly on a nearby chair. He stood naked before her, his enormous penis sticking out rigid as a bar of iron.

The door of the room opened and a small dapper-looking man came in dressed in a black pinstriped suit. His neatly clipped mustache and the sides of his hair were white. He was carrying a camera with a flash attachment. Closing the door behind him, he positioned himself so he could get the naked man and the woman in the viewfinder. The camera clicked.

Kneeling down, the naked man tore the skirt and pants off the writhing woman. She raised her legs and crashed her heels against his chest, sending him reeling back onto the floor. She looked down at his sprawling body, a look of savage pleasure on her face. Slowly the man got to his feet, then crashed his open hand across her face. A smile flickered on his lips as, taking her thighs under his arms, he pulled her toward him and thrust his penis deep into her soft, receptive vagina. Her eyes flew wide as her body jerked forward against him. She struggled desperately as he pounded into her but was held helpless by the viselike grip around her thighs.

Then slowly her violent contortions subsided, and her movements changed to synchronize with his. Now he was varying the pace of his strokes, his powerful hands caressing her breasts; and all the time the dapper little man was excitedly scuttling around taking his photographs.

For twenty minutes this went on. Three times the woman's body shuddered in violent orgasm until finally the man bent forward and clasping her breasts brought himself to climax.

He got to his feet and, still naked, went out of the door and up the stairs to the bathroom where he took a quick shower. When he returned to the room, the little man was on his knees jerking into the woman like a dog in heat.

The man put his clothes on without haste, keeping his back to the two of them. Then he turned to make his way to the door, and as he passed the woman, she looked up at him and winked with one eye.

The man picked up a brown manila envelope on the table by the front door, slipped it into his pocket and let himself out.

As he walked the distance back to his car, Günther Kraske resumed his tuneless whistling.

Gartmann parted from Cramer under the horse chestnut tree in the *Kottenforst* and made his way back to his car. As he drove back to the center of Bonn, his feelings were mixed. His meeting with Cramer had been satisfactory in every respect save one. They had agreed that Günther Kraske would set up a new neo-Nazi group to be named Group 666. He would recruit its members from among the extreme right-wing members of the *Korps*, the dueling fraternities at the universities. They were used to strong discipline and hard work, and, most important, many of them were intensely nationalistic. Skillfully led, they could be turned into highly efficient and dedicated killers.

Gartmann's one cause for irritation was Cramer's patronizing contempt for him. One day he would show the professor what real men of action could do.

But as he approached the turnoff to the brothel, his humor improved. Now at least he could get rid of Renate Schultze. The leftist terrorists were dominated by women, and he had needed her to deal with them. But now . . . !

Back in his office Gartmann jabbed the intercom button. "Frau Brusche, get hold of Günther Kraske. I want to see him immediately."

"Yes, Herr Gartmann. . . . Renate Schultze is downstairs. She wants to see you. It's urgent."

"Send her up."

Renate Schultze came through the door, her eyes blazing. "Where the hell were you last night?"

"That's my affair," Gartmann answered with indifference.

"Like hell it is! I suppose you were up to your balls in that English pussy." She stood glaring at him.

"Sit down, Renate," he said easily, relaxed in the knowledge that this was the last of her tantrums he would have to put up with.

Renate sat down and relaxed. The hell with Gartmann's sex life. She had a business proposition to make. "This terrorist business is a mess," she said. "Unless we do something pretty dramatic, it's going to fall apart."

"Dramatic?"

"Yes. Something which will rock the German people and attract new recruits . . . *good* ones."

"I take it you have something in mind," Gartmann said. He was enjoying the situation. He hoped she had a good idea; it would hurt all the more when he pulled the carpet from under her and told her they'd quit the terrorist business as of half an hour ago.

Renate blew smoke through her nostrils and looked at Gartmann mildly. "How about," she said, very casually, "how about exploding an atomic bomb under the Bundestag?"

The smug look died on Gartmann's face, and his mouth fell open. Two thoughts flashed through his mind simultaneously: it was an impossible idea, but Renate was *not* in the habit of making ridiculous suggestions. He regained his composure. "Very good, Renate. A brilliant idea. Just a trifle difficult to implement, I fancy."

"Not really," she answered coolly. "Only a little bomb, but enough to turn the German parliament into a hole in the ground."

"And how do you propose to get hold of this *little* bomb? I hope you don't imagine Moscow will provide one. If it was discovered, it could start a nuclear war, and I don't think they would like that." He gave a tight smile.

"I'm not an idiot, Bruno. I'm not talking about a big, sophisticated military bomb. Something small and crude. The sort of thing that can be made with a small quantity of the right kind of uranium, simple laboratory equipment, and a lot of expertise. Moscow could let us have the uranium. *I* will supply the expertise."

"*You* supply the expertise?"

Renate continued. She explained about the American girl and her father.

By chance, Renate had captured Barbara Maxwell. She was going to put that chance to good use. Barbara Maxwell would become a hostage—to lure her father to her rescue.

"It's feasible," Gartmann said thoughtfully, "But perhaps you'd like to clarify what you mean by *you* will supply the expertise?"

"It's very simple, Bruno. *I* have the American girl and the letter. Without the letter you can't get the father over here, and without the girl you won't have the means to, shall we say, *persuade* the father to make the bomb. At one hundred thousand marks you'll be getting a bargain. Fifty thousand for the letter, another fifty thousand for giving you the girl when you've successfully kidnapped the father. It's a very reasonable proposition. I could ask for the whole hundred in advance. Think about it."

Gartmann had already thought about it. He wanted that bomb.

"How do I know you've got the girl?" he asked.

"Don't be a fool, Bruno. Have I ever set up a deal and not delivered? The girl's somewhere safe from everyone, including you!"

Renate Schultze got to her feet and walked out of the office.

Gartmann watched her go with a look of triumph. He went to the cupboard and poured himself a large glass of Schnapps. Fantastic! Launch Group 666 with a nuclear explosion at an American base! Kill Americans, Cramer had said. My God, there'd be a few killed all right. And by a German atomic bomb! It would rock NATO to its foundations.

He swallowed the Schnapps and smacked his lips, and a heavy scowl came to his face. If he told Cramer, the little runt would take the credit for it. That was the way intellectual weasels like Cramer operated.

Gartmann refilled his glass and studied the clear liquid. Then the corners of his mouth began to twitch as he recalled something his father had said, drunk on the occasion of his appointment to the East German politburo. "Always remember, my boy, we have powerful friends on our side . . . even in the West. People you would never expect. Industrialists and financiers . . . people like Baron von Richter."

Gartmann felt his pulse quicken. Richter Industries were major participants in the French-German consortium developing the Super-Phoenix fast breeder nuclear reactor. However, first there was the question of feasibility. Could such a bomb *really* be made? His valued client from the Federal Ministry for Atomic Research, Dr. Vister, would know about such things. Dr. Vister would receive an unexpected, but assuredly welcome, invitation to a "Gartmann-Nacht." Then he would discuss the question with him—casually, as a matter of academic interest.

Gartmann smiled with satisfaction and settled back to wait for Günther Kraske. . . .

Two blocks away Günther Kraske parked the BMW and made his way to Gartmann's office. He nodded a perfunctory greeting to Frau Brusche.

"He'll see you right away," she informed Kraske.

"Ah, Günther, sit down, sit down," Gartmann said warmly as Kraske entered. "Schnapps?"

Kraske shook his head and took a manilla envelope from his pocket and tossed it onto Gartmann's desk.

Gartmann glanced at the document inside and raised his eyebrows. "How did you get this? It's classified 'Eyes Only: Ministry of Defense.' "

"I have an arrangement with a woman who has a rape fetish married to a senior guy in the defense ministry who can't get it up unless he watches his wife being screwed. He's keen on photography too. He gives her three hundred marks so she can enact a little rape scene with me. That gets her going. Then he does his thing!" Kraske stopped and lit a cigarette.

"But the document . . . ?"

"Simple. The woman keeps the three hundred and gives me copies of documents her husband brings home instead. He doesn't know, of course, but what's the harm? They both have a ball, she gets the money, we get the documents. Everyone's happy." Kraske bared his teeth, which was about the nearest he could get to a smile.

Gartmann grinned appreciatively. "How long have you been doing this kind of work, Günther?"

"Two years."

"You enjoy it?"

Kraske gave a sour look. "It's ruining my sex life. Another year of it and I'll be as bent as the rest of them."

"You'd like a change?"

"I'd like a change."

"Killing?"

"People?"

"People."

Kraske bared his teeth again. "Why not. It's got to be better than winding myself up every morning like a clockwork bull. . . . Who do I kill?"

"Americans."

"I'll have that drink now."

Gartmann handed him a glass, then explained about Group 666. He made no mention of the atomic bomb. "First of all, however," he ended, "I want you to go to America. I have a little job for you over there."

"I'd like that," Kraske said. "I've never been to America."

THREE

Big Sur, California

David Maxwell opened his eyes. In the stillness of the bedroom he could hear the gentle sound of the Pacific breakers on the Malibu beach. It took a lot of money to wake up to that kind of music.

Taking care not to disturb the sleeping woman beside him, he slid out of bed, went to the bathroom, and closed the door quietly behind him.

It was 6:30 A.M. If he hurried he could make the three hundred miles up the coast to Big Sur to meet his father for lunch at Nepenthe. He didn't want to be late.

He stepped under the shower and soaped himself vigorously, then reached for the shampoo and massaged the suds into his thick, blond hair. For a few moments he stood watching the rivulets of soapy water stream down his lean muscular body. Stepping out of the shower, he grabbed a towel.

The door opened. She was tall, sleepy, beautiful, and naked. "What are you doing?" she asked with a yawn.

"Going," he said.

"Oh, for God's sake, David, you've only just come!" She opened her eyes wide.

"There's an answer to that," he said with a grin and reached for the toothbrush.

"Bastard," she said. "Is that all you think I'm good for?"

David turned to her, his expression serious. "No, you're good for a lot of things, but with other people. The only thing we've got in common we do in the sack. I'm not knocking it. It's beautiful."

"Not just for the day?" She was standing behind him, her long fingers moving down his body. "We could picnic on the beach . . . or whatever."

"Not even whatever," he said. "I'm meeting my father for lunch."

"Your *father*?"

David Maxwell twisted round to face her. "Yes, my father. We get along well together. Up here." He touched his forehead.

As David drove north along the coast toward Big Sur, he felt a growing sense of excitement at the prospect of the long and stimulating lunch with his father which lay ahead.

It was a regular thing. They met on the last Saturday of each month, and together explored in conversation the frontiers of scientific knowledge. Inevitably, as the lunch wore on, his father would turn the conversation to his obsession with the dangers of nuclear proliferation and the book he was writing urging yet more stringent controls on the dissemination of nuclear expertise.

On one such occasion his father had laughed and said, "You know the Big Sur Chamber of Commerce, the way they describe this place? Somewhere to slow down, meditate, and catch up with your soul. I guess they got it wrong. For me, it's been where my soul caught up with me." And then his father had smiled ruefully and fallen silent.

Now, as David drove through the narrow Carmel streets, he wondered if perhaps his father bitterly regretted a lifetime dedicated to the development of atomic weapons. And if now he lived in some kind of inner torment, desperately trying to warn the world against the monster he had helped to create. To atone, at least in some small measure.

David parked at the side of Nepenthe, walked through the restaurant, and out onto the crowded ocean-view terrace. He ordered a large Scotch and settled down to wait for his father. After an hour and two more Scotches he left.

He pulled off the highway and followed the dirt road up to his father's place set among the trees on the hill rising up from the rugged coastline.

David pressed the doorbell, waited, then fetched the spare key left under a stone behind the bole of an old cypress tree.

Maybe his father had forgotten. More likely, he had been held up some way. David sat in the comfortable wicker chair by the window, facing out across the treetops toward the ocean, and waited.

Another hour passed.

It was hot. He went into the bathroom to freshen up. He looked up from the wash basin and noticed his father's toilet things were missing from the glass shelf. Suddenly the empty house took on a new significance.

Upstairs in the bedroom were the unmistakable signs of hasty packing.

Maxwell returned to the wicker chair. It didn't make sense. His father had gone away. Without calling him at Livermore to let him know. Without leaving a message at the restaurant. Without leaving a note for him in the house.

It wasn't like his father. He was a meticulous man. And he didn't let people down. Especially not his son.

Apprehensive, David tried to think. Then it occurred to him. A long shot but worth a try.

At the desk he flipped the pages of his father's personal telephone diary and found the number of Mrs. Jones, the woman who drove up every morning from Carmel to bring groceries and take care of the household chores.

"Mrs. Jones?"

"Yes."

"David Maxwell."

A short, embarrassed, "Oh," then silence.

"I'm at my father's place, and it looks like he's gone away. Did he happen to tell you where?"

The sound of a sharp intake of breath, then, "Yes. He's gone to visit his brother in Seattle. Said he'd be away about a week." The words spoken carefully . . . nervously.

"Mrs. Jones, I'm coming over to see you right away."

The door of the small house on the outskirts of town opened before David had time to press the bell. Mrs. Jones was short, plump, with a round face and kindly, blue eyes. She showed him into a small and neatly kept sitting room.

David remained standing. "Why did you lie to me, Mrs. Jones?" he said.

"Lie!"

"About my father. He hasn't got a brother. Not in Seattle. Not anywhere."

She caught her breath and her eyes widened. Then she slumped heavily into a chair and looked up at him with a worried expression. "I knew it. I knew something wasn't right. That *man*—" She broke off and shivered.

David was on his knees in front of her. "Now, from the beginning, Mrs. Jones. Tell me," he said quietly.

"I was at your father's house this morning, cleaning up, and this man came. When I opened the door and saw him, I froze inside. I guess you could say he was good-looking, but there was something . . . an evilness about him. . . . I can't describe it any other way. I wanted to shut the door on him and run. Can you believe a thing like that?"

David nodded. "Go on."

"He had a foreign accent. German, I would say. Asked to see your father. I left them together and got on about my business. Can't have been more than fifteen minutes later when I heard the outside door shut. And then your father came into the kitchen. I swear I never saw a man look so bad. Drained, like a ghost, and shaking all over. He just looked at me and then turned and went upstairs. I called after him, but he didn't take any notice. A short while later he called me into the library. He was still shaking, and his voice was a whisper. He said he was going to visit his brother in Seattle. I doubt he even knew what he was saying. Then he gave me an envelope. It's addressed to you."

"Where is it?" David's tension made the words a harsh command.

She rose unsteadily, went to a cupboard and returned to her chair holding a white envelope. "He said I was to keep it, but if I didn't hear from him within a week, I was to call you and have you come over and collect it right away."

David tore the envelope half open and a photograph fell out. He picked it up and the shock of what he saw drained him of strength. Barbara, naked, was standing against a bare wall. Just in view to one side of her head was a hand and a wrist—a woman's. The hand was holding an automatic a few inches from Barbara's head. David saw the terror on Barbara's face, and his shock turned to rage.

He ripped the envelope open. Inside were two letters. First, he read the one addressed to him from his father. Its message was brief and terrifying: He had had a visit from a German—Mrs. Jones could describe him. The German represented people who were holding Barbara prisoner. He had been instructed to be at an address in Bonn—twenty-two Teufelstrasse—within twenty-four hours. If he failed, or if he told *anyone* where he was going, Barbara would be killed. That was all he had been told. On receipt of this letter, seven days would have passed since he had left for Germany. David must assume the worst and hand the matter over to the proper authorities.

The other letter, in Barbara's handwriting—or a perfect facsimile of it—pleaded for her father to do as the German instructed and everything would be all right. She *knew* it.

For an instant David stood motionless.

He knew nothing. Except he was needed—at twenty-two Teufelstrasse in Bonn, West Germany.

FOUR

Bonn, Germany

The man was well over six feet tall, with iron gray hair and icy blue eyes, and weighed a hundred seventy-five pounds.

His name was Baron Friedriech von Richter.

The baron had just completed a workout in the gymnasium of his mansion situated on the top of a small hill ten kilometers outside Bonn, that would have taxed the strength and endurance of a man half his fifty-two years.

The baron walked to the end of the gymnasium and entered the shower. The water was cold, bracing and he felt a warm glow of satisfaction as he dried himself and put on a robe.

He was a strong self-disciplinarian: a fit body was necessary for an alert mind. The baron prided himself on having both, and with reason.

The gymnasium phone rang, and the baron walked briskly to the wall set and picked up the receiver.

"Herr Baron . . . ?" It was the voice of his male personal secretary. "There is someone named Herr Gartmann who wishes to speak to you. It is urgent."

"Who is he?" Von Richter asked curtly.

"I don't know. All he will say is he has a matter of

the utmost political delicacy to discuss with you."

Von Richter frowned. "Put him through."

"Baron von Richter?"

"Yes."

"We haven't met, but my name is Bruno Gartmann."

Something clicked in Von Richter's mind hearing Gartmann's full name, but he remained silent.

"I would appreciate the opportunity to discuss something with you in private," Gartmann continued.

"I'm a very busy man, Herr Gartmann. What is it you want to discuss?"

"It is a very private matter, Herr Baron."

Von Richter raised his eyebrows in annoyance. What could a man like Bruno Gartmann possibly want with him? "I'm afraid I am too busy." He was about to replace the receiver.

"A very *political* matter," Gartmann said quickly.

Von Richter was silent for a moment then said, "Very well. Be here in an hour's time. Bring some form of identification for the guards at the gate."

"Thank you, Herr Baron."

Von Richter put down the phone thoughtfully. He began to walk slowly toward the dressing room. It was odd, to say the least, that Gartmann should want to see him. He knew who Gartmann was—the cheap little SSD man who ran the brothel—and it was inconceivable that Gartmann should know more about him than was public knowledge. And yet Gartmann had used the word "political" in a very special and disturbing way. Von Richter began to dress with a growing sense of unease.

The Richter industrial and banking dynasty had

risen like a phoenix from the ashes of the First World War.

In 1921 the Chief of the Army High Command, General Hans von Seecht had struck a bargain with Lenin for the joint manufacture of armaments and military training in Russia, activities forbidden in Germany under the terms of the Treaty of Versailles.

At the time the Richter family had been a private banking house. But their involvement in financing the Russian venture, followed by the crash rearmament of Germany under Hitler, led to the establishment of a vast industrial empire. Their ties with Russia remained close. And even up to 3 A.M. on June 22, 1941, when the German army hurled itself across the Russian frontier, the Richter industries were producing machine tools destined for Russia under trading agreements endorsed personally by Hitler and Stalin.

After the war, trading ties with Russia were renewed. In time, on the premature death of his father from war wounds, the reins of the empire passed to the brilliant thirty-year-old son, Friedriech von Richter.

Under the influence of his father, Friedriech's education had been broadly based, for his father believed the survival of great industrial dynasties depended on being able to discern and predict the inevitable tides of history.

After studying English, French, and Russian at Heidelberg, Friedriech had attended the Sorbonne in Paris to read history and philosophy. His education had been completed at the Harvard Business School.

At age thirty-five Friedriech von Richter was

elected to the Bundestag where he seized every opportunity to propound his perception of the future course of history, a scenario which became known as the *Richterlehre*, the Richter doctrine.

Central to the doctrine was the evident fact that the Russian economic system had failed. And that, faced with intractible domestic problems, the Russians would seek a way out by foreign conquest. They would occupy Western Europe and the Middle East. Although America would be alerted to these dangers, the slow and due process of her democratic system would prevent her from mobilizing her resources in time to intervene decisively. With America isolated, Russia would prepare herself for the cataclysmic and inevitable war with China. A war which would start some time during the first decade of the twenty-first century, the devastation to both participants on a scale unparalleled in history.

The inescapable conclusion emerging from this scenario was that it was in the interests of Russia—and of course, in the interests of the Richter dynasty—that there be a rapprochement between Western Europe and Russia. A united Europe of half a billion people, comprised of highly industrialized and technologically advanced countries, would be the greatest concentration of power in the world. It could direct the course of history, it would solve Russia's economic problems, and it (and it alone) could contain the Chinese.

Von Richter dedicated himself to the task of persuading the Russians that the Realpolitik of history demanded that they form a powerful union with Western Europe; not conquer it. And since the Russian leaders were hard-nosed pragmatists, he did not consider his task impossible. Pragmatists were always more amenable to reason than idealists.

All this was public knowledge about Baron von Richter. However, what was known to only a few was the existence and activities of the *Weisse Kapelle*, the "White Chapel," a secret organization formed by Von Richter and comprised of influential politicians, industrialists, and members of the military from Germany, Britain, and France who shared his vision of history.

Clandestine meetings between members of the *Weisse Kapelle* and senior Russian Party officials were initiated. Because of his trading connections with Russia, Von Richter himself was able to make frequent visits to Moscow without arousing suspicion. In time, he was on first name terms with four of the eleven members of the Politburo, including the head of the KGB. Without committing themselves openly, they nevertheless conveyed to Von Richter that they sympathized with his ideas. They made it clear, however, that the older members of the Politburo would never accept his proposals. But, with the passage of time when the old men died, the situation might become very different.

It was hardly surprising therefore, that, as he finished dressing in the gymnasium, Von Richter should be feeling disturbed by a telephone call about a "political" matter from a junior and distasteful member of the SSD like Gartmann.

But as he drove out to Von Richter's estate, Gartmann felt quite different. He was triumphant. He had Dr. Maxwell. Now all he needed was the uranium, and very soon he would show that intellectual weakling Cramer and all the rest of his breed what a man of action could achieve.

At the gate of the estate Gartmann showed his driving licence to one of the two guards armed with submachine guns; he was expected: the guard waved him through.

On the way up to the house he passed two more armed guards patrolling the grounds. Someone as wealthy as Von Richter was a priority target for a kidnap attempt by any one of the terrorist groups.

A man dressed in the black uniform of a butler answered the door and led the way into the spacious library.

"Herr Gartmann?" Gartmann turned to see the imposing figure of Von Richter as he entered.

"Yes, Herr Baron." Gartmann extended his hand, but it was not accepted.

"What is your business?" Von Richter did not invite him to be seated.

Gartmann had considered carefully how he should approach the reason for his visit. Boldness and directness were the only ways to deal with a man of the baron's stature he had decided. "Herr Baron, it may surprise you to know I have impeccable references in East Berlin and Moscow."

"Your point, man?" The harshness of the baron's voice disguised the disquiet he was feeling: it was all too evident Gartmann knew at least something of his Moscow connection.

"The point, Herr Baron, is that a part of my . . . *activities,* shall we say, is to make American forces feel unwelcome in our country. I need your help to acquire a small quantity of enriched uranium 235."

Von Richter's iron self-control prevented no more than the slightest dilation of his pupils from betraying what he felt at that moment. Two thoughts were uppermost in his mind—both shattering in their implications. How did Gartmann, a menial SSD officer, know enough about him to think he could make this approach? The man was mad! What he was contemplating was unthinkable!

An atomic attack on American troops! It could start a world war! And this . . . this *imbecile* was playing around with the idea. . . . He had to be stopped. But not by him—by the SSD, by Moscow if necessary!

"Herr Gartmann," he said, "I have no idea what you are talking about, *nor* do I wish to know. You will leave now." He pressed the bell for the butler.

The butler appeared, and the baron spoke: "One more thing, Gartmann. In future I do not think you will find your references in East Berlin and Moscow are quite as impeccable as you imagine. Now—get out of my house!"

As Gartmann drove back into Bonn he felt humiliated and angry. The aristocratic swine of a baron had treated him like dirt! He was like Cramer and the rest of them. Pirouetting around like a bunch of fairies keeping their hands clean while men like him shoveled the shit and got the results. And as for that bitch Renate and her crazy idea for an atomic bomb —Christ! She would get what she deserved now.

But underlying his humiliation and anger was fear. He had acted without authority in kidnapping Dr. Maxwell. Investigations would be conducted. The

SSD—perhaps Moscow—would want to know how he knew about Von Richter. They would look into his whole operation in the minutest detail. He could not survive such an investigation.

"I don't get it," said Wilfried Linke, chief of the BND—West German counterespionage—replacing the telephone. He looked at his assistant across the desk with his thick black eyebrows raised.

His assistant grinned. "The minister?"

"Yes." Linke shook his head and banged his forehead with the palm of his hand. "I-just-don't-get-it," he repeated.

"Well, come on, give. What did he want?"

Linke ran the fingers of one hand through his thinning hair. "The minister wants us—has *ordered* us—to pick up a woman named Renate Schultze and question her."

"About . . . ?"

"About where she was on the night of the twelfth of this month."

"And . . . ?"

"And *nothing!* That's it. Except we're to act as if we don't believe her, no matter what she says. Then release her."

"Is that all? No indication of what's behind it?"

"None."

"Who is she, this Schultze woman?"

"A whore at Gartmann's."

"The *minister* told you that!"

The two men looked at each other for a long moment, then Linke shook his head. "No, nothing like that. I'd wager any amount you care to name the minister's never been near Gartmann's place. It's not his scene. I doubt he's ever been near his wife come to that."

"The guy's crazy," the assistant said.

"Yeah . . . like a fox," Linke said dryly. "Get the woman."

It was four o'clock in the afternoon and raining when Renate Schultze emerged from the offices of the BND. She ran three blocks along the wet street and ducked into a bar and ordered a large Schnapps. *What had they wanted? What did they know?*

For an hour they had questioned her. Where had she been on the night of the twelfth? *The night she had killed the runaway terrorist boy in Frankfurt!* They couldn't know. They *didn't* know, or they would have been more specific.

She gulped down the Schnapps and ordered another.

But why the incessant, repetitive questioning: *Where were you? You're lying, try again. Where were you?* They didn't know—but they *must* suspect something!

She downed the second Schnapps and left the bar. As she made her way to Gartmann's office, he was also drinking. Heavily. He looked at her with bloodshot eyes as she entered. "Stupid bitch," he snarled.

Renate ignored his insult. "I'm getting out of the country," she snapped.

The urgency in her voice communicated to Gartmann, and for an instant he forgot his own anger. "Why? What's happened?"

She told him, and Gartmann felt the invisible net

of uncontrollable events tightening around him. He had to cut the strands where he could. Eliminating identifiable areas of risk. Reduce vulnerability. Renate was right. She must go. He could not hope to maneuver against an SSD investigation while under pressure from the BND.

"When are you going?" he said.

"Tonight."

"Where?"

She looked at him. "It's better you don't know."

He nodded. "I want Dr. Maxwell's daughter before you go. We can't have her on the loose talking her head off."

"Of course."

"Where is she?"

"That information costs you twenty-five thousand marks. Remember?"

"You're in no position to make terms."

She narrowed her eyes. "Nor are you."

Gartmann bit his lip. "All right. But where is she?"

"I'll meet you tonight at ten-thirty at the intersection of Adenauer Allee and Welckerstrasse on the road to Koblenz. Bring the twenty-five thousand. I'll lead the way in my car."

"In your car?"

"Yes. I'm not returning to Bonn. I told you. I'm getting out."

She left, and Gartmann picked up the telephone.

The two cars came to a stop in front of a small, broken-down farmhouse standing on the edge of a wood. There were no lights at the windows, nor any others signs of habitation.

Renate glanced at the briefcase in Gartmann's hand as he got out of his car. "The money?" she said.

"The money," he said curtly and followed her to the door.

A young man answered the knock, recognized Renate and stood back to let her enter followed by Gartmann.

The room, lit only by a night candle, was bare save for two camping chairs and a table on which was a small transistor radio, a pack of cards, a camera, and a revolver. The windows of either side of the room were screened by old blankets. On the floor next to the door was a blue sleeping bag and, nearby, two crates of beer.

"How's the girl?" Renate said, looking at the man with distaste. He was young and good-looking, if you liked that kind of thing—a fleshy mouth and long eyelashes any woman would envy.

The man shrugged. "She's all right."

"I hope so," Renate gave him a hard stare. He was a pimp and, like most of his kind, a coward. He lived off the substantial earnings of one of the girls at the brothel. He had worked for Renate before.

"The girl's in the kitchen. I've put her to bed." The man scowled and nodded to a door.

Gartmann took two paces toward the door. "Hold it, Bruno!" Something in Renate's voice made Gartmann whip round in alarm. She was standing there, a pistol in her hand.

"What—what are you doing, Renate?" Gartmann's voice trembled.

Renate smiled maliciously. "Oh, come on, Bruno. You know the rules of the game. I've got a car full of money out there and another twenty-five thousand in your briefcase. In two hours I can cross the French frontier by one of a dozen country lanes without even being stopped. Then on to Switzerland and a Swiss bank. From there . . . anywhere I choose in the world."

"Exactly; that was what we both had in mind, wasn't it?" Gartmann smiled ingratiatingly.

"It's what *I've* got in mind, but not you, Bruno. Your rules say I won't live for five minutes after I leave this place. *If* I leave this place. Do you think I'm a fool? You can't let me live; I know too much."

"Listen to me," Gartmann pleaded. "Didn't I take you out of that cheap café. Give you beautiful clothes. Make you rich! In the name of God, Renate, let's talk this over! work something out."

"The hell you made me rich," Renate's voice was loaded with venom. "I made *you* rich. You owe your rank, your money . . . everything to me. And you were going to throw me out for that English whore. *You think I don't know!* Renate's voice rose to a crescendo of bitter hatred, and her finger tightened on the trigger.

There was no noise, merely a momentary look of astonishment in Renate's eyes before she toppled forward onto the floor, the gun clattering on the bare boards beside her.

The two men stood motionless, Gartmann's face sagging with relief, the boy's next to him deathly white.

Twenty seconds later the door opened and Günther Kraske came in, an automatic with a silencer in his hand. He smiled at Gartmann with bared teeth, then stuck a cigarette between them. He seemed amused.

Gartmann looked toward the window with the broken pane and the blanket pushed slightly to one side. "Thank God," he said to Kraske.

The boy turned to Kraske with a smile. The smile died on his face as Kraske fired and the boy slumped to the floor.

Gartmann walked to the door, his knees weak with shock. For an instant he leaned against the door before turning to Kraske. "My God," he said, his voice hollow. "You'll never know how close that was."

There was a flicker of life in Kraske's eyes, then very casually he said, "You were never in any danger, comrade. I was there all the time. I heard everything." He paused and shook his head sadly. "The Schultze woman looks like a good lay. It was a pity to kill her."

For a moment Gartmann stared at him. Then he said, "Get rid of the mess and get the girl out of here." He turned on his heel and walked out into the night.

Gartmann came out of the bathroom in his robe, a large brandy in his hand, feeling a lot better. At least he had eliminated the Schultze problem. After a good night's sleep he'd address himself to his other problems. The American girl and her father. Meantime, there was more to life than problems.

He walked to the ice bucket, put his brandy down, and poured himself a glass of champagne. He crossed to the woman lying naked on his bed and lay down beside her. "You wanted a bigger apartment," he said.

"You haven't—" the woman looked at him expectantly.

"Yes. I've sent Renate away. I was tired of her. You can have *her* apartment."

Judy Sinclair smiled with delight. "Oh, how absolutely marvelous. You *are* a darling, Bruno."

"Then thank me nicely . . . darling." Gartmann reached up for her hair and pulled her down on him.

FIVE

Bonn, West Germany

"Twenty-two Teufelstrasse," David Maxwell said to the taxi driver at Bonn airport. "And hurry."

The white-haired driver shrugged. Typical American, he thought. Always in a hurry. The way the *Amis* were during the war. Too much rushing; not enough thinking. Not like the British: so much thinking that by the time they made a move, the whole situation had changed. Funny—the way people were so different. He stamped on the accelerator and shot across the front of a Mercedes limousine and into the center lane.

The old man was wrong about David Maxwell. He had done all the thinking he needed. The conclusion, inescapable: Barbara and his father were in danger. Great danger. The explanation? Unattainable without more information. The source of the information: twenty-two Teufelstrasse.

The taxi came to a stop with a jolt outside the apartment building.

"Fast enough?" the old man grinned at David.

"Yeah," David said. "Thanks."

He gave the driver a generous tip, then stood looking at the apartment block.

Inside twenty-two Teufelstrasse, Günther Kraske was reading a paperback he had bought at LA International Airport. He was lying in a comfortable chair with his feet up on a low stool, the inevitable cigarette clenched between his teeth.

For a moment he lowered the book and glanced up at Barbara Maxwell, who was seated with her back to him by the window, gazing out at the scattered shreds of white cloud drifting across the blue sky.

Inasmuch as Kraske liked or disliked *anyone,* he quite liked this American girl. She'd had a rough time, but she hadn't cried, thrown hysterics, or done anything stupid the way most women–and men–did in her situation.

Barbara tried to concentrate on watching the slowly changing shapes of the white clouds in the sky. She was more frightened than she showed.

The doorbell rang.

Kraske put on his jacket to cover the gun in his shoulder holster. He gave Barbara a meaningful look, then went through the door, closing it behind him, and down the short corridor to open the front door.

David Maxwell pressed the bell again and kept his finger on the button.

The door opened, and Maxwell was looking at a big man with a hard stare.

"Is Barbara here?" he said.

Kraske's eyes narrowed, scrutinizing David's face.

"I'm David Maxwell . . . Barbara's my sister. Is she here?" David repeated, sensing the wariness behind Kraske's eyes.

"No–she's not here," Kraske said, choosing his words carefully. "Can I help you?"

"I had a letter from her with this address," David lied.

"Sent to you *in* America. Your accent, it's American."

"That's right," David answered.

"That probably explains it," Kraske said. "I moved in only a couple of days ago. I don't know who was here before. Maybe your sister."

"The apartment's rented?"

"Yes."

"Could you tell me who owns the apartment? She may have left a forwarding address."

Kraske hesitated. "Sorry, I can't do that. I'm sharing the apartment with a friend. He made all the arrangements. He's gone to Berlin for a few days. Try the post office—they may have her new address."

"Can you contact your friend in Berlin? In case he knows her address?"

"I don't know where he's staying. Try the post office."

Kraske started to close the door, then opened it again. "Ah, Mr. Maxwell. Tell me where I can contact you. If my friend calls from Berlin, he may have something on your sister."

"I haven't checked in anywhere yet. I came straight from the airport."

"I see. Are you familiar with Bonn?"

"My first visit."

"What do you want? Somewhere exspensive, low priced, or something in between?"

"In between, I guess."

"Then try the Hotel Daufenhof. You'll like it."

"Thanks."

The door shut, and David walked away, his mind racing. The man knew something. The way he'd said, "No, she's not here," like he was keeping his options open. The natural response would have been, "She doesn't *live* here." And the quick follow on, "Can I help you?" The guy had been fishing for information. And the all too helpful suggestion of the hotel. So he'd know where to contact him . . . *find him!* There was something else too. A sense of evil about him—the way Mrs. Jones had said.

A cab passed. He waved it down. "Hotel Daufenhof," he said.

Kraske picked up the phone and dialed. "We've got a problem," he said.

Gartmann's stomach turned over. He already had problems. "What?" his voice shook.

"Dr. Maxwell's son has turned up."

"*W-h-a-t!* Maxwell's *son!* Where?"

"Right here . . . at the apartment."

There was a long silence. Then, "I don't believe it."

"You'd better. He said he had a letter from this address."

"Impossible! You idiot, you . . ."

"Shut up, Gartmann. I didn't set this mess up. You did." There was no anger in Kraske's voice, merely impatience.

Gartmann was silent, the claws in his stomach tightening. With David Maxwell on the loose, the whole situation could blow up in his face. "You'll have to kill him," he said at last. "And quickly. Before he goes to the police."

"I know," Kraske said flatly. "I'm going to–quickly."

As Gartmann put down the receiver, Judy Sinclair appeared at the door, a provocative smile on her face. "Hello, darling," she said. "I just popped in to see if you wanted company tonight."

Gartmann looked at her speculatively, then said, "Yes. Get the cognac out of the cabinet. I need someone to talk to."

David Maxwell finished unpacking at the Hotel Daufenhof, had dinner in the downstairs restaurant, and was now pacing his room, considering his next move. The man at Barbara's address would contact him sooner or later. The question was, what action should he take before that happened? The phone rang and he almost jumped.

"Mr. Maxwell?" A woman's voice.

"Yeah."

"Mr. Maxwell, you don't know me, but it's important that I see you this evening. I can't explain now, but it would be best if we met in your hotel room."

Some instinct made David say, "No. I'll meet you in the hotel bar."

"Mr. Maxwell, your hotel room would be . . . safer."

David didn't think so. "The bar," he repeated.

A pause. "Very well. If you insist."

"I do."

"Ten o'clock then," the woman said and hung up.

David put the phone down, knowing he'd made the right decision. All the players in this game knew more than he did. And that had to include the woman. His room was private—too private. Elementary precautions were necessary, essential.

At five minutes to ten he went down to the bar, gave his name to the barman, ordered a Scotch and soda, and selected a table in an alcove at one end of the room.

He sipped his Scotch. The woman's voice had been upper crust English. Very. That didn't tell him anything except that *maybe* she was upper crust English.

"Mr. Maxwell." David looked up. Christ, she was beautiful. Tall, perfect features, shining long blond hair, and wearing an exquisitely tailored creamy white silk suit.

"Judy Haverford," Judy Sinclair said, extending a slim hand.

David rose and took her hand. A very firm grip for such an elegant lady, David thought.

"Drink?" He watched her sit down and cross her long, shapely legs.

"I've ordered one, thank you."

"What can I do for you, Miss Haverford?" David said sitting back and examining her face, particularly her eyes. They were wide-spaced and green with an almost unnatural brightness, the way a brilliantly colored orchid seems strangely unnatural in its exotic beauty. But there was far more to them then that, David decided. They were intelligent eyes. Calculating. And at that moment they were scrutinizing him at least as acutely as he was her.

"I'm afraid you are going to find what I have to say hard to understand, Mr. Maxwell. But I would urge you to consider my advice with the utmost seriousness."

Maxwell listened carefully. There was no other way of regarding this woman. "And what is your advice?" he said and was surprised to find he had lowered his voice.

"Get out of Germany, Mr. Maxwell. Now. Tonight. Any way you can."

Maxwell hadn't known what to expect. But not this. "Why?"

"Because unless you do, it is most unlikely you will be alive tomorrow morning," she replied evenly.

The waiter arrived with a large, neat Scotch. She sipped it and eyed Maxwell while he tried to take in her astounding statement.

"Don't you think that needs some explanation?" David asked. "And who exactly are you?"

"It won't matter when you're dead."

"Right now I'm not dead," David said. "So let's get this straight. You're a complete stranger, yet you know who I am and where to find me. Your warning means either you don't want me to be killed *or* you want me out of Germany. Which?"

"Both, Mr. Maxwell." She leaned forward, and David caught the subtle fragrance of her perfume. "I can't explain much, but this I will tell you. As I'm sure you realize, it's connected with your father and your sister. There is nothing you can do to help them. Absolutely nothing. Do you understand?" She looked at him earnestly, then sat back, adding, "But you're going to try. And that's why you're going to be killed."

"Are you telling me if I went to the police, it wouldn't help my father and sister? And it wouldn't help keep me alive?"

"I'm telling you more than that, Mr. Maxwell. If you go to the police, you will be pronouncing the sentence of death on your father and sister. And maybe you will still be killed."

"Look . . ." David gripped the edge of the table. "Just *who* are you?"

"I can't tell you, Mr. Maxwell, but I beg you *please* get out of here. There's more at stake then even your family."

"Paging Mr. Maxwell." A young fresh-faced boy passed the alcove with "Mr. Maxwell" chalked on a board attached to a short pole.

David jumped to his feet and waved to the boy. "I'm Maxwell," he said.

"Telephone for you, *mein Herr*. You can take it in the lobby."

David turned to Judy Sinclair. "I'll be right back. You'll wait?"

He caught a fleeting look of anxiety in her eyes before she said, "Yes. I'll wait."

In the lobby he picked up the phone. "Maxwell."

"Ah, Mr. Maxwell. I'm glad I got hold of you. I'm the man you spoke to this afternoon. By good luck my friend has just phoned from Berlin. I asked him about your sister."

"And?" David prompted.

"He knows where your sister is but it seems to be a rather delicate matter. I can't talk on the telephone."

"Where then?"

"I suggest you come to the apartment again. In case you haven't got your bearings yet, it's directly across the park from your hotel. Five minutes' walk. It'll be quicker than taking a cab at this time of night."

"I'll be right with you," David said.

David returned to the bar. "Miss Haverford, I have to leave you. Something urgent's come up."

"Please, Mr. Maxwell, Don't go *anywhere*. Don't do anything. Just get out of Germany, I beg you." She was on her feet, standing close to him.

"Sorry, Miss Haverford. You know where you can contact me again if you want to." He turned and walked quickly out of the bar.

As he hurried beneath the trees in the darkened park, he tried to put the beautiful Miss Haverford out of his mind. The only thing he knew about her for sure was she *did* want him out of Germany. For reasons unknown.

His immediate concern was Kraske. He wasn't going to his apartment. They would talk in a nearby bar or on the street, but not in his apartment.

He approached the lights at the other side of the park and quickened his pace. About five yards ahead of him, the broad trunk of a giant chestnut was silhouetted against the streetlights.

The crack of the shot was crisp and sharp, like a firecracker. David spun to his left where the shot had come from. In the glow of the light spilled between the trees from the street, she was unmistakable. Not her face, but the tall figure of a woman dressed in white.

Maxwell ran. Back into the park, not toward the street where he would be an easy target silhouetted against the lights. He stopped running at the entrance to his hotel.

Breathlessly, he went into the bar. Miss Haverford wasn't there. Naturally.

In his hotel room he called the operator and got the telephone number of the apartment in Teufelstrasse. He dialed, the phone rang . . . and rang. There was no answer.

David replaced the receiver.

Now he knew two things. Miss Haverford was in cahoots with the man at Teufelstrasse. And Miss Haverford wanted him out of Germany . . . or in Germany, dead.

SIX

Bonn, West Germany

General Wade Horton sat down in the comfortable leather chair and stretched his legs in front of him. He did not know who owned the house he was in, but he was sure it was not the occupant of the chair opposite him—Colonel Ivanov, the Russian military attaché in Bonn.

The Russians would have selected the house with great care. A private meeting between the deputy commander of NATO forces in Central Europe and the Russian military attaché was, to say the least, unusual.

Not that this was their first secret meeting. The first had come about much the way the general had expected. Three days after he had returned to Brunssum from Naples he had received an anonymous phone call. His caller had spoken briefly, referring only to "the memento you left in the garden of our consulate in Naples," and then suggested a time and address on the outskirts of Bonn "where the matter can be discussed."

As suggested, the general had driven the short distance from Brunssum to Bonn, and there he had met Colonel Ivanov.

The colonel was tall and slim and had a long, aquiline face and delicate-looking white skin. But what had impressed the general was his obvious, acute intelligence and air of competence: very considerable competence.

Eventually the general had told the colonel every detail of the horror of that night in Naples. The colonel had listened in silence, then said, very quietly, "What is it you want, General?"

The general had spoken the one word, *"Vengeance!"* And in the general's eyes the colonel had seen a look of inhuman ferocity which, for reasons he could not understand, had sent a cold chill down his spine. "How?" he had replied in a whisper.

"That is for you to work out," the general had replied. "In a situation of military crisis, I can give orders affecting the whole defense of Western Europe. Orders which will be obeyed without question. Do I have to say more?"

The colonel had been overwhelmed by the enormity of the general's words. The implications were incalculable. But he knew he must be cautious. "Have you any proof of what you have told me?" he had said at last.

"Tomorrow is the end of the month," the general replied. "Frau Gensert's lawyers will not receive their usual message from her; they will release her letter to the SSD. It will be all the proof you need."

"Encouragement, but not proof, General. It is conceivable your intelligence people uncovered Frau Gensert, killed her, fabricated your story, and have made arrangements for the letter to be sent. After all, General, we cannot overlook the possibility that this is a bizarre and elaborate trick to discredit the veracity of the information your son gave us on the Sosus system."

The general had fixed the colonel with the hard, uncompromising eyes of a man who knew his strength. "Then find some other way to convince yourself I am not lying. I am handing you the biggest opportunity that will come your way if you live for a thousand years."

The colonel had known the general was right. And that was why, as the two men met for the second time, impatiently waiting in an adjoining room was Dr. Korznikov, senior analyst at the Lenin Institute of Psychiatry in Moscow. His orders were as clear as they were daunting—*to assess in twenty-four hours whether the general could be relied upon beyond doubt to commit an act of betrayal against his country of immeasurable proportions.*

"Drugs!" the general exclaimed when the colonel had explained what was intended.

"I regret it should be necessary, General. But there is no other way. We have to be convinced. We have the letter from Frau Gensert to the SSD, but it is not enough."

"The truth drug?"

"And possibly other drugs. The truth drug is not always one hundred percent reliable. You will cooperate?"

"If it's the only way."

"The *only* way. I will fetch the doctor immediately. You will understand the administering of drugs is not a matter for amateurs."

As they were introduced, the general nodded

curtly at the doctor, with his thinning silver hair and bushy eyebrows.

"I suggest we start immediately," the colonel continued quickly and led the way to a living room at the back of the house.

"The couch, please," the doctor said waving his hand with its stubby fingers toward a chaise longue covered in crimson velvet. "Take your jacket off and roll up the sleeve of your right arm, please, General."

Dr. Korznikov pulled up a chair and sat beside him. Then, feeling for a prominent vein, he slowly injected a solution of sodium thiopentone, his eyes riveted on the general's face: the quality and rate of injection had to be sufficent to obliterate the general's mental censors, but not enough to induce narcotic stupor.

Then began a series of questions covering every detail of the general's story; the doctor speaking in a quiet, firm voice, the general answering in a slow monotone.

Every detail checked.

From behind the chaise longue the colonel smiled triumphantly. He gave a thumbs-up signal to the doctor. The doctor scowled and shook his head irritably, then rose and gestured for the colonel to join him some distance away by the window.

"We've got him!" the colonel whispered excitedly. "He's *ours.*"

"No, comrade, we have not got him—not yet. My instructions are to establish that a dedicated professional soldier can be relied upon to commit a *monstrous* act of betrayal against his own army.

When the time comes for him to carry out this act he may pull back. Intention and act are not the same. I must know more about the general and his motivations before I can be certain he will *act.*"

The doctor returned to the general and began to question him again, taking him back through his life. The general responded freely and without stress to questions about the death of his wife, his military career and his combat experience in Korea and Vietnam.

"Now imagine the time when you were a little boy, a *very* little boy, as far back as you can remember," the doctor continued. "Tell me about your father."

At first the general spoke calmly, saying that his father was always good to him, strict but fair. He always made time to be with him—gave him a baseball kit for his fifth birthday and played with him in the garden, even took him fishing. "And then—" The general stopped abruptly and stared fixedly in front of him.

"And then," the doctor prompted softly.

"He *was* a good father." The general's tone was defiant.

"Always?" the doctor coaxed.

"Always!" The general turned to face the doctor, his eyes full of anger.

"Of course," the doctor said soothingly. He rose and beckoned the colonel to the window again. "He's hiding something," he said. "Something so deep-seated even the drug won't allow him to speak of it. It must be very important to him and, if my experience is anything to go by, possibly very important to us."

The doctor began to pace up and down, stroking his chin. After several minutes he stopped and said, "I don't like it. The risks are great. I know nothing of the general's medical history. To introduce another drug into his system?" He shook his head. "The effect on him is totally unpredictable."

"Risks have to be taken, Comrade Doctor. Our orders are from the Kremlin. What drug do you have in mind?"

"Mescaline. It's a hallucinogenic drug. Under its influence some patients will act out wish-fulfilling fantasies. I have an instinct about the general. If the mescaline works, I think we may get what we want. But we must wait a few hours to allow the drugs already in his system to dissipate to some degree at least."

"It's essential?"

"That's my opinion."

"You'll want to remain with him while you wait?"

"Of course."

"I'll bring you some sandwiches and coffee."

"Yes, thank you."

After taking in the sandwiches for the doctor, the colonel went to the study and called the Russian Embassy. Yes, he was assured, Baron von Richter had already left for Riga as arranged.

The colonel returned to the kitchen where he sat deep in thought. He could think of no reason why Von Richter was wanted in Riga so urgently; nor why he himself was to fly there immediately as he was in no position to report on the general.

Shortly after three o'clock the doctor declared himself ready to proceed, and the colonel took his position behind the chaise longue.

"What are you doing?" the general said opening his eyes and raising himself on one elbow as the doctor took his arm to administer the injection of mescaline.

"Just one more, then we will be finished," the doctor answered reassuringly.

The general sat back, and the doctor injected the mescaline.

After a short while the general felt himself going hot and cold. His body began to tremble, and his eyes darkened over as the pupils dilated. Then he heard the doctor speaking—he could see him clearly but he seemed to be sitting a long way from him. "You were happy with your father, General; then something happened. What was it?"

The general swiveled his head from side to side slowly and began to speak. "I was six and I heard my mother and father quarreling. My mother was screaming and laughing at my father, saying he wasn't my real father. It was some other man. I was too young to understand what she meant at the time. My father left the house the next day. He never came back."

Abruptly the general fell still and silent. The colonel looked questioningly at the doctor who raised his finger to his lips to indicate silence. After a few moments the general began to tremble again, his facial muscles working savagely in anger. For an instant he stared at the doctor, *and he saw the face of his father*! Without warning, his hands shot like a bullet to grasp the neck of the doctor. The doctor's chair crashed to the floor, and the general was astride him, his powerful hands tightening around the doctor's throat. "You treacherous bastard. I'm going to kill you," he yelled.

The colonel had his arms around the general's neck, heaving with all his strength to drag him off. But the general had the power of a madman. In desperation the colonel leaned back, then brought the side of his hand down onto the general's neck with all his weight behind it, terrified (though he had no choice) that he might kill the man. The general felt nothing. He slumped forward onto the doctor.

The colonel heaved him off the gasping doctor. "Are you all right, comrade?"

To his amazement the colonel saw a wide smile light up the doctor's face as he said, "Magnificent! Absolutely *magnificent*! Here. Help me up." He held up his hand, and the colonel pulled him up. Then still gasping, he fumbled in his bag, found a hypodermic, and slammed the needle into the general's rump. "That'll keep him quiet for a while. We don't want anything to happen to him; he's a prize specimen."

"Do you realize, comrade," the doctor continued excitedly and waving a forefinger at the colonel, "in my whole life I have seen it only twice. A perfect textbook case!" He beamed at the colonel again.

"Perhaps I could share in the cause of your good humor?" the colonel said.

"Yes, of course, my dear colonel. The general and his father had a very close relationship. Then his father deserted him without his knowing why. An experience so traumatic, he couldn't bring himself to talk of it even under the sodium thiopentone. But under the mescaline the general relived the experience."

"But why is this all so important?"

"Because, Colonel, it explains why the general is prepared to commit such an act of treachery against his army. You see, he could not allow himself *consciously* to feel anger—he *loved* his father. So he did what young children very often do in such a situation: he internalized the anger in the shape of guilt. *His* guilt. *He* must have made his father do this terrible thing. But repressed underneath, like a boiling volcano waiting to spew out through some crack in the earth's crust, his anger has remained buried, wanting vengeance against the man who had shattered his world. Repressed aggression is too mild a way to express such a force."

"I still don't see the connection between this and—" The colonel interrupted.

"Obvious. The army gave the general what his father had destroyed. An authoritarian world. Strict but fair. And, above all, a *predictable* world in which the rules and the consequences of action are known. And then it happened, the same way as it had happened with his father: the army betrayed him by killing his son. He cracked—and now the volcanic forces are loose, and there is no way of stopping them. He *is* reliable. He *will* act."

"No reservations? You know how important it is."

"None."

"So he *is* ours."

"Yes, Colonel, *all* ours."

SEVEN

●

Riga, U.S.S.R. of Latvia

On the Baltic Sea, some twenty kilometers from Riga and high above the rocky coast, there stands an imposing stone mansion. The land from the mansion slopes steeply toward the sea, studded here and there by massive outcroppings of rock. Between these grow a wide variety of trees and scattered among them are ten freshly whitewashed stone villas, each one surrounded by a well-tended garden full of flowers and shrubs.

The setting and accommodation would be ideal for a luxury vacation complex. In fact, it is one of several retreats in the Soviet Union used by the eleven members of the Politburo when they feel it necessary, or pleasurable, to escape from Moscow for a while.

The mansion and the villas are more than ample to accommodate the members of the Politburo together with their senior aides, their guards, and their servants.

Inside each villa are freshly cut flowers, bowls of fruit, a fully stocked liquor cabinet, and a selection of foods and wines from all over the world. A phone call to the main building will supply any further needs the visitor might have.

It was ten o'clock in the evening. The baron had finished a superb meal of Beluga caviar, venison, and fresh peaches expertly prepared and served by a waiter in a brilliant red uniform. With a snifter in his hand, the baron stood at the open door of the villa breathing the cool night air. Not far distant he could hear the somnolent lapping of the waves against the rocks.

Lights appeared at the window of the adjacent villa. The baron wondered who the new arrival was. He had been for a walk around the grounds shortly before dusk, and most of the villas appeared to be already occupied. He had seen people hurrying between the villas; two had been dressed in the uniform of chief marshal of the Soviet Union. And being shepherded into one villa by a severe-looking woman in a long black skirt, a group of four young girls in their early teens.

The baron took one last breath and closed the door. He flipped through the magazines, found the current edition of *Der Spiegel* and began to read. But he found it hard to concentrate. His mind kept returning to the perplexing question of why he should have been summoned to what was obviously a politburo meeting of a very unusual nature.

Lost in thought, he gave a start at the sound of the doorbell. To his surprise, his visitor was Colonel Ivanov.

"Good evening, Baron. As your new neighbor, I thought it might be sociable to drop in for a nightcap . . . if it's convenient of course."

"Come in, dear Colonel, do come in." The baron's smile was genuine, though it did cross his mind to wonder why the colonel should visit him so soon after the tiring journey from Bonn.

"What will you drink?"

"Some of that splendid Napoleon brandy."

The baron poured the drinks, and the two men seated themselves in the comfortable chintz-covered armchairs. "Have you been called into the presence of the Mighty Ones yet?" the colonel asked, smiling and nodding his head in the direction of the mansion.

The colonel knew the answer to his question. But a note of humor and shared mystery seemed the best way to carry out the instructions he had received directly from the KGB: to visit the baron immediately and set him at his ease as much as possible.

"No, not yet. To be honest, I have no idea why I'm here."

The colonel laughed. "That makes two of us," he lied.

A moment of embarrassed silence followed before the colonel said, "I have just had a most unusual experience, Baron. I think it will interest you. A very senior NATO commander offered to cooperate with us, and we had to find out if his offer was genuine. The whole business was quite fascinating."

The colonel described the methods Dr. Korznikov used to pry open the secrets buried in General Horton's mind. He made no mention of the General's name nor of the events which had taken place in Naples.

The baron was very interested, and from time to time he interrupted with questions. As he was not without knowledge in the use of drugs, he wondered why the Russian psychiatrist had taken the considerable risk of administering the different drugs in so short a time. Clearly, the Russians had been in a great hurry. The same urgency, in fact, as applied to his own summons to the politburo meeting.

Nor did he miss the reference to baseball which the colonel let slip when describing the NATO commander's childhood. A minor slip, the baron thought, and totally understandable in view of the colonel's fascination with the case. Obviously, the very senior NATO commander was an American.

"That's an astounding story," the baron agreed and rose to refill their glasses. The phone rang. The baron handed the glasses to the colonel and went to the phone. "Yes . . . in about five minutes . . . yes, he's with me. I'll tell him." The baron replaced the receiver. "That was *your* lord and master," he told the colonel with a slight smile. "KGB Chairman Grechko."

"What did he want?" the colonel feigned surprise.

"He and the foreign minister are coming down to the villa in about five minutes."

"I wonder what they want."

"I wonder," said the baron, taking his glass from the colonel.

The two men sat in uneasy silence, sipping their brandies and carefully avoiding each other's eyes.

The doorbell rang, and the colonel rose to answer it. Chairman of the KGB, Vladimir Grechko was a short, chunky man with powerful features, thick gray hair and a mustache to match. He entered the villa followed by the tall, angular, and balding foreign minister, Aleksei Burov. As they greeted him, the baron detected a forced air of cordiality tinged with embarrassment. Both men looked exhausted.

When the visitors had their drinks, Burov sank into a chair with a long groan, stretched his legs out, and drained his glass. He looked at the baron. "You know how long we've been at it? Eighteen hours a day for the past five days. I could sleep for a week." He let out a long sigh.

"You're getting old, comrade," Grechko said in a voice like coarse gravel. "You want to sleep, ha! . . . And you know what that dog Karpov will be at right now? Filling himself with vodka while a couple of ripe Georgian girls display themselves. Then he'll be at them for half the night like a mad bull. In the morning he'll look as if he's slept like a baby all night. The man's seventy! He's inhuman! And what about Moslov?" he grinned slyly.

Burov shot Grechko a quick warning glance, and Grechko contented himself with a hoarse chuckle. The phone rang. The colonel took the call, said a few words, excused himself to the group, and left.

When the door shut, Grechko looked at the baron. "As you know, Burov and I and several other members of the Politburo had hoped, as you do, there could be a peaceful coming together of our two countries and the formation of a united Europe. I regret this is not to be. We are to take the other path."

The baron hesitated before using the word, but there *was* no other word. "War," he said quietly.

The two Russians nodded.

"An irrevocable decision?" the baron asked.

"Totally. The debate is over. We have lost. The final decision has been made. There are too many powerful and logical arguments for war. As you know, Baron, there is no doubt we can win a European war. Our General Staff is completely confident, and our intelligence information tells us it is a view secretly shared by NATO commanders."

"But the losses, the devastation!"

"Acceptable." Grechko punched the word out. "The Americans are at last beginning to realize the danger they are in. The sleeping giant is stirring. The possibility exists they will embark on a crash arms program. If they do, we are lost. An attempt to keep up with them would bleed us dry. Our economy would collapse. These are the hard facts of reality we have to face. We must strike now before it is too late. As the Americans would say, we must cash in our chips while we are still ahead and unify Europe by force of arms."

There was a long silence. The baron understood only too well the power of the arguments he had just heard. At last he said, "Why are you telling me this? Aren't you afraid I might warn my people?"

It was Burov's turn to speak. "No, Baron, you are too intelligent to do that. The losses in this war on both sides will be horrendous. It will be a quick war, but a war of attrition. And since we outnumber you so heavily in men and armaments, we must win. The truth is, the quicker it is over, the better. If you warn your people, you will be doing them a great disservice. It could only prolong the struggle and cause even greater suffering and devastation to your country. The outcome would be inevitable."

"Then why–"

"Because we want your help to reduce the suffering . . . on both sides." Burov was standing close as he spoke, the bottle of brandy in his hand poised over the baron's glass. The baron nodded, and Burov poured, saying, "The crucial time will be the first forty-eight hours. That is when NATO will have to make the decision whether or not to use tactical nuclear weapons to try and stop us, If they do, the destruction in the area of battle–mainly West Germany–will be colossal. It will not affect the final outcome, of course, for our forces are far better equipped to fight in a nuclear environment than NATO's. But, we would rather avoid the losses inevitable in a nuclear conflict.

Burov replaced the bottle of brandy on the table and looked at Grechko who tented his fingers and put them to his chin. "For the sake of your country," Grechko said, "and ours, we are asking you to use the influence of the *Weisse Kapelle* to ensure that nuclear weapons are not used."

"How? . . . Precisely?"

"Among the members of the *Kapelle* you have many politicians with large financial and media interests capable of influencing governments and public opinion. Start a campaign immediately against the *first* use by NATO of nuclear weapons in the event of war. I need hardly tell you that such a campaign will be well received by the public. And in view of the lack of a firm policy on this matter among the NATO governments, public opinion will prove decisive. And–"

The baron only half-listened while Grechko, with

his accustomed thoroughness, went into the details of his proposal. His thoughts were occupied by entirely different considerations. A peaceful rapprochement between Germany and Russia was one thing. Germany's economic power would make them equal partners in any such arrangement. But Russian *occupation* of a defeated and devastated Germany was an entirely different matter. The destruction of both his country and the Richter dynasty was not a prospect the baron was prepared to contemplate.

The baron's mind—that unique mixture of vision and discipline—was already at work. The germ of an idea. A collection of disconnected threads, the raw material from which the fabric of an idea might be woven, began to form in his mind.

Grechko was still speaking. "Will you help us make this war as quick and as painless as possible?" he concluded.

The baron remained silent. At last he said, "I am sympathetic to your ideas, but I have a counter proposal to make."

In unison the eyes of the two Russians narrowed.

"However," the baron continued, "I have hardly had time to formulate my proposal in detail. I suggest we meet here again at seven o'clock tomorrow morning. I take it that will give you sufficient time to consider my proposal before reporting back to your comrades in the Politburo?"

Grechko spoke first. "What possible alternative can there be?"

"It's either war or peace, Baron. There's no going back. No alternative," Burov echoed.

"I think there may be an alternative," the baron

replied, "which is neither war nor peace. An alternative both our countries will accept."

The Russians stared at him blankly.

"Now, gentlemen, if you will excuse me, I have some thinking to do." The baron rose to his feet, and the Russians did likewise. "Good night, gentlemen," the baron said at the open door. "I will see you at seven o'clock."

Grechko and Burov left without speaking. They could think of nothing to say. Nothing at all.

The baron put on a light topcoat and went out into the cool night air. A brisk walk along the cliffs would clear his head. He stood on a small promontory, gazing out over the calm sea bathed in moonlight. Then, breathing deeply, he followed the cliffs for exactly ten minutes before turning back to his villa.

The pathways zigzagged between the villas, but a glimpse of the brightly lit mansion from between the trees was enough for him to keep his direction.

As he passed one villa, he heard the sound of raucous laughter. The door suddenly slammed open, and two naked men were framed in the entrance. They were struggling violently, kicking wildly, arms flailing. A shout of agony as one pair of hands found their target, the opponent's testicles. The two men collapsed, thrashing on the path. A second later four more naked figures appeared at the door: two men and two women. They were laughing uproariously at the struggling bodies on the ground. And on the heads of the two women were the unmistakable peaked caps worn by chief marshals of the Soviet Union.

Quietly the baron stepped off the path into the shadow of the trees.

Another two hundred meters, he estimated, and he would be back at his villa. Again he heard a scream, but there was something about the sound which made him hesitate. It was the high-pitched scream of a girl; a very young girl. His every nerve jarred as the screams increased in anguish and intensity. He moved quickly to the side of the villa and peered through the slats of the only partially closed venetian blinds. Revulsion turned his stomach.

Now he knew why Grechko and Burov had refused to talk in his presence about the sexual proclivities of Politburo member Moslov.

One of the very young girls he had seen that afternoon—hardly more than a child—was stripped naked and lying stretched prone at the end of a bed. The woman was there too, grimly forcing the girl's head and shoulders downward. And standing behind the girl was Moslov, the alcoholic perspiration dripping from his brow as he ferociously rammed his penis into the girl, his eyes glazed with lust.

The baron decided he did not like the nightlife of the High and Mighty at their peaceful and beautiful retreat on the Baltic Coast. In his villa, he poured himself a large brandy, then, placing a chair by the open door, began to think.

As he knew would happen, he found that the thoughts which had first entered his mind while listening to Grechko had already begun to grow and take shape. Among them were three major ideas, and he concentrated on them, examining and developing them.

By the time the birds started to sing their dawn chorus, he had woven them into a pattern in which each thread had its strengths and weaknesses. With luck and infinite skill, the fabric could be made to hold together; *it would work.*

The baron closed his eyes and slept.

Later that day, five hours after his early breakfast meeting with Grechko and Burov, the baron walked slowly to the cliffs and climbed down the steep rock face to the sea's edge. There he stripped naked and dived into the icy waters of the Baltic. For an hour he swam steadily, his mind blank, aware only of the relaxing hypnotic rhythm of his muscles. And when he eventually emerged from the sea and returned to his villa, he felt a calm confidence in the plan he had outlined to Grechko and Burov.

The three strands consisted of the *Weisse Kapelle;* the American general who wanted to humiliate his own army; Bruno Gartmann, who wanted to make atomic bombs in West Germany. They would all work together to achieve the baron's goal.

It was an intricate and ingenious plan. The difficulties were enormous, but not insurmountable. Many men would have to die. Betrayal and treachery were the very core of his plan. The baron believed that the moral principle of the ends never justifying the means was a self-indulgence only idealists could afford; men who cared about the future could not be squeamish.

Now all the baron could do was wait. Everything depended on the eleven men cloistered in the mansion on the hill, discussing the future of Western Europe

—the future of two hundred and fifty million people.

Dusk had begun to fall when Grechko and Burov stood once more at the door of the baron's villa, smiling and jubilant, each carrying a bottle of champagne. They both congratulated the baron heartily with warm embraces. "Your proposal has been approved," Grechko beamed. "In fact the party leader went so far as to say he was 'enthusiastic'! And he is not a man given to praise."

The baron extricated himself from their arms and said, "The glasses, gentlemen. I suggest you fill them."

The bottles were opened and the glasses filled.

"Now to business," Grechko said. "There are, of course, conditions."

The baron looked at him without expression. "Naturally," he said.

"*All* contact with the American general will continue to be made by us."

"What I expected," the baron agreed, sipping his champagne.

"The actual manufacture of the atomic bombs will be *your* responsibility," Grechko continued. "And it is imperative all activities are made to appear attributable to the neo-Nazis. *Everything* you do must seem to threaten Russian interests as much as the Americans."

"Obviously," the baron replied impatiently. "And you are prepared to make the necessary arrangements in East Germany—*including* the sacrifice of your own men?"

"Agreed." Grechko drew a notepad from his pocket and glanced at it. "The uranium," he said. "That will not be supplied by us. Not directly. It will be stolen in such a manner as to point the finger of responsibility to West German sources."

"How?"

"It is better you don't know," Grechko replied. "However, you can be sure it will be traced to Western sources."

"And the country of operation?" the baron asked.

"Zambu, on the coast of South West Africa."

The baron considered this, then replied, "A good selection. The logistics will be comparatively easy."

"That is what we thought. Now, the name of the operation. The party leader has chosen it himself: *The Coda Alliance*."

The baron smiled wryly. Evidently the party leader had a taste for music. A coda is an independent, often elaborate, passage of music introduced after the natural conclusion of the main work. A sort of surprise. "An apt choice," he said.

"Precisely," Burov said with a sly grin. "The West will think events have reached their natural conclusion. Then we spring the Coda. The coup de grace."

"And the timing?"

"The twentieth of June."

"But that's little more than three weeks away," the baron protested.

"It has to be, Baron. If your operation is not successful, the original intention to invade at 3:30 A.M. on the twenty-second of June will be put into effect."

The baron raised his eyebrows quizzically.

"Correct," Grechko said, answering the baron's unspoken question. "Our chiefs of staff have a sense of humor. It is the anniversary of Hitler's attack on *our* country. Now, one last point. I said the party leader was enthusiastic about your plan. So enthusiastic he wants you to have an incentive to succeed. You have his word that, if you *fail,* the Richter dynasty will cease to exist. Completely!"

EIGHT

Bonn, West Germany

Earlier that morning, as the baron was climbing out of the sea onto the rocks after his swim, David Maxwell finished his breakfast in the hotel.

He had spent a restless night, half waking, half sleeping, in a twilight world of nightmares and indecision. He had been warned to get out of Germany or die. And to prove her point, the beautiful Judy Haverford *had* tried to kill him in the park. He *should* go to the police. But the photograph of Barbara with the gun at her head was ever present in his mind, as was the way his father had left for Germany without even telling *him,* let alone the police. However obscure their meaning, they were warnings he could not ignore.

Through the windows of the breakfast room he could see sheets of torrential rain drenching the sidewalk in a thousand spurts of water, and across the street the branches of the trees waved crazily in the gusting wind of a freak May storm.

Maxwell rose from the table and took the elevator to his room. The only immediate course of action was to go back to that apartment, to the man who had suggested he cross the park in order to set him up as a target for Judy Haverford.

He took his raincoat from the closet and was about to leave when the phone rang.

"Mr. Maxwell?" David recognized the precise English enunciation of Miss Haverford.

"Yes."

"You were nearly killed last night."

"I'd noticed," David said. "I was there. Your night shooting leaves a lot to be desired, I'm glad to say."

"Mr. Maxwell, this is not a time for jokes."

"Really! What is it a time for?"

"Getting out of Germany, Mr. Maxwell."

"I got your message last night, Miss Haverford—if that's your name, which I doubt."

"Then for God's sake be sensible and get out!"

David was silent for a moment, then he said, "I think we're wasting our time, Miss Haverford. I have no wish to get myself killed. On the other hand I have no intention of leaving here until I have found my sister and my father. In short, Miss Haverford, I want information, not bullets."

A long pause. Then, "I can't give you information, but I can give you a promise. If you do anything except get a taxi directly to the airport, you will be dead by the end of this day."

"That's all, huh?"

"That's all, Mr. Maxwell. Except, Good-bye."

Maxwell took the elevator down to the lobby and tried to make sense of the cultured Miss Haverford, or whoever. She had warned him, tried to kill him, and now she was warning him again. Why make it so complicated? Why didn't she just concentrate on the killing bit!

Outside, it was still pouring. After waiting fifteen minutes for a taxi, he gave up and started to walk. But not across the park. Not even in daylight. It would take him about twenty minutes, but he wasn't short on time; he was short on answers.

The streets were half empty. People were either taking shelter inside until the storm blew over or riding in the taxis he couldn't get. He leaned forward into the blustering wind and felt the water trickling down the back of his neck.

He came to a corner where a small crowd was huddled under the awning in front of a restaurant, avoiding the downpour and vainly stepping out into the rain every now and again in search of an empty taxi.

David halted under the awning to mop the back of his neck with his handkerchief and pull up the collar of his coat. The blow came from behind him, just above his ankles, sweeping his legs from under him and sending him sprawling onto his face on the sidewalk.

The sound that came a second later was unmistakable. The urgent spewing of bullets from a submachine gun; a continuous staccato of shattering, metallic vibrations, the sound of death. And then came the screams and the shattering of glass.

Maxwell flung his body round to face the sound of the firing. Through the blur of the downpour it was impossible to be certain but for an instant he thought he saw the face of the man from the apartment peering through the window of a fast disappearing black limousine. The man had something white around the top of his head—a bandage, perhaps.

David staggered to his feet, and a look of horror came to his face. It was like a film of a mass execution. Only it wasn't a film. The fusillade of bullets had raked the people huddled under the awning.

For an instant David stood watching, unable to take in the reality of such carnage. Then he was filled with an unthinking, blind rage. He began to run. Across the road and into the park. The grass was sodden and slippery under his feet. He skidded to the ground repeatedly as he forced himself with every ounce of strength and breath to cross that park and reach that apartment. *That* apartment! The only point of contact he knew with a network of death. And when he got there, *he-did-not-care-what-happened! Somebody, somehow, was going to pay!*

His heart pounding, gasping for breath, David reached the apartment. Ignoring the bell, he raised his fist and slammed it against the door, time and time again. It remained closed. Still in a frenzy of impotent rage, he seized the door handle and crashed his shoulder against the solid oak panel. The unlocked door flew open.

Maxwell's momentum carried him halfway down the narrow corridor. He regained his balance and rushed on into the room at the far end. It was empty! He looked around quickly. The room was spotlessly clean. Empty ash trays, the furniture freshly polished. Not a spot of dust or—Maxwell quickly realized—fingerprints!

He opened the adjoining door into a bedroom. The bed was bare, the closets empty.

Maxwell raised his fist and in helpless rage crashed it against the door of the closet. He stared at the torn flesh of his bloody knuckles. And again he saw the shattered and bleeding bodies under the awning. Then he was filled with a chilling fear: Barbara and his father were in the hands of people who were prepared to commit acts of coldblooded mayhem to kill one man. Him! *He* had been the target, and only fifteen minutes after the lovely Judy Haverford had promised his death. She delivered! If he hadn't tripped he . . . Maxwell frowned. He *hadn't* tripped. He had *been* tripped. Deliberately. Expertly. He stared blankly at the blood dripping from his knuckles onto the boards of the floor.

"What are you doing in here?" a voice demanded from behind him.

Maxwell turned sharply to face the man at the door. "Nothing," he replied.

"That's not good enough," the man said advancing toward Maxwell. "I am in charge of the apartments and—"

"Get the hell out of my way," Maxwell said and shoved the man aside.

The man was still yelling at him as he went out of the door of the apartment.

He walked down the street and hailed a passing taxi.

"Where to?" the driver asked.

"I want a hotel," Maxwell answered. "A cheap hotel . . . a very cheap one."

The driver detected Maxwell's American accent and noted his expensive clothes. "Sure that's all you want?" he said with a suggestive leer.

"No, I want a gun . . . and ammunition," Maxwell said.

The driver's eyes narrowed The man was not a terrorist, that was certain. He was a well-dressed American who wanted a gun. And well-dressed Americans who wanted guns were likely to have money. A lot of money. "A thousand marks," he said.

Maxwell nodded and climbed into the taxi. He needed time, just a short time, to think. To think, he had to be alive. To be alive, he had to have a hideout. And maybe, in a place like Bonn, a man like him needed a gun.

He had never fired a gun, and he hoped he would never have to.

NINE

Bonn, West Germany

It was six-thirty in the evening. Gartmann bent his bulky body and reached in the cabinet for another bottle of Schnapps; his second of the day. Returning to his desk, he filled his glass and drank deeply. He rested his head against the high back of the chair and closed his eyes wearily. A few days ago he had been in control. And now? Things could not be worse.

The men from the SSD Special Investigation Department were due in Bonn the next morning. The baron hadn't wasted any time.

After careful consideration, Gartmann felt he could handle any inquiries into his discovery of the baron's Moscow connections. He would attribute his knowledge to rumors. But regretfully, he just could not reveal his source—someone at a drunken party with fellow officers of the SSD a year ago on a visit to East Berlin.

The investigators might not accept this explanation. But they could not positively disprove it. He would, of course, be found guilty of monumental bad judgment for approaching the baron. He would undoubtedly be immediately sent back to East Germany and be punished. But his father's patronage would ensure that his punishment was not too severe.

But his imminent return to East Germany meant he would have no choice but to reveal to the investigators that he had kidnapped the eminent American Dr. Maxwell and his daughter. This act, carried out without approval of his superiors, would be regarded as a crime so blatant that his father would be able to do little to protect him against the consequences.

He had considered killing the doctor and his daughter and disposing of their bodies. But the arrangements necessary to do that were complicated and would involve other people. Inevitably, the investigators would find out. And they would recognize it for what it was—a high risk operation with serious ramifications carried out in an attempt to cover up his crime.

And there was David Maxwell.

His omission to report, even to Cramer, the danger from David Maxwell . . . Gartmann dared not even think of the punishment appropriate for this crime! If he was to salvage *anything* out of the terrible mess he had created, Maxwell must die! Before the morning, when the investigators from the SSD arrived. Before Maxwell went to the police.

And, thank God, there was a chance he could do this. In a way that would satisfy even the investigators of the SSD. Maxwell would die at the hands of the neo-Nazi Group 666.

As he had expected, after the attempt on Maxwell's life in front of the restaurant, Maxwell had not returned to his hotel—a man who was being pursued so persistently and violently would at least go into hiding. A few inquiries and a handful of marks had elicited the information from his hotel that they had received instructions from Maxwell to pack his things for collection by a taxi driver. The taxi driver had been followed; the location of Maxwell's hideout in the cheap hotel on the outskirts of town established.

And at that very moment, as Gartmann poured himself yet another glass of Schnapps, he knew Günther Kraske was preparing the ceremony for the initiation of the first young killers of Group 666. Their first victim: David Maxwell.

It *couldn't* go wrong this time. Maxwell had a charmed life, but all good things come to an end. *They had to!*

Half an hour later Gartmann was still slumped in the chair, the bottle of Schnapps on his desk half empty. Gartmann wasn't feeling good, and he wasn't feeling bad. He was nearing that never-never land where there was no feeling at all.

The phone rang. Gartmann grunted but made no move. It kept ringing. He scowled and reached clumsily for the receiver. "Yes," he said.

"This is Baron von Richter."

Gartmann was stunned. "Who?" he said.

"Baron von Richter," repeated the baron. "I want to see you at my home tonight. Ten o'clock. You will be there, yes?"

"Yes, of course, Baron," Gartmann stammered.

The phone went dead leaving Gartmann staring at the receiver in his hand. Von Richter! Wanted to see him! What in God's name for? And he had contacted him *direct*!

He replaced the receiver and focused his bleary

eyes on his watch. Seven-twenty. He had to collect his wits, get sober. Unsteadily he made his way to the bathroom and, leaning over the basin, forced two fingers down his throat. He kept the pressure up until he had emptied his stomach. Then for ten minutes he stood under the cold shower before phoning down for a pot of black coffee and a pitcher of fresh orange juice.

By ten o'clock as he drove up the long driveway to the baron's house, his mental faculties were alert, if not finely tuned.

The butler showed him to the library where the baron greeted him warmly: an unexpected reception which did little to calm Gartmann's state of agitation.

"Drink, Herr Gartmann?" the baron asked as Gartmann seated himself.

"Mineral water, thank you, Baron!"

"How very sensible." The baron smiled at Gartmann benignly. "There's an envelope on the desk addressed to you. Perhaps you would be kind enough to read it while I get your drink."

Gartmann collected the envelope, sat down, and opened it. His eyes were drawn like a magnet to the signature at the bottom of the letter—KGB Chairman Grechko.

The letter was short, merely stating he had been assigned to a mission of the greatest importance and would henceforth take his orders from Baron von Richter. He read it three times, then gazed at it blankly.

"Your drink," the baron seated himself opposite Gartmann. "I owe you an apology," the baron began, aware that his first task was to restore Gartmann's confidence and sense of importance. "When you first came to see me, I regret, I was rather hasty and did not consider the full potential of your idea. I had rather a lot on my mind at the time. I hope you will forgive me."

To be spoken to in such a deferential way by a man of the baron's standing, and a man who was in the confidence of the chairman himself, was all Gartmann needed for an instant ego-fix. "Of course, of course, Baron, I fully understand," he said sitting upright in his chair.

"Good. I'm afraid I am not empowered to tell you the ultimate purpose of the plan we are going to work on together. That is known only by myself and a few of our friends in the Kremlin. This is only prudent: I'm sure you will agree."

Gartmann nodded.

"We are going to take your idea of the neo-Nazi Group 666 detonating an atomic bomb in an American base and expand the scale of the operation. There are going to be three bombs. Clearly, it is imperative that the West be convinced that Group 666 acted entirely on its own. There must be no suspicion whatever of any Russian involvement. Western intelligence services must be misled into believing that Group 666 was totally responsible for *manufacturing*, as well as using, the bombs. This is why we have chosen Zambu as the place to make them."

Gartmann frowned. "Zambu?"

"A small, independent Marxist state on the West Coast of Africa. It is common knowledge that the

President and his government are mere puppets and the country is controlled by Russian KGB 'advisers.' Now the plan is this."

The baron leaned forward confidingly; Gartmann drew closer.

"Group 666 is going to seize power from the Russians in Zambu *by force*. By this means we shall prevent any possibility of a suspected link between the Group and Russia."

"But how? Group 666 is not strong enough to—"

"I will tell you how. First, you will smuggle Dr. Maxwell and his daughter to Zambu. Do not use established SSD and KGB conduits. Arrange it through one of your criminal connections."

Gartmann smiled slyly. "That will be easy enough."

"Next," the baron continued, "through the same connections recruit one hundred French mercenaries for an attack on Zambu. Security is not necessary. On the contrary. Make sure it is known that Group 666 is behind the operation. You follow me?"

"Not entirely," Gartmann answered slowly. "The mercenaries will know the attack on Zambu is a fake."

"It will *not* be a fake. The mercenaries must be good, experienced fighting men. Ex-French paras, preferably. The KGB in Zambu will put up strong resistance. Their defense must not be successful. *That* would be a disaster."

Gartmann stared at the baron. "Kill our comrades in Zambu?"

"Unfortunate, but necessary. It is the whole essence of our plan to convince the outside world that Russia is innocent in this affair. Of course, there are many other facets to the plan which I cannot tell you. But your part is clear so far, I hope?"

"Yes," Gartmann answered suppressing his excitement.

"Good. There is one other thing you must do. Ensure the activities of Group 666 in West Germany are on the maximum scale possible."

Gartmann was growing in confidence. "Read the newspapers tomorrow, Herr Baron. Group 666 is going to be launched on a scale that will fully satisfy you."

"That is good," the baron replied with an appreciative smile, "because the name of the whole operation is the Coda Alliance. You are familiar with the word 'coda'?"

"Yes."

"The main 'movement' of this political piece of music will take place in West Germany and Zambu. But the coda—the unexpected—will come from the East. The KGB will, shall we say, *replicate* the activities of Group 666 in East Germany."

"Literally?" Gartmann raised his eyebrows.

"Literally. The KGB will kill their own servicemen in the name of Group 666. In addition, reports will be leaked to the media of fictitious secret meetings between the East and West branches of Group 666 to discuss unified action to rid *all* Germany of foreign troops—American and Russian. You see, my dear Gartmann, the activities of Group 666 in East Germany form the very foundations for the Coda. . . . More than this I cannot tell you at present. You had better leave now. We both have many things to attend to."

The baron rose to his feet.

Gartmann left the baron's house totally perplexed, but elated. He, Bruno, was working on an assignment authorized by the chairman of the Russian KGB himself! The baron had treated him with respect. Deference, even! They were using his idea about the atomic bombs! Christ, that would show that little intellectual creep, Cramer. And as for the investigators from the SSD, they would certainly be told to mind their own business.

He stamped on the accelerator. *Now* for Judy Sinclair. Jesus, he was going to screw her head off.

TEN

Heidelberg and Bonn, West Germany

On the flat top of a steeply sloping and wooded hill to the west of the city of Heidelberg, are the ruins of a thirteenth century castle. Neglected for many decades, the crumbling moss-covered walls jut up among the trees like the jagged stumps of broken teeth. Only the southwest tower, covered in ivy, still rises above the tops of the leaf trees; and pervading the whole ruin is the smell of the damp decay of ages.

It is not an inviting place, and visitors to the ruins are few. Occasionally in the high summer, when the moss is dry, young couples from the surrounding villages seek the seclusion of the castle to spend quiet moments together. For most of the time, however, it is left to its slow decay unobserved.

But not on this night.

In the center of the ruins, marked out by the remainder of what long ago were four-foot-thick walls, is the main hall, and at one end of this, sunk twenty feet into the ground but no longer hidden by the floor of the hall, is a large crypt, once secret, now open to the sky.

The scene in the crypt would not have been unfamiliar to the Teutonic Knights of the Third Reich.

Under a blazing torch implanted high on each wall was draped a huge flag of the swastika, the top and bottom segments of this infamous symbol each containing the figures 666 in red.

In the exact center of the crypt was an oblong stone plinth—once the focal point of some long-forgotten ritual in ages past—now worn with time to no more than a couple of feet high. Arraigned along and facing one side of the plinth stood six men, each with an armband matching the flags on the wall.

Standing on the plinth was Günther Kraske, his face covered with a black mask, and behind the mask, a smile.

For an hour he had been addressing the six silent figures. Their eyes gleamed bright with intoxication when the torch on the wall behind him flared in the night breeze, and Kraske knew he had them. He had transported them from the realms of reason into the mad twilight of unthinking, emotional commitment.

His task had not been difficult. All in his audience were members of the dueling fraternity at the university, dueling being deemed to teach courage, discipline, and honor; it was also thought to foster that unique sense of racial heritage, *Gemeinschaftsgefühl*, that could be so easily perverted into a blind commitment to a common purpose, no matter how hideous its ultimate expression.

Standing at the end of the row of six men facing the oblong plinth was a tall young man, Karl Bauer, his blue eyes riveted on the masked face of Kraske. He did not know the identity of the man behind the mask, and he did not care. The man spoke a language he understood, reviling the petty squabbling of Bonn's corrupt politicians and the undermining of Germany's *volkischer* tradition by the mindless plastic materialism of the Americans. Materialistic democracy was not a creed for *men*, not for *Germans*! Germany's destiny was greater, its rightful place in history yet to be achieved. . . . And above all, the man had talked of *action*!

On a signal from Kraske each of the six stepped forward in turn into the flickering light to stand immediately in front of the plinth. Each spent about five minutes with Kraske, their conversation a low whisper, and at the end each was handed two objects which Kraske took from a leather box by his side on the plinth—the old SS dagger given to all members of Hitler's Schutzstaffeln with the words "Blood and Honor" engraved on the hilt, and a 9 mm automatic with twenty rounds of ammunition.

Last in line was Karl Bauer, and now came his turn. Kraske handed him the dagger. "Unsheath it," he commanded.

Bauer obeyed.

"Hold it by the blade in your right hand, hilt upwards, and repeat after me: "I, Karl Bauer, pledge my blood and my life to the cause of Group 666 and swear henceforth to sacrifice all for the freedom of a united Germany and the rightful historical destiny of the Fatherland."

Bauer repeated the oath of allegiance.

"Kiss the blade," Kraske ordered.

Bauer pressed the cold steel to his lips.

"Now listen to me well," Kraske said. "You have

taken the oath, but it will not be consummated until you have killed with the dagger in the name of the Fatherland. These are your orders."

Bauer listened attentively, then departed through the dark passageway under the ruins of the castle. He emerged among a thicket in a wood on the side of the hill. By the light of the moon he picked his way down to where his Mercedes coupe was parked. As the powerful engine sprang to life, he felt the thrill of excitement flood through his veins. *To kill for the Fatherland!* The car leaped forward, and with a squeal of tires he headed for the Autobahn leading to Bonn.

Kraske waited five minutes, then ducked into the passageway. He felt confident. He knew—as had the ancient Order of Knights, Emperors, Caesars, Archbishops, and Dictators throughout history—that men are not moved to sacrifice themselves by abstract ideas, but by the emotional power of mysticism and ritual.

Nevertheless, there would be no chance of error. None.

As Karl Bauer reduced speed from a hundred-sixty kilometers an hour down to sixty to take the turnoff from A61 Autobahn in Bonn, David Maxwell looked at the luminous dial of his watch. Three o'clock, and he felt wide awake.

He punched the pillow and turned onto his side. The old bed creaked under his weight. For God's sake, he thought, he'd made his decision, so why in hell's name couldn't he relax and go to sleep. He knew why not. Because out there—somewhere—Barbara and his father were in terrible danger.

He was safe—for the time being at least. Half the population of Bonn were set on killing him, but no one could trace him, at least not until morning. And in the morning he would be heading right for the American Embassy. While he still had time. While he was still alive and able to do something to help Barbara and his father. He had the gun with him, on the floor by the bed. It made him feel safer. Not that he expected to use it; he was not even sure he knew *how* to use it.

Maxwell didn't like danger, and he didn't like problems he couldn't resolve. He heaved himself onto his back and tried to empty his mind by relaxing his body. He wasn't sure he heard anything, but something made him open his eyes, look toward the door. Then he sensed a presence in the blackness of the room. A board creaked—right beside the bed! Maxwell's reaction was instinctive and instantaneous. He threw himself to the side of the bed and reached down groping for the gun on the floor. He felt a blow on his chest like the kick of a horse, and for an instant he was still, poised on the edge of the bed, the breath knocked from his body. Then he was desperately groping again, and his fingers touched the heavy metal of the gun. In the blackness he heard unhurried footsteps retreating toward the door. He found the trigger and fired—once, twice, and a third time—in the direction of the footsteps. Then the strength drained from him, and he collapsed off the edge of the bed onto the floor. Then there was blackness.

Downstairs in the lobby, Günther Kraske was waiting. He had followed Karl Bauer to the hotel. Bauer's instructions were to consummate his initiation into

Group 666 by killing the American, Maxwell. But Kraske was not taking any chances. There must be no mistakes this time. Kraske was going to *see* the dead body of Maxwell.

At the sound of the shots, Kraske raced up the stairs. The door of Maxwell's room was open. He found the light switch, and one look was all he needed. Group 666 had their first dead hero; Bauer was sprawled on the floor on his face, blood and brains oozing from where the back of his head had been torn off.

And lying beside the bed on his back, the front of his pajamas drenched in blood, the SS dagger deep in his chest, was one very dead American by the name of David Maxwell.

Kraske turned and saw the small group of sleepy-looking people at the open door. "Police, police, call the police!" he yelled, shouldering his way through the stunned group.

Fifteen seconds later he was walking slowly down the street, whistling between his teeth.

It could not have worked out better. A dead martyr and a dead Maxwell. Neat.

ELEVEN

Bonn, West Germany
Chequers, England

Wilfried Linke, counterintelligence chief of the West German Federal Intelligence Service—the BND—reached for the light switch beside his bed and picked up the ringing phone. His wife gave a small sigh of protest and turned away from the light.

The conversation lasted ten minutes, with Linke doing most of the listening. He replaced the receiver and slid out of bed. "Where are you going, Wilfried?" his wife asked still half asleep.

"Important business."

His wife groaned. "Not again. What time is it?"

"Nearly four-thirty."

"Oh, my God. Try not to wake the children."

Linke grunted and went into the dressing room. Five minutes later he was heading downtown. More crazy instructions from the minister, he thought bitterly. Didn't the man ever sleep?

At the hospital the doctor was expecting him and escorted him rapidly to a private room. A man lay in the bed, his head and chest bandaged. The man was David Maxwell.

"What's the extent of the injuries?" Linke asked.

The doctor shrugged. "He was fortunate. Very fortunate. The dagger glanced off his breast bone and was deflected along the outer face of a rib. It's a flesh wound; nasty but not serious. My guess is he was lying on his side when the blow was struck."

"Why is he unconscious?"

"It appears he fell after being struck and hit his head against an iron radiator on the wall beside his bed. There's a deep gash, but the X ray shows no sign of a fracture. He should regain consciousness before long."

"The minister's spoken to you?" Linke said.

"Yes."

"Is it safe to move him?"

"With care."

"Right. I'll send two of my men in hospital uniforms. Have an ambulance waiting but don't worry about a driver: I'll supply one. I want him out of here as soon as possible."

The doctor nodded.

"And don't forget to inform the police of his death. Keep him under sedation. I don't want him asking questions or screaming to someone for help."

"It's very irregular."

"Tell that to the minister."

Maxwell opened his eyes in the bedroom of a private house on the outskirts of Bonn. A BND safe house. His head throbbed, the pain focusing at one point at the back. He raised his right arm, and a sharp pain shot across his chest and shoulder. Looking down, he saw the bandage across his chest. Yes, he remembered now: the shadowy figure in the darkness of his hotel room and the sudden blow on his chest. He wondered what he had been hit by . . . with. Gingerly he raised his left arm and touched his head—more bandages. He lowered his arm and tried to think. A head wound. He could not account for this.

A deliberate cough to his left made him turn his head sharply. Searing pain in both head and chest made him wish he hadn't. A man was sitting by the bed smiling pleasantly—gray hair, bags under the eyes, mottled skin, a goatee . . . about fifty. "I'm glad you're awake, Mr. Maxwell," the man said.

"Where am I?" David asked.

"In a nursing home."

"You're a doctor?"

"Yes. How do you feel?"

"Suppose you tell me what's wrong first," Maxwell said.

"Knife wound in the chest; concussion which lasted about thirteen hours," the doctor replied.

"I feel fine," Maxwell said.

The doctor grunted. "Perhaps, but you must remain in bed."

"What for?" said Maxwell. "I can walk, can't I?"

"It's best," the doctor replied. "We want to make sure there's no reaction from the concussion. You're a very lucky man, Mr. Maxwell. If the knife had gone in straight, you'd be dead."

"I want to sec someone from the American Embassy. Right away. Will you fix it?" Maxwell said.

The doctor hesitated, then replied, "Why, of course. I'll see to it." He left the room and returned a few minutes later carrying a small tray with a glass of water and a tablet on it. "The Embassy says they will have someone over within an hour," he said placing the tray beside the bed and handing the water and tablet to Maxwell. "Take this," he said.

"What is it?" Maxwell said.

"An antibiotic. A simple precaution against infection in the wound."

Maxwell swallowed the tablet.

"I'll leave you now so you can get some rest," the doctor said.

The door shut and Maxwell settled back to wait. He hoped the Embassy would get someone over quickly. Before the German police arrived and started asking questions. He wanted to talk to his own people first. Then it occurred to him to wonder why he was in a nursing home, not a hospital. And then he was asleep. The tablet worked fast.

Two days later an ambulance drew up in front of a large private house on the outskirts of Bonn.

The driver got out, opened the rear door of the ambulance, then disappeared into the house. A few minutes later he emerged, accompanied by two men carrying a stretcher. Lying on the stretcher was the unconscious body of David Maxwell.

The stretcher was eased into the ambulance, and the two men took their places inside. A minute later the doctor with the goatee climbed in beside the two men.

The ambulance moved off.

Two hours later the ambulance drove onto the tarmac of the U.S. Seventeenth Air Force Base at Bitburg and came to a stop near a C-130. The unconscious Maxwell, accompanied by the doctor, was transferred to the C-130 which then taxied to the runway and, after being cleared, took off into the afternoon sky.

Two hours later the C-130 came to a stop at the U.S. Third Air Force Base at Lakenheath in England where Maxwell and the doctor were transferred to another waiting ambulance.

A hundred-mile drive through the green English countryside brought them to a large Tudor mansion in the county of Buckinghamshire. As the ambulance stopped to be checked at the gate of the estate, Maxwell's eyelids twitched. The doctor watching him let out a sigh of relief. Keeping a man under sedation and having him come around at a predetermined time called for skill and no small measure of luck.

As Maxwell was lifted from the ambulance and carried into one of the large reception rooms in the mansion and laid on a couch, he began to emerge through a woolly haze into consciousness: enough to know that he existed, that something was going on around him, and that his head ached—but not enough to care.

"Mr. Maxwell, Mr. Maxwell." David felt someone gently patting his cheeks. He opened his eyes and recognized the face of the man sitting beside him holding a cup toward him. "Coffee. It will make you feel better."

David closed his eyes. Confused as he was, his first instinct was to get as firm a grip on the situation as he could before showing he was conscious. The man speaking to him was the doctor who had looked after him: he knew *that*. The doctor who had given him the tablet. Before he had fallen asleep; too quickly. He remembered *that*!

David opened his eyes wide. "What the hell's going on. . . ." He trailed off as he saw he was in totally new surroundings: a massive room with antique furniture; through the window, lawns and trees.

"Drink," the doctor prompted. "You'll feel better."

David took the cup and sipped the hot coffee. "Where am I?" he said.

"Chequers, in England."

"Chequers?"

"It's the country house of the British Prime Minister."

David stared, dumbfounded.

"It's true, Mr. Maxwell, though I can't tell you why you're here. I don't know myself. My instructions are to get you functioning physically and mentally as quickly as possible. You've been under sedation for several days. You'll be feeling weak and stiff, so when you've finished that coffee, I want you to try walking. Take it easy at first."

"The hell I will. I want to know what's going on. I've been—"

The doctor interrupted. "You're wasting time, asking me. Now," he took the cup, "get to your feet. Gently."

David stood up with effort. He began to walk and felt the stiffness in his legs and the muscles of his back. He reached the huge bay windows and turned. "What about this?" he pointed to his chest.

"Nothing to worry about. Stitches where the knife went in but no damage to the muscle tissue."

The door opened and a gray-haired man with a back like a ramrod looked at David. "Would you be good enough to follow me, sir."

David followed the man as he led the way along a wide corridor. He stopped before the double doors at the end and opened them with a flourish. "Please go in, sir."

David stepped forward. The center of the room was occupied by a large mahogany table. Around the table six men were seated, all looking at him with only slightly disguised curiosity. David recognized one of them, the white-haired British Prime Minister sitting at the head of the table.

"Sit down, will you please, Mr. Maxwell," the Prime Minister said, gesturing to an empty chair at the end of the table.

"Now let me introduce you," the Prime Minister continued. "On your left, Herr Linke, head of German Intelligence. Next to him, Mr. Johnson, the American Ambassador here in England. And next to him, Brigadier Smetelton, head of MI6 British Intelligence."

The Prime Minister turned to his left. "On your right, Monsieur Perchard, head of SDECE French Intelligence, and finally, next to you Mr. Mason, deputy of CIA operations in Europe."

David realized he should have been a little in awe of such company. But he felt totally calm and at ease; perhaps because the drugs hadn't worn off or because recent events had considerably reduced his capacity to experience surprise.

"We have a great deal to tell you, Mr. Maxwell, and I would ask you to listen most carefully," the Prime Minister stated. "When we have made the situation clear to you, we are going to ask you to do something quite extraordinary. Unfortunately, the time constraints are such that we will require an immediate yes or no answer from you. To help you understand the importance of what you are about to learn, I must tell you we have every reason to believe the Russians have embarked on an operation which threatens the security of the whole free world. They must be stopped and we believe *you* are uniquely placed to help do this. Now. To start explaining the situation, I will turn the floor over to the head of MI6."

The head of MI6 was a tall, lean man, completely bald, with large, protruding ears. Although he was well into his fifties, his face was unlined and when he looked at David, it was with the most calm blue eyes David had ever seen.

"Mr. Maxwell," he began in a low considered tone, "I am going to describe a world which you will no doubt regard with great distaste. A world in which people like myself have to make cold-blooded life-or-death decisions about innocent people. I would ask you to bear in mind that we do not take such decisions without a good deal of soul-searching and anguish. To get to the point, we have known for several days not only that your father and sister have been kidnapped; but by whom, and indeed exactly where they have been held captive for most of the time."

Maxwell stared, aghast. Then anger flooded through him. "And you did *nothing* to release them!" His eyes were blazing with fury.

"As I said, Mr. Maxwell, we have to make painful decisions. But I must remind you of the Prime Minister's words: we are faced by a possible threat to the security of the whole free world. For reasons which will become apparent later, it is a reasonable assumption your father has been kidnapped because of his experience in nuclear weapons—"

"And my sister?" David interrupted fiercely.

"The bait. And possibly—I say only 'possibly'—as a lever to make your father cooperate with his kidnappers."

This thought had not occurred to David. He controlled his voice carefully before asking, "Who are the kidnappers?"

"The SSD, the East German Arm of the Russian KGB."

"And why didn't you rescue them if you know where they are?" David tried to keep the anger out of his voice.

"Because, Mr. Maxwell, we don't know what the Russians are up to. But as long as we know where your father and sister are, we have leads to follow. If we rescued them, the SSD would in all probability replace your father by someone we have no tabs on. Your father is expendable to the Russians, but to us he is a vital connection we have to hold on to."

"Vital connection! You mean he's expendable to you *too*!"

"I don't make the rules of the game, Mr. Maxwell, but I do have to play by them. Please try to understand."

David's brain was clearing, and immediately a dozen questions formed in his mind.

"The man who tried to kill you in your hotel," Herr Linke of the BND addressed David, "he was a member of Group 666, a neo-Nazi organization controlled by the SSD. In your case they failed. Unfortunately, five American servicemen *were* killed by the group that same night. And, incredible as it may seem, the group claimed to have killed a similar number of Russian servicemen in *East* Germany. Our intelligence has confirmed this claim to be true!"

David frowned, not understanding.

The Prime Minister spoke. "Yes, puzzling, isn't it. But there are even more perplexing developments. Monsieur Perchard," he turned and addressed the head of French Intelligence, "would you continue please."

The head of the SDECE raised his bushy eyebrows, passed a hand through a thatch of black hair, and fixed his dark gaze on Maxwell. "I don't know if you are aware of the fact, Monsieur Maxwell, but France is one of the main countries from which mercenaries are recruited. Mainly for operations in Africa. France has many ex-colonies in Africa and still retains investments worth hundreds of millions of dollars in these countries. Whenever the SDECE hears mercenaries are being recruited, it is our policy to infiltrate their numbers with one of our agents." He smiled briefly. "To keep an eye on what is happening to our investments, you might say. Recently, we learned that a new mercenary operation is being mounted. For obvious reasons the sponsors of these operations usually try to keep tight security on their identity. In this instance, security has been lax to the point of suspicion. Group 666 are the sponsors, and the objective of the mercenary attack is a country called Zambu . . . a Russian puppet state!"

"Furthermore," the head of the SDECE continued,

"we have evidence that the mercenaries have been in contact with the leader of the Zambu Liberation Front, an organization based in Paris. The leader of this organization is a man called Yanu. Until four years ago, Yanu was the pro-Western President of Zambu. Then, with Russian backing, he was deposed in a coup by his son, Monato, who is now the Russian-controlled president of the country."

"So you see," the Prime Minister interjected, "we have leads which suggest the apparently nonsensical possibility that a Russian controlled neo-Nazi group are going to use mercenaries to overthrow their own man, Monato, and replace him with Yanu."

"*And,*" the SDECE chief added, "two French nuclear engineers are going with the mercenaries."

"The final piece of information we received yesterday is the most curious of all," the Prime Minister said. "A ship, the S.S. *Lander,* carrying a cargo including enriched uranium, has disappeared off the west coast of Africa."

David looked incredulous. "Disappeared?"

"Yes, vanished. An emergency air and sea search of the area where the ship was last known to be located has drawn a complete blank. There were five other ships near the estimated position of the S.S. *Lander.* Four of them have been identified as belonging to well-known and reputable shipping lines and have been contacted by radio. The fifth is the S.S. *Burgh,* registered in Liberia. So far, attempts to trace its owners have failed. At this moment it is on a course for South West Africa. Its destination could be Zambu."

"Wait a minute," David said. "Are you suggesting that . . . the *Burgh stole* the uranium and *sank* the *Lander*?"

"Incredible, I know," the Prime Minister answered. "But totally feasible."

David was silent for a while, the meaning of the evidence being presented to him—and his reason for being there—becoming clearer. At last he said, "And you believe it is possible my father . . . and sister . . . may be abducted to Zambu. Is that it?"

"No." The word was rapped out by the CIA man. David turned to face him as he added, "The fact is, Mr. Maxwell, they are already there."

"What?"

"They were being held in apartments in Bonn. MI6 had them under full surveillance. I won't go into details, but their surveillance teams were fooled. Mainly because the people who got them out of the apartments were completely unknown to MI6; in no way connected with the SSD. They suspect the operation was set up by a crime syndicate."

"So how do you know they're in Zambu?"

"From CIA agents in Zambu. Once we learned of the destination of the mercenaries and possible destination of the S.S. *Burgh*, we made an educated guess. Air traffic in and out of Zambu is minimal. The airport is little more than a landing strip. It's a pretty primitive country. We had telescopic photographs taken of all passenger arrivals. Your father and sister arrived in a military aircraft . . . from Angola, we think."

"How are they?" David asked anxiously, but relieved to know at least they were alive.

"From the photographs they look okay. That's all we know. You see, Mr. Maxwell, yesterday morning the government of Zambu—that means the Russians—gave all foreigners just twelve hours to get out of the country. That includes our agents. We've been shut out."

David was silent again. He could sense the atmosphere of tension and expectancy from the men around the table. They were all absolutely still, almost holding their breath, it seemed.

"We've *got* to get agents back there," the CIA man said very softly. "God knows what the Russians are up to, but it has to be very big. It's too elaborate to be anything else."

David turned. He knew what was coming: But it was ridiculous. . . . Impossible!

"We want you to go into Zambu, Mr. Maxwell."

"You've got to be joking." It was all David could think of to say.

"I was never more serious in my life. You won't be alone, but we need *you* in there."

"Why me? I don't know a thing about the way agents operate."

"You've got all the right qualifications, Maxwell. Look—I'll level with you. Until you moved hotels MI6 were trying to keep you out of trouble. Not because they cared a damn about you but because they were scared to hell you would foul things up for them. Panic the SSD into replacing your father with someone else, and they'd lose contact with the situation. So, when Group 666 tried to kill you, we transferred you from hospital to a BND safe house and put it out that you were dead. As far as the SSD are concerned, their kidnap operation is still clean. Incidentally, when did you learn to shoot like that?"

"Like what?"

"Hell, you nearly took the guy's head off!"

David felt sick. The sudden revelation that he had killed a man was bad enough, but the flip way the CIA man talked about it. . . . "That was one hundred percent luck," he said. "I didn't even see him."

"Luck, the most important qualification of all in our business. Nobody gets by for long without it. We call it survivability. People either have it, or they don't; you can't be taught it."

"Stop trying to sell me," David answered sourly. "My *real* qualifications for the job are (one) you want a nuclear physicist who has the expertise to assess exactly what they're doing with that uranium, and (two) you're going to tell me that if I want to help my father and sister, I'd better accept your proposition. Right?"

"You are, of course, absolutely right." It was the American ambassador who answered. "And it is my duty to make it plain that I do not consider it proper that any untrained civilian should be asked to put himself at such risk. The dangers are unknown, but clearly they are considerable. We do not know what is going on in Zambu, nor have we the slightest indication of what might take place in the future."

"That's understood, Mr. Ambassador," David replied. "The fact is, I have no choice. I have to do anything I can to help my family. My answer is, Yes."

The CIA man didn't try to hide his smile of triumph. "I knew you'd come across, Maxwell."

"On two conditions," David said. "I am going as a

private American citizen, not as an employee of the CIA. The distinction may not make any difference to you, but it does to me."

"No problem," the CIA man said quickly.

"Secondly," David went on, "I don't know who else is going on this little trip, but I'm not prepared to take *orders* from anyone; advice, yes; orders, no."

"Maxwell, I said you had survivability, *not* experience. It's no picnic you're going on. Split-second decisions may have to be made. Someone with experience has to make them and know they will be obeyed."

"Then you've got a problem," David said.

The American ambassador smiled faintly and addressed the CIA man. "You've forgotten. Mr. Maxwell is going as a civilian; he doesn't have to take orders."

The CIA man bit his lip. "Okay, if that's how you want it."

"That's how I want it," David said.

"You've made a most courageous decision, Mr. Maxwell," the Prime Minister spoke. "You take our thanks and our prayers with you."

"Thank you, sir," David said. "When do I go? . . . And how?"

"First we have to get you fit and give you some basic training," the CIA man said.

"And then?"

The CIA man hesitated, then said, "Well, since the Russians have expelled all foreigners and strange white men can hardly infiltrate a black country, there *is* only one way in. You're going to hijack a commercial jet and crash in on them."

"You mean, hijack—for real!"

"Yeah, you got it, Maxwell."

TWELVE

Loch Naird, Scotland

Maxwell gasped for breath and looked up the steep scree slope which separated him from the summit of the mountain. His combat fatigues had been torn in half a dozen places by the jagged rocks ascending the rugged mountain. A Russian AKM 7.62 mm assault rifle was strapped across his shoulders.

Ten yards farther up the scree, almost at the summit, another figure similarly attired and equipped paused and turned to yell at him, "Keep moving, you idle bastard."

David gritted his teeth and, half blinded by the perspiration streaming into his eyes, started the final ascent. Standing firmly on the summit, the man above him was waiting. He extended his arm to give a helping hand. As David reached for the hand, the man raised his foot and aimed a vicious kick at his chest. David fell flat on his face, and the leg shot out above his head. Flinging himself onto his side, he grabbed the leg and heaved with all his strength. The man toppled and plunged through the air, but before striking the scree twenty feet below, his body had twisted so that, with his head tucked forward into his chest, he landed on the side of his right shoulder and somersaulted down the scree.

David did not even turn to look at the falling man. He heaved himself up the last few feet and began to run along the flat ridge of the summit. A hundred yards on he threw himself to the ground in the prone position. He raised the AKM to his shoulder, flicked the fire selector to "cyclic," took a deep breath, and squeezed the trigger evenly. In exactly three seconds the magazine was empty. Thirty rounds had torn into the wooden replica of a man's head and shoulders set between two rocks eighty yards ahead of him.

Placing the AKM on its side in front of him, David lowered his cheek onto the bare rock and lay gasping for breath.

"Thank Christ! You made it. I thought you never would."

He rolled on his back and looked up into the face of Stan McGregor. There was a gash on the side of McGregor's face, and David guessed he had caught it on a jagged piece of rock as he had somersaulted down the scree.

"Next time I'll throw you so you won't stop till you hit the bottom of the goddam mountain," David answered unsmiling.

McGregor grinned. "Music to my ears, boy. Music to my ears," he said, then walked off to inspect the result of David's shooting.

David sat up and shook his head from side to side. It was crazy. *Impossibly* crazy. Only a short time ago he had been living a civilized life at Livermore where keeping fit was something called tennis, swimming, or golf. Civilized. Where physical aggression was something you watched on television. Safe. Sensible. And now he was living in a broken-down stone cottage on the edge of Loch Naird in the black rugged highlands of northwest Scotland. With no running water, no heat, and in the company of a Scots-American madman named McGregor whose one ambition was to turn him into a one hundred percent fit, aggressive, murderous, inhuman being. And he was succeeding!

Not that McGregor had made a secret of his intentions. When David had arrived, he had advanced to meet his instructor who was standing by the door of his cottage. "David Maxwell," David had said holding out his hand.

"Stan McGregor," the other man answered and slammed him across the face with the back of his hand. Totally unprepared, David had stumbled and fallen. McGregor stood over him looking down at him with expressionless black eyes. "Now what do *you* do?" he said.

David just stared. He couldn't believe it.

"I'll tell you," McGregor said. "You swing at my ankles with your right foot. With any luck I fall down. Then you kick me in the stomach with all the strength God gave you. Then, if you're still winning and I haven't done anything to interfere with your plans, you get me by the throat and bang my head on the ground until I know better than to hit you in the face." He held out his hand to help David to his feet. David took his hand. He didn't know exactly how it happened, it was so quick: McGregor had hold of his wrist with both hands and was pushing his head into the ground with a booted foot on his neck. "Maxwell,

I'm trying to tell you something," McGregor had said quietly. "Don't ever trust me."

McGregor released David. "Come on inside," he said. David hesitated. "Come on, will you. I'm not going to do anything smart. Not for a while."

David clambered to his feet. "You call that *smart*!" he said.

McGregor turned to him, and David saw in his face the same hard, black, and uncompromising ruggedness he saw in the craggy mountains rising up behind the cottage. "Where we're going, it's smart," McGregor said.

Inside the spartan cottage McGregor lit a cigarette. "My only vice," he said, then fell silent scrutinizing David's face. At length he said, "We're going into a situation in Zambu we don't know one goddam thing about. We could be there for a day, or a year. We don't know. Maybe the Russians will welcome us with caviar and champagne, but don't bet on it: they have less attractive customs. I've got five days to teach you enough to give you a half decent chance of staying alive no matter what."

David remained silent. Despite McGregor's slightly unorthodox and painful way of greeting him, he found he was responding to this man. David respected professionalism, abhorred amateurism . . . in the laboratory or anywhere else. If a man was doing a job, let him do it well or forget it. McGregor exuded confident professionalism.

McGregor dropped his cigarette on the floor and ground it out with the heel of his boot. "If I am any judge of character, Maxwell—which I am in my own limited barbaric field—you've got a fatal flaw. You lack instinctive aggression. You've got five days to correct that."

David smiled. "Suppose I don't want to."

"Then suppose you go outside and kill yourself right now," McGregor answered.

David grinned. "Look McGregor, I understand what you're saying. But there is no way I can change my basic nature just like that . . . like flipping a switch, for God's sake."

"Wrong, Maxwell. You know who make the best fighting men? Not aggressive thugs, not men who have been brutalized, but intelligent men—often sensitive men—who, for *whatever* the reason, have made the decision that they must commit themselves totally to winning. It all happens up here"—McGregor tapped his forehead with his fingers—"wars, battles, hand-to-hand combat; nine times out of ten they're won or lost in men's minds."

"And you really believe I can accomplish this instant character transformation?"

"Yes. From now on I am likely to attack you physically at any time. Mostly when you're in the least advantageous position to defend yourself. You've had a small sample of it already. It gets worse. The rules of the game say you can do the same to me. The rules of war say you've got five days to learn to do it. To psyche yourself into flipping that switch."

"I'll believe it when it happens," David answered.

"Count on it," said McGregor and lit another cigarette. "Now," he continued, "weapons. Zambu's knee-deep in Russian hardware. We'll concentrate on three simple weapons: the AKM assault rifle, the Makarov pistol, the RGD grenade. Your rifle . . . you live with it: you don't move one inch, night or day, without it; not even in the cottage. Remember, the rifle can get along fine without you; but there will be times when you won't even be able to take another breath unless you have it with you. Do I make myself clear?"

David nodded, suppressing a smile. Where in God's name did they get people like McGregor from, he wondered. Then–more seriously–he wondered exactly who McGregor was; and where he'd picked up his apparently very considerable knowledge of how to survive in some distinctly hostile environments.

If Maxwell *had* entertained any doubts about the seriousness of McGregor's approach to his training, the next few days would have put him right. They ran: up the mountains, down the mountains; all the time carrying rifles and spare magazines of ammunition. And when David's muscles and lungs told him he couldn't go any further, McGregor told him he could; and he did. They swam in the Loch, the shock of the freezing water knocking the breath from David's body as he dived in. And in the evenings McGregor instructed him how to strip and clean the AKM and the Makarov, or taught him how to fight with his hands, knees, elbows, and feet, and with a knife. And all the time David was under the impression McGregor was hurting him a great deal more than was necessary.

By the third day David found he was looking at McGregor with something not far removed from dislike. A state of mind not improved when in the afternoon as he was crossing a cascading mountain stream by means of a fallen tree just strong enough to bear his weight, McGregor loosed off a burst of AKM which shattered the tree sending David crashing into the icy water.

And there was the time they were throwing grenades and McGregor stuck one down David's tunic, then ran for cover. David fished the grenade out and threw it, and it *did* explode. "You goddam idiot!" David screamed at him, "you could have killed me." McGregor hadn't even smiled when he replied. "Listen, Maxwell. If you aren't smart enough to get one of those things out of your tunic when you know it's only got a four-second fuse, then hell, I don't want even to cross the street with you, let alone go to some lousy place called Zambu. I'd rather you *were* dead."

And finally there was the time when they were using a grappling iron and rope to climb a fifty-foot cliff. They'd run ten miles carrying full equipment to get there, and David was pretty near exhausted. "I'll go up first," MacGregor said. "Give you time to get your strength back." Then it was David's turn. There were hardly any footholds, so it was almost a case of hauling himself up with his arms. He arrived at the top gasping, his arms limp with fatigue. McGregor looked at him for an instant, then he whipped the butt of his rifle into David's stomach. David fell to the ground wincing with pain, too weak and exhausted to defend himself from the rain of blows from rifle butt and boots. Then, with a flick of his wrists, McGregor reversed the rifle and plunged the bayonet into the ground within an inch of David's throat. David stared at McGregor with horror. McGregor bent low, his face six inches from David's. "Dumb bastard," he said and spat in David's face.

For the rest of the day David had reasoned with himself. McGregor was doing it deliberately. He *knew* that. It wasn't important. He was learning how to survive, and that was all that mattered. McGregor was trying to turn him into a savage. The hell with McGregor . . . and all he stood for. McGregor was going to lose.

And that was how it was until McGregor's boot came crashing toward his chest at the summit of the scree. When he grabbed McGregor's leg and heaved him somersaulting down the scree, it wasn't a decision. It was a reflex.

McGregor returned from inspecting the target Maxwell had cut in half with thirty rounds from the AKM. David was still on the ground, feeling his ankle with his hands. He pulled a face. "I think I've sprained my ankle: it hurts like hell." He grimaced with pain.

"Jesus! That's all we need." McGregor's face was clouded with concern. He knelt to feel the ankle. David raised his foot and crashed his boot into McGregor's stomach sending him sprawling. Then he crashed down on the prostrate man's stomach with both knees and squeezing his throat with both hands pounded his head on the ground. He stopped, then spat into McGregor's face. "Dumb bastard," he said and got slowly to his feet.

McGregor groaned and wiped the spittle from his face. "I love you, boy. You-really-have-made-it. Flipped that switch. . . . Right on." And for the first time since they had met, David saw a broad smile on the face of Stan McGregor . . . Instructor extraordinaire in the gentle arts of survival.

McGregor scrambled to his feet. "From now on out, no tricks. Right. The game's over. We don't want to arrive at Zambu a couple of cripples."

After a swim in the Loch to clean up, McGregor slapped David on the back. "You've earned a break. There's a quiet inn down the coast a bit. We'll drop in and sink a few jars of malt whiskey."

The inn was quiet: half a dozen men and a couple of women sitting talking in soft highland voices. David felt conspicuous, slightly embarrassed, in his battle fatigues. But the "natives" didn't even look at him.

"What's your posion?" McGregor asked.

"Glenlivet," David answered.

"It's good," McGregor agreed, "but if I were you, I'd ask for the recommendation of the landlord. *We* Scots are a bit canny. There's a few malt blends never leave Scotland. They reckon they're too good to waste on foreigners." He winked at the landlord who reached for a bottle on the shelf and poured two glasses of almost clear liquid.

McGregor raised his glass. "Here's to you, boy," he said and took an appreciative sip from his glass.

David responded and not for the first time wondered about McGregor. Despite his habit of calling him "boy"—something David found it impossible to take exception to—McGregor couldn't be more than five years older than himself. And there were the scars on his body. He had counted ten when they'd been naked swimming. Who *was* he?

"Some of the finest folk in the world around here," McGregor interrupted David's thoughts. "If you want company, they'll take you to their hearts. And if you want to be alone, they take no offense."

"What about these?" David pointed to his battle fatigues. "They don't seem impressed."

"Why should they? The SAS use the place for training."

"SAS?"

"A British outfit . . . Special Air Service. . . . a sort of elite commando unit. No more than about five hundred men. Their identities are kept secret. Operate alone or in pairs. Never in uniform. The British haven't got much military clout today, but wherever there's trouble in the world, they like to have men on the ground. Find out what's going on. Lend a hand sometimes."

"They're good?"

"I wouldn't like to be against them too often."

Praise indeed, thought David. "And you, McGregor?" he said. "Are you CIA?"

"No . . . free-lance."

"But you're working for them? Right now?"

"Yeah . . . contract basis."

David frowned. "A mercenary?" he hazarded.

For the briefest of moments David saw anger in McGregor's eyes. "No, *not* a mercenary," he replied between tight lips. "I'm very particular about the kind of work I do. And who I work for."

McGregor placed his empty glass on the bar and nodded to the barman. "Tomorrow you meet the third member of this little party. It's a woman," he said.

"A woman!" David exclaimed.

"Yeah, why not?" McGregor replied calmly. "There's nothing you can do she can't do ten times better. And there's a few things she can do you could never do."

David remained silent. "And one thing," McGregor continued, "when you meet her, don't stare the way you are now. If you do, most likely she'll break your arms."

THIRTEEN

Loch Naird, Scotland

The following day was cold with a thin drizzle misting over the Loch like a fine veil. David went to the window as he heard the approaching sound of a vehicle. A Land-Rover was lurching across the rock-dotted grass, the driver somehow managing to avoid the bigger rocks which would have torn the bottom out of the vehicle.

"Some lunatic's trying to total a Land-Rover," David said turning to McGregor who was still eating breakfast.

"That'll be her," McGregor said without looking up.

David opened the door and waited. The Land-Rover jolted to a stop, and a young woman jumped out. She was dressed in tight jeans, knee-length boots, and a thick woolen polo-neck sweater which reached halfway down her thighs. Her long blond hair was tied simply behind her neck.

She could have been any young woman, sensibly dressed for the weather.

She wasn't. She was the beautiful Miss Haverford.

The woman who had warned him in Bonn to get out of Germany, then tried to kill him in the park.

David blinked several times, rapidly.

"Hello, darling," she smiled and winked at David, then stepped forward through the door forcing him to step back to make room for her.

"How are you, Stan?" she said to McGregor. There was an easy familiarity in her voice.

"Great . . . and you?" McGregor answered.

"Just fine. I think I'll take a little practice before this drizzle turns into a downpour. See if I can still hit a mountainside at ten yards."

McGregor grunted.

David watched while she slung a PK light machine gun over one shoulder and an AKM rifle over the other. Then she picked up two long boxes of ammunition in each hand and walked out of the door.

"Do you know who that is!" David stared at McGregor.

"Sure. Judy Sinclair. She's the third party."

"The hell she is!" David exploded. "Her name's Haverford, and she tried to kill me in Bonn."

"I doubt it," replied McGregor. "If she tried to kill you, you'd be dead."

"I tell you, she did. And her name's Haverford."

McGregor rose, and when he spoke, there was a hollow coldness in his voice. "Listen, boy. I have one of the best reasons in the world to know her name. And it's Sinclair . . . Judy."

"I don't think I'm getting through to you, McGregor," David said angrily. "She's connected with the SSD scene in Bonn. I'm damn certain of it."

"Connected is a pretty loose word."

"Yeah. You mean perhaps she was *free-lancing* for the SSD at the time!"

"Maybe she was at that," McGregor said with a smile. "It's a funny old world."

"Not from where I'm standing, it isn't."

McGregor sighed. "Listen, Maxwell, just relax. I *know* who she is. So there's been some confusion. . . . She'll tell you about it in her own good time. Don't worry."

David felt some of the tension going. McGregor couldn't be wrong. Not *that* wrong!

"Let's get moving," McGregor said. "Play ball with grenades."

The evening was weird. They ate in almost total silence, yet David detected not the slightest strain between McGregor and the woman. On the contrary, their silence—like their meeting—was one of familiarity.

After the meal Judy attached a night-sight to one of the AKMs and went out without another word.

Twenty minutes later the sound of distant firing broke the stillness. "Taking it all a bit seriously, isn't she?" David commented.

"I like to think so," McGregor answered, rising to his feet and going to the closet. He rummaged for a few moments, then faced David, a bottle of whiskey in his hand. "Drink, Maxwell?" he said, and poured generous mcasures into two mugs. He passed one to David, then sat down. "Here's to the one that got away," McGregor raised his mug.

"Who's fishing?" David said.

"All of us. Life's a big lake. We try and catch what we can and sometimes the big one gets away."

McGregor fell silent and in the soft light of the

lantern David saw in his eyes a sadness. Then the look was gone, and McGregor said: "Tomorrow we split for a couple of days. We'll meet up again in London. At Heathrow Airport."

David frowned. "That sounds a bit casual. Doesn't hijacking an airplane call for detailed planning?"

"The planning's been done," McGregor answered. "Judy has the details. You're going with her when we split. She wants to explain a few things to you. Now, let's talk about Zambu. You know anything about it?"

"Not a thing."

"Right then, listen. . . ."

McGregor talked on about the terrain, vegetation, people, the political setup.

The next morning David awoke to see McGregor bending over the fireplace cooking breakfast. On the table was the bottle of Scotch. Empty! There was no sign of Judy.

He got up and stood by the open window. It was a beautiful day. Across the still waters of the Loch the morning sun was rising into a clear blue sky above the rugged mountains. And emerging from the shallow edge of the Loch was the naked figure of Judy Sinclair.

"Here," McGregor was standing beside him holding the AKM. He tapped the telescopic sight attached to the rifle. "Have a good look," he said with a smile. "You won't regret it."

David raised the rifle and squinted through the sight: she was running toward the cottage with long flowing strides, every part of her body balanced and relaxed, forming a perfect symmetry of movement, her breasts were high and firm, her stomach as flat as a young boy's, and the muscles of her long thighs undulating with a sensuous fluency.

Before David realized, she was through the door. "Good morning, David," she said. "I hope you didn't miss." She looked at the rifle.

"Not a thing," he said.

"Good," she replied smiling. "We leave at ten; I suggest you change into your civvies."

"Where are we going?" David asked.

"Oh, I thought it would be nice if we saw more of the highlands. The scenery is absolutely beautiful."

"Why not?" David answered.

Everything was loaded, and Judy sat behind the wheel of one of the Land-Rovers. David and McGregor stood by the other. "Be on your way, boy," McGregor said extending a hand. "You take the high road and I'll take the low road—only be damn sure you're at Heathrow Airport dead on time." They shook hands, and David climbed in beside Judy.

Maxwell turned to Judy but before he could speak she said, "No questions, David. I'll explain everything later. Relax and enjoy the scenery."

As they drove through the grand and bleak country toward Inverness, with the snowcapped heights of Ben Wyvis on their left, Judy talked of her love for the highlands. "Whenever I can, I come up here," she said. "The peace, the stillness . . ." She stopped the Land-Rover. "*Listen* to the silence," she said. "It's as real as sound and in a way quite beautiful. If you listen to it for long enough, you lose your awareness of self. Somehow the silence embraces you, and you become a part of it—of the universe. It sounds ridiculous, but silence makes me believe in the existence of a deity. Something far greater than ourselves."

David looked at the beautiful woman beside him—machine guns, silence, and deities: it was a very strange combination.

"You have Scots blood?" David asked.

She laughed. "Not a drop. English on my father's side, Irish on my mother's."

At Inverness they lunched on freshly caught trout and roast venison, then drove south and arrived at the village of Luss on the edge of beautiful Loch Lomond shortly before seven o'clock.

They entered an old inn where a gray-haired woman greeted Judy effusively and, with a glance at David, asked, "Your usual room, Miss Sinclair?"

"Yes, Mrs. Malcolm, that will be fine, thank you," Judy said and turned to David. "You go up and take the first bath. I want to have a word with Mrs. Malcolm."

As David wallowed in the luxury of a hot bath, he could hear McGregor saying, "It'll make you soft, boy. Soft!" And then it occurred to David to think that maybe McGregor had himself wallowed in that same bath.

"Come on there—get out and make way for a lady," Judy stood at the door. "I'll join you downstairs in the bar."

The bar was warm and cozy. David sat by the window nursing a malt whiskey. Judy came through the door. She was wearing a long dark crimson silk gown which flowed with the elegant lines of her body. "Where did *that* come from!" he said as she sat down.

"Is that the most flattering thing you can say," she asked with a teasing pout.

"Hell, no, you're . . . it's beautiful. But–"

"Mrs. Malcolm keeps a few things for me here. Now, what's that you're drinking?"

David told her.

"Well, at least McGregor taught you something," she laughed.

"How about you?" David asked.

"How about me, what?"

"Did McGregor . . . teach you *your* drinking habits?"

She was silent for a moment, then said, "No–McGregor taught me a lot of things, but drinking wasn't one of them."

"I see," David said.

"I doubt if you do. But let's talk about something else. I want to set the record straight. I *am* the woman who warned you to get out of Germany."

"I know," David said. "That's not what's bothering me."

"I am also the woman you saw running in the park," she continued. "Only I wasn't trying to kill you. . . . I saved your life."

"How the hell–?"

"Behind a tree in front of you a man was waiting to kill you. His name is Günther Kraske, and he's SSD. It was *him* I shot at–not you. Unfortunately I only wounded him. A head wound, enough to stun him and drop him to the ground, that's all."

David described the man he'd met at the apartment where Barbara had been held captive, the man he'd seen looking through the back of the car with a bandage round his head after the attack on him outside the restaurant.

"Yes, that's him. And for the record, I also saved your life at that restaurant."

"It was *you* who pulled my feet from under me?"

"Yes—the truth is, Mr. David Maxwell, after you refused to leave Germany, I spent a great deal of time and energy I could ill afford trying to stop you from getting yourself killed."

"Why?" he said. "Seems to me I was getting in *everybody's* way! The SSD's *and* our people's."

Judy Sinclair looked at him thoughtfully for a long time.

"I'm not sure I've worked out the answer to that," she said. Then she added, "However, it was fortunate, wasn't it. Otherwise we wouldn't have you in Zambu to help us."

David looked into his glass and raised his eyes to hers. "What were you doing in Bonn? . . . apart from keeping me alive?" he said.

There was another long silence before she answered. "Some while ago British intelligence began to suspect that a brothel in Bonn was being run by the SSD. They had to penetrate the brothel and find out if their suspicions were right. I was given the assignment."

"Are you telling me you were a—"

"Shut up, David, and listen." David saw the slight trembling of her hands and the defiant way she tossed her head back. "Eventually I became the mistress of the man running the brothel, a man called Gartmann," she continued speaking carefully. "The details aren't important except that to do it, I had to get rid of the mistress he already had." She paused.

"Get rid of?" David said quietly.

"Yes. You see, I suspected she was involved in a terrorist incident in Frankfurt, so I arranged for German Intelligence to pick her up and question her about it. As I anticipated, she panicked and decided to leave Gartmann." She paused again. "I also knew that Gartmann couldn't let her leave. . . . He *had* to kill her." She looked David straight in the eyes. "In other words, I killed her."

"I think I need another drink," David said. The days with McGregor had been games. Shooting at objects . . . learning to kill, but not killing. Now he was talking to a woman who had committed cold, calculated . . . murder! He felt emotionally disorientated. Unsure of his feelings.

He returned with the drinks. "Yes," he said.

"Once I became his mistress, I knew almost everything he did. I was given an apartment in the brothel. I was able to bug his office and his phones. That's how we found out about your father and sister . . . and the plans to send them to Zambu."

David was staring at the liquid in his glass. He looked up sharply. "How did you get into this—this business?" he said quietly.

"That's a long story," she answered, "but when I look back, I suppose there was something inevitable about it. My father came from a military family. For the past hundred years, at least one of the sons of the family was a professional soldier in the British army." She laughed. "I think we Sinclairs have been careless enough to spill blood in just about every country in the world. My father and my brother were in the army. My brother was killed when he was nineteen–a stupid accident on a mortar range. I was only twelve at the time, and from them on my father treated me as if I were the boy he had lost. He taught me how to shoot, hunt . . . even unarmed combat. I grew up a real little tomboy. Then when I was twenty, my father was killed. You see he was a member of the SAS, the–"

"Yes, I know, the Special Air Service. McGregor told me about them," David interrupted.

"He was killed in Yemen, in the Middle East. For reasons I'm not prepared to explain, I knew who killed him. I loved my father–a typical Electra complex, I suppose." There was a bitter edge to her laugh. "So I went to Yemen, and I killed my father's murderer. It caused a lot of embarrassment to the British government, but they managed to keep the whole thing quiet and get me out. When I was back in England, I was approached by British Intelligence, MI6. They suggested I work for them. As the saying goes: it seemed like a good idea at the time. I accepted. So there you are: now you know the story of my short life."

"Maybe," David answered feeling the gaps in her story were in some way more significant than what she had told him. And he still wondered how an intelligent, beautiful, and undeniably sensitive woman could bring herself to use her body and kill–even in the interest of her country. Then he remembered how McGregor had said it was intelligent men who, once they had made the commitment, made the most ruthless and efficient fighting men. Maybe there was a reason for this. He wasn't sure.

But it was not the time to question her about it. He could sense she had had to force herself to tell him as much as she had. And he wondered why she *had* told him so much—so much about herself. There had been no need for it.

"It's your turn, David," she said interrupting his thoughts. He looked up and saw the watchful anxiety in her eyes. "Tell me about yourself. More than is in your dossier."

David's eyes narrowed. "I have a dossier?"

"Of course," she smiled. "But only a little one . . . so far."

"If I can help it, it's going to stay that way."

"I hope so." Her face was serious.

"Personal information?" David said, curious.

"A little," she teased.

"I'm not sure I like that," David said.

"A private sort of person? Like to keep to yourself?" She was smiling.

"I guess so."

"That's what it says in the dossier. Says you're hung up on your work and don't socialize much. . . . Apart from the little harem you have scattered along the West Coast, that is. Apparently they think you're good at it, but you're not the marrying kind."

"Good at what?"

She raised her eyebrows. "Why ask me? I don't know what you do to your women."

"You mean those women talked about *that*! Who to?"

"The FBI. And, as you put it, *that* is the one thing women will always talk about, in case you didn't know."

"What else is in that dossier?" David asked irritably.

"You get full marks for fitness and mental agility. And they think you're quite good for a beginner."

"What at?"

"Surviving . . . violence."

"Now let's get this straight," David leaned forward. "I'm the nuclear expert. If there is any violence around, you and McGregor can take care of it. It's your department."

"You may not have any choice."

David was silent, the photograph of Barbara in his mind's eye. "I know it," he said and was silent again.

Judy touched his arm lightly. "And I know you're a very private man who doesn't like talking about his feelings. Now, let's eat."

They went into the dining room, and people's heads turned to follow the beautiful woman whose eyes turned emerald green in the candlelight when they sat in their booth.

And as they continued to talk during dinner, Judy's questions began to focus on his work.

"Could your father really make atomic bombs in Zambu?" she asked. "Even with the help of the two French nuclear engineers. I mean, doesn't it need massive facilities—laboratories, plant, equipment . . . people?"

David's answer was emphatic. "No—my father could do it on his own. The only reason I can think of for the two nuclear engineers is that they want the bomb

—or bombs—in a hurry. The engineers can do the heavy work far quicker than he could."

"It *can't* be that easy otherwise—"

"I didn't say it was easy," David cut in. "I said my father could do it—so could a few thousand other people around the place. I promise you."

Judy was shaking her head.

David leaned forward. "Look: do you *really* want to know?"

"If I can understand. Physics wasn't exactly my strong subject at school."

"I'll keep it simple. But believe me, to my father it *is* simple."

David called the waiter and ordered a couple of liqueur whiskeys, then turned back to Judy. "Okay," he said. "The only problem, and the reason why small countries, criminals, terrorists, and nuts all over the world aren't making atomic bombs, is you have to get your hands on the right kind of uranium. What's called weapons grade uranium—highly enriched uranium 235."

"What about all the nuclear power reactors? They use uranium."

"Right. But you can't make bombs from it. Most nuclear power reactors use fuel which contains uranium 235 enriched—concentrated—to a level of three to four percent. But to make atomic bombs, you need weapons grade uranium—uranium enriched to as high as a *ninety* percent level. Okay?"

"So far."

"Okay. Now there's only two uses for weapons grade uranium. One, obviously, to make nuclear weapons. The other, for reasons it would be too complicated to explain, to fuel small test or pilot reactors used by universities and countries familiarizing themselves with the technology of full-scaled commercial reactors. The ship that disappeared had a consignment of uranium destined for this purpose as part of its cargo. So whoever stole it *has* weapons grade uranaum. The rest is straightforward."

"Straightforward?" Judy said accepting her liqueur whiskey from the waiter. "Isn't uranium enriched to ninety percent dangerous to handle without elaborate equipment? . . . Radioactive?"

"You could carry it around in your pocket for weeks, and it wouldn't do you any harm. It's only when the stuff explodes that the radiation is released."

"And . . . ?" Judy asked.

"And what?" David answered.

"How do you actually *make* the bomb?"

"It'll bore the pants off of you."

"No—I really want to know," Judy insisted.

"Okay. Only don't say you didn't ask for it. . . . To get an atomic explosion you need a certain minimum quantity of weapons grade uranium in one lump. This quantity is called the 'critical mass,' because it's the amount of uranium necessary to self-generate fission—a chain reaction of splitting atoms which is what an atomic explosion is. Okay?"

Judy sipped the thick, sweet liqueur and nodded.

"But—for reasons too complicated to explain right now—the size of the critical mass depends on the type of bomb you're putting together. My guess is they'll make a pretty crude bomb; something like the one dropped on Hiroshima, only smaller. It's called a gun type bomb. And for this type of bomb the critical mass will be around forty kilograms."

"What's that in pounds?" Judy asked.

"About ninety pounds. Uranium's heavy stuff. Ninety pounds is no bigger than a football. So . . . the trick is to put two slugs of uranium—both smaller than the critical mass—into each end of a half-inch thick steel cylinder and keep them apart."

"How long would the cylinder be?"

"Oh, about four feet would be enough. . . . Then you put a couple of ounces of chemical explosive behind one of the slugs of uranium inside the cylinder. When you detonate it, the explosion shoots the slug down the cylinder to join the other slug and, whammee! you've got a critical mass."

David was silent for a moment, then he said quietly, "In other words, you've got something like a one kiloton explosion—the equivalent of a thousand tons of TNT."

"As simple as that." Judy looked at him incredulously.

"There's a few more details, but nothing complicated. *Making* the bomb is simple; it's getting hold of the weapons grade uranium that's difficult."

Judy was silent, her gaze fixed on the table. Then she raised her eyes to meet his, and he saw the anxiety in them. "Would you write all that down for me—including the details you left out?" she asked.

"Why sure, but why?" He looked at her questioningly.

She reached out and put her hand gently on his. "David, do you really understand what you have got yourself into . . . ? That there is every possibility you may be killed." Her cool fingers pressed on his hand.

David's eyes were locked with hers And he realized the answer to her question was, no. Danger, yes, but the reality of death, no. It had not really occurred to him.

"So that's why you want it written down," he said.

She nodded.

"Then I'd better take care of myself," he said squeezing her hand. "Because I don't think you've quite graduated in my subject yet."

"Nor you in mine," she answered.

They went up to the bedroom, a tension between them. He, uncertain of himself—of everything: wary of being manipulated, not sure about people, motives . . . right and wrong. She, hesitant, frightened . . . afraid of doing wrong, of *being* wrong—for him.

He closed the door, and for a moment they stood apart, and he saw the searching in her eyes. She stepped close to him and slowly raised her hands to touch his cheeks, and in her eyes he saw a vulnerability, a fear of rejection. She pressed her lips to his, softly at first, then with a hungry urgency. And David knew he was not being manipulated: she wanted him as much as he did her. The difference between technique and desire was beyond words, beyond doubts.

He took her in his arms and felt the softness of her body, and the demanding pressure of her pelvis. Then he picked her up and carried her to the bed, cradled in his arms.

For a moment she lay still, her eyes still searching his. As David undressed hurriedly, his eyes still on her, she slowly peeled her long dress upward and over her curved thighs and the tops of her stockings until she lay exposed, offering . . .

David knelt beside her on the bed and unbuttoned the top of her dress, releasing the naked firmness of her breasts. He lowered his head and caressed her nipples with his tongue. As she arched beneath him, he pulled her dress from her body, then lowered his head to her thighs, taking her round buttocks in his hands.

She began to moan, rocking slowly at first, then rapidly, moved by a frenzied force. With a wild shout she reached for him and pulled him up and then as he entered her warm softness, he too let out a shout of ecstasy.

He could not control himself. Within minutes he had exploded inside her. He looked into her now soft eyes. "I'll do better next time," he said and smiled. "It's been a long time."

She returned his smile and reached down for him. "Then let's catch up," she said.

FOURTEEN

Heathrow, London
Frankfurt, West Germany

The Terminal Three departure lounge at London's Heathrow Airport was packed with the usual assortment of holiday and business travelers.

Sitting at one of the rows of easy chairs was a man of about thirty-five. He was obviously a business man, a successful one. His well-cut dark blue suit was unmistakably Savile Row. He adjusted his horn-rimmed glasses, took out a sheaf of papers from the black leather briefcase on the seat beside him, and began to scan the pages. From time to time he made a notation on one of the pages with a gold pen.

At a plastic-topped table some distance from the businessman a young woman, wearing a wide-brimmed red hat with attractive glimpses of curling hair, raised a cup of coffee to her lips. On the floor beside her was a model's bag. She sipped the coffee, pulled a face of mild distaste, then resumed that vacant stare which is the attractive woman's defense against the probing of men's lascivious eyes.

Behind her, leaning on the bar, an untouched beer in front of him, an athletic-looking man in his late twenties glanced at the flight indicator board. He was casually but expensively dressed; a light brown suede jacket, open-necked fawn silk shirt, dark brown trousers and suede boots, with a thick gold chain around one wrist—something to do with films or television perhaps. Beside him was a brown leather case.

All three people had one thing in common. Having had their hand luggage searched and passed through the metal detector, they had gone to the toilets. There, each had looked for the cubicle with a cross scratched just below the handle. Inside the cubicle they had stood on the toilet seat, removed the cistern lid and from inside removed a waterproof plastic bag containing a fully loaded gun. A cleaner, who was recently employed by the airport authority and who would shortly be leaving to perform some other simple but useful job for MI6, had deposited the guns in the cisterns earlier that morning.

The voice over the public address system requested all passengers for the TWA flight for Frankfurt to proceed to gate number 20.

McGregor replaced his papers in the briefcase and took off his glasses. Judy Sinclair stopped looking vacant and picked up her model bag. David Maxwell took a sip of beer and reached down for his leather grip. The three of them made their way to gate 20 and boarded the Boeing 707.

As the plane left the ground and leveled off at 30,000 feet, David Maxwell glanced across the aisle at McGregor, who was studying some papers resting on the briefcase on his lap. To Maxwell, a Savile Row suit and glasses didn't quite go with his image of McGregor, but then, not everyone had just spent five days in Scotland with him.

Over his shoulder David took a quick glance at

Judy and began to think about the fabulous night they had spent together; and the day after, exploring the wooded islands of Loch Lomond in the boat Mrs. Malcolm had insisted they use without payment. There had been a strange hesitancy about her manner with him which was totally out of keeping with everything else he knew about her. It was hard to understand. As for his feelings about her . . . he simply didn't know. A jumble of conflicting emotions.

Abruptly his thoughts changed. *He was about to hijack an airplane!* It seemed ridiculous. Unreal. McGregor had said he had "flipped the switch." He wondered if he really had. A plane, a gigantic piece of complex machinery, full of people—*lives*—and they were going to take command of it by crude violence. *It was obscene!*

His hands were trembling, and perspiration began to form on his forehead. And then disgust was overcome by another thought. *He was losing his nerve!*

"Are you all right, sir?" A hostess was bending, peering anxiously at his white face. Jesus! Five minutes from Frankfurt, and some guy was going to be sick all over the place. Or worse. She could do without that.

David shook his head. "Yes, I'm fine thanks. Something I ate, I guess."

The hostess moved on with a silent prayer.

"Are you *sure* you're all right?" McGregor was leaning across the aisle, his hand on David's arm. David looked into McGregor's eyes. They weren't comforting or sympathetic. They were ice cold, their message loud and clear: you let us down now, Maxwell, and I'll kill you!

And in McGregor's eyes David saw the truth. There were two worlds; the normal world of the people around him in the plane and the new world of violence of which he was now part. He had crossed that bridge, and there was no going back. Too much depended on him—McGregor, Judy. . . . His father and Barbara. . . . And God alone knew what else.

"Sure. I'm okay. No sweat. Relax," he said and he felt his fear subsiding.

As the plane landed and swung around off the runway to taxi to the disembarkation berth, McGregor burst into the flight deck. "Stop this goddamn bus. Now!"

Three heads swiveled to look at him, too astonished to obey his order. "Stop this fucking thing, I said. Right here!"

As the copilot opened his mouth to speak, McGregor hit him on the side of his head with the automatic. Not enough to do him any permanent damage but enough to convince the pilot that the man with the gun was serious . . . and violent . . . and he'd better obey.

The engine cut out, and as the brakes locked, the plane stopped with a slight jolt

"Inform the central tower you've been hijacked. Tell them to stand by for further instructions. That's all," McGregor snapped.

Back in the cabin only those passengers in the front realized what was going on until David stood in the middle of the aisle and shouted, "Attention, everybody. Stay in your seats. Do not remove your seat belts." There were a few gasps, a woman let out a short, tight scream, but most of the passengers were frozen in shock, their eyes riveted on the gun in David's hand. "Look behind you," David shouted. Eighty heads turned to see Judy at the rear of the plane, also with a gun in her hand. "Now listen to me," David continued enunciating each word clearly. "We-do-not-want-to-hurt-you. If you do *exactly* what I say, no one will be harmed. Is-that-clear?"

David turned to one of the hostesses. He spoke calmly. "I want you to get the women and children out of the plane. Understand?" The hostess nodded. "Break open the emergency exit and use the escape chute."

It took the well-drilled hostesses less than fifteen minutes to evacuate the women and children.

David addressed the remaining men passengers. "Anyone with a medical or health condition liable to make another long flight dangerous, raise their arms."

Fifteen men raised their arms. David guessed three-quarters of them had good health but quick wits. It didn't matter. The essential was to make sure that no genuine case remained on board. "Okay, get out of the plane," he ordered.

They did. Very quickly.

About thirty-five men remained. "Fill the seats at the front of the plane. *Now!*" David ordered.

Judy followed behind as the men moved up front, then walked between them and joined David. "Very professional," she whispered. "I'm impressed."

"I'd make a good drill sergeant, eh?" he grinned.

Judy winked. "A credit to any guards' regiment."

"I've a feeling the rest of it isn't going to be like a parade ground."

Judy smiled. "Just pretend it is. . . . It helps."

David addressed the silent men, still dazed by the speed of events. "The lady's going to look after you for a while. If any of you have dumb macho instincts, forget them. She shoots a whole lot better than I do."

David slammed the emergency exit shut, then stood at the door of the flight deck. "How's it going?" he asked McGregor.

McGregor pulled back through the door. "Just dandy. How about you?"

"No problems."

"Good. I've given them our terms: a list of nine left-wing terrorists to be released from German prisons and delivered to us here together with five million Deutsche Mark in cash by midnight. If they don't deliver we kill one hostage every fifteen minutes after midnight. Refueling starts one hour earlier."

David looked at his watch. It was 11:30 A.M. "It's going to be a long wait," he said.

"Don't let it bother you. Nothing can go wrong so long as the dudes out there keep absolute silence. If they can't talk, they can't exchange smart ideas. Okay? I'm going to keep with these guys here. They're trained to be smart without talking."

David was right. It was a long wait. Every now and then he took a quick look out of one of the windows. The preparations were impressive. He estimated there were a hundred soldiers positioned strategically around the building facing the plane; he knew each one was a sharpshooter with telescopic sights. And as the daylight began to fade, the powerful beams of six searchlights ranged on top of the airport buildings focused on the aircraft pouring light through the windows.

* * *

In Bonn other preparations were taking place in the office of the German chancellor, and although David knew what their outcome would be, he did not know exactly how they would be handled.

Apart from the gray-haired Chancellor himself, there were three men present: the secretary of state, the minister of the interior, and Colonel Körner, head of Grenzschutzgruppe 9 (GSG9)—the antiterrorist commandos who had successfully stormed and captured hijacked airplanes three times in the past.

The smallness of the meeting was not only a reflection of the Chancellor's customary autocratic use of his constitutional power, it was a measure of the dire need for impenetrable security to surround the proceedings. Only one man present, the Chancellor himself, knew of the true nature of the hijack operation and its place in a mission vital to the security of the West.

"It's the best—it's the *only* plan I can come up with for an immediate attack, Herr Chancellor," Colonel Körner said, shifting his wiry frame on the chair, "But I don't like it. We know nothing about these hijackers. Nothing! Except, according to the passengers they released this morning, they are pretty calm and efficient. We *should* wait. . . . Let them sweat it out until they get tired and their nerves start getting frayed."

The square-shouldered Chancellor looked at the colonel with the implacable stare for which he was so noted. He spoke quietly, "I appreciate your concern, Colonel, but in my judgment we cannot afford to wait. It is precisely *because* they are so calm and efficient that I believe if we do nothing, then at precisely fifteen minutes after midnight the first dead body will be thrown out of the plane. *I will not let that happen on German soil.* Nor will I give in to their demands. I have spoken personally to the President of the United States, and he is in full agreement with my views. You will carry out the attack as planned. Agreed, gentlemen?"

The question was a formality.

When the men had left, the Chancellor took a sheet of paper from a drawer in his desk and in a clear bold hand wrote the exact details he had just agreed with Colonel Körner for the attack on the hijacked aircraft.

Waiting in an antechamber next to his office was Wilfried Linke, head of German counterintelligence. The Chancellor entered the chamber and handed the sheet of paper to him. "What can you do about it?" he said.

Linke read in silence. Under the circumstances Colonel Körner's plan of attack was good, he thought, but everything depended upon split-second timing. The hijackers had demanded that, before the refueling started, the searchlights be switched off and kept off. The refueling crew were to bring a steel ladder with them and place it against the open door of the aircraft. Then, the nine released terrorists—with the ransom money—were to be taken by bus to a point ten yards from the aircraft. From there they would disembark, one by one, at thirty-second intervals and climb the ladder into the plane.

Linke grunted. The hijackers were taking no chances. If a standard stairway had been used, it might have been possible for a group of commandos to storm up it. *Nobody* was going to storm up a ladder! He continued reading:

Colonel Körner proposed staffing the bus with nine of his own men, suitably dressed to pass for the terrorists in the dim light. He himself would disembark first armed with a pistol and a concussion grenade—a device designed to produce maximum flash and noise without dispersing metallic fragmentation which might kill not only the thrower but, in this instance, the hostages.

He would throw the grenade from halfway up the ladder. A second later, a commando in the bus would flash a torch as a signal for the searchlights to be switched on, sending their powerful beams pouring into the entrance and windows of the aircraft. Their purpose would be twofold: to add to the blinding effect of the concussion grenade and to illuminate the inside of the plane so when the colonel hurled himself through the entrance, he could pick his targets. The moment the searchlights came on, the commandos in the bus would rush to his support.

Linke raised his eyes to the Chancellor, his face grave. "There is only one thing we can do to *ensure* the colonel's plan fails," he said. "Would you add the following notation to the letter, please, Herr Chancellor."

Linke dictated the sentences.

"Who will do this?" the Chancellor asked when he had finished writing.

"I will," Linke answered. "I am the one man who can go where he wants in the airport without being challenged. Besides, there will be an official enquiry when it's all over and I am above suspicion."

"Agreed." The Chancellor handed the letter to Linke. "You are *sure* the American will get it?"

"He'll get it, Herr Chancellor."

"And the attempt to rescue the hostages will appear genuine, *beyond all possible doubt*? It is imperative the Russians have not even the minutest cause for suspicion. They will have their agents—somewhere—watching the whole thing. Our agents must get into Zambu, their mission unsuspected. If the Russians are making bombs there, God alone knows what's at stake."

Linke smiled grimly. "That at least we can be sure of. It *will* be genuine. After all, the colonel and his men know nothing of our intentions."

"Regrettable," the Chancellor murmured. "But necessary. No risks can be taken. I have kept the truth even from some of my own ministers."

The interior of the Boeing 707 was bright as daylight. David spoke to McGregor. "These damn lights are getting on my nerves."

McGregor glanced at his watch. "They'll be switched off in ten minutes when the refueling starts. Meantime, think of the picture the television viewers are getting. Dramatic, eh? This is strictly a publicity operation."

Maxwell returned to Judy who was guarding the hostages. "Any trouble?" he asked.

Judy smiled. "No, they're being good as gold. I think they've got the impression we're serious."

David let out a long breath. "I don't think they're as scared as I am. I'll be glad when we're out of this place and in the air again."

Suddenly the cabin lights came on followed a few seconds later by the extinguishing of the searchlights.

"Here," McGregor called to David. "Keep an eye on the crew."

David went to the flight deck while McGregor opened the exit door of the aircraft. Ten seconds later through the glass of the cabin David saw the fuel truck coming over the tarmac toward the aircraft.

At the open door McGregor waited. A minute passed, and there was a slight bump against the bottom of the opening, and McGregor saw the glinting top of a steel ladder resting there. Swiftly, gun in hand, he descended the ladder and moved to the fuel truck.

"Who's got the letter?" he barked.

One of the men took an envelope from inside his overalls. At the last moment he had been given the letter and told it contained the German government's reply to the hijackers' demands. He was to hand it over to the hijacker who supervised the refueling. He did so—gladly.

McGregor returned to the plane, opened the envelope, and read the letter written by the Chancellor describing the impending attack by GSG9. Then he went forward and hauled up the ladder as far as it would go into the body of the aircraft before joining David on the flight deck. "Okay, get this thing moving to the end of the runway ready for takeoff," he said to the pilot.

"Where are we going?" the pilot asked.

"I'll tell you when we're airborne. Now, move it!"

The engines burst into life, and the 707 taxied slowly to the end of the runway.

"Right, hold it here. . . . Keep the engines ready for a quick takeoff. And when he says 'go,'" McGregor pointed to David, "get this bird into the air. Fast."

McGregor pulled David to one side. "Now listen, Maxwell. In five minutes a lot of things are going to happen. No matter what, stay where you are and wait until I shout 'go.' Then make damn sure these jokers get this thing in the air. That's *all* you have to do. Got it?"

David nodded, and McGregor went to speak to Judy.

From across the airport, the bus with Colonel Körner and his commandos on board began to move toward the 707. The colonel noted with relief that a bank of black clouds was about to obscure the moon. He smiled grimly. At least God was on their side; the rest depended on split-second timing—and luck. It always did.

On the flat roof of the airport building Wilfried Linke crept softly until he stood behind a man crouched over one of the searchlights. Raising both hands he clamped a chloroform-soaked pad over the mouth of the crouching figure.

For a few moments the man tried desperately to reach backward for Linke's head; then the chloroform took its effect and he was still.

In an instant Linke was on his feet and behind the searchlight. He peered through the infrared sight which Colonel Körner had ordered be affixed to each of the searchlights. When they were switched on, there would be no time to probe for their target; they must illuminate the plane instantly.

Through the sight Linke saw the bus coming to a halt, and Colonel Körner emerge from the side exit.

Lying on his stomach inside the plane, his hand six inches from the ladder, McGregor also saw the colonel leave the bus. His muscles tensed.

As he advanced toward the ladder, the colonel knew the moment of truth had arrived. Within seconds the fate of the hostages—and perhaps his own life or death—would be decided. Six feet from the ladder the colonel took a deep breath and steadied himself. He took two more steps and froze. First one searchlight—Linke's—then another, then in quick succession four more—their operators acting on reflex, thinking they had missed the signal—bathed him, the bus, and the plane in brilliant light.

The colonel's thought processes were instinctive and as rapid as a computer. The searchlights were the signal for his men to leap to their feet, fully armed, and dash to his aid. At that moment they were in full view of the hijackers! To turn back now would at best mean failure; at worst a bullet in the back. The colonel lobbed the grenade into the plane from where he stood.

Lying in the plane McGregor was equally surprised. Not by the searchlights—he had been expecting them. For him, they were the signal to get to his feet, *obviously* see they were under attack, slam the ladder away, and shout "Go!" for the plane to take off.

What *did* surprise McGregor was the colonel's speed of reaction: the black blob of the grenade coming toward him at that instant was clearly visible in the brilliant light. Instinctively, he clapped his hands to his ears and shut his eyes. But the shock waves from the explosion stunned him momentarily. Long enough for Colonel Körner to reach the top of the ladder. McGregor fired, and the colonel dropped out of sight, a bullet through the head.

McGregor heaved the ladder clear of the plane. "Go!" he yelled.

"Move it!" David yelled at the pilots, and the engines roared to a crescendo.

McGregor was standing beside David. "What in God's name happened?" David shouted as the runway lights flashed by the accelerating aircraft.

"Something went wrong," McGregor replied.

"And . . . ?"

"I had to shoot one of them."

David stared at McGregor.

"There's a price for everything, Maxwell. And a brave man just paid the price for courage. If you want someone to blame, hang it on the people who made this little joyride necessary. Now go back and check on Judy."

David moved slowly back along the aisle to Judy. "Are you all right?" she asked, seeing his ashen face.

"I don't know," David answered. "McGregor killed one of those poor bastard commandos. They didn't even know—" He broke off and looked into her eyes . . . searching for an answer; for some sign of sanity.

Judy touched his hand gently. "Remember this,

David. McGregor *always* does what's necessary—without hesitation. And no matter what the cost. *Believe me.* I know." For an instant, there was bitterness in her eyes.

FIFTEEN

Zambu, Africa

The Boeing 707 cruised at 40,000 feet on a bearing given the captain by McGregor; the clear sky surrounding an unlimited expanse of stars. Peaceful.

"How long is the flight?" David handed McGregor a cup of coffee and leaned against the door of the flight deck. The air still held the acrid smell of the concussion grenade.

"Total flight time about seven hours," McGregor replied.

"What's the plan?"

McGregor looked at David with blank eyes. "Plan? . . . We land; what else?"

"For God's sake, you've got to have something worked out."

"Maxwell, this isn't a goddamn laboratory. We're going into a situation we don't know a thing about; how the hell do we *plan*! We play it by ear. . . . We go in on a prayer."

"Doesn't sound too much different from some of the laboratories I've worked in," David grinned.

McGregor gave a short laugh. "That's what I always figured. . . . Now go to the back of the plane. We each get two hours sleep. You're first."

For about thirty seconds David had time to think about the attack by GSG9 and McGregor. It was a whole new ball game, and he didn't like the rules. He didn't think he'd ever adapt to them. He didn't want to. Then his eyes closed, and he slept.

At six in the morning David was standing guard over the passengers, most of whom were asleep. At the far end of the cabin he could see Judy who was also sleeping. On the flight deck McGregor spoke to the captain. "Radio for permission to land at Hono," he said. Hono was the capital and the only town of any real size in underdeveloped Zambu.

The captain grimaced. "They won't give us permission to land. It's Russian controlled, and the Russians are signatories of the Hijacking Agreement."

"Yeah, I know. Don't worry your sweet head about it—just do it," McGregor said.

The captain shrugged, "Okay!" He nodded to the copilot. "Do what the gentleman says, Sam."

Three minutes later the copilot spoke without looking up. "Permission refused. . . . And they want us out of their airspace."

"That's fine," McGregor said, "now that we've got the protocol over with, go in there and land."

"We can't," the captain replied.

"Why not?"

"The runway isn't long enough."

"The hell it isn't," McGregor sounded bored. "I know *exactly* how long it is. It's tight, but possible. So stop arguing and concentrate on landing this thing. Just imagine what you're going to look like if you get it wrong."

"I'll have to make a low pass over the airfield first . . . have a good look at the runway."

"Naturally," McGregor spoke tersely.

As the plane lost height, David knelt on a seat by one of the windows behind the passengers. McGregor was still on the flight deck, Judy up front guarding the passengers. It hadn't escaped David that his active participation in the hijacking operation had been kept to the minimum possible. And it wasn't difficult to guess why: in the event of trouble, he wasn't trusted to act swiftly or ruthlessly enough: to kill without hesitation. He knew they were right.

Below David saw open savanna: flat terrain covered with tall green grass, dotted with clumps of trees. Very soon the land sloped downward in a long escarpment and then leveled off again, and they were passing over a dense forest of tall trees; and winding like a snake through the forest, the muddy waters of a river making its way to the sea.

The trees thinned out to be replaced by a short stretch of scrubland, and there, with an abruptness which took David by surprise, they were above the airfield: a single runway with a small building and control tower to one side of it. Then came a stretch of about a mile of thin scrub before the plane flashed across the town.

From his side of the plane David could scc a widc road extending from the airfield right through the town to the water's edge, then branching east and west along the coast. The town itself, comprised of one- and two-story buildings, stretched westward in David's vision for about three miles and then ended abruptly in scrubland which shortly gave way to a tree-dotted landscape with widely separated two-story white stucco houses situated here and there—the residential area of the few privileged rich.

The plane crossed the coast road and was above the large lagoon around which the town was situated; then it flew out above the open ocean. It banked to the right and began the long half circle which would bring it in line with the airfield runway. David crossed to the other side of the plane to get a complete view of the town.

The lagoon was shaped like the top of an anvil: about one mile wide at the sea entrance, then arcing out on both sides to a width of about four miles. At the west end of the lagoon was a harbor: a collection of warehouses, three cranes, and an assortment of small coastal vessels moored alongside. Anchored a couple of hundred yards from the harbor's edge was a large vessel, and as the plane dipped for its approach, David clearly saw its name: *Burgh.*

Ahead, about half a mile before the airfield, the river flowed to empty its muddy waters into the blue waters of the lagoon at one end of the harbor.

The plane crossed the river at a hundred feet, and a few seconds later the landing wheels touched down. The plane came to a stop two feet from the edge of the runway.

"That wasn't so bad," McGregor grinned at the captain.

"You'll never know," the grim-faced captain answered.

"Call it an occupational hazard," McGregor said. "Now get this thing off the runway."

"Any particular place you'd like me to put it? . . . We aim to please."

"Yeah. Drive it to the reception committee," McGregor answered pointing toward the men clustered outside the airport building.

The copilot spoke. "The control tower says to get the hell out."

"Tell him you'd like to but you're on the wrong end of a gun," McGregor said.

The plane taxied to within fifty yards of the reception committee: some black, some white, all armed.

"Hold it here," McGregor ordered.

The plane stopped.

"Now get back with the passengers . . . all of you," McGregor commanded the crew.

They obeyed.

McGregor followed them as far as the beginning of the passenger aisle, then took a grenade from his pocket, pulled the pin, and lobbed it through to the flight deck. After the explosion he smiled at the captain. "I like it here," he said. "I aim to stay for a while."

It had all happened quickly and efficiently. The reception committee had disarmed them, put them in a truck with a couple of silent guards: white . . . and Russian. Then they had been driven to the center of town and into a small square at one side of which was a solid gray stone building.

Inside was a big open area with a dozen desks occupied by white men. "KGB headquarters," McGregor had remarked quietly as they marched past and into an inner office. The man sitting behind the desk was short, stocky, and as angry as anyone David had seen in a long while.

He introduced himself as Colonel Smirnov. Then in broken, but totally adequate, English he informed them that the Russian government regarded hijacking as one of the most barbaric crimes possible.

Futhermore, he did not believe for one moment they were the least bit concerned with obtaining the release of imprisoned German terrorists. It had been nothing more than a clumsy scheme to rob the German government of five million marks under the guise of political motives. It had happened before; it was not going to happen in Zambu . . . not while he was in charge. They would be returned to Germany to face trial just as soon as transport could be arranged.

David paced up and down their cell with growing irritation. It was about twelve by ten feet and completely bare with floor-to-roof steel bars through which he could see the shirt-sleeved Russian guard sitting with his feet up on the desk staring fixedly at Judy. David wished he wouldn't, but it didn't seem to be bothering Judy: she was sitting propped against the wall, her wide-brimmed red hat tilted over her face, to all appearances asleep.

McGregor was also propped against a wall. He seemed to be asleep. David looked up at the grilled window set a little above head height at the back of the cell. He crossed to it, reached up and clasped the bars, and hoisted himself to peer out. An empty high-walled compound; an exercise area, David imagined. He lowered himself.

The guard's eyes flicked back to Judy.

David stood for a moment glaring at McGregor. He'd make one last attempt: one final effort to get some sense out of McGregor. So far all he had got was, "It'll work out; don't worry. Relax." How could he *relax*!

All the elaborate planning, the death of the German commando, had been for nothing! And how could the two of them be so relaxed? *Asleep!* Is that what being a professional meant? Maybe . . . but they didn't have a father and a sister whose safety—*lives, maybe*—were at stake.

David slumped down next to McGregor. McGregor grunted and opened his eyes. "Get some sleep while you can, Maxwell; you're going to need it."

David looked at him angrily. "For the last time, McGregor, will you tell me what's going on?"

"For the last time, Maxwell. . . . No."

"For God's sake, why not? This whole thing's fallen apart, and you don't seem to give a damn."

"On the contrary, the operation's been a total success . . . so far. We're here, aren't we?"

"In a prison! . . . About to be shipped back to Germany!"

"I said don't worry; we're going to get out."

"How?"

"Listen, Maxwell, there are a few things you don't know. First, Colonel Smirnov thinks we're no more than a bunch of decadent pirates. It's my guess he knows less about what's going to happen in this place than we do, so he's got no reason to be suspicious about us. But before he ships us back to Germany, he's going to check with Moscow. How long that takes depends on their communications system. But it's possible the colonel will get instructions to interrogate us, let's say . . . thoroughly and quickly."

"So?"

"I don't want you telling the colonel how we're planning to get out of here."

David was puzzled. "Why would *I* tell them?" he asked.

"You might not, only I'm not taking any chances. I don't know your breaking point."

David frowned. "Breaking point?"

"Yeah. Thorough and quick interrogation is a euphemism for quick and brutal torture. Nothing subtle—just a lot of pain. I know my breaking point; I know Judy's. It would take them quite a while to break us. . . . You, I know nothing about."

David felt his anger rising. "You think *I* would talk when my father and sister are—"

"Cool it, boy," McGregor placed a hand on David's arm. "I'm not insulting you. Standing up to pain isn't a simple matter of willpower. Everyone's got a different pain threshold. What's unbearable to some people is tolerable to others. There's only one sure thing—no more than one in a million people can take all the pain that can be handed out without breaking. The Gestapo proved that during the war. Forget the heroics. . . . People break!"

David considered this. McGregor had a point. Why extend the risk to him, an unknown quantity. "Okay," he acknowledged. "But *when* do we get out?"

"Not even that," McGregor answered. "Now, do like I say; sleep."

At three o'clock David saw McGregor get to his feet and glance at his watch. Judy raised the brim of her hat, looked at McGregor, stretched her arms and legs, then settled down again.

As the minutes went by, David detected a growing tenseness in the lines on McGregor's face as he walked up and down.

Abruptly McGregor stopped in his tracks. Then he moved to stand under the small grilled window, listening. Judy was watching him. McGregor turned to look at her. As far as David could see, nothing passed between them, yet Judy got to her feet and went to stand by McGregor. After a second or two she nodded, almost imperceptibly, then returned to her position on the floor by the wall.

Once again David speculated about Judy and McGregor. They spoke to each other only when circumstances demanded it. Physically, Judy seemed to maintain a certain distance from McGregor. Yet they also seemed linked by a subtle bond of understanding and communication.

Then David heard the distant sound of an approaching aircraft. As the sound came nearer, he realized there were two planes, the pitch of their engines similar but distinguishable.

Soon he heard the whine of landing aircraft.

Then silence.

At first the firing was spasmodic. Rapidly it rose to a cacophony of rifle and machine-gun fire interrupted by the dull thuds of grenades and mortars.

A man from the outer office poked his head hurriedly around the door and shouted something in Russian to the guard. A minute later car doors slammed outside and tires screeched as three cars took off in rapid succession.

The guard moved his chair so he could see both the prisoners and the door. He sat down.

"The mercenaries?" David said.

"Yeah," McGregor answered.

"You were expecting them?"

McGregor nodded. "Our hijack operation was timed to coincide with the mercenary attack."

"And *they* are going to rescue *us*?" David asked.

"Not *they*—one of them."

"One!"

"Yeah. He's a bit exceptional."

"My God, I hope so," David said, his voice heavy with skepticism.

"And this is what you wouldn't tell me? That the . . . a mercenary is supposed to get us out of here?"

McGregor looked at David with cold indifference. "In case you haven't noticed, Maxwell, it hardly looks as if the Russians here were expecting the mercenaries. But we know from French intelligence the Russians recruited the mercenaries using Group 666 as a front. Right? Which means the Russians have Colonel Smirnov set up as a fall guy. Doesn't make sense, does it?"

"No," David agreed.

"So the only way we're going to find out what Moscow's up to is to let their plan develop. . . . *Not* foul it up for them; which is what might have happened if Colonel Smirnov had exposed you to enough pain to make you tell him about the mercenaries. Savvy?"

David nodded. The sounds of fighting rose to a crescendo, then abruptly ceased. After ten minutes of silence, bursts of fire broke out, gradually moving nearer through the town. Then came the sounds of brakes from outside the building. A burst of automatic fire in the front office reverberated through the building, followed by heavy footsteps approaching down the corridor to the cell.

The guard moved swiftly to stand against the wall to one side of the open door.

"Hit the deck," McGregor grabbed David's arm, pulling him down. Judy was already flat on the floor.

It took only three seconds, but to David it was like slow motion. A round metallic object came through the door, bounced on the floor, then skidded a few feet before stopping, still spinning on one side of its oval surface. The guard saw it and hurled himself through the open door, firing from the hip. Then another long burst of automatic fire, and the guard's body came flying back through the door, just off the ground and doubled up like a crumpled sack. A blinding explosion enveloped the flying body. A fragment from the grenade struck one of the bars of the cell and whinned into the back wall.

David looked up as two men in camouflage tunics and para boots burst into the room, submachine guns at the ready. Without glancing at the shattered remains of the body on the floor, their eyes went straight to the occupants of the cell.

"Who are you?" one of them asked in French, his heavy eyebrows raised in surprise. "Russian?"

"No, English," Judy replied quickly in English. "And those two," she pointed, "Americans."

"Ah! The hijackers." The man smiled with understanding. "The Boeing. . . . what a mess!"

Judy smiled back.

"Hey, Jacques, bring that black bastard, the President, here," the mercenary shouted over his shoulder.

David's eyes were glued on McGregor.

McGregor's eyes showed nothing.

An enormous African, well over six feet tall and a good two hundred eighty pounds, wearing traditional robes of scarlet and blue cloth, came through the door, a mercenary prodding him forward with a submachine gun.

"A companion for you," the mercenary addressed Judy. "President Monato of Zambu." He grinned.

The African was pushed into the cell, and the door locked again.

The three mercenaries stood for several minutes eyeing Judy. Eventually one said, "Let's get going." Reluctantly the other two followed him out.

"Do you speak English?" David addressed the African.

"I was educated at Oxford University in England. They speak rather a lot of English there." The African smiled; a gentle, good-natured smile, David thought.

"What happened?" David said.

"The mercenaries came to my home on the outskirts of town where I was meeting with my ministers. They slaughtered the ministers but my bodyguards held out long enough for me to escape. I was captured trying to reach a small coastal cruiser I have moored in the lagoon. I fancy my imprisonment here is no more than a short stay of execution."

"Keep quiet, you two," McGregor spoke urgently.

David listened. From down the corridor could be heard the sound of angry voices in argument. Then there was silence, and David saw the narrowing of McGregor's eyes. Footsteps came toward them from the corridor, and the three mercenaries reappeared.

Their eyes were fixed on Judy.

The bottom fell out of David's stomach. There was no mistaking the men's intentions; the expression on their faces said it all.

David looked swiftly at Judy. She was returning the men's gaze with calm eyes. For God's sake, David thought, *doesn't she know*!

One of the mercenaries unlocked the cell. "Come here," he said to Judy, his voice hoarse.

Judy walked out of the cell. There was a moment of hesitancy before the men seized her and tore off her clothes.

David watched in amazement: she had made no sound, no attempt at resistance.

She stood naked, except for the wide-brimmed red hat still on her head. A provocative smile came to her face. "Gentlemen," she said, "never in my hat." The mercenaries held back astonished while Judy nonchalantly removed the hat and tossed it on the floor. Then she reached up and pulled four long pins from her hair and lifted her wig off rcvcaling hcr natural blond hair tied tightly at the back of her head to accommodate the wig. "One more second, please, gentlemen," she said. She reached up, fiddled with something at the back of her head, and as she lowered her arms, her hair fell free. And in her right hand, deftly removed from their sheaths hidden in the now freed knot of natural hair, were two inch-long steel pins, each tipped with a poison which brought death within seconds of entering the blood stream.

The three men seized Judy by the arms and legs and spread-eagled her on the desk.

One of the mercenaries groped feverishly with his trousers, his glazed eyes fixed on Judy's body, the other held her down on her back with two enormous hands clamped on her upper arms, her forearms hanging loosely over the edges of the desk. The third stood beside the desk, his brutal face contorted with sadistic anticipation.

David watched in horror . . . then in astonishment as one of Judy's loose forearms whipped up and her fingers struck the right hand of the man holding her down. For a second the man looked at her in angry surprise. A look which almost instantly turned to a bewildered frown before his hands slipped from Judy, and he staggered back, his face twisted in pain.

The man between Judy's legs stopped, his pants around his knees, his stomach bare, and stared in amazement. Like a whiplash, Judy arched her body up and forward and the forefinger and thumb of her right hand struck the exposed stomach. He swore and raised his fist to strike her face, but his arm stayed in the air. His face convulsed in pain, and he too staggered back to collapse on the floor writhing in agony.

Judy was on her feet, standing across the desk from the third mercenary. With a roar of rage, he dived with outstretched arms for her throat. Panic seized

David as he saw Judy make no attempt to avoid her attacker. As his hands grasped her throat she rolled onto her back taking the force of his weight with her. Then a piercing scream of agony came from the man. He stumbled to his feet, his hands clasped to his face.

As Judy sprang for one of the submachine guns lying on the floor, the man took his hands from his face, still screaming. David nearly vomited. One of his eyes was hanging on his cheek by a thread of muscle, expertly gouged from its socket by Judy's thumb.

The man clasped his hands to his face again, but they fell to his sides as he spun around under the impact of the burst from the submachine gun as Judy fired. Then she whipped the gun around and with a burst of fire raked the body of one of the already dead men lying on the floor.

"Attention!"

Judy froze. Two more mercenaries stood at the door, their guns leveled at her. The one who had given the command was short and dark, Corsican probably. The other, a bearded giant of a man.

He quickly examined the three dead men and spoke quietly to his companion who then withdrew.

"Dress yourself," the giant ordered, pointing to Judy's torn clothes.

Judy did the best she could to clad herself with her torn garments.

"Inside," the giant ordered.

Judy entered the cell, and as she did, David once again sensed some unseen communication between her and McGregor.

The giant mercenary left. A minute later another man appeared and, apparently oblivious of the carnage around him, sat down on a chair, a rifle across his knees and lit a cigarette in his mouth.

"I'm sorry," Judy said quietly to McGregor but not so quietly David didn't hear it. *What the hell was she talking about,* David thought. *Sorry!* For Christ's sake, she'd nearly been raped and killed. *And she was saying sorry!*

"Forget it," McGregor replied. "They would have killed us all afterwards anyway. . . . They always do. . . . It makes them feel better." He gave a humorless smile.

David was seething with fury. *Was that all McGregor could say? "Forget it!"* What the hell did he mean anyway? Forget what? David turned away gritting his teeth, fighting to control his fury. It was no time to make a scene. But later . . . ! (If there ever was a "later.")

McGregor moved to stand under the window at the back of the cell. A speck of something white—unseen by anyone—appeared on the sill of the window, then gently fell down the wall to the floor. McGregor put his foot on it; eyed the guard; casually bent to pick it up. He turned his back on the guard, opened the pellet of paper, glanced at it, then shoved it into his mouth and swallowed it. He went across to Judy, spoke to her, and returned to the window.

"Monsieur." Judy was standing at the bars of the cell, beckoning to the guard, even less well clad than the scanty remains of her clothing would have allowed. "A cigarette, please, Monsieur."

The guard scrutinized her for a moment; got to his

feet and crossed to her. He smiled slowly as he looked at her naked breasts and held out the pack. Judy took a cigarette, put it to her lips, and leaned forward to accept the proffered light. "*Merci,*" she said.

"*Avec plaisir,*" the guard replied with a lecherous grin and turned his back to return to his place.

At that instant McGregor's hand shot up above his head, the palm open and facing outward between the bars of the window. A round metal object was thrust into the open hand from outside the bars, and the grenade was safely in McGregor's pocket. McGregor looked at his watch, then went to speak to the black president. Monato moved to sit at one corner of the cell away from the outer wall.

"Maxwell," McGregor was standing next to David, his back to the guard. "Go and sit next to Monato. In about sixty seconds Judy and I are going to join you. When we do, hit the deck and stay down until I tell you to get up. Got it?"

David nodded. He had learned enough about McGregor not to waste time asking questions in situations of imminent danger.

Judy's eyes were on McGregor. McGregor's eyes flicked to his watch then to Judy, and the two of them threw themselves headlong to join Maxwell and Monato on the floor in the corner.

The guard got to his feet, frowning at this strange behavior. A second later the building shook with the force of an explosion. At the far corner from where the four prostrate figures lay, the outer wall of the cell erupted, sending a hail of shattered bricks and stone spewing into the cell.

Maxwell heard Monato let out a groan and saw his hand go to the side of his head.

The cell was filled with dense swirling clouds of thick dust.

"Keep down," McGregor yelled and, rising to his knees, tossed the grenade through the bars toward the now crouching figure of the guard barely visible in the choking dust.

This time Maxwell felt the shock waves from the explosion as fragments of the grenade whined through the air.

"Move it!" McGregor slapped Maxwell on the shoulder, and David scrambled to his feet. Through the dust he saw a hole of light, about two by three feet, in the outside wall of the cell.

"Hold it, Maxwell!" David turned to see McGregor dragging Monato's heavy body by the shoulders across the floor. "Give me a hand with this guy," McGregor shouted. David took Monato's feet and they carried him toward the hole.

"Why do we want *him*?" David asked breathlessly.

"Because if he's alive, we're going to need all the friends we can get," McGregor answered.

McGregor went through the hole first, then hauled Monato through. David crawled through after them to see the giant bearded mercenary hoisting Monato's body into a jeep, the engine running. Crouching by the hole was Judy, an AKM in her hands. Near the jeep, McGregor was reloading a bazooka—the weapon, David guessed, which had been used to blast the hole in the cell wall.

"Grab yourself an AKM and get in the passenger seat," McGregor yelled. David vaulted into the vehicle.

It was piled with weapons: AKM's, submachine guns, boxes of ammunition, and grenades. He slammed a magazine into an AKM as the bearded giant sprang with incredible agility into the driver's seat. At the same moment he heard Judy loose a round through the hole in the wall. Then she backed away toward the jeep, firing from the hip.

McGregor climbed into the back of the vehicle, the bazooka in his hands, followed swiftly by Judy. The jeep leaped forward toward the gate.

"The only way out is past the front of the building," McGregor was shouting at Maxwell as the jeep swung through the gate into the road. "It's packed with very upset mercenaries. . . . We're going to blast our way through them. Fire at anything in uniform."

"Judy," McGregor gestured toward the bazooka, and Judy crouched down at the side of the jeep facing outward. McGregor raised the bazooka and placed the barrel on her right shoulder to be grasped and held firm by her waiting hands.

As the jeep careened around the corner, David saw mercenaries pouring into the street from the building.

The bearded giant flung the jeep across the road to mount the sidewalk furthest from the building.

"Fire!" McGregor screamed, and David poured automatic fire into the clustered mercenaries. He felt the impact of displaced air as a stream of bullets whipped past his head when the mercenaries returned his fire. At that point the entrance of the building erupted in a brilliant orange flash as McGregor fired and a bazooka missile struck the wall behind the mercenaries.

David stopped firing as the explosion sent bodies flying into the air. "Keep firing, you dumb bastard!" McGregor screamed seizing an AKM and opening up.

Now they were opposite the entrance, a mass of dead and staggering bodies enveloped in smoke and dust.

The bearded giant half stood up, with one hand on the wheel, and flung his right hand forward. A grenade went like a bullet straight through the open entrance of the building.

A minute later the jeep was around the corner into the main street and heading north toward the airfield.

"Don't fire at anybody unless they open up first," McGregor commanded. He then spoke to David: "Maxwell, meet Leopard—maybe now you'll agree he's a bit exceptional." The bearded giant turned to give Maxwell an embarrassed smile.

David agreed. He also wondered at the way McGregor, Judy, and now this Leopard, had acted as a perfectly rehearsed team . . . as if they had worked together—many times.

A group of mercenaries came into view down the street, staggering and swaying, with bottles in their hands. As the jeep passed, Leopard waved and shouted something David didn't understand. They waved back, hooting and laughing, pointing at Judy. One made an unmistakably crude gesture. And David realized that until the events back at the headquarters were known, a man with as outstanding an appearance as Leopard was the best passport to safety they could have.

"How's Monato?" McGregor spoke to Judy, who

was on her knees with the black president's head in her lap.

"Not too bad. A piece of flying stone must have caught him on the head. His breathing is all right. He'll get his senses back soon."

"I hope so," McGregor said. "We need him to guide us to a good hideout. You can bet your sweet life there's a truck filling up with mercenaries right now with nothing on their minds except killing us."

Then McGregor spoke to Leopard. "Head up to the scrubland between the town and the airfield. Go left through the scrub until you hit the river. If we follow it north, it should take us into forest. By that time let's pray Monato's hale and hearty . . . and talking."

They reached the rough dirt track running along the side of the river and followed it for a mile until they were opposite the airfield about half a mile to their right. The land between the river and the airfield was flat with scattered clumps of shrub; but not enough to screen them from view.

"I hope to Christ there's no radio contact between their headquarters and the airfield," said McGregor.

"There is, *mes amis*," Leopard replied with a rueful smile.

"Terrific," McGregor said grimly.

Past the airfield the banks of the river began to heighten steadily as they climbed the escarpment. Ahead, the river still continued on a level course for a couple of miles until, clearly visible, it cascaded over the edge of the escarpment in a sheet of tumbling water and rising spray.

McGregor was looking over his shoulder, aware

they were totally exposed, also, that any pursuing vehicle would be clearly visible.

Suddenly McGregor clapped Leopard on the shoulder. "How the hell did that goddamn thing get up there?" he said pointing to the sky behind them and the speck of a helicopter.

Leopard took a quick look. "At least five mercenaries can fly a copter," he answered. "I recruited only the best."

"Jesus!" McGregor said in disgust. "Did you have to be *so* thorough?"

"It was necessary, *mon ami,*" The captain . . . the dark one like a Corsican . . . he is KGB. I could not have fooled him."

"With that thing breathing down our necks we're never going to find a hideout," McGregor said. He was silent for a moment, then said, "See that large rock ahead, fifty yards at two o'clock? Make for it."

The jeep lurched to a stop behind the boulder; a slab of gray rock about five feet high. As McGregor and Leopard lifted Monato to lie beside the rock, he groaned. "Thank Christ," McGregor breathed. "He's coming around." He turned to Judy. "Stay with him. See if you can make him talk. We want a hideout with air cover . . . *not* in one of his people's villages, but not too far distant from one."

Leopard had hauled the bazooka from the jeep and was loading it. McGregor spoke rapidly to David. "If they do it by the book, that copter will come in close for one good look. Then they'll pull back out of range, keep tabs on us, and guide their hoodlum pals on the ground to where we are by radio. Okay. So we've got just about two seconds to knock it out of the sky when it comes in close."

Leopard passed the bazooka to McGregor then grabbed a couple of AKMs from the jeep and handed one to David. McGregor rested the top of the bazooka barrel on top of the rock, then spoke: "Maxwell, lie flat at one end of the rock. Don't show yourself but watch that copter. When it gets within four hundred feet, shout."

David peered round the edge of the rock. The copter was about a half mile distant, following the track by the river at a height of five hundred feet. Its first view, David realized, would be of an empty jeep. Not until it was directly overhead would the five of them be visible behind the rock.

Suddenly the copter began to dip down toward the jeep like a swooping bird. It leveled off at a hundred feet and came straight toward them. David held his breath, knowing the timing was crucial. If McGregor exposed himself too soon, the copter could jerk skyward like a dragonfly, at an angle and speed which would give McGregor no chance. But if he left it too late, McGregor would not have time to get a shot off.

"Now!" David yelled.

McGregor rose, his feet planted firmly apart. Through the sights he saw the copter approaching almost head on. He "aimed off" twenty feet ahead of it and squeezed the trigger. Two seconds later the helicopter seemed to stall in the sky as if it had flown into a brick wall. Then there was an explosion like a clap of thunder and the air was full of flying pieces of metal. A second explosion followed, and the plunging, twisting machine was enveloped in flames, black smoke pouring skyward as it plummeted to the ground.

As the blazing wreckage hit the edge of the river bank, briefly it teetered before toppling down the steep bank into the river. A plume of smoke and steam shot up above the bank in one dense cloud to dissipate skyward . . . and then there was nothing.

David saw McGregor and Leopard exchange winks, and he wondered just what it took to make McGregor happy.

"How's Monato?" McGregor was stooping, speaking to Judy.

"In the land of the living and very informative," she answered. "He knows just the place we want." Monato nodded his agreement and got unsteadily to his feet.

Guided by Monato, they followed the track up to the waterfall where the land leveled off and scattered trees indicated the beginning of the forest. They kept to the river's edge for another ten minutes, the forest thickening all the time, and came to a wooden bridge.

"How much farther?" McGregor asked Monato.

"Across the bridge and then perhaps two or three miles," he answered.

They crossed the bridge, and McGregor told Leopard to stop.

"Everybody out and unload the jeep," McGregor ordered. "We'll make it on foot from here. There'll be a truckload of murderers a few miles behind us who could follow wheel tracks half way across Africa."

They distributed the weapons, ammunition, and grenade boxes among them. McGregor drove the jeep slowly toward the edge of the river. A few yards before it reached the bank, he jumped. The jeep plunged into the river. "I hate good equipment to get in the wrong hands," McGregor said to no one in particular. "Now let's get moving. Monato, you lead."

David realized he was carrying a good two hundred pounds: a weight he could scarcely have got off the ground before Scotland. He hated to think what McGregor and Leopard were carrying: each was festooned with enough weaponary to equip a small army. Even Judy, covered in little more than her underclothes, the few strips of cloth that remained from her elegant dress, and, still wearing the flimsiest fashionable shoes, was heavily laden.

At the front marched Monato who, despite his rotund appearance, moved with surprising agility, holding the long, brilliantly colored robes clear off the ground, revealing feet clad in brightly embroidered sandals.

As the group progressed, the trees became tall and closer together, their thick leaves joining at the top to form a solid canopy blotting out the sunlight; below in the half light the ground was blanketed with a dense undergrowth of vines, fallen trees and giant ferns. Yet somehow Monato managed to navigate through this solid mass of tangled vegetation.

Abruptly the trees ended, and in front of them they saw a flattopped rocky hillock rising twenty feet above the floor of the jungle and about forty yards in diameter—as if a giant rock had fallen from the sky into the middle of the jungle.

"This is it," Monato said. "It will be more comfortable and healthier than the wet floor of the jungle."

"How did you find it?" McGregor said, looking around doubtfully.

"I used to come down here as a young boy," Monato answered. "You could say I found it by a long remembered instinct."

McGregor frowned. "But how are *we* going to find it?" he said.

Monato smiled. "I thought of that, my friend . . . Here. follow me." He led the way across the flat top of the rock to the far edge. Below, was a narrow stream. "In the dryseason that stream is empty; even now in the wet season it is no more than a foot deep. If you follow its course for about four miles, it joins the main river half a mile north of the airfield.

"On the wrong side of the river?"

"Yes, but two hundred yards down river is a ford. Even now the water is only waist deep."

"Perfect," McGregor said.

"I thought you might think so . . . Mr. McGregor?"

McGregor smiled and extended his hand. "I'm afraid there hasn't been too much time for formalities."

Monato gave a slight, dignified bow of acknowledgment as they shook hands. A ritual he repeated as McGregor introduced the remaining members of the party. "You were very brave, young lady," he said to Judy as he took her hand.

"A case of necessity, Mr. President."

"Please call me Monato. It *is* my name after all . . . and I am inclined to believe my title of President is now . . . defunct, shall we say." He turned to McGregor. "Mr. McGregor, if you wish to do anything while it is daylight, I suggest you do it while you have time. Darkness comes very swiftly in this part of the world. The sun will set in less than an hour."

As darkness fell, McGregor called them all together. First he spoke to Monato. "I don't doubt you're wondering what the hell's going on, Monato. To tell you the truth, so are we. I'd like to tell you who we are; unfortunately I can't do that. But I can promise you we mean your country no harm."

"I have seen enough with my own eyes to convince me of that," Monato said solemnly.

McGregor asked, "That large ship in the harbor, the *Burgh*—has it been unloaded yet?"

"No. It has been there three days. I can see it across the lagoon from my residence. I have been wondering what its cargo is."

"And do you know anything about the Americans who arrived here recently? A man named Dr. Maxwell and his daughter, Barbara."

"I have not heard of them."

McGregor hesitated before he continued. "Monato, we have things to talk about; it would be safer if you didn't hear them. I'd be obliged if—"

"There is no need for explanations or apologies," Monato interrupted getting to his feet. "To put matters at their simplest, I am, after all, labeled a Marxist. I don't know who you are, but I doubt if your political sympathies lie in that direction."

Monato turned to leave, then paused and faced McGregor again. When he spoke, it was with a quiet dignity, "I am sure you think me naive, Mr. Mc-

Gregor, but when I let the Russians come to my country, I sincerely believed they would help my people. Zambu is a very poor country, and the Russians made many promises. By the time I realized they wanted my country only as a base to infiltrate the richer and more important countries of Africa, it was too late."

Monato paused and looked around in the gloom at the silent group squatting on the ground around him. The rain had started, and the heavy raindrops, falling on the leaves, sounded like the sharp cracking of twigs. From all around came the night noises of the jungle.

"The Russian secret police," Monato continued, "had taken control of my country. I was their prisoner. So you see, I am not quite so enthusiastic a Marxist as perhaps the outside world believes. I will do what I can to help you—I owe you that for saving my life. I can only pray your motives for being here are better than the Russians'."

Monato turned and went to sit apart from them.

McGregor spoke abruptly. "Right, let's take a look at what we've got. Leopard, you say the mercenary captain who was with you when you found us is KGB?"

"Yes. He organized the whole operation. I was his lieutenant. It was not difficult for me to discover where he was getting *his* instructions from. I planned to get you out of prison by more subtle means—some way to make it look like you really were a bunch of lunatic hijackers. But when I saw Judy surrounded by three corpses, one of whom showed no visible cause of death except for a small pin sticking in his wrist, I knew it would not be long before the captain made the same discovery. Hijackers don't carry such sophisticated methods of dispensing death. He would have known right away you weren't legit . . . probably would have guessed you were agents. So I had to bust you out before he put you under the kind of protection I couldn't break through."

Maxwell was listening in silence. Now he knew why Judy had said she was sorry to McGregor after killing her three would-be rapists. She had known it had blown their cover as hijackers. And he knew why, after killing the third of the men, she had turned the submachine gun on the two already dead: to try and make it look as if they had died from rather more obvious causes.

"Right," McGregor was speaking. "So by now the Russians know we're Western agents and we're here to find out what's going on. But what the hell is going on? One thing's for sure: Colonel Smirnov wasn't expecting the mercenaries."

Judy spoke. "What *exactly* were your orders, Leopard . . . concerning the Russians, I mean."

"In one respect, unusual. Mostly on this kind of operation nobody bothers with taking prisoners: they are just an embarrassment. But we had firm orders to take prisoners. Right now there are about sixty Russians safely locked up in one of the airport buildings."

"What about the ship in the harbor?" David asked. "If our information is correct, it's got a Russian crew."

"*Had* a Russian crew," Leopard replied. "We stormed the ship. The crew were well armed. They put up strong resistance. The survivors are out at the airport with the rest of the Russian prisoners."

"The ship's unguarded?" Maxwell said.

"No, a couple of mercenaries on board."

"What about my father and sister?" David said. "Monato didn't know anything about them."

"Doesn't mean a thing," McGregor answered. "If my guess is right, they were sent out of town before this thing began. Too valuable to risk getting them killed by all the shit that's been flying around." He turned to Leopard. "What time are the mercenaries scheduled to fly out."

"Tomorrow evening."

McGregor was silent for several moments, then said, "The only thing for sure is that the Russians are playing a very serious game with themselves called 'If You Don't Know, You Get Killed.' Colonel Smirnov, his men, and the crew of that ship *didn't know*. Why?"

"Because," Judy answered, "When those mercenaries get back home, they are going to spread some pretty convincing news that the Russians have been thrown out of Zambu."

"Right," McGregor said. "And it's a fair guess they're going to be replaced by neo-Nazis who are acting as a front for the Russians. Kinda crazy, isn't it?"

"What happens to the Russian prisoners?" Maxwell said.

"Probably get flown out tomorrow night after the mercenaries have gone, then back to Russia," Leopard answered. "No one will know."

"The lucky ones. . . ." McGregor gave a short laugh.

"About forty Russians weren't so lucky," Leopard said.

McGregor was silent for a moment, then said, "Okay, we take one thing at a time. Tomorrow we find out for sure what's on board that ship."

As David lay down on the bare rock to sleep, the rain was falling in a steady downpour. It didn't matter because the temperature was only a few degrees below the daytime temperature of seventy-five. The hard rock bed and the fact he hadn't eaten all day didn't matter either—not after Scotland.

But before the monotonous beating of the rain on the thick foliage of the jungle sent him to sleep, he had time to think back to that bright morning in Malibu when he had awoken to the gentle sound of the Pacific breakers.

So much had happened since then.

And out there, somewhere in the blackness, his father and Barbara. And a ship. And the reason for it all? He fell asleep and dreamed he and Judy were running along the sea edge, laughing and kissing under the bright sunlight. And then they fell into each other's arms in the warm surf. And then he realized the surf wasn't seawater at all. It was warm, thick, foaming blood. And he woke up with a scream and stared into the blackness of the jungle.

SIXTEEN

Moscow, U.S.S.R.

At eight o'clock Moscow time—a few hours before dawn would awaken the five sleeping figures sprawled on the rock in the Zambu jungle four thousand miles away—Colonel Ivanov waited impatiently at the entrance of his hotel for the Zil limousine which would take him to the offices of KGB Chairman Vladimir Grechko.

The colonel had traveled the previous evening from Bonn to Moscow to report on his dealings with the mad American General Wade Horton, deputy commander of NATO forces in Central Europe.

The Zil arrived, and the colonel got in. After a fifteen-minute drive they arrived at Dzerzhinski Square, and the driver opened the door. The colonel muttered his thanks and made his way up to the offices of the chairman, where an efficient-looking male secretary escorted him to a door, knocked, and gestured for the colonel to enter.

Seated in easy chairs at one end of the room were the chairman and foreign minister, Aleksei Burov. They had obviously been in deep conversation. Now their eyes were fixed on the colonel as he advanced toward them.

"Be seated," the chairman said, waving to a chair. He passed a stubby-fingered hand through his cropped gray hair and got straight to the point. "Well, Comrade Colonel," he said, "can you assure us the American general is prepared to carry out his part of the Coda Alliance Operation?"

The colonel crossed his legs and began to speak, choosing his words carefully. "Acting on your instructions, Comrade Chairman, I have had a series of meetings with the general. At our first meeting I told him I wanted his reactions to a purely hypothetical scenario. I put it to him that if the commander of NATO forces was to meet with an unfortunate accident, then temporarily he, the deputy commander, would be in sole command of these forces."

There was a quick knock on the door. The secretary entered and handed the chairman a sheet of paper which he rapidly scanned, then put aside on a small table. "Continue," he said looking up at the colonel.

"I then asked him if, assuming this situation were to arise, and if we were to provide him with a sufficiently sound reason for ordering the immediate evacuation of all major American bases, would he give such an order. I explained that although this would not be followed by hostilities between ourselves and NATO, it would nevertheless guarantee the humiliation of his army in the eyes of the world."

"And his reaction?" The chairman's glance flicked momentarily to the piece of paper on the table.

"Most surprising," the colonel replied. "I had thought he would want some assurance that the rightness of his decision to order the evacuation could not be challenged. . . . To protect himself. However, this does not appear to worry him. His only concern was to be convinced that we really could provide a reasonable pretext for the evacuation. Naturally, I was able to reassure him about this. Evidently he is not worried what happens to him. Only that his army be humiliated."

"The man's *mad,*" the chairman said derisively.

"Precisely. The man *is* mad," said the foreign minister quietly. "His actions and his behavior under analysis have made that abundantly clear."

"So Colonel, you have no doubts about his reliability? If you are proved wrong . . ." There was no need for the chairman to complete the sentence.

"No doubt whatsoever," the colonel replied. "But may I ask how the other parts of the operation are progressing?"

"In all aspects save one, satisfactorily," the chairman answered thoughtfully. "A special cadre of our security services is operating secretly in East Germany under the guise of a branch of the neo-Nazi Group 666. They have killed twenty-seven of our own Soviet servicemen and are demanding the withdrawal of all Soviet forces from East Germany."

"You mean the newspaper reports are *correct*? Our men have *actually* been killed!" the colonel asked in surprise.

A look of impatient irritability flickered over the chairman's face. "Of course. Do you think we would take the slightest risk of Western Intelligence discovering that Group 666 is not genuine? . . . However we do have a problem. Earlier this morning I received a message from Von Richter to say the mercenary operation in Zambu has been successfully completed. I have now received a communication," he picked up the sheet of paper from the table and waved it in the air, "from one of our own agents who went with the mercenaries to keep an eye on things. Those hijackers from Frankfurt are Western Intelligence agents . . . and they have escaped into the jungle."

"I don't like it," the foreign minister said, stroking his chin nervously with a bony hand. "Why have Western Intelligence taken such elaborate measures to get their agents back into Zambu?"

"Their ingenuity is to be admired. I had not expected it, I must confess. I thought we had effectively shut their agents out. But the reason for their excessive curiosity is not hard to understand. We made no secret of the neo-Nazi backed mercenary operation. On the contrary, we made sure they heard about it. They will have suspected that the uranium from the S.S. *Lander* was in all probability 'stolen' by the S.S. *Burgh*. So," he turned to face the colonel, "if you were in their position, what conclusions would you have come to, Colonel?"

"Conclusions? None. But anxiety and concern: considerable. The need to find out what is going on in Zambu: imperative. The activities of Group 666 in West Germany have become the talking point of the whole nation. So far thirty-eight Americans have been killed, including five women and three children. American servicemen are now confined to their bases. Relations between Bonn and Washington have never been worse. But," the colonel paused and looked intently at the men, "if I were in Western Intelligence,

I would still suspect the possibility of a Russian connection. Firstly, because the stealing of the uranium required facilities and organizations not normally available to an underground terrorist organization such as Group 666. Secondly, because I would take a lot of convincing that the expelling of all foreigners from Zambu by Russia was merely coincidence."

"A very accurate summary of the situation," the chairman said appreciatively. "However as regards your first point—the facilities required to steal the uranium—we have directed the finger of suspicion at powerful German industrial interests. Attempts by the Atomic Energy Agency to trace the ownership of the S.S. *Burgh* have conveniently come to a dead end with a small West German shipping company. The company and its records have suddenly vanished—except for a few forged documents which link it with large German industrial concerns owned by men with known extreme right-wing sympathies. An investigation will show this link to be a deception, but by then it will be too late. And to finally destroy all suspicion of a Russian connection, we shall shortly have eye-witness accounts of the mercenaries when they return to tell of the bloody fighting to overcome Colonel Smirnov and his men."

The foreign minister listened to all this with growing surprise. Not once had the chairman referred to the effect on their plans of the unexpected and potentially disastrous presence of Western intelligence agents now in Zambu. "The hijackers . . . Western agents!" he started.

"Do not alarm yourself, comrade," the chairman silenced him quietly. "I have been thinking about them. They are not a threat. On the contrary, we can use them to our advantage."

The foreign minister looked at him blankly.

"Let us analyze the situation," the chairman continued calmly. "At seven-thirty this evening local time, the mercenaries are due to leave Zambu. At eight, armed members of Group 666 fly in and take control of the country. If the agents are not caught—even if somehow they discover atomic bombs are being made—what harm can it do? It will confirm what we want them to believe—that Group 666 is making atomic bombs with the secret backing of German industrialists."

The foreign minister paused, then said, "Aren't you forgetting Colonel Smirnov and his men who are being held prisoners? They are to be flown out and brought back to Russia. If the Western agents witness this peaceful exodus, their suspicions of a Russian connection will be confirmed."

"Precisely, comrade!" The chairman's blunt features glowed in a smile of total satisfaction. "So we have a God-given opportunity to kill the Russian connection stone dead. Colonel Smirnov and his men are . . . expendable!"

The chairman continued to smile, but the foreign minister and Colonel Ivanov felt a chill run through them.

SEVENTEEN

Zambu, West Africa

Maxwell stirred, stretched his arms which were still half asleep, caught his wrist on a jagged edge of rock, and sat up fully awake. He looked at his watch—6:30 A.M.

The sun was already hot, the rain-soaked undergrowth of the surrounding jungle steaming in the heat.

At the edge of the rock where the rain-filled stream rushed by, David saw McGregor, Judy, Leopard, and Monato in conversation, squatting in a group. As David clambered to his feet, McGregor detached himself from the others and came to join him. "Sleep well?" he asked with a grin.

"Never better," David replied. "It's luxury after the cold of Scotland."

"Don't bet on it," McGregor said. "The humidity is above ninety percent, you'll sweat like a pig day and night. Don't bother trying to get dry: there's no way. Rain or sun, makes no difference: your clothes stay soaked."

David's stomach rumbled with hunger. "I don't want to go soft on you," he said. "But is there anything edible around here?"

"No, but we're working on it. Monato says there's a village about four miles from here. His uncle is the chief. Leopard and I are going with him to see what we can rustle up in the way of food and suitable clothing. We're not exactly dressed for the occasion."

David looked at his own tight-fitting pants and sports shirt, the crumpled bottom half of McGregor's immaculately cut business suit and his mud-splattered silk shirt and the remaining fragments of Judy's haute couture dress. Only Leopard in combat gear looked as if he had any business being in the middle of an African jungle. David smiled, "Looks like we just dropped right out of an airplane," he said.

"Monato's sending men from his uncle's village into town to look out for your father and sister," McGregor said. "If my hunch is right, once the mercenaries get the hell out, they're going to turn up—and so are Group 666, bringing Yanu as their front man to replace Monato as president."

"And then what?" David asked.

"I don't know. We're still playing it by ear. After we get food and clothes, the first move is to check that ship. That's your job . . . with Leopard. As far as possible we're going to operate in pairs. That way if there's a wipeout, at least there'll be two of us left."

"Charming," David said.

"We're mixed up with some pretty charming company. . . ."

McGregor turned and went back to join Leopard and Monato. A few minutes later David watched them disappear down the side of the rock and out of sight into the jungle. Then with a shock, he realized he could not see Judy.

For an instant he felt the impulse to cry out for her. Since their brief, intimate time together by Loch Lomond, he had not had time to think about his feelings for her. Nor had she encouraged contact of any kind. She had created an invisible gap between them. A distance more real than space, time, and substance could ever effect. In its way, a distance as intangible and powerful as the closeness between her and McGregor and even Leopard.

He ran to the edge of the rock overlooking the stream. In the muddy water, twenty feet below, was Judy. She was lying in the stream fully clothed, her back to him. And within easy reach, just behind her on the bank, was her rifle carefully placed on its side.

David slid down the rocky slope to stand by the water looking down at her.

She turned her head and smiled up at him: and in her eyes he saw the same uncertain vulnerability and tenderness which had been so much a part of their intimacy at Loch Lomond.

For a moment he was confused: the sudden bridging of the gulf between them was disorienting. "You're being very modest," he said, forcing a laugh.

She glanced at her tattered clothes. "Not modest . . . cautious. I'd rather not have to run around the jungle naked. That would be *very* immodest. And very uncomfortable, even with *these* on." She raised a long slim leg from the muddy water to show she was still wearing her flimsy shoes.

"Danger? Here?" David laughed.

For an instant her eyes clouded, then she smiled again. "Come on," she said. "Get yourself into this glorious mud."

She winked at him. A playful wink, but with a serious intent.

David slid into the water beside her.

There was an incredible sensuousness about it all: the soft warmth of the water, the savage heat of the sun beating down from the brilliant sky, the fecundity of the steaming jungle all around, the screeching of the birds in the trees. They were all of a oneness; a violent assertion of life, an overwhelming blind cry *to be! To exist!*

Judy was reaching under the water, and her hand emerged holding her flimsy pants. She threw them onto the muddy bank, then flung herself on top of him, kissing his face and chest with wide open lips, her green eyes made brilliant by the wildness of her desire. "Take me, David—for God's sake, take me." The words were hoarse.

David seized her and flung her onto her back, pinning her against the slippery bank.

He thrust savagely into her and a wild cry came from his gaping mouth and she began to moan, squirming in the slippery mud of the bank.

Behind Judy's head, David saw her carelessly thrown pants and beside them her rifle. And in them he saw the stark symbolism of life and death, and he was gripped by a sudden frenzied urge to assert *life*. The body beneath him was no longer Judy Sinclair; it was life! And he thrust into her with increasing savagery, driven only by some blind, primordial instinct of human survival. The supremacy of creation over death.

When he came, he let out a cry of triumphant joy as he felt his seed flood into her.

He withdrew, still in a trance, and sat back on his heels in the water, his chest heaving, his body trembling.

He opened his eyes, and she was leaning up on her elbows, her body covered in the mud, looking at him. In the deepness of her eyes he saw that she had understood!

She smiled softly and took his hand. And they lay in the river side by side, neither speaking until they were cleansed of the thick mud of the bank. Then David was standing beside her, wanting to speak, but she shook her head and said, "Not now, David. . . ."

She slung her rifle over her shoulder and David watched in silence as she picked her way up the side of the steep rock. He knew he was alone again, but he was happy.

Shortly after noon the other three returned from the village with food. They ate in silence, hungrily stuffing the highly seasoned mixture of cold cereals into their mouths with their fingers.

"Let's get down to business," McGregor said when they had finished. "Monato's uncle sent men into town while we were at the village to spread the word to look for your folks, Maxwell. They brought back a stack of combat gear stripped from dead mercenaries. Also, they brought a supply of these." McGregor reached down and produced a knife with a six-inch razor-sharp blade. He handed it to David. "Unless you've no option—absolutely no option—any killing has to be silent. We're going to be in and out of that town quite a few times, but the fact that we're still around and haven't taken off to escape across the frontier has to be a secret for as long as possible. You with me?"

David nodded.

"Right. Now I want you to memorize this." McGregor took a jagged stone and began to scratch the surface of a flat piece of rock. It was a crude map of the area showing their location in relation to the lagoon, the harbor, the town, the airfield, the river, and other salient features of the terrain.

David studied it for a few minutes, then said, "Okay. I've got it. Now what?"

"According to the chief's men, the mercenaries are having a party to celebrate their departure: drinking, raping, looting—the usual. Leopard says they have two guards on the ship, but the chances are they won't be watching that carefully. That'll make it easy for you and Leopard to get aboard and take a look at the cargo."

David wondered exactly what McGregor's definition of "easy" was.

"You leave in fifteen minutes," McGregor said.

David grunted and went to select his gear. He found a pair of boots that fit, pants that were baggy at the waist, and a tunic with a deep red band of dried blood running diagonally across the chest punctured by four neat holes about the size of a dime.

He selected a 9 mm Makarov pistol from Leopard's store, inserted eight rounds into the magazine, slammed it into the butt, yanked the slide back forcing a round into the chamber, then pushed the safety catch up into "safe." He shoved the pistol firmly into his belt, filled three more magazines, and put them into his pockets.

With the knife McGregor had given him he cut a strip of material from a spare tunic and wound it tightly around the blade of the knife. This he jammed firmly under his belt at the back of his right hip; easily accessible but pointing safely downward and outward.

He stood up. Judy was in front of him, her eyes cast down at the ground. "David," she said, "promise one thing." She raised her eyes to his and David saw they were full of anxiety. She went on quickly, "Forget every decent instinct you've ever known. Never hesitate for an instant to measure the rightness or the necessity to kill. Remember, a dead man can do you no harm—but a moment's hesitation can bring death. For me, David. . . ." She left him suddenly.

David felt angry. For God's sake, hadn't he proved himself in Scotland! Hadn't he done everything asked of him so far! Didn't she think he had learned *anything*!

And then he heard the voice of Leopard. "Time to go, *mon ami*."

Together they slithered down the rock slope to the stream and, with Leopard in the lead, started to walk along the narrow bank. David knew the route from McGregor's map. For about four miles they would follow the stream through the jungle until it joined the main river. There they would turn south, keeping parallel to the main river until they reached the rear of the harbor—an assortment of brick and tin warehouses and behind them, the squalid shanty dwellings of the harbor workers. They would skirt right around the rear of the harbor to a point on the sea shore half a mile from the entrance to the lagoon. The S.S.

Lander was anchored a few hundred yards from the shore, just inside the lagoon.

As they struggled down stream, they were able to walk on narrow muddy strips of bank for short distances only. Most of the time the jungle came right to the stream's edge forcing them to walk knee-deep through the water.

An hour passed, and David felt every step becoming a conscious effort to force his muscles to obey his purpose; to free each foot in turn from the cloying mud of the stream's bed and lift it above the surface of the water for the next step forward.

His uniform clung to his body. It was soaked with perspiration. The sweat pouring down his forehead streamed into his eyes, making them sting with salt.

Ahead of him Leopard pushed forward at a relentless pace, not once glancing back. Maxwell guessed that the philosophy of men such as Leopard was simple and uncompromising. Concessions to weakness were neither asked for, nor given.

By the time they reached the junction with the main river, Maxwell's muscles were screaming for respite. More than ever, he understood the reason for the merciless assault upon his body during his training by McGregor in the mountains around Loch Naird.

Keeping a screen of thick scrub between themselves and any possible observer from the airfield half a mile to their left across the river, they ran the two miles south before turning to make the seven mile semicircle through the edge of the jungle behind the harbor area.

By the time they reached the beach, David's body

had ceased to protest, driven on by brute determination. Mind and body were one, and Maxwell felt that unique euphoria experienced by athletes when they find for the first time that they are able to push themselves to unthinkable realms of exertion.

They stopped under a cluster of palm trees about twenty yards back from the sandy edge of the calm sea. Leopard spoke for the first time. "We will follow the beach as far as we dare toward the entrance of the lagoon. From there we swim. A distance of a mile perhaps. And once we are on the ship, . . ." Leopard hunched his enormous shoulders in a Gallic shrug, "we shall see, *mon ami*. We shall see."

As they walked through the palm trees toward the harbor, the light began to fade rapidly into night. A half-moon appeared and threw its watery light over the still sea. The occasional yelp of a dog or the cry of a baby came from the nearby shanties to their left behind the harbor.

Leopard stopped, picked up a thick log from a fallen tree, and tucked it under his arm. Three hundred yards farther on he stopped again and pointed through the palm trees.

David looked in the direction indicated and saw the dim, low outline of a row of shanties. For an instant the silence was broken by the angry shout of a man's voice followed by the scream of a woman and the piercing cry of a baby. Then silence.

"Happy families . . . the same the world over," Leopard whispered with a grin, then lowered the log to the ground. "Put your gun and knife on this," he said taking a length of cloth from inside his tunic and spreading it on the ground. Leopard placed his own weapons on the cloth and, making a bundle of them, took some twine from his pocket and bound the bundle firmly to the top of the log.

"Strip—everything except your underpants," Leopard said quietly.

They stripped and hid their clothes under a cluster of fallen palm leaves. Then each took an end of the log and waded into the sea. With one hand steadying the log, they propelled themselves slowly around the jutting sandbar which formed the lip of the lagoon and the entrance to the harbor.

When it first came into view, the ship was four hundred yards away; with the deck bathed in light, the superstructure was brightly silhouetted against the black unlit shapes of the harbor buildings across the lagoon behind it. Even the rippling water around the ship was bathed in the spill of the ship's brilliant lights.

They reached the area where the lights began to illuminate the surface of the water, fifty yards from the ship. Leopard was treading water, his eyes fixed on the ship. "Can you see anything?" he whispered.

"No," David answered as the sound of a drunken burst of laughter came floating clearly across the water.

"They're behind the bridge. Probably the captain's quarters," Leopard said. "See the shore boat, at the bottom of the boarding ladder? We'll make for that."

David grunted his acknowledgment, noting that the bottom half of the ladder and the boat were in shadow, screened from the deck lights by the overhanging side of the ship.

"Now!" Leopard whispered urgently and plunged

his free arm into the water, his feet breaking the surface thrashing to drive the log forward.

David responded instantly.

Now speed was paramount, silence secondary! to cross the bright stretch of water where discovery could mean certain death.

Their lungs bursting, they reached the bottom of the ladder, their necks strained backward and their eyes riveted on the side of the ship. Listening. Waiting.

But no face appeared. No stream of bullets tore down into their exposed heads. David heaved a silent sigh of relief as another burst of laughter came from high above them.

Silently they guided the log to wedge it between the bow of the shore boat and the side of the ship. Then Leopard ripped the twine from around the log with one powerful wrench and unwrapped their weapons. Reaching up he placed them silently in the shore boat, then grasping the side of the boat heaved himself effortlessly into it.

A second later David was beside Leopard. He took the knife in his left hand, the gun in his right. Leopard touched the hand with the gun. "Remember, *mon ami,*" he whispered. "Use it only if there is no other way."

Swiftly they crept up the ladder, paused momentarily to scan the open deck, then climbed the two flights of steel steps to the bridge. It was deserted; but from somewhere nearby came more laughter, followed by a crash and the splintering of glass.

"Follow me," Leopard whispered and stealthily led

the way along a row of brightly lit, square portholes the size of small windows.

Leopard dropped on all fours and crawled below the first porthole. Rising to his feet, he peered cautiously through the glass. He pulled back sharply and gestured with his thumb for David to take a look.

Slowly, David peered through the porthole. For a second he was frozen in horror, then he jerked his head back and a cold anger filled him. He hadn't counted. He didn't want to count! The big cabin was crammed with naked bodies. Dark skinned women of all ages being savaged in every conceivable way by God alone knew how many mercenaries.

Maxwell was sick with revulsion.

Leopard had crawled back beside David and was pulling him by the hand toward the bridge. "Where is the uranium likely to be?" he asked softly.

"I don't know," David answered dully.

"Mon Dieu! Think," Leopard hissed.

"I tell you I don't know. . . . Probably in one of the aft holds near the derricks."

"Then start looking. *Vite.* While those pigs are still having their sport. *Allez!"*

"Those women . . ." David started.

"Forget them." Leopard gripped his arm tightly. "We can't help them."

David nodded silently then made his way below decks and through to the aft holds. He knew what he was looking for, and he found them. Rows of steel drums marked "FISSILE MATERIAL" and underneath these words the international markings which indicated the contents were highly enriched uranium 235.

He made his way back swiftly, and as he reached the crew's mess, he heard the raucous laughter and shouting still coming from the captain's quarters. Halfway across the room he froze. Coming through a side door, a crate of liquor on each shoulder, was an enormous man—stark naked—his body almost covered in thick black hair.

He looked at Maxwell in surprise, his dark eyes taking in the gun and the knife. For an instant he scowled, then a vicious grin spread across his swarthy face. *Merde . . . un petit hijacker, oui?*

David raised the gun threateningly: the gun he knew he couldn't use without pronouncing his own sentence of death. One shot and the mercenaries would be down within seconds.

He was trapped, with an ape of a man.

The mercenary had assessed Maxwell's predicament with equal accuracy. His grin broadened. He advanced, his eyes gleaming, his thick mouth twisted into a contemptuous sneer. He would wring the neck of this *petit poulet.*

Six feet from Maxwell he stopped and lowered one of the crates to the deck. He swiveled his shoulders as if to lower the other. Instead, he hurled the crate. David jumped to one side, but the flying crate struck his left forearm, sending a jagged pain shooting up his arm: the knife fell from his hand.

With a roar the man bounded forward. Maxwell brought the butt of the gun down toward the man's bull head with all his strength. But the blow was anticipated: the man jerked his head to one side, and the butt crashed down on his shoulder. Maxwell saw the grimace of pain and the fury in his assailant's eyes before two powerful hands seized him by the throat in a grip of iron.

Maxwell grabbed the thick wrists and with the strength of desperation strained to break the tightening grip on his throat before the pressure on the carotid arteries on the side of his neck finally cut the supply of oxygen to his brain and consciousness left him.

Through a haze of pain, his eyes bulging, Maxwell saw the wall only a few feet behind the mercenary. With his head swimming in blackness, the last vestiges of consciousness fading, he willed his muscles to obey and, raising his arms to grip the biceps of the mercenary's outstretched arms, pushed forward with every fiber of his remaining strength.

The mercenary, believing his *petit poulet* to be all but dead, was caught off guard and staggered back against the wall. He snorted derisively at the swelling face in front of him and increased the pressure of his grip. Maxwell, his vision the blinding white which precedes blackness and death, raised his feet and placing them on the wall to either side of the mercenary's waist, pushed backward in what he had already calculated might be the last act of his life.

The combined force of Maxwell's weight and the force of his thrusting legs toppled the surprised mercenary, and in a wild effort to regain his balance he released his grip on Maxwell's throat. Maxwell crashed to the deck on his back. For a split second the mercenary teetered; then, his arms flailing the air, he fell forward and down toward Maxwell. While the mercenary's body was still in the air, Maxwell raised his knees and slammed them with all his remaining strength into the falling man's solar plexus.

With a gasp of agony the mercenary landed on top of Maxwell and rolled off to lie beside him. He turned on his side, his face contorted with rage. *Cochon!* he spat seizing Maxwell's throat again. Maxwell thrust under the mercenary's arms and grasped the thick hair on the man's chest with both hands. Then, using his grip on the hair for leverage, he slammed his forehead against the bridge of the mercenary's nose.

As McGregor had told him back in Loch Naird, the effect was instant and catastrophic. The mercenary let out a yell of pain and his hands fell from Maxwell's neck. His nose was split wide open to the bone, blood spurting down his face, and for an instant he was stunned. And in that instant Maxwell rolled to his left and, grabbing a bottle from the crate nearby, he raised it and crashed it down onto the mercenary's head.

Maxwell rose shakily to his feet, searched for and found his knife and gun, then made for the door. He stopped and slowly turned to look at the body of the mercenary . . . lying motionless and silent. For how long? A few seconds, a few minutes—long enough for Leopard and him to get away? There was no way of knowing. Even if they did get away, the fact that they were "operating," as McGregor had put it, and the possibility they had discovered the uranium would be known.

But he couldn't do it!

Not kill a helpless man.

Then he remembered Judy's words. "Forget every

decent instinct you've ever known. . . . Remember, a dead man can do you no harm. For me, David."

He must do it!

Slowly he turned.

It took all his strength to drag the groaning mercenary to a steel closet in the corner where he could hide the body; the *dead* body. The man opened glazed eyes, trying to focus as David knelt beside his naked body. Then he saw the knife in David's hand.

And David saw the pleading in his eyes.

David closed his eyes, about to plunge the knife into the man's bare gut.

He opened them again. He would not do it the easy way. He would pay the highest price he could for this act of murder.

He looked into the terrified eyes of the man. And as he plunged the knife down, he saw in them the silent scream that comes with the certainty of imminent and violent death. And as the knife pierced the soft flesh below the ribs and penetrated up to enter the heart, David stifled the cry that came to his own lips.

He withdrew the knife and remained kneeling beside the dead man, his body shaking in an agony of shock and revulsion.

How long he remained there he did not know. His next memory was a touch on his shoulder and the urgent tones of Leopard's voice, "*Mon Dieu!* What are you doing? Praying for his soul?"

David, startled, opened his mouth to speak, but Leopard spoke again. "Did you find the uranium?"

David nodded.

From the deck overhead came the thudding of boots.

"Then let's get out of here. The mercenaries are making ready to leave. I was afraid you would stumble into them, so I came to find you. Take the dead man's feet and we'll get him out of sight below decks."

Fully alert now, David hastened to obey, and together they carried the naked corpse down a flight of steps to the crew's quarters. Leopard opened a cabin door and backed in. "Dump him on the bunk," he directed.

"What now?" David said.

"We stay here until they're gone. They won't be wasting time looking down here for one of their numbers—even if they miss him."

"The women?" David asked.

"You killed *that* brute? *C'est formidable!*" Leopard replied ignoring his question and nodding appreciatively at the corpse on the bunk and moving to the porthole. "Come here," he said. "They're on their way."

David joined him by the porthole. Still caught in the lights from the ship, the small boat packed with men was heading for the harbor jetty. At the back, one hand on the rudder, the other holding a bottle and waving it in the air rhythmically from side to side as if conducting a group sing stood a tall mercenary. "The boys have had a good party," Leopard said and turned away.

They waited twenty minutes to give the mercenaries time to get well clear of the harbor, then, securing their weapons on the log again, swam back to their clothes.

As they covered the seven miles back skirting the

harbor toward the river, Maxwell's mind was blank. He did not want to think. He was not ready to think. *He would not think!* Not yet.

They turned north along the bank of the river at a point directly across from the airfield.

Suddenly the silence was shattered by the sound of airplane engines bursting into life. And then two strings of runway lights stabbed across the darkness of the airfield.

Seconds later, first one, then another aircraft roared down the runway and up into the blackness of the night sky.

"There they go," said Leopard as the sound of the engines faded into the distance. "Mercenaries . . . the hyenas of war."

A mile farther on Leopard stopped in his tracks and turned to grab Maxwell's arm. "You hear it?" he said.

At first David could hear nothing, then he picked it up: the distant sound of approaching aircraft.

"Quick. Back to the airfield," Leopard said, turning on his heel and breaking into a run. "We passed the ford across the river a quarter of a mile back," he shouted over his shoulder to Maxwell.

Even in the darkness the ford was easy to locate by the dip in the river bank, scooped out by the passage of feet for thousands of years.

Across the river a half mile sprint through the low clumps of scrub took them to the far side of the airfield.

They lay flat, observing the small building a hundred and fifty yards directly opposite them across the airfield. Atop the building was a brightly lit, all-round glass control tower. Three men were clearly visible. Two were black and were, David assumed, responsible for operating the landing lights and the rudimentary radio traffic control system.

The third, standing looking out over the airfield, was in the combat gear of a mercenary; he was the Corsican-looking KGB man, a submachine gun cradled in his arms.

The plane roared in to land. "What's the KGB man still here for?" Maxwell shouted.

"See the hangar next to the tower," Leopard bellowed back. "That's where the Russian prisoners are. If my guess is right, he's stayed behind to make sure they get out safely. . . . I imagine he will go with them. When Group 666 arrive, all they will find is *dead* Russians."

The plane came to a stop twenty yards from the tower, and the KGB man and the two black controllers placed steps against the exit. The door of the plane opened and a figure appeared dressed in the uniform of Group 666: knee-high jackboots, breeches with a wide leather belt, a khaki shirt, and black tie.

"*Mon Dieu!*" Leopard was staring in amazement. "*What* are they doing here before the Russians have even got out?" They watched in silence as about forty similarly dressed figures, all armed, descended the steps. It was not possible to see their features, but to David they had the unmistakable air and gait of very young men—boys almost.

"Christ, they're kids," he said.

Leopard looked at him sharply. "Kids! There are not enough of them, and they have not had the combat experience to deal with the Russians like the mercenaries did. But that is *all* they lack—numbers and experience. Everyone of them has killed in cold blood—American servicemen, their wives and children —to earn the privilege of being a member of Group 666. By instinct they are killers—not *petits garçons.*"

And, at the head of the group assembled near the airplane, Günther Kraske would have agreed with Leopard's assessment of his "boys." Particularly as to the nature of their instincts.

As was his habit when he was happily engaged, Kraske was whistling between his teeth as he stepped forward to greet the puzzled KGB mercenary. They exchanged passwords. "You're an hour early," the KGB man said to Kraske. "Our comrades are still here . . . in the hangar."

"It doesn't matter," Kraske said with an air of indifference.

"But if your Germans see our comrades fly out, they will be suspicious."

"It doesn't matter," Kraske repeated. "The keys to the hangar, please, comrade." Kraske had a pistol in his hand.

The KGB man's eyes narrowed as his hands moved to the keys at his waist. Then Kraske shot him in the heart.

"What the hell's going on?" David whispered to Leopard as the man slumped to the ground.

Leopard shook his head and shrugged in bafflement. "I have no idea, *mon ami,* no idea at all."

The two men lay watching as Kraske approached the hangar, unlocked the padlock, and walked back to join the men of Group 666 who were standing in a row facing the hangar about twenty paces away from it.

Slowly the giant doors were pushed open from inside, and the Russians began to emerge, the wounded supported by their comrades. At first they smiled and talked excitedly to each other, but gradually silence fell as they stood in a bewildered group facing the motionless row of uniformed figures.

Colonel Smirnov stepped forward and called out in Russian. There was no answer. He called again, and the prisoners huddled closer together, sensing the dreadful event that was about to happen.

The word came from Kraske. "Fire." And the Nazis raised their submachine guns, a deafening orchestration of death as the scythe of bullets cut through the Russian prisoners until the last man fell. In the silence that followed a billow of smoke from the guns drifted slowly up to disappear in the blackness of the sky above.

David lay numbed, his face buried in the earth.

"*Allez!*" Leopard was grasping his shoulder. "Let's get out."

Maxwell had no sense of time, no awareness of his aching body, no real consciousness of his existence, as they made the exhausting journey back up the stream to the rock. His mind was filled with a black mist of horror, a nightmare too terrifying to be recollected.

Maxwell lay on the rock. Numb.

Vaguely he heard the hushed whispers of Leopard, Judy, and McGregor. Next he heard McGregor's voice close to him. "Leopard says you did well, Maxwell."

David opened his eyes and saw the dark silhouette of McGregor kneeling beside him.

He looked at McGregor with blank eyes. "Did well?" he thought. What did such words *mean*? In comfortable offices, chauffeur driven cars and in expensive restaurants, men in Bonn, London, Moscow, and Washington were talking in the euphemistic, cliché-ridden language of politics and foreign policy, then returning to their luxurious homes and, for some, the warm embrace of their families.

But here, thousands of miles away, in a little known African country, the reality of the talk was being acted out in bloody murder, rape, and massacre. How could any man "do well" in such a hell of violence.

" 'Did well'?" he echoed McGregor's words aloud.

"Yes . . . you survived."

"Survived," he repeated in a hollow voice. He remembered the words of the CIA man at Chequers telling him he had "survivability."

But David Maxwell knew it was not the truth.

The man who had come from California to Africa had not survived.

It was only the beginning.

EIGHTEEN

Zambu, West Africa

A three-tongued fork of lightning streaked to the ground, bathing the glistening wetness of the jungle with a dazzling brightness. Maxwell turned as the crack of thunder shook the rock beneath him, then came echoing back from the distant mountains as a wave of rumbling sound.

McGregor shouted to make himself heard above the second clap of thunder. "Good news, Maxwell. Monato's people have located your father. He's held in a warehouse down at the harbor."

"And Barbara?" Maxwell shouted back.

McGregor shook his head. "No sign of her. They're still looking. . . . Take Judy with you to the warehouse. This afternoon. A guide's coming."

"I want to go to my father now."

"This afternoon," McGregor insisted. "Yanu's being installed as president, and there's going to be a big celebration. Free liquor. Monato says everyone in town will be a raving maniac. They brew their own gin, and it's lethal."

Maxwell turned to Monato. "Who wants to celebrate in this?" He raised his eyes to the storm.

"Where would *you* rather be?" Monato replied.

"Huddled in a shanty with a leaking roof and your belly empty, or drinking gin in the rain?"

"Yeah," Maxwell agreed.

By four o'clock, when the guide arrived, the rain had ceased, but the low clouds were still black and threatening.

Instead of taking the long route down the stream, the guide led Judy and David through the jungle by hidden paths cutting a good four miles off the journey. When they reached the beach, they continued along the palm-fringed shoreline until they came to the spit of sand that was one side of the entrance to the lagoon.

To their left was the harbor front. It was deserted, as were the native shanties behind it. But from the brightly lit town across the lagoon came the deep throbbing of drums. Yanu's inauguration celebrations were well under way.

The guide tapped Maxwell on the shoulder and pointed with a long, thin arm: "There."

To one side of the S.S. *Burgh*, now only dimly lit, was the dark outline of a large warehouse with a triangular roof.

The guide pointed to the ground at his feet. "I wait," he said.

Maxwell nodded. Crouching low, he and Judy moved forward across the sand to the shelter of the stone harbor wall. No sound broke the silence save a faint racking cough from a distant shanty; someone left behind, no doubt too near death to profit even from the anesthetic of Yanu's gin.

Maxwell jumped so his elbows were resting on the wall, his head just visible above it. The huge sliding doors of the warehouse were partly open, a weak spill of light streaking the dark harbor front.

Effortlessly, they pulled themselves up and over the wall, then moved swiftly into the shadow of the building adjoining the warehouse. Slowly, gun in hand, Maxwell crept toward the open doors. He felt the touch of a hand on his shoulder. "I go first," Judy whispered. Maxwell shook his head and continued forward. Pressing his cheek against the edge of one of the doors, he moved his head to peer inside.

Halfway down the large empty warehouse two uniformed members of Group 666 were seated on packing cases playing cards on an upturned oil drum. On the floor beside them were submachine guns. One of the men took a sip from a bottle, made a face of disgust, and passed the bottle to his companion, who declined the offer with an equally expressive face.

Soundlessly, Maxwell slipped between the doors. "Don't move!" he barked.

The two men looked up in frozen astonishment at the battle-clad figure holding a pistol the way only men who know how to use them do.

"On your feet!" Maxwell ordered.

The men rose slowly, eyeing Maxwell warily.

"Move that stuff over to the doors!" Maxwell commanded, pointing at the crates and oil drum.

The two men hesitated, seeing no reason for such a command.

"*Move* it!" Maxwell barked.

The men hastened to obey, and on Maxwell's instructions arranged the items as if they had been playing cards only a few paces inside the doors.

"Sit down," Maxwell ordered. He moved behind

the seated men, and the bare butt of his pistol descended on the head of first one and then the other. The two men fell sprawling to the ground.

Swiftly Maxwell removed their watches, emptied their pockets, pulled the rings from their fingers. He took the bottle of gin and forced some of the liquor down the throats of the unconscious men, each in turn.

Then he took his knife and slit their throats. First one, then the other.

They had killed innocent American families.

They had mercilessly gunned down helpless prisoners.

They were men who had chosen to live by the sword and had died by the sword.

Maxwell turned away, satisfied their death would be seen as the act of local native thieves.

His face was drained white as he bent to pick up the two submachine guns. But he felt nothing. Absolutely nothing. The hideous events of the past weeks became a blur in the continuing violence. *Because it was necessary.*

David Maxwell, the man of peace from California, was no more.

Judy was watching, and David tossed her one of the guns. "Quick, follow me." She heard his words and obeyed.

At the back of the warehouse was a steel door, bolted shut. He pulled the bolt free and opened the door.

Maxwell stood blinking in the brilliant light before he saw a face, familiar yet so different. Sitting at a desk with papers made dazzling white by the glare of the bulb suspended from the low ceiling, his father stared at him with uncomprehending eyes. His mouth was working soundlessly to form the words his confused brain could not supply. His gray hair was now snowy white, his gaunt features were skeletal.

David paused in shock, then said to Judy, "Watch the door."

"David!" His father found the word.

"Yes. Listen to me, Dad." He crouched by his father's side. "There's no time for explanations. None. Understand?"

His father shook his head.

David grasped the thin wrist of the old man and squeezed it gently. "Just answer my questions. Are they forcing you to make atomic bombs?"

His father gave a slight nod.

"How many?"

A pause. "Three." The voice was reed-thin.

His father raised his eyes, and David saw in them the revelation of unbearable pain. "They've got Barbara." The words were little more than a whisper.

"Where?"

"I don't know—they said something about a hospital." Then he let out a cry of hopeless despair. "*How could I choose?* They tortured her. *Here!* In front of me. Terrible. . . ." his voice trailed away.

"You had no choice," David reassured him.

"How can a man choose between the agony of his daughter," his father's suffering words poured out, ". . . the agony of his own daughter against making bombs that could kill so many unknown people. How can you weigh blood, loyalty, and love against cold statistics. Only the devil could conceive of such a choice." He looked pleadingly at David. "In the name of heaven, what would God say?"

"You had no choice," David repeated firmly.

"No, you are wrong," his father answered. "I *had* no choice while Barbara was here. Suffering. But since then I have had time to think . . . to make the right decision. I shall make their bombs, and they will torture Barbara no more. And then I will detonate one —here, where *we* are. The statistics *are* the morality. *That* is the only right decision."

David called urgently for Judy to join him, then said, "Dad, do you know who these men are?"

"German, dressed like Nazis."

"Is there any one man who is in charge—a leader?"

"Yes. He just stood there, watching as if . . ." His father faltered, then continued. ". . . As if it meant nothing to him. The pain, the screams. . . ."

"Can you describe him?" David asked, glancing at Judy.

His father hesitated. "Tallish, dark hair, young . . . perhaps thirty." His father shuddered. "The coldest, blankest eyes I've ever seen—blue."

"Was his name ever mentioned?" David pressed.

His father shook his head.

David turned to Judy. They both knew the description fitted Kraske, but it could fit thousands of other men.

Judy bent low and spoke softly. "Dr. Maxwell, was there anything unusual in this man's behavior—odd gestures, mannerisms, anything like that?"

The old man did not have to think before he answered. "His whistling. As if he was bored by the awful. . . ." He broke off and then recovered his composure to continue. "Not a tune—a sort of hissing between his teeth."

"It *is* Kraske," Judy looked at David. "It has to be. He whistles like that when he's enjoying himself."

"Are you certain? You know how much depends on it."

Judy spoke again. "Dr. Maxwell, did this man smoke?"

"Yes."

"How?" Judy said.

The old man looked puzzled, then understanding showed on his face. "Ah yes—I see what you mean. He clenched the cigarette between his teeth. Sort of aggressive, macho."

"I'm certain," Judy said. "The description, the whistling, the way he smokes. It's too much to be coincidence."

David turned to his father. "How badly is Barbara hurt?"

"Physically, nothing she won't recover from in time. I couldn't let it go on." He shuddered again. "But God knows what it's done to her mind."

"The bombs . . . what type?" David asked quickly, conscious that discovery of the dead guards could come at any moment.

"Elementary gun type. About a kiloton yield," his father answered sensing his urgency.

"When do they want them finalized by?"

"Six P.M. in four days' time."

"They were that precise?"

"Yes."

"Any other specific instructions?"

"Only that they have to be designed to fit into

crates not exceeding five feet ten inches high, the sides not more than two feet six inches."

"Can you design the bombs so they won't function?"

"I've thought of that. But they have two French nuclear engineers here. I've talked to them. They couldn't design the bombs themselves with any guarantee they would work, but they know enough to check out any basic design defects. They've spelled that out to me. They've got a copy of the Los Alamos critical mass summaries, so I can't even fool them on the thickness of the neutron reflector."

David nodded, then rose to his feet and looked around the small room. The walls were plain brick. There were no windows. At the top of the back wall was an air vent—a horizontal series of metal slats about an inch apart cemented into the wall. David placed a chair against the wall and stood on it to peer between the slats. It was dark, but he could see enough—a small patch of open ground behind the warehouse, then the outline of shanty dwellings.

He returned to crouch beside his father. "Now listen, Dad. I haven't time to explain, but I want you to do these things. First, complete the bombs within half an hour of your six-thirty deadline. Not before. Slow down on the work if necessary. Second, if there are any changes in the plans—type, size, number of bombs, the completion time—write the information on a piece of paper and stuff it between the slats of the air vent after dark. If anything comes up on the last day, it's vital you have the information there before six-thirty. Okay?"

"I can see no problems," his father answered.

"And lastly, Dad, do *not* detonate one of the bombs here in Zambu. I said I can't explain, so you'll have to trust I know what I'm doing. But if you want a good moral reason, I'll give you one. God willing, these bombs will never be used—anywhere. If they are, think of it this way. The Zambus are a backward and defenseless people. Over the centuries all we have given them is slavery, disease, exploitation, and war. To give them our most sophisticated of all diseases—lethal doses of radiation—would be the ultimate moral crime. If three people from our so-called civilized world have to die to save each Zambu, we owe it to them. You can't refute the moral logic of that, Dad, and I know it."

David got to his feet and bent to embrace his father's shoulders. "Good-bye, Dad. God willing, we'll meet again."

"I suspect God has rather different plans for me," his father replied with a faint smile.

"Yes," David said and went to the door followed by Judy.

On the journey back neither Judy nor David spoke. David, because his mind was racing, planning what he knew must be done. Judy, because she was still numbed by the sight of David slitting the throats of two unconscious men.

They reached the rock to be greeted by McGregor. "It's still a Russian operation," David said.

"Holy Jesus! You know what that means?" McGregor said. "The Russians ordered their own prisoners killed just to throw *us*!"

McGregor was silent, and when he finally spoke, there was an awe in his voice Maxwell had never heard before. "What in the name of God are the Russians playing at? They've sacrificed their own men to fool us into believing that Group 666 are making bombs. *Three bombs!* What in hell can they do with three bombs that's so important?" He shook his head. "They've got enough of their own bombs in Russia to destroy half the world."

"I know," David said. "So whatever they've got in mind, it's got to be pretty momentous. And we've got to find out. Before it's too late. Now get Leopard over and I'll tell you what we're going to do."

NINETEEN

Zambu, West Africa

"We've got to go into Germany *with* those bombs," David said.

"With the bombs?" McGregor echoed.

"Yes. There's no other way we can find out how the Russians plan to use them. What their ultimate objective is. Stop them trying some other way."

"I wouldn't argue with that," McGregor answered. "But how the hell do we ride those bombs into Germany?"

"One thing we know for sure," David said. "They're in one hell of a hurry. As soon as Group 666 arrived, they unloaded the uranium and got my father working on the designs in no time flat. They're working to a precise deadline—6:30 P.M. in four days time—which means they are tying in with an equally precise operation to get the bombs out of here. Right?"

"Reasonable assumptions," McGregor conceded.

"The dimensions given my father for the bomb containers are small and specific. So they're not planning on using large transportation like a ship or a truck. That leaves an aircraft, a supposition supported by their evident requirement for speed. Judging from the dimensions of the containers, it's not a large plane with a loading bay—it's not a large aircraft of any kind. Those containers are designed to fit through the door of a medium-sized plane, an executive jet maybe."

"And we're going to hitch a lift with the bombs," McGregor said, his voice neutral. "Care to tell us how?"

"In principle, yes. To work out the details, we need more information. Nothing we can't get from Monato and his people. But the basics are straightforward. First, you and me," David nodded at McGregor, "arrive at the back of the warehouse at six o'clock, half an hour before the deadline for completion of the bombs. It'll just about be dark enough for safety. We check the air vent to see if my father has left a message about any last minute change of plan. Then, if possible, we break my father out. By 'if possible,' I mean if it can be done without alerting the Nazis and prejudicing the rest of the operation."

There was a silence. Then McGregor said, "You realize that if we don't get him out, he's going to be killed? They're not going to leave him around alive once they've got the bombs."

"I know," David said. "So does my father, and he's prepared for it."

McGregor shrugged. "He's your father."

"That's right," said David and continued. "While we are at the warehouse, Judy, Leopard, and Monato take up a position in hiding among the scrub directly across the airfield from the control tower. Leopard takes the bazooka, and Judy a light machine gun. They wait for us. We move on into the town and rescue my sister from the hospital. Group 666 will be more than busy moving and loading the bombs onto the airplane. I doubt there will be more than a couple of men at the hospital watching over a girl. Then we join Judy and the others, and Monato takes Barbara back to his uncle's village and waits for Judy and Leopard to join them later. From there they escape through the jungle over the frontier. They make it back to the American Embassy in Bonn the quickest way possible."

"The bit about us getting aboard the plane with the bomb?" McGregor prompted.

"We get hold of a couple of Nazi uniforms."

"No sweat," McGregor commented casually.

"After handing Barbara over to Monato, we make it in the darkness to the airfield building. The crew of the plane will be there—probably only a pilot and a copilot. We seize them at gunpoint and force them to take off with us onboard."

"And what will a bunch of hoodlums in Nazi uniforms and armed with submachine guns be doing while we're fixing ourselves a lift?" McGregor asked mildly.

"Praying," said David. "As soon as we grab the crew, we signal for Leopard to loose off a missile into the side of the building and Judy to spray the top of the entrance with tracer. That's when we tell your hoodlums that if they make one wrong move, the next load comes through the door."

For the first time since he had known him, Maxwell heard McGregor chuckle. "I like it, Maxwell. I like it very much. You've been doing some thinking since you left your father—haven't you, boy."

"It helps keep my mind off my problems," said David.

"Yes, doesn't it, though," McGregor replied with a grin. "But one little problem. What happens if we screw it up and don't make the plane?"

"That's *our* tough luck, McGregor. We're all expendable on this operation, unless I've got it wrong."

"That's not what's bothering me. I mean, what happens to those bombs?"

"We've got a fail-safe. Judy and Leopard plaster the plane with rocket and machine-gun fire. With full fuel tanks, it'll explode into a fireball. The bombs may be crude as far as atomic devices go, but they're put together with precision, or they don't work. The explosion and heat will foul them up so they never work."

"And the uranium?"

"Nothing. It won't be affected. It could be salvaged and used to make other bombs. But at least Judy and Leopard can get back and report what's going on. Leopard can pick out the registration number of the plane through the infrared night-sight on the bazooka. That may give a lead. And Barbara has been held prisoner long enough—she may have heard names, recognize faces. At least we will have gained time and opened up lines of investigation."

"Okay," McGregor said looking at Judy and Leopard, "before we make comments, let's think about it. We'll get some sleep now and meet in the morning."

Maxwell was awoken the next morning by a hand shaking his shoulder. He opened his eyes to see McGregor kneeling beside him. A little distance away, the other members of the party were eating breakfast.

"Before we get together to talk over your plan, Maxwell," McGregor said, "there's a couple of points I want to settle with you privately."

Maxwell rubbed his eyes. "Go ahead," he said.

"It's possible that plane isn't going to West Germany. Could be they're going to fly to a Communist-controlled country. They could do this, and we couldn't stop them. We can threaten the pilots, but we can't shoot them. Not both of them. So if this happens or if we lose control of those bombs for any reason at all, you should know I'm going to pull the pins on a couple of grenades while we're still in the air. Curtains. You go along with this?"

"Naturally," Maxwell said.

"Fine. And I'm going to make myself a petrol bomb. Just in case we land in West Germany and something still goes wrong. A burning airplane is hard to hide. But the chances are, we'll burn with it. Still okay?"

"Still okay."

"Let's eat," McGregor said.

After breakfast they sat in the welcome hot sun and discussed Maxwell's plan. Very little was said. Leopard could see no flaws in it. He had a few questions about weapons, that was all. Judy said she approved of it but remained curiously silent otherwise. It was agreed McGregor would meet with Monato to obtain a detailed layout of the hospital and Barbara's location within it. Also, a layout of the airport building. Then the meeting broke up.

McGregor left with Monato for his uncle's village

while Leopard started on his self-assigned daily task of stripping and cleaning the weapons.

Judy was sitting on the edge of the rock, her hands clasped around her knees, staring down at the stream. For a minute David stood beside her. Her long, fair hair, normally so glistening and clean, hung in sweat-darkened clusters, sticking to the skin at the back of her neck above the rim of her tight-fitting T-shirt soaked with perspiration.

David sat beside her. "What do you think of my plan?" he said. "You didn't say much." He leaned forward and turned his head looking at her, trying to penetrate the blank, withdrawn barrier of her eyes.

"It's very good," she answered simply, not looking at him.

"I'm overwhelmed by your enthusiasm," he teased.

She turned slowly to look at him, and in her eyes he saw an inexplicable sadness. "I said it was very good," she repeated, an emptiness in her voice. "As good as anything even *McGregor* could come up with."

David was silent, puzzled by the way she had used McGregor's name—as if it caused her pain. Then, very deliberately he said, "If I was half as good as McGregor, I'd be pleased."

She averted her eyes from him. "David, do you remember when we were in Scotland how you told me you hated violence. But McGregor had taught you how to cope with it. 'Flipped the switch,' as McGregor called it. Remember?"

"Sure I remember."

"Well, it isn't as simple as that. You're not like

McGregor." She hesitated. "And God knows what it did to him."

"You're not making sense."

"Listen to me, David." She looked at him steadily. "I watched you when you slit those two men's throats. It wasn't easy, was it?"

"What do you expect. It's not every day—"

"No, listen to me, David—please. The next time it will be easier, until you think you don't feel anything at all. And that's when it happens—to men like you anyway. They snap inside. They think they've learned to control their decent instincts, but nobody can really change like that. And suddenly they realize what they've done—what they've become—and they can't face it. The conflict destroys them. Some, the luckier ones, take to the bottle. The really unlucky ones commit suicide. Believe me, David, I've *seen it.*" She was on her knees clutching his arms, her fingers digging into his flesh. Her eyes were filled with a wild kind of desperation.

"What about you . . . and McGregor?" David said, aware that only some powerful emotion could have made her say what she had at a time like this.

Her hands fell from his arms, and she lowered her eyes. "We're different," she said.

"What is it about you and McGregor?" David asked, his voice gentle.

Judy was silent for a long time, then she said very quietly, "We're married."

"Married! I . . ." David found no words.

"McGregor and Leopard were with my father when he was killed in Yemen," Judy hurried on. "Before he died, my father asked McGregor to break the news to me. I fell in love with him. Not very surprising, I suppose. In some ways he was like my father . . . and doing the same kind of work. I was young, and it all seemed very glamorous." Judy wiped the tears from her eyes and tossed her head back.

"Anyway," she continued, "we were married shortly after British Intelligence persuaded me to work for them. Several times after that we worked together with Leopard. The last time was in Afghanistan. McGregor had to choose between putting my life at extreme risk and taking a chance on jeopardizing the success of the mission. He chose to put my life on the line. But afterwards I got the feeling he hadn't had to make a real choice at all. McGregor's brutally professional. I don't mean cruel. But he will sacrifice anything . . . anybody, if it is necessary to achieve his objective. Maybe we need men like McGregor. Probably we do. But it was something I couldn't live with, not within a marriage. So we called it a day and separated."

"But you went on working for British Intelligence."

"Yes. Finding out about McGregor killed something inside me. I was afraid to trust anyone; even more afraid to trust my own emotions." She gave a short bitter laugh. "People with dead emotions are way ahead in our business. And that's how it was until . . ."

"Until?"

She turned to face him, her tear-filled eyes searching his. "Oh, David, don't you understand what I'm trying to tell you? I love you, but I'm terrified about what's going to happen to you. The *real* you inside."

She threw her arms around David and held him tight against her trembling body.

David cupped her face in his hands and looked into her yearning eyes. "Trust me," he said softly. "Nothing is going to happen to me, I promise."

Their lips met, and then she buried her face against his chest, holding him yet more tightly. For she understood only too well how the brutal violence that lay ahead could destroy any man. Not his life, perhaps, but his soul.

David rose and, taking her hand, pulled her to her feet. Monato had told him of a waterfall of crystal-clear water cascading into the muddy stream, its source somewhere in the mountains to the north. He led her there, about half a mile up the stream.

Her tears had ceased, but she held on to his hand, and for the first time in his life David felt a deep protectiveness, an overwhelming need to be close, to be enduring . . . to love.

They stood for a while under the cool waterfall. And then they embraced . . . their enjoyment of each other's bodies was slow, sensuous, sometimes demanding and urgent. There was a new closeness, a commitment, the joy of love given and love taken.

The waiting passed swiftly. Each day they slipped away to the waterfall where they would talk, make love, or simply lie under its refreshing cascade. But although they did not speak of it, they knew their brief, idyllic respite from reality was the prelude to dangers which neither of them might survive.

Perhaps it was this suspension of time, David thought, that had led him so swiftly to fall in love with this strange woman. He prayed they might both live to test their love in more peaceful times.

McGregor was aware of the relationship which had developed between Judy and David. They made no attempt to hide it; he was glad. In his own way he still loved his wife, but he had long ceased to believe his "own way" was good enough. He had come to know that marriage, perhaps even love, could never be a part of his life. He was glad it was Maxwell. He liked the man.

Each day he went with Monato to his uncle's village to tie up the details of their plan. They also checked with the man who paid nightly visits to Maxwell's father to see if he had left a message in the air vent of his room. There were no messages.

Leopard was content to fulfill his limited but vital role. He was, among many other things, a weapons specialist: the best.

On the third night, guided by one of Monato's men, he went up-country. There, out of sound of the town, he checked the setting of the infrared night-sights on the bazooka.

Destroying the plane loaded with bombs–should it be necessary–would be child's play under normal circumstances. But if there should be a crosswind, he would need all his skill. The Russian RPG–7 rocket launcher was a good weapon, but one had to be familiar with its quirks. A strong lateral wind could grab a hold of the stabilizing fins on the rocket and direct it upwind, yards off target. Or, once the rocket's booster had burned out, the wind could drag it downwind, again far off target. Allowance had to be made for such eventualities; a matter of judgment based on experience, two qualities which Leopard possessed in abundance.

But Leopard knew that, should it be necessary to destroy the plane, his responsibility would be an onerous one. The consequence of failure, unforgivable.

While not attending to the weapons, Leopard was content to keep his silence, sitting against a rock sucking an empty pipe and thinking of his cottage on the hillside near Grasse in Provence. For it was there, with his wife and six children around him and a bottle of red wine beside him, that he was at peace with himself and the world.

However, peace had its price. And two or three times a year Leopard would leave for one of his *petits voyages,* his little journeys, as he told the children. And on these journeys, the man with the nom de guerre of Leopard changed from the amiable giant his children knew to one of the most formidable men of war available to Western intelligence.

It was on the evening of the third day, as McGregor and Maxwell were going over details of their part in the action, that David said, "Aren't we relying an awful lot on the loyalty of Monato's people? It could take only one of them to have betrayed us, and we've *no* chance."

"If we had to rely on their loyalty, you'd be too right," McGregor replied. "They haven't even got a word for loyalty in their language. But we've got something going for us a lot more effective than an abstract idea like loyalty."

McGregor paused to stretch his arms and legs before lying back and looking up at the star-filled sky. "Truth is," he said, "our culture and values don't mean a thing to the Zambus. They still believe in the power of ghosts, spirits, sorcerers, medicine men, and witches. And when I say they believe, I *mean* it. You'll never make sense of a thing they do unless you understand this. The thing they fear most is having a curse laid on them by someone senior to them in their own family—a father, grandmother, whoever—or someone higher up in the village hierarchy. A curse laid on someone by Monato's uncle would frighten them to death. They'd figure even the most powerful—and expensive—white magician couldn't protect them from it."

"What are the curses supposed to do?" David asked.

"There's no *suppose* about it," McGregor said. "Mostly it happens. The guy gets injured; one of his wives or children die or—if he gets really unlucky—his crops fail. When you're living near starvation level, that's bad news. Not surprising they've got different values to us. Against a curse from Monato, they figure they've got *no* chance. Fact he isn't president any longer doesn't mean a thing. He's the chief of the tribe, and that's what counts. They rate politics as a game played for profit by the powerful men in the towns. Nothing to do with them."

"So if one of them betrayed us, they would be scared Monato would lay a curse on them—is that right?"

"Yeah—best security in the world."

The two men fell silent for a while, then McGregor said, "Monato had one of the village witches do a prediction on this little deal of ours."

"What happened?"

"The guy killed a chicken and played around for a long while with bits and pieces from its inside."

"And?"

"He wouldn't say."

TWENTY

Zambu, West Africa

"What was all that about?" Maxwell asked McGregor.

They were standing behind a high clump of scrub a short distance from the line of shanties which separated them from the back of the warehouse. Their two guides, just returned from a reconnaisance of the building, had spent the last few minutes talking to McGregor in a mixture of pidgin English and hand signs.

"Nothing much," McGregor said in the gathering gloom of nightfall. "The front of the warehouse is lousy with Germans loading crates into a truck."

Maxwell stiffened: the sudden realization that the bombs were no longer an idea. They existed! Packed in the containers was enough power to wipe out a major city.

Maxwell checked his watch. Six twenty-five. He had told his father to put a note in the air vent by six-thirty if there were any last minute changes in his captors' plans. "Let's check the air vent," he said.

Led by the guides, they slipped between the shanties and crossed the patch of grass to reach the wall of the warehouse directly below the slatted air vent.

McGregor braced his back against the wall and

locked his fingers between his legs, palms upward, to form a stirrup.

Maxwell placed one foot in the stirrup and heaved himself up. The slats of the vent were six inches above his head. With one hand he carefully felt between the slats. There was no note. Maxwell breathed a sigh of relief. They would not have to make any changes in their plans. He whispered down to McGregor who then raised his cupped hands even higher so Maxwell could see between the slats. David hoped for one last glimpse of his father.

Straining his neck, he peered into the lighted room and saw his father lying on an iron bed set beside his desk. David winced at the expression on the old man's face, tormented and despairing. He understood just how much suffering it had cost his father to make those bombs soon to be let loose in the world.

"Dad," he called softly.

His father gazed around the room in bewilderment. When Maxwell called again, he craned his neck to peer up at the air vent, and a smile came to his face. He rose unsteadily to his feet and began to shuffle toward the wall. Abruptly he stopped and turned his head sharply to the door. A second later he had moved back to the bed with the speed of desperation and was lying prone, his eyes staring at the door.

It opened, and Maxwell saw what his father had heard. A man was standing there, a submachine gun cradled in one arm. The man was whistling between his teeth. The man was Kraske.

David watched in frozen horror as Kraske sauntered across to the bed and stood looking down at his father, his face without expression. Then, quite casually, he raised the gun and raked the outstretched body on the bed until the magazine was empty.

Maxwell's stomach convulsed, his mind was torn with the pain of hatred and impotent anguish as he watched his father's cold-blooded execution.

Maxwell stepped to the ground, his legs trembling.

McGregor did not need an explanation. He had guessed. He seized Maxwell by the arm and steered him, stumbling, back through the shanties and into the scrub.

Maxwell had come to terms with the inevitability of his father's murder. But to see it! And to see it done by a man who showed such cold indifference to life! *Kraske!* Maxwell was overwhelmed by blinding rage, an all-consuming hatred demanding retribution. *Revenge!*

He heard McGregor's voice. "I'm sorry, Maxwell. Nothing else I can say. . . . We'd better get moving."

Maxwell nodded.

They made fast progress back around the harbor area and up along the bank of the river to the ford. As they waded across, McGregor stopped briefly to reach to the bed of the river and his hand emerged, holding a rock the size of a large orange.

They followed the river bank down toward the town passing the airfield on their left. Approaching the first scattered bungalows, they heard the distant sound of an airplane. The sound came closer, and the landing lights on the airfield behind them sprang into life, illuminating the base of the low, black clouds drifting in from the sea. The first heavy drops of rain fell as the plane screeched in low overhead to land. The sound of its engine died, and the landing lights were extinguished.

Keeping a steady trot, the guides followed the back streets toward the hospital. The rain began to sleet down, and they abandoned any attempt at caution. In the darkness, a casual observer would see only the shapes of four men huddled together, hastening to some destination and the shelter of a roof.

The hospital was a low, white-stucco building set back from the road behind a high stone wall.

Swiftly the four of them climbed the wall, and jumped, landing silently among the thick bushes on the other side. Taking shelter under the hospital porch, twenty yards from the bushes, a German stood with a submachine gun slung over one shoulder and a bored look on his face.

His expression changed to one of surprise and mild amusement when he saw the black figure of one of the guides emerge from the darkness to stand in front of him jabbering excitedly and pointing wildly toward the bushes.

He jerked back with a scowl as the guide grabbed his arm and tried to pull him off the porch.

Inside the small reception area a black nurse watched from behind a desk. The guide rushed over to her and spoke rapidly. The nurse rose and approached the German. "You speak English?" she asked.

"A little," he replied.

The nurse pointed to the bushes. "There . . . a man . . . like you." She touched the swastika on the man's arm band The German nodded his understanding.

"Man, hurt bad . . . much blood," the nurse finished.

The German frowned and slipped the gun from his shoulder. He remembered the incident when they had first arrived when the two men guarding the American at the warehouse had been robbed and murdered. "Black bastards," he muttered, cautiously approaching the edge of the bushes.

He sensed the presence of danger by his side. But before he could react, the stone in McGregor's hand had crashed to the base of his skull, shattering the vertebrae and breaking his neck instantly. He slumped noiselessly to the ground.

A knife to the heart would have been as quick, but the uniform was required—without bloodstains.

Then the guide dashed out of the bushes and spoke to the nurse who was watching curiously from the porch. A badly injured man was in the bushes, the guide said. Should he be moved before receiving medical attention? Her expert advice was needed.

The nurse returned quickly to her desk and grabbed the storm torch from the wall behind it. Accompanied by the guide, she hurried through the torrential rain.

Before the beam of the torch could penetrate the bushes, the guide wrenched it from her hand and, clasping one hand tightly around her mouth, forced her into the bushes. The two guides set about gagging and binding her with cloth and twine.

Within minutes the dead German had been stripped, and McGregor stood in his uniform. He slung the submachine gun over his shoulder, safety off; then, grasping the dead man under the armpits, he dragged him, feet trailing along the ground, to the hospital entrance.

Maxwell and the guides moved swiftly in the darkness to take up their positions under the second window along the left side of the building.

Inside the window, the light was on, the red cotton drapes drawn.

Inside was Barbara.

McGregor, walking backward, dragged the dead man past the deserted reception desk and around the corner into the corridor which led to one of the hospital's two wards. Six yards down the corridor behind him, McGregor knew, were swing doors and through them a short stretch of corridor with a private room to the side. Beyond was another pair of swing doors leading into the main ward where a solitary night nurse was on duty—with a telephone beside her on the desk. And in the short stretch of corridor, standing outside Barbara's room, was a German guard. An obstacle, to be removed and the source of the uniform for Maxwell.

McGregor backed into the swing doors, forcing them open and, without turning his head, shouted to the guard. "Here. Help me with this man." McGregor's German was perfect. He had rehearsed the words repeatedly with Maxwell.

The guard, had he seen McGregor's face, would have recognized him as not being one of his own. But McGregor's back was to him, and he did not see his face. Instead he saw the lifeless form of a white man dressed only in underclothes being dragged toward him by a compatriot.

He rushed to be of assistance.

"He's slipping," McGregor's words were urgent as he deliberately released his right hand from under the man's armpit. The guard stooped to grab the man before his head could hit the stone floor. McGregor shifted the weight of his body onto the balls of his feet and struck down onto the bent and exposed neck of the guard with the back of his hand.

The guard slumped forward across the dead body of his compatriot; it was a silent, bloodless, and instant execution.

McGregor placed his hand on the door handle to Barbara's room. He did not know what to expect when he opened the door. How severely had the girl been tortured before her father had given in? How had she been treated after her torture?

He had prepared himself for two eventualities. If she reacted to his sudden appearance normally, he would quickly reassure her and they would escape through the window. If she was hysterically uncontrollable, he would quickly kill her. Silently, and with great regret. He would tell Maxwell he had found her dead. Maxwell would have to accept it; there would be no opportunity for investigation or inquiry.

McGregor was *not* prepared to prejudice their swift and undetected progress to the airfield in an attempt to save the life of one person. He had agreed to come to the hospital for one reason only: it was a place where there were two Germans, isolated from their comrades, whose uniforms could be removed with the minimum risk of alerting those at the airfield.

He opened the door. Barbara was not in the bed. She was on the floor in one corner of the room, dressed in a hospital gown, her hands clasped around her knees as she rocked from side to side, a low moaning coming from the back of her open mouth.

And in her eyes, nothing. No surprise; no fear. Nothing. Just a blank, uncomprehending emptiness.

Quickly McGregor dragged the bodies of the two dead Germans from the corridor into the room and shut the door.

He began to remove the German's uniform, his eyes flicking to examine the eyes of the still moaning girl. To make *some* assessment of her condition. Would she remain oblivious, but silent? Or, if he attempted to lift her through the window, would she become hysterical?

He unbuckled the German's belt and spoke her name. She looked at him blankly.

Fifteen yards away in the main yard the night nurse finished bandaging the leg of the man sitting on the bed. Standing impatiently watching was another man. Both men wore the uniform of Group 666.

The injured man had caught his leg between the side of the truck and one of the bomb containers while they were loading the bombs at the warehouse. Fifteen minutes ago the truck had dropped them off at the hospital on its way out to the airfield. The fit man would help his injured companion back to their billet.

Since the murder at the warehouse, Group 666 moved in pairs. Never alone.

The bandaging completed, the wounded man limped to the door.

Outside in the empty corridor the injured man winked at his comrade. "Guess where Müller is?" he said with a leer.

"I don't have to. He's screwing the ass off the American bitch. They've all been at her."

The two men exchanged sly glances and quietly approached the door.

McGregor had made his decision. The girl was beyond reach; shocked, catatonic. He would get her out the window. The possibility of complications, a degree above zero. No more.

Suddenly the door opened wide. The two Germans stood staring, momentarily unable to take in what they saw: two dead bodies and a man in their uniform with a face too mature to be one of them.

McGregor dived for the gun he had placed on the bed. As he swiveled to fire the door slammed.

Now, every second—every hundredth of a second—counted. The difference between life or death, between a successful mission and God alone knew what! Once the two Germans collected their wits, they would pour a fusillade of fire through the closed doors and then nothing, absolutely nothing, in the small room could survive for more than a fragment of time.

McGregor grabbed the Germans' clothes, flung open the window, and dived headfirst out into the blackness. In the spill of light from the window he saw the ground in time to hunch and land on his shoulder, then somersault to his feet. He dived to the wall.

"What happened?" Crouching against the wall, Maxwell stared in amazement.

"Keep quiet!" McGregor snapped and placed his hand over Maxwell's mouth to reinforce his command.

Maxwell shoved his hand aside angrily. "Barbara? . . ." he started and was silenced by the thunderous burst of fire pouring into the room. The air filled with the sound of ricocheting bullets and the shattering of the glass window above them, and a shower of splintered glass spewed down upon them.

Then there was silence.

McGregor rose to stand at one side of the window, listening. In his right hand was a fragmentation grenade, the forefinger of his left hand crooked in the pull ring.

At the sound of steps in the room he pulled the pin, counted to two then tossed the grenade through the window. Exactly one and a half seconds later the deafening sound of the explosion came like a shock wave, and fragments from the grenade whined through the window into the dark night.

"Move!" McGregor yelled.

They reached the street, and McGregor spoke quickly to the guides who then took to their heels. "We don't need them anymore," he said to Maxwell. "Now let's get to that airfield. We're going to have to change our plans."

"What's happened to Barbara?" Maxwell said hoarsely, without moving.

"What the hell do you *think*'s happened? She's dead," McGregor replied. "I'll explain later. We've got to get out of here."

But Maxwell wasn't listening. His father's death. Now Barbara! *"You killed her!"* he screamed and raised his arm.

The movement from McGregor was swift and expert. The four rigid fingers of his right hand sank into Maxwell's solar plexus. The air shot from his lungs, and he sank to his knees in agony.

"Listen to me, you goddamn idiot," McGregor hissed between clenched teeth. "There was nothing else I could do. Get it? *Nothing!* If *you* had gone into that hospital in my place, you and Barbara—*both*—would be dead. And I would be under that window with my head shot off. Now, *move*!"

Maxwell got to his feet, breathing heavily. He had no reason to doubt the truth of McGregor's words, and the anger born of grief which had erupted against McGregor was replaced by a cold hatred for the unknown men who had made such things possible. Even Kraske was unimportant—a vile and warped fool being used. But somewhere there were men, *and they would pay*! "Let's go," he said.

They reached Judy and Leopard hidden in a shallow hollow, screened by low scrub on the edge of the airfield, just as the rain stopped.

McGregor took the bazooka from Leopard and, peering through the night-sights, began a methodical examination of the airfield and the building directly across from their position.

Judy lowered herself to lie beside David. "Where's Barbara?" she whispered.

Not turning his head, David said the one word, "Dead."

Judy stretched out her hand to cover his and squeezed gently. But there was no pressure of response, no indication from him of a closeness and a sharing of grief. And she knew that at that moment there were no words that could reach him.

In time, perhaps. But not then.

McGregor slid down into the hollow. "There's no chance we can sneak in dressed like a couple of Nazis and grab the pilots. When they get the bad news about the hospital, they'll be alert as hell . . . and they'll start throwing guards around the place like confetti. We're going to keep it simple and crash in on them."

No one spoke, McGregor continued, "Leopard, have they finished loading the bombs?"

"Yes. Three large crates and one small one."

"The small one will be the detonators and timing devices to arm the bombs," David interjected.

"Refueled the plane?"

"Immediately they landed," Leopard replied.

"And the plane's a Falcon?"

"Mystère Falcon 20. Made in France, used all over the world," Leopard elaborated. "Crew of two. Eight to fourteen passenger seats—depending on the configuration—or cargo conversion."

"Which is it? Cargo or passenger?"

"Passenger," Leopard replied with a frown. "There's a quick-change kit which converts one of those things to cargo in less than an hour. They haven't used it. The crates are across the top of the seats. I've seen them through the fuselage windows with the night-sights. Why do a stupid thing like that? *C'est fou!*" Leopard shrugged heavily.

"They'll have a good reason," McGregor said. "And we'll know what it is when we get to Germany. Now all of you, listen to me."

Methodically McGregor began to spell out what each of them must do.

Suddenly the sound of shouting drifted across from the brightly lit building. McGregor reached for the bazooka and, raising himself to the edge of the hollow, began to inspect the airfield. After several minutes he slithered back and said, "They've got the bad news already. They're sending guys out to patrol the perimeter of the airfield and have placed guards in front of the building and around the plane. . . . Judy, the ones around the plane are your pigeons. Knock them off fast. And for chrissakes, don't hit the goddamn plane"

Judy nodded.

"Leopard, you'll have to move back or the perimeter guards will walk in on you."

A grunt from Leopard.

"Okay, let's go," McGregor said, and he and Maxwell rose to a crouch and headed back into the scrub.

Judy slithered forward on her stomach and began the long, exhausting elbow crawl across the open airfield. Resting across the inside of her elbows was the RPK machine gun, complete with bipod folded back and clipped to the barrel, a seventy-five-round drum of ammunition: a total weight of over fifteen pounds.

With a whispered "*Bonne chance,* my little angel," Leopard watched her go, then picked up the bazooka and a case of six rockets.

Two hundred yards back from the edge of the airfield was a small hillock. No more than ten feet above the surrounding ground, but high enough to give a clear field of vision above the scrub.

Leopard positioned himself on top of the hillock and, raising the bazooka sights to his eye, began a careful scrutiny of what would soon be a field of violent battle.

First he picked out the right-hand corner of the building–McGregor and David's first destination. From there he panned left across twenty yards of windowless brick wall to come to the first lighted window. Inside he saw the heads and shoulders of three men sitting around a table. Two were in white shirts—the pilot and copilot of the plane whom he had seen get out of the plane when it landed. Now they had been joined by a third man in uniform.

Leopard kept panning left across the arrival and departure area; first a window then the entrance, and on the other side, another window. He estimated there were about fifteen uniformed figures inside, standing in small groups, a couple by one of the windows looking out.

Then followed another short stretch of blank wall before he picked up the truck which had brought the bombs. And a few yards to the left of that, out in front of the hangar which abutted the building, the sleek outline of the Falcon with the guards positioned around it.

At the far corner of the hangar, the rear half of it visible, stood the fuel truck.

Leopard grunted with satisfaction. The moon was still obscured by the heavy cloud, but the rain had stopped. And far more important, the wind had dropped. At a range of four hundred yards he could foresee no difficulty in hitting his designated targets.

He prepared three rockets for firing, inserted one in the muzzle of the bazooka, then swiveled right again to locate the corner of the building where McGregor and Maxwell were due to arrive. He waited for them to appear in his sights.

Out on the airfield Judy reached her objective. A spot two hundred and fifty yards directly down the concrete runway from where the Falcon was standing. Her position was totally exposed, her only protection the darkness. Behind her were another two hundred yards of bare runway, and on either side of her the flat grass of the airfield.

Still lying on her stomach, she unclasped the bipod and set the machine gun up pointing toward the Falcon. Her arm muscles were trembling with the exertion of the long crawl as she squinted through the sights. One by one she searched for and located the six guards around the plane. But when the moment for action came, there would be no time to search for targets. The guards had to die within seconds.

Judy rested the butt of the machine gun on the concrete and waited.

As McGregor and David came around the corner of the building and into his sights, Leopard adjusted his position to follow them as they moved swiftly in the shadow of the wall until they reached the edge of the spill of light from the first window. There they stopped and crouched.

Leopard traversed until his sights picked up the back of the fuel truck beside the hangar. He took his time lining up the sights; the need now was for accuracy—the need for urgency was to come.

He squeezed the trigger, and the noise of the ejecting rocket was like a crash of thunder in the still night.

As Judy raised the machine gun to her shoulder, the truck, still half full of high-octane fuel, exploded into a brilliant white ball of fire. Streaks of blazing fuel burst into the air like a fountain of light.

The airfield was brighter than day.

Within five seconds Judy had got off three one-second bursts of eleven rounds each, aiming at chest height to avoid the low wing of the Falcon. Three guards to one side of the plane spun like out-of-control tops, then fell to the ground.

The guards on the other side of the plane stood transfixed. The almost simultaneous sound of the rocket, the explosion of the fuel truck, and the bursts of machine-gun fire, all from different directions, were too fast for their minds to register. Judy aimed and fired again, this time in one continuous burst, and the three men died before they had even moved.

Judy reached to set the fire selector at single-shot, and Leopard's second rocket crashed through the entrance of the building and exploded against the back wall. Half the men inside died instantly; the remainder were wounded or stunned.

The guards stationed outside the entrance ran headlong across the airfield. With no destination, they ran to escape the hell that had erupted around them.

Judy fired once, then once again, and they were sprawled dead on the runway.

Fourteen men had died within twenty seconds of calculated mayhem.

Sitting with the two pilots, Günther Kraske had leaped to his feet at the sound of the exploding fuel truck and dashed for the door. As he opened it, the force of the rocket exploding in the entrance knocked him back into the room. He got to his feet and struggled to the window, then leaped back as the glass in front of him was shattered by the barrel of a submachine gun and a voice shouted in German "Don't move!"

Kraske stared in confusion at the face behind the gun. A face grim with hatred. A face he remembered but couldn't place. For an instant Maxwell's finger tightened on the trigger as he faced his father's murderer. But even more quickly he realized that the man *must not die*. Not yet.

He was the Russian connection!

The *only* connection.

The pressure on the trigger eased.

Moving along the wall, McGregor had reached the main entrance. He lobbed two grenades through the door shattered by Leopard's rocket, waited for the explosions, then dashed into the dust-filled darkness and devastation.

Stumbling and slipping on the unseen bodies of the dead and the wounded, he found the room where Kraske and the two pilots stood motionless, their eyes riveted on Maxwell at the window.

McGregor cursed as he saw the man in uniform. For chrissakes, did Maxwell think they were taking prisoners! He raised his gun.

"Hold it!" David yelled. "He's the one who killed my father. We need him."

McGregor lowered his gun instantly.

And Kraske realized why he recognized the face at the window. David Maxwell! The man he had seen lying on the bed in Bonn with a dagger sunk deep in his chest. He had been killed—the newspapers had confirmed it! Then, at the pit of his stomach, Kraske knew that something had gone wrong, very wrong . . . way back along the line somewhere.

McGregor prodded Kraske with his gun. "Get moving," he said.

With McGregor behind them Kraske and the two pilots picked their way back through the debris and bodies, the only faint light coming through the windows from the burning fuel truck.

Ahead of him Kraske saw the dull metallic glint of a submachine gun lying across the chest of one of the dead men. Deliberately, he stumbled and fell across the dead man, his hands grasping for the gun, his fingers feeling for the trigger. He swore aloud as if annoyed by his own clumsiness. But as he whipped onto his back to fire, McGregor knew the swift movement in the darkness was not the normal reaction of a man fallen by accident. McGregor fired. Kraske's body arched briefly in a spasm of death, then was still.

"What the hell was that? Where's Kraske?" David asked quickly as the two pilots emerged from the door.

"Kraske tried to get smart. He's dead."

"We wanted him *alive*!" David yelled.

"You think I don't know," McGregor's voice was steel. "Now get moving to the plane—or do you want Judy killed too."

Out on the runway, still brilliantly lit by the burning truck, Judy's life hung in the balance. Unaware that David and McGregor had already penetrated the building, the men patrolling the perimeter had been able to locate only two sources of the attack, the crash of the bazooka from somewhere in the darkness of the scrub and the prostrate figure of Judy out on the runway.

Six of them ran in the direction of the bazooka. The others turned their attention to Judy. She was beyond the range of their submachine guns. To attempt to cross the wide expanse of open airfield would mean certain death. They dived for the cover of the scrub and circled swiftly around the perimeter to bring her within range.

Judy swiveled around on her stomach to face the near edge of the perimeter from where the attack would come. She set the fire selector to automatic and waited.

She would not survive such an attack, but they were going to pay a heavy price for her life. She glanced quickly up the runway and saw the four figures climbing into the Falcon. She wondered how long it took to start the engine.

Inside the Falcon, Maxwell settled the same question without ceremony. "Forget the takeoff checks," he yelled. "Get it moving or I'll blow your heads off."

Fifteen seconds later the twin-turbofan engines burst into life, and the plane taxied forward.

"Stop by the figure lying on the runway," Maxwell shouted.

Judy jumped to her feet and grabbed David's outstretched hand. He pulled her aboard and held her warm body tightly against his as the plane taxied on to the end of the runway.

From his vantage point Leopard let out a long sigh of relief as he watched the plane turn at the end of the runway and rev, ready to take off.

His relief was short-lived. Five men were running from various parts of the perimeter, converging on the machine gun Judy had left on the runway. One burst from this high-velocity weapon fired into the cabin of the Falcon as it came down the runway on takeoff, and that would be an end of it. Even concentrated fire from their submachine guns might be enough.

Leopard raised the bazooka and aimed, holding his fire until the five men would be grouped near the machine gun. They all had to die.

At the bottom of the hillock he heard the breaking of scrub followed by a short exchange of conversation. He had only seconds before his inevitable discovery. He held his breath and steadied his aim as the tension sent the blood pulsating through his body.

On the runway, one man had thrown himself down behind the machine gun; the others were only yards away. Leopard squeezed the trigger, then reached to reload his weapon. He heard the scrambling of feet coming up the hillock. He dare not move. He had to be sure. He had a split second to see the jagged flash of the explosion on the runway and the men around the machine gun tossed high into the air; then a deafening metallic crack from behind engulfed him. Blinding light filled his vision, then nothing.

Two Germans stood on the hillock, gazing down at the lifeless body of the bearded giant.

The man named Leopard had made his last *petit voyage.*

TWENTY-ONE

Tripoli, North Africa

On the cramped flight deck of the Falcon, Maxwell rose from his crouching position behind the two pilots.

Half an hour had passed since their desperate take-off, and now they were cruising at 450 miles an hour, 40,000 feet above the empty deserts of central Africa. The most economical height and speed for the Falcon necessary, as the pilots had explained to Maxwell, if their fuel was to last them until they reached their destination of Tripoli on the Mediterranean coast of Africa.

In fact, the pilots had been only too eager to explain everything—everything they knew. What little equanimity they had retained through the holocaust at the airport had been rapidly eroded by the grim, hard faces of their abductors and Maxwell's short but eloquent command to "talk or die."

They had talked.

Maxwell edged his way down the narrow trench aisle toward the back of the plane. Two of the bomb containers occupied the full length of the port side of the plane. They were attached to the tops of the seats by bonds of thick rope slotted through steel hasps screwed to their undersides. The other container was similarly attached to the three starboard front seats. A small box containing the detonators and timing devices was in the luggage space immediately aft of the flight deck.

Judy and McGregor occupied two of the remaining three seats at the rear. Maxwell sat down between them. "Seems the pilots think they're smuggling arms into West Germany for Group 666—machine guns, bazookas, and ammunition. While we've been away the Group have been conducting a small-scale terrorist war against our servicemen. Same in East Germany."

"How did they react when you told them they had atomic bombs on board?" Judy asked.

"I didn't tell them. It would have made them too scared to go through with their operation."

"Which is?" McGregor prompted.

"The pilots are employed by a company named *Adlerflugwerkedienst*. It's a commercial outfit which operates aircraft for private owners who don't want the hassle and overheads of providing their own backup facilities, full-time pilots, and so on. When the owners aren't using their aircraft, they're hired out to defray costs. A few days ago the pilots were approached by a man with a proposition."

"Do they know the identity of that man?" McGregor interjected quickly.

"No. And at the time they didn't care. The man said he had chartered the Falcon from *Adlerflugwerkedienst* to make a completely legitimate flight to Tripoli and back. Once they got to Tripoli, the man said, arrangements had been made for a further flight out to Zambu and back, no questions asked and without even filing a flight plan."

"A totally undocumented and unrecorded flight, in other words?" McGregor said.

"Right. And when we reach Tripoli in about four hours' time, they refuel and complete the legitimate return flight to Frankfurt."

"So Tripoli has been fixed," McGregor said. "Air traffic control, customs—the lot. That means government involvment. I guess the Russians asked their Libyan friends to do them a favor. It wouldn't be the first time. But you can bet your sweet life the Libyans don't know what's on this plane." McGregor paused, then said, "Okay, so far, so easy. Now what about the difficult bit. Going into Germany we're on a regular flight plan—there's no other way a plane like this *could* get into Germany. As soon as we hit European airspace, air traffic control will keep tabs on us all the way to Frankfurt. And at Frankfurt there's *no way* they can fix customs. So how do they get the bombs through?"

"We don't reach Frankfurt," Maxwell answered. "About a hundred miles south of there the pilots report engine failure. Air traffic control at Frankfurt will see them lose height, then drop out of vision below radar level at about four hundred feet. There's a disused airstrip twenty miles west of this point good enough for a Falcon to make an emergency landing."

McGregor shook his head. "*Twin* engine failure," he said. "Who do those pilots think they're going to be fooling. When the aviation authorities . . ."

"The pilots won't be around to answer questions," David cut in. "There'll be a car waiting at the airstrip to take them directly to Frankfurt Airport. With false passports they take an early morning flight and end up in Argentina. Their money is already out there, and they have the promise of help to set up their own cargo outfit. Makes sense. They're only young kids, a couple of years out of the German air force. No family responsibilities. And the old brigade Nazis still have plenty of connections in South America."

"It's cool, but it does not make sense. Not all the way down the line," McGregor replied. "The guy who hired the Falcon disappears. Right? So the German aviation authorities end up with a mystery—a Falcon sitting on a disused airstrip with two perfectly good engines and no pilots. *Adlerflugwerkedienst* can't explain a thing. The only weak link is the pilots. Argentina, hell! They're *dead.*"

"Could be," David said.

"For *sure,*" McGregor replied. "But it's academic now. They've got themselves into a whole new scenario. What did you tell the pilots?"

"What we agreed. That we were working for the BND. If they cooperated with us, it might knock five years off their sentences."

"And they believed you?"

"Right now they'd believe anything. But it's logical anyway."

"Okay. Then let's look at the logic of what happens when we get to that airstrip. What time are we scheduled to arrive?"

"Four o'clock. Just before dawn—one hour's stopover at Tripoli to refuel, then two and a half hours to the airstrip. At Tripoli the pilots have to give a radio message to someone confirming their estimated time of arrival in Germany."

McGregor's face clouded. "Why?"

"My guess is the people in Germany are working to one helluva tight schedule. They have to unload the bombs and make them disappear before air traffic control at Frankfurt have the air full of helicopters looking for a crashed Falcon. Timing's critical. An ETA sent from Zambu would not be accurate enough. . . . And from our point of view there's a more important reason. Kraske was supposed to have radioed their departure on schedule from Zambu. He was just about to do it when we disturbed him. If we want the people in Germany to be ready and waiting for us, we've *got* to confirm from Tripoli."

"Do the pilots have any idea who the radio contact in Germany is?"

"No."

"Okay, let's plan our action. They're going to have eight to ten men meeting the plane—to move the containers out fast. Most likely they'll be Group 666. And armed. But there will be at least one SSD man among them. No way are the Russians going to risk a foul-up at this stage. That's the man we've got to grab. The only way we can do this is get the lot of them. Then the BND can sort out the SSD man, and the balloon goes up on the Russian connection. With Kraske dead there's no other way of *proving* the tie up with the Russians . . . or finding out what their objective is."

"The trick being," Maxwell said, "to catch them all —remembering there's not going to be much light around."

"Right," McGregor agreed. "Any suggestions?"

"The landing will be pretty rough, I imagine," Judy said looking at David.

"According to the pilots, rough but not hazardous."

"Bad enough to put a lot of strain on the fuselage and make it plausible that the exit door jams?"

"I guess so."

"Then suppose we jam the door from the inside. The reception committee will rush to try and help free it from the outside. And you can depend on it that the SSD element will be right there with them. They're not going to stand back and watch their plans go up in the air because of a jammed door!"

McGregor was smiling. "I like it," he said.

"Then," Judy continued, "one of us opens the door with a submachine gun very much in evidence. At the same moment one of us breaks out through the emergency exit onto the wing with another submachine gun. That should wrap them up nicely."

"Beautiful," McGregor said appreciatively. "I'll take the door, and you, Judy, go through the emergency exit."

"Wait a minute," David protested. "*I'll* take the emergency exit."

"The hell you will," McGregor said. "That emergency exit is only about two feet by one and a half. Judy can get through it in no time flat. You'd never make it fast enough. And if there's any trouble, we need some delicate shooting. We want them all alive. Remember? Wounded if we have to. But *not* dead.

Judy can pick cherries off a tree with a submachine gun. But . . ."

"All right, all right," David said. "You've made your point."

McGregor looked at Maxwell steadily for a few moments, then said, "But there is something you can do, Maxwell. If anything goes wrong with our plan, we've got to cover ourselves so Group 666 don't get near those bombs. I'll give you the gasoline bomb. If necessary, you throw it and then you toss a couple of grenades around to guarantee this thing goes up in very quick flames. Attract the helicopters that'll be out looking for it. Will you do it?" McGregor fixed David with hard appraising eyes.

"What makes you think you have to ask?" David said quietly.

"Dying in action is one thing," McGregor said. "Usually you don't have too much choice about it. Committing suicide isn't as easy."

"You don't have to worry," David answered.

McGregor gave a quick smile. "No, I guess I don't."

At half past midnight under a brilliant moon the Falcon taxied into a bay at Tripoli Airport to refuel.

One of the young pilots climbed out and walked the short distance to the back of a nearby maintenance shop. He lit a cigarette and drew on it, his face furrowed in thought. For a minute or two he gazed up at the star-filled sky and breathed the warm night air. And he thought of the sweet life in Argentina—the money, the women, the beaches around Buenos Aires . . . the freedom!

Then his stomach turned over as he thought of ten years in a German jail.

He would be thirty-five when he got out.

Broke, disgraced, his prospects gone. . . . A life thrown away!

He felt sick.

But there *was* a chance. A gamble. And he must decide now. Before it was too late. He had *not* told Maxwell all the details of their landing in Germany. In the first moments after the panic of takeoff, some things had not even occurred to him. And when Maxwell had asked him for an instrument, an artifact of some kind that could be used to jam the door shut, some instinct had told him to remain silent.

The pilot looked up at the glittering stars again. A jammed door. A delay. Essential to the plans of the men from the BND? Possibly. *Probably.* And if there was *no* delay? And if the men in Germany were warned of trouble? Who could tell what might happen.

My God, it *was* worth the gamble. What was the risk of a few more years in prison compared to the chance of freedom and a life full of promise.

He flung his cigarette to the ground and took the paper from the breast pocket of his flying jacket on which were written the identification code and ETA of the plane in Germany. Holding it against the green-painted steel shutters of the maintenance shop, he took a ball-point pen from his pocket and in the light from the moon added the words: THREE HOSTILE PASSENGERS ON BOARD.

Then he gazed up at the infinite space of the sky and took a deep breath. It was done. Now, at least, *there was hope*!

A quiet cough behind him made him turn sharply. A man stood a short distance behind him. The pilot spoke *the* words. The man made the correct response. The pilot handed the man the paper, then turned and walked back to the plane. A new lightness in his step.

In Bonn Gartmann sat slumped in a chair, a glass in his hand. On the table beside him was a bottle of cognac, a telephone, and a pad and pencil.

For the first time since he had been entrusted with part of an assignment which Baron von Richter described as "of momentous significance," Gartmann had been drinking. Heavily. For five hours. Ever since the message from Kraske confirming the departure of the Falcon *had not arrived!*

The message that would have sent him speeding down the Autobahn to a disused airstrip south of Frankfurt where men were waiting to unload the bombs. Where three of Von Richter's helicopters, painted the muddy green of U.S. army helicopters, were waiting; operated by East German air force pilots who had crossed into West Germany "on business"—according to their papers. They had return tickets back to the East. They wouldn't need them. But they didn't know.

With a trembling hand, Gartmann raised the bottle to refill his glass. The telephone rang. He picked it up, and a voice spoke. A series of numbers. Nothing else. He jotted the numbers down on the pad beside the telephone.

As Gartmann began to decode the message of the numbers, he was overwhelmed with relief. The Falcon was at Tripoli. It would reach Germany on schedule. Thank God! Only a few numbers remained. He decoded the word *hostile* and frowned. Hostile?

THREE HOSTILE PASSENGERS ON BOARD

Gartmann stared blankly at the five words he had written, his mouth hanging open.

It was impossible!

He reached for the phone and dialed.

He was forbidden to make direct contact with the baron under any circumstances. But no such disastrous circumstances could have been foreseen!

Fighting to control his voice—ignoring the baron's initial anger at his breach of security—Gartmann relayed the terrifying contents of the message from Tripoli.

Then the baron spoke again, his voice now calm, soothing. There were only three hostile passengers. *Only three.* They could be dealt with; by means already at their disposal. Gartmann must hurry to the airfield to warn the waiting men and issue new instructions.

Gartmann put the phone down and hurried out, his confidence restored.

The baron replaced the receiver and went to his gun room. He selected a high velocity hunting rifle and slipped two boxes of ammunition in his pocket. In the garage he started the powerful engine of his Mercedes.

He would be there, at the airfield—hidden out of sight.

Ready. In case anything went wrong.

Nothing must stop them now.

They were too close.

Within hours the first act to change the map of Europe would burst upon the world.

For a moment the pilot imagined the scene at Frankfurt air traffic control after his terse report of engine failure, followed by radio silence. They would be watching the plummeting white dot on the radarscope. In a few seconds the alarm would go out and the search for the crashed aircraft would begin.

At a thousand feet he saw the faint white streak of the Rhine River in the blackness below. He leveled off to 400 feet and followed the river north.

Maxwell swallowed hard to clear the deafness caused by the rapid descent of the plane. He checked the buckle on his safety belt for the rough landing ahead. Under his rump on the seat he felt the bulge of the gasoline bomb wrapped in cloth, placed there for easy access—and safety—during the landing.

The pilot saw where the river bent sharply westward at an angle of forty-five degrees. At the crook of the bend he banked tightly onto a due west course, dropped to 300 feet, and throttled back to a hundred miles an hour, five miles above stalling speed.

Beside him the copilot peered out of the starboard cabin window. Vaguely he could distinguish between the solid blackness of the forest land, interspersed by the lighter tones of fields and grassland. He nudged the pilot and pointed to the flashing beacon almost directly below. The pilot nodded and put the plane into a tight turn to lineup on the beacon.

As the plane approached the beacon head-on, the pilot lowered the landing gear and dropped to 100 feet above the woodland. Abruptly the trees gave way to open space, and the pilot "flared out," lifting the nose slightly to reduce the rate of descent and then gently throttling back. Fifteen seconds later the landing wheels touched the ground.

Standing in front of one of the helicopters, Gartmann tensed. Nearby eight members of Group 666 watched as the braking parachute flared out behind the Falcon when it lurched over the uneven ground toward them. All were armed with pistols; two held grenades ready for use.

Only fifty yards away, lying behind one of the trees which marked the edge of the airstrip, Baron von Richter squinted through the sights of his rifle. He had left his car hidden in the woods back down the rough track leading to the airfield and now he approached silently, his presence unknown. He lowered the rifle, satisfied that there was just sufficient light to select and hit his targets. If necessary.

As the Falcon came to a stop within yards of the most forward of the three helicopters with the flashing beacon atop, the two men with grenades sprinted toward the passenger doors.

The pilot leaned forward and, with his left hand, moved a switch. The plane reverberated with the sharp crack of the explosion which tore the door from the fuselage and sent it flying into the air. McGregor was the first to realize what had happened.

Judy had been right. The landing *might* have jammed the door. A fact those who had planned the operation had *not* overlooked. They had inserted small strips of plastic explosive which tore the door free from its housing. Maxwell's attempt to jam the door had been futile.

It was the knowledge of this fact that gave the pilot hope as he gazed up at the starry sky over Tripoli.

A second later four CS gas grenades exploded with dull thuds in the aisle beside McGregor and the others. In an instant the confined space was filled with dense white gas. They choked, their lungs seared by the acrid gas. With blinded eyes, tears streaming from them, they struggled to free themselves from their safety belts before they were suffocated.

Coughing uncontrollably, Maxwell found his seat belt, released it, then blindly groped for the gasoline bomb. But as his hands grasped it, he was overwhelmed by dizziness, his brain cut off from life-giving oxygen. He collapsed in his seat, and the bomb fell and rolled harmlessly into the aisle. Behind him McGregor had also freed himself. With lungs bursting, he first felt around on the floor under Maxwell, then around his seat for the bomb. As his senses began to leave him, he knew he had only a few seconds before he too passed out. If there was any hope of stopping the bombs from being unleashed, it was outside the plane. Summoning every last vestige of his remaining physical and mental strength, he grabbed Maxwell by the collar and dragged him through the solid wall of whiteness to the exit. Together they fell to the ground coughing and retching, their convulsing lungs fighting for oxygen. Beside them was Judy.

"Bring them over here," Gartmann ordered from a few yards back, an automatic in his hand.

Their pistols were taken from them and still gasping and half-blinded, they were dragged and dumped down in front of Gartmann. He looked at the huddled bodies. He was surprised to see one of them had the long hair of a woman. Curious, he moved closer and bent to look at her. Judy blinked up at him through swollen, streaming eyes, and there was an instant of mutual recognition. McGregor, seizing this brief opportunity, lashed out with his leg and cut Gartmann's feet from under him. With a yell of anger, Gartmann fell onto his back, the automatic flying from his hand.

McGregor staggered to his feet. The figures grouped around the exit of the plane, waiting for the gas to clear, were a blur, but that was all he needed. He knew what he must do. The code by which he lived *demanded* it.

He stumbled toward the men, his hands thrust deep into his pockets.

Judy saw him. She held her breath. For she *knew!*

McGregor's mouth gaped, fighting for the air he so desperately needed. Only a few more yards and he would reach the plane—and the men there. *The men who must die.*

They turned their attention away from the plane to stare curiously at the unarmed, battle-clad man staggering toward them, his hands in his pockets.

A few feet away and in the dim light they saw his face clearly. A face so grim and hard, born of a commitment beyond their understanding, they saw in it the imminence of death.

Then he was among them. His hands high above his head. In each hand he held a grenade, the pins levered free while in his pockets. Just for an instant they saw on McGregor's face a look of total contempt.

Then the frozen silence was shattered by the simultaneous explosion of the two grenades.

Maxwell saw the bodies hurtling in the air, to lie scattered and still upon the ground. For a brief moment he was stunned. McGregor had died as he had lived.

Ruthless.

Uncompromising.

Gartmann was still sprawled on the grass, unable to believe what he had seen. Maxwell sprang upon him, and his hands found his throat. "Find the gun," he yelled to Judy.

Wiping her eyes to clear her vision, Judy began to search the grass. A dull glint caught her eyes, and she stooped to examine it. There was a sharp crack, and it was as if a slight breeze had touched the hair at the back of her neck. But it was not a breeze; it was a high velocity bullet. Instinctively Judy flung herself to the ground and yelled to David who had frozen at the sound of the shot, just as he began to stand up over the unconscious body of Gartmann. "Keep down and make for the plane."

Maxwell hit the ground and the two of them wriggled through the grass toward the plane.

Baron von Richter rose to his feet from his hiding place and tried to pick out his targets, but they were lost in the grass and the dimness of the light. He ran toward the plane.

A moment later Maxwell and Judy rose to their feet on the other side of the plane and, looking under its belly, saw the approaching figure with the rifle.

"Make for the trees behind us," Maxwell said.

"Keep the plane between us and the guy with the rifle."

Once in the trees they stopped and looked back. The man with the rifle had stopped and was looking in their direction. Then he turned and disappeared behind the plane.

"Stay here," Maxwell said then crawled back to the edge of the trees. If his hazy recollection was right, the helicopter was only about ten yards from the trees at the end of the airstrip. He wanted to be sure. Then he caught his breath as he saw what he had not registered in the desperate events since they had landed—there were *three* helicopters!

He returned to Judy. "Come on," he said. "I think we can get close enough to get a good look at the man with the rifle. He's got to be the SSD boss man. We'll work around through the trees to behind the helicopters."

"Helicopters?" Judy asked with surprise.

"Yeah, three."

"Perhaps they intend hiding the bombs separately in case—"

"Maybe," Maxwell cut in, but a more ominous thought was already forming in his mind. "Let's go," he said.

Baron von Richter assessed the situation swiftly. Whoever the fugitives were, they were unarmed. They could not intervene. They had only one option: to escape and sound the alarm.

Of the eight men from Group 666, seven had been killed by the grenades and the eighth had but a few minutes to live. The pilots, too, were dead.

That left five of them: himself, Gartmann (who was sitting up clutching his throat), and the helicopter pilots. It was enough. He thanked God Gartmann had survived; only he and the man named Kraske, who had failed to arrive in the plane, knew how to arm the bombs.

They unloaded the bombs from the plane and carried one to each of the helicopters.

Each time, from the nearby trees, Maxwell and Judy saw the face of the baron, but neither of them could identify him. They withdrew silently back through the woods until they reached a rough track. With any luck it would lead them to a road. They broke into a run, their lungs and throats rasping with soreness from the gas. Suddenly Maxwell grabbed Judy's arm. "Hold it," he whispered.

Ahead among the trees, to the side of the track, was the dark outline of a car. They approached it silently, then crouched watching and listening, but there was no sign of anyone in or near the car.

David tried the door. It opened.

The baron heard the engine of his car burst into life. Momentarily he was annoyed with himself for leaving his key in the ignition.

He guessed who the occupants of the car were. But it did not matter. It was a minor problem: he could take care of it later.

All that mattered at that moment was to get the bombs armed and loaded! Then no one could stop the momentous tide of events that would engulf the world!

On instructions from Gartmann, the pilots removed the center panel from one end of the first bomb container. Then with trembling hands Gartmann reached inside and unscrewed the plug in the base plate of the bomb. Taking a detonator from the separate box, he set the timing device and screwed it back in place of the plug.

The operation was repeated with the other two bombs, the timing device being set according to their destinations.

The bombs were now armed.

Then the three containers were lifted and placed under the helicopters and the special hooks on the ends of their rescue hoists attached to hasps on the containers.

The baron went to collect his rifle and returned with it slung on his shoulder.

Gartmann looked up at him nervously. The moment had come when he *had* to tell the baron he had been recognized by one of the escaped agents. He still couldn't really believe it. The English whore—an agent! But he could not deny the evidence of his eyes, nor the look of recognition in *her* eyes.

"It would be inadvisable for me to return to Bonn," he started, trying to sound casual, to minimize the import of what he was about to reveal. "I'm not certain, but I suspect I might have been recognized by one of the escaped agents." He did not elaborate further. "It would be best if I returned to East Germany immediately—just as a precaution."

The baron looked at Gartmann for a moment, unslung his rifle, raised it and shot him through the forehead. The baron turned to the nearest pilot. "Put his body in your helicopter and drop it in the river after you have disposed of the bomb. *After* the bomb. Understand?"

The pilot nodded. He certainly had no wish to make a diversion to the river *before* he had disposed of the bomb.

Then the baron turned to the second pilot. "I will come with you, and you will drop me off near a small town five miles north of here. I will show you where."

As the baron climbed aboard the helicopter, he looked across at the Falcon surrounded by dead bodies and gave a smile of satisfaction. It had all worked out very well. Better even than the original plan. If further proof was needed that the bombs were the work of Group 666—which he doubted—then the dead bodies around the plane would supply it. As for Gartmann, it no longer mattered that he had been recognized. His body would never be found. Never. And very shortly there would be *no one* outside Moscow who knew of his connection to the Russians.

The helicopter rose slowly, and as the bomb left the ground, the weight of it on the rescue hoist activated the first movement of a two-stage, slip switch fuse. Connected to the fuse were ten pounds of plastic explosive packed neatly inside the engine housing. A rather clever device, the baron thought. It would dispose of the helicopters and pilots most effectively —after they had delivered their deadly cargoes.

Maxwell swung the Mercedes off the track and onto the road. He gunned the car to a hundred and twenty kilometers an hour and looked at his watch. It was four thirty-five. Incredibly, only thirty minutes had passed since the Falcon had landed.

He turned to look at Judy. "McGregor was a very brave man," he said.

She gave a half smile. "Brave? Yes, I suppose so. But I don't think he would have called it that. I think he would say he did it because . . . it was necessary."

"That's one way of looking at it," David said.

"*His* way," she answered and turned her head away, the silent tears welling to her eyes.

Ten kilometers along the road they reached a small town, and David slowed down to scan the buildings on either side of the main street. Above the entrance to a stone building he saw the sign he was looking for: POLIZEI. He braked hard, pulled over, stopped, and got out followed by Judy. He took a quick look at the licence plate of the car.

The night duty officer looked up at the two apparitions coming through the door. A man—and a woman! —dressed in battle fatigues, their faces haggard, their eyes swollen and red. He rose from his chair and leaned across the desk, his hand a few inches from his pistol.

David spoke slowly, giving weight to every word, hoping to break down the skepticism with which he knew his words would be received. "My name is David Maxwell," he said. "The woman's Judy Sinclair. We are working for Herr Linke, head of the BND. It is absolutely imperative I speak to Herr Linke immediately."

The officer regarded David doubtfully.

"Listen!" David said, the tension exploding within him. "*Right now there are three helicopters in the air somewhere around here carrying atomic bombs. Got it! Atomic bombs! Now, get onto the BND. For God's sake! Before it's too late!"*

The police officer blinked rapidly. The man was *crazy*! There was something in his eyes; something that was dangerous. He reached for his pistol.

Maxwell's arm shot out like a whiplash. The officer's hand was gripping the butt of the pistol. It stayed there, and then his wrist was lifted and dashed against the desk like a piece of soft rubber. He let out a yell of pain, and the pistol clattered onto the desk.

Maxwell seized it and leveled it at the officer. "You have precisely five seconds to get on that phone before I kill you," he said between clenched teeth.

The officer hurried to the phone and dialed. His words were garbled, but he got the essentials across. He put the receiver down and looked at Maxwell with staring eyes. "They will call Herr Linke at his home and ask him to call you here—if he thinks it is important." The officer finished the sentence quickly and bit his lip, his eyes riveted on the pistol.

"We'll wait," said David.

The duty officer in the control tower at the U.S.A. Air Force base at Ramstein—headquarters of the Fourth Tactical Air Force—gazed out across the wooded landscape surrounding the base. The first weak rays of sunlight whitened the cloudless sky to the east. It was going to be another beautiful summer day. He wished he wasn't going to waste so much of it catching up on his sleep.

The officer was surprised by the sight of a helicopter, about a mile away, skimming feet above the treetops. He frowned and turned to a sergeant. "We have any copters out?" he said.

"No, sir. Not right now."

"Then what the hell's that?"

The sergeant followed the direction of the officer's pointing arm. "Could be some idiot army pilot's lost his way, sir," he suggested with a grin.

"Not even the army can get *that* lost," the officer replied and reached for the binoculars.

The pilot of the helicopter knew (as a result of meticulous testing in East Germany under similar conditions) that he would become visible to the Ramstein control tower at one mile—forty seconds flying time. He also knew that American airbases did not have air defense systems against low flying aircraft. Not that they would have used them if they had—not in peacetime against one small unidentified helicopter.

The pilot looked at Gartmann's dead body and pulled a wry face. He could have done without the job of dumping the body in the river. It would mean a diversion to the river before reaching the RV in the forest to the north where they were to land and be picked up by car. He didn't like it. Getting into Ramstein was the easy part; the trouble would start when he left it. At the final briefing it had occurred to him to ask what would happen to the helicopters after they were left at the RV—their identity could be traced. He had been told that would be taken care of, and he didn't doubt it would. Still . . . he could have done without the diversion.

"It's got no identity markings," the officer yelled, lowering the binoculars. Ten seconds later the helicopter was over the center of the airbase. "There's a crate slung under it. In the name of Christ, what's going on?" The officer was staring at the sergeant.

"Santa Claus maybe," the sergeant joked and grinned again.

The helicopter settled the container to the ground. Then, by dropping a few inches lower, detached the open hook of the rescue hoist from the hasp on the container. The release of weight from the hoist completed the second movement of the slip-switch, and the fuse was activated with a ten-second delay.

"It's got to be a goddamn joke." The officer was shaking his head from side to side. "But I'll tell you this: . . . I-am-not-amused."

The helicopter swooped upward—for ten seconds—then there was a sharp crack, like the burst of a small caliber shell, and the air was suddenly full of flying pieces of metal. The helicopter plummeted to the ground fifty yards clear of the bomb . . . where it could do it no damage.

Men were running from all directions. Within minutes the puzzling object was circled by several hundred curious men.

Two men tried to lift the container from either end. "Jesus! This thing's heavy enough to be a bomb," one joked with a grimace as he lowered his end. "You crazy," the other laughed. "Who'd do—"

A sudden and deathly hush fell on the circle of men. *They knew who'd do a thing like that!* Group 666 had already killed six men from the base and two of their wives!

"Get the hell out!" someone yelled, panic in his voice.

As one man, they ran.

Seconds later the first atomic device to be detonated on German soil exploded with the force of one thousand tons of TNT. And in the holocaust of heat, blast, and radiation thousands of men, women, and children died instantly. The entire base, with its squadrons of F–15 Eagles, ceased to exist. The forest around the base erupted into fire like kindling.

Gartmann's body, the pilot, and the helicopter vanished from the face of the earth.

Thirty miles away David heard the explosion. "Oh my God! Oh-my-God!" He buried his hands in his face. He had been waiting for it, living in terror from the moment he had seen *three* helicopters. From the moment he realized the Russians had done the unexpected—with hindsight, the obvious: they had not *hidden* the bombs; they had used them immediately. Before they could be traced. Before they could be stopped.

The telephone rang, startling David. He had been listening for two more very different sounds.

"For you, Maxwell—Herr Linke." The police officer said regarding David with a new respect.

David took the receiver. "Herr Linke?"

"Yes, Herr Maxwell. I got some crazy garbled message about atomic bombs already in the country."

"One's just exploded," David said and heard the sharp intake of breath from Linke. "Two more are going to do the same any minute now." There was an icy coldness to David's voice now. "Group 666 will claim responsibility, but the Russians are pulling all the strings. It's their party."

"How do you—"

"I'll be in Bonn in two hours," David interrupted. "I'll tell you about it then. Meantime close down on Gartmann's operation. And take this car licence number down." David spelled out the number of the baron's car. "Got it?"

"Yes."

"Trace the owner and arrest him. Use any pretext. He's the big man . . . the Russian connection. We've got to expose him before it's too late."

"Too late?"

"Yes, Herr Linke. The Russian party has only just begun. . . ."

TWENTY-TWO

Brunssum, Holland

General Wade Horton leaned out of bed and pressed the button to silence the bell of his alarm clock. It was 5:00 A.M. exactly.

He stretched, yawned, and waited for the bedside phone to ring. He knew it would ring, and he knew why.

Under normal circumstances the call would have been taken by General Holger Buddenberg, commander of Allied Forces Central Europe. But the general was in no condition to take the call. He was in the morgue.

The previous morning he had gone for his customary hour of horseback riding before breakfast. He had later been found at a lonely spot lying on the ground with his neck broken. He must have been thrown by his horse. The KGB agent who had held him at gunpoint, ordered him to dismount, and then expertly broken his neck and bruised his back, had already returned to Moscow.

Now General Horton lay staring up at the white ceiling, his mind a blank. Waiting. For the phone to ring.

Although his name would go down in history for

the part he was about to play in this day's events, he felt nothing.

For he was insane.

Totally!

The world of reality no longer existed; the affairs of nations were meaningless. His mind was a vault emptied of all reason. Filled only by hate. Demanding only vengeance against the army which had betrayed his son.

Justice would be done.

The phone rang. He let it go on ringing for several minutes, then, reaching out slowly, took the receiver and said "Yes."

The voice at the other end was calm, the speaker selected and trained to be totally controlled in the face of all eventualities. He spoke in a flat monotone, giving the general all the available information. Three massive explosions, believed to be atomic, at Ramstein, Kaiserslautern, and Wiesbaden; cause of the explosions: not known; possibility of delivery by Russian aircraft or missiles: negative; casualties: not known, but undoubtedly heavy.

The general was equally calm: he would be at headquarters directly; meantime all NATO bases should be directed to carry out an immediate search for unusual objects within their precincts. Action to be taken in the event of any such object being discovered: immediate evacuation of all personnel.

The general replaced the receiver, summoned his chauffeur, ate a light breakfast, and got into the waiting car.

He instructed the driver to get him to headquarters quickly.

In fact, the general was not in a hurry; he was awaiting certain imminent developments. He checked his watch. He would reach headquarters around six-fifteen. Fine.

The hum of tense voices silenced as the general entered the room full of staff officers. "Sit down, gentlemen," the general said as he seated himself at the head of the table.

"Have you heard the latest news, sir?" A British staff officer spoke.

The general's hard brown eyes narrowed. "*Latest* news?"

"Yes, sir. On German radio. Group 666 have claimed responsibility for the atomic explosions. They threaten further explosions at American bases within twenty-four hours—unless the order is given immediately that all foreign troops be withdrawn from German soil."

There was not a flicker of change of expression on the general's face as he heard this incredible news. Not that the men around the table with their eyes riveted on him had expected it—he was that kind of man: cool, imperturbable . . . professional.

"Have we any indication how they got these bombs into our bases?" the general asked.

"No, sir." The speaker was an American three-star general. "But we're pretty sure how they *didn't* get in. There are no reports of low flying aircraft in the close vicinity of the bases at the time. Nor of explosions immediately prior to the detonation of the bombs, which rules out the possibility some sort of short-range missile launchers were used."

"Helicopters?" General Horton suggested, his face still impassive.

"One report from German civilians near the base at Wiesbaden shortly before the explosion. But nothing after the explosion. We can forget about helicopters, sir. They might sneak in at dawn without being heard, but they would have been heard and seen by thousands of people after the explosions. No one was asleep after the big bangs!"

General Horton nodded his agreement. "So we must assume the bombs were sneaked into our bases some other way."

"Yes, sir. Hundreds of tons of supplies go into those bases every day. A lot of it from civilian sources. For all we know there are bombs sitting inside other bases right now, just waiting to be detonated by radio."

The general pursed his lips and his eyebrows came together as if in concentrated thought. "Okay, gentlemen. I'm ordering the immediate evacuation of all bases in Germany. Get everybody out and do it fast."

"Sir. With due respect, shouldn't we clear that first with—" The three-star general initiated the suggestion with a frown of concern.

General Horton cut him short. "Forget the red tape, General. I'm in command, and I'm responsible for the lives of three hundred thousand servicemen and about the same number of wives and children. Under no circumstances am I going to make them sweat it out after that radio broadcast and then maybe have them die. Get them out! We'll take care of the command politics later."

TWENTY-THREE

Bonn, West Germany

Shortly after 7:00 A.M., one hour after the staff officers had dispersed to carry out General Horton's orders for evacuation, David and Judy entered the office of Wilfried Linke at the offices of the BND in Bonn.

Linke rose to greet them. For an instant his gray eyes flickered over their exhausted faces and tattered battle fatigues.

"Have you traced the car?" David said quickly.

"Not yet. I am expecting to hear from the police any time now. While we are waiting tell me everything."

Speaking rapidly David began to describe the events of importance since they had boarded the plane at London Airport.

Linke listened intently, only taking his eyes off David's face to take two short telephone calls, his terse replies revealing nothing concerning the subject of his calls.

"You are both to be congratulated," Linke said when David finished. "You have acted with great courage and ingenuity. You have my sincerest condolences on the death of your father and your sister. . . .

And you, Frau McGregor, on the death of your husband. He was a courageous man."

Linke rose from behind his desk and paced the floor in silence for several minutes. He stopped to face them. "I regret I have some disappointing news. One of the calls I took while you were talking was from the police. The owner of the car is Baron von Richter, one of our most respected politicians and industrialists; his credentials are impeccable. Strictly off the record, the baron reported the car stolen from outside an apartment we know to be occupied by his mistress."

David's heart sank. Christ, what a fool! He should have known. Of course the car was stolen. He had been insane to expect men bent on mass murder to drive around in their own cars!

"What about Gartmann's people?" Judy said.

Linke began his pacing again. "They are under interrogation, but I doubt if anything will come from it. They are all small fry." He halted and gave an embarrassed cough before continuing. "The fact is, we have to face the possibility that the Russians are not involved in this thing."

"*What!*" David leaped to his feet in amazement. "Are you out of your mind!"

"With all respect, Herr Maxwell, I must suggest that the events of the last week are more likely to have impaired your judgment than mine."

David was shouting now. "And I *imagined* I saw Kraske kill my father? . . . And Judy didn't *really* recognize Gartmann?"

Linke returned to his seat and looked at Maxwell,

his pudgy fingers forming a "V" under his chin. "I suggest we examine the situation *rationally*, Herr Maxwell."

David lowered himself to his seat, his eyes blazing.

Linke continued. "First, the question of motive. What can the Russians gain from the explosions of three atomic bombs? And there *are* only three bombs; *we* know that. Of course, temporarily, there will be considerable embarrassment between our two countries. But in the end sanity will prevail; American forces will not pull out of Germany. The Russians will have gained nothing. But if their complicity were discovered, detente would finally be dead. And, my dear Herr Maxwell, you know what the Russians call detente—the creeping surrender of the West. They do not want *that* to end."

David could not deny the logic of Linke's reasoning. Neither could he deny the evidence of his own eyes. "I saw Kraske kill my father," he said. "*That* was fact. You're merely theorizing."

"But good theories," Linke replied leaning back in his chair. "And consider what you call 'fact.' Imagine you are a member of the jury. Would you believe—beyond all reasonable doubt—the evidence of a man who had spoken to another man only briefly at the door of an apartment and then claimed he recognized that same man . . . through the slats of an air vent! Or the evidence of a woman who said she recognized a man she caught no more than a glimpse of . . . in the half light of dawn and half blinded by CS gas!"

"It *was* Gartmann—beyond all reasonable doubt." Judy angrily brushed her hair back from her face.

Linke leaned forward, his elbows on the desk. When

he spoke, his voice was patient, understanding. "Believe me, I know you are convinced you are right. You have both been through the most terrible experiences. But now we must be coldly analytical. You saw uniformed members of Group 666 callously gun down helpless Russian prisoners. Does that suggest Russian complicity?"

"I don't know, for chrissake," David said his voice flat, a weariness flowing over him—the exhaustion, the tension, the *horror* of the past twenty-four hours and of Zambu! And now the frustrating dry logic of Linke!

"Probably we will never know what the Russians' real intentions were," Linke said. "It is obvious that at some stage they lost control over Group 666; devoured by the monster they themselves created, so to speak. . . . It may interest you to know that the number of attacks on Russian troops—verified attacks—in East Germany have been even greater than those on your servicemen in this country. Tomorrow I am myself meeting with East German officials in Berlin to discuss methods of coordinating our antiterrorist operations. And the Bundestag is considering introducing the death penalty for terrorists. What more can be done?"

"So that's it. . . ." Judy said bitterly.

Linke shrugged. "What else, Frau McGregor? We have no evidence. . . . This man Kraske is dead. . . . Gartmann has disappeared. . . . There are no leads to follow. What could I do even if I did believe the Russians are involved?"

David fixed Linke with tired eyes. "Let me tell you something," he said. "As a scientist I am trained to work within the tight discipline of known facts. To think logically and objectively. But during the past weeks I have learned something else. When you are dealing with people, not measurable facts, logic is pretty near damn useless. The unexpected almost always happens. The only way you can survive is to follow your instincts and be prepared for anything. So if I were you, I would quit theorizing and start using your imagination: assume the Russians *are* involved, then think what their next move could be. Because, believe me, they are going to make one!"

TWENTY-FOUR

Bonn, West Germany

Wilfried Linke might have been short on imagination, but there was nothing wrong with his sense of propriety or his organizational ability. Herr David Maxwell and Frau Judy McGregor had been booked into separate hotel rooms—without an adjoining door—but with an adequate collection of new and expensive clothes.

David lay back on the bed, exhausted. But sleep did not come easily. Thoughts, recollections, emotions flooded his mind in an unfocused kaleidoscope of images and sensations. So much and such terrible things had happened . . . and for what? In time he became overwhelmed by a numbing sense of foreboding and drifted uneasily into sleep.

He awoke with a scream of rage and hatred. The shattered body of his father lying ripped open under the hail of bullets was still before his eyes.

David struggled to sit up, his whole body soaked with perspiration. Rising unsteadily, he stumbled into the bathroom. He leaned on the washbasin, breathing deeply, staring at his face in the mirror: he was a vision of hatred. Stooping, he splashed his face with cold water, and slowly the passions within him subsided. He shuddered.

He pulled back the drapes and looked out of the window. At once, the deep foreboding which had been with him as he fell asleep flooded back. Cars caromed by, and the front of the hotel was bedlam. Scores of people were fighting around two taxis. He watched just long enough to see one taxi pull away, its rear door open as the occupants kicked and punched at the arms and faces of those still trying to drag them out.

Immediately, David turned to the radio and switched it on. He stood transfixed as he listened to the newscast:

East German radio reports that three atomic bombs have been exploded in Soviet bases in East Germany. . . . Thousands of Russian troops have died. . . . NATO surveillance confirms that the reports are authentic. . . . Responsibility for the explosions has been claimed by Group 666. . . . The bombs appear to have been made in West Africa. . . .

David felt the blood drain from him. There *were* only three bombs! And they had been used in *West* Germany! The Russians had deliberately killed thousands of their own men *with their own bombs*!

There was no other explanation.

A slaughter of their own people.

David snatched up his clothes and began to dress hurriedly as the newscaster went on:

Moscow has announced it has no alternative but to occupy West Germany to root out and destroy the Nazis who are operating from the West. . . . It claims this is not an act of war, but rather a police action necessary to restore stability to central Europe. . . . The occupation will commence at midnight. . . . Provided there is no resistance, negotiations can begin for the reunification of Germany and free elections throughout the country. . . .

Maxwell turned the radio up. The newscaster continued:

At an emergency session of the Bundestag many leading politicians have urged that resistance to the Soviets would be futile. . . . American troops are scattered far from their bases and their armaments. . . . German and other NATO forces would face certain destruction. . . .

In view of this "suicidal" situation, certain senior staff officers of the Bundeswehr have spoken out in support of this view.

Prominent among those in the Bundestag urging that this should not be regarded as a catastrophe, but an historic opportunity to finally resolve the East-West conflict in Europe, Baron von Richter who . . .

Maxwell's hands froze in the act of putting on his jacket.

Baron von Richter!

The man whose car had been stolen.

Stolen!

He whipped his jacket on and rushed out to bang on Judy's door.

She opened it, her eyes still heavy with sleep.

He pushed her back into the room and slammed the door. "Don't ask for explanations; there's no time. When you were in Bonn with Gartmann, did you have criminal contacts? People who can supply guns?"

She stared at him blankly for a minute. "Yes, but—"

"Then get two. *Anything* with silencers. Then meet me as quickly as you can *outside* Linke's. . . . Now get dressed and get moving."

Judy was wide awake now; too experienced to waste time asking questions. But as she went for her clothes, the thought flashed through her mind that this was the way it had been with McGregor.

Maxwell grabbed for the phone and dialed. "Herr Linke?"

"Ja."

"Maxwell."

A silence.

"Have you done some thinking?"

A pause. "Yes . . . I have, Herr Maxwell."

"You've checked the time the car was reported stolen?"

"There's no point now. You could prove nothing, even if we had time. And there is *no* time. . . . There is nothing we can do. . . ." his voice trailed off.

"Maybe I can do something."

"One man? Impossible!"

"Maybe, but will you do it? Check on the car!"

"Yes. But it won't make any difference."

"Something else. Have your men check on Von Richter's movements. I want to know where he will be two hours from now. And," David continued hurriedly, "I need your advice—something only you can tell me."

"Oh! . . . What?"

"Not on the telephone. Send a car to pick me up. There's not a chance in hell of getting a taxi. Tell the driver I'm wearing a dark blue jacket and black pants. I'll be on the sidewalk a hundred yards east of the hotel. If he comes any nearer, he'll get mobbed. We've got a riot going on here."

"Are you sure you're not wasting my time, Herr Maxwell? I've already told you nothing can be done. Baron von Richter—*assuming* you are right about him—has moved too fast. We can't touch him."

"Maybe *I* can touch him," Maxwell answered. "But I *must* talk to you first."

"Very well."

"And a photograph of the baron. I want to see one," David added.

"Yes. But—"

David slammed the phone down.

Then he crossed to Judy's bed, removed one of the sheets, and tore off several strips and put them into a plastic bag.

Judy was ready. She looked ravishing in a long, tight-fitting black skirt and cream silk blouse with flowing sleeves.

David looked at the skirt. "It's not going to be *that* kind of a party."

Judy kicked one long leg shoulder high, and he saw the parting of the hip-length slit down the skirt. "It's for all occasions," she grinned.

He put his arms around her waist, pulling her gently to him. "I wish to God I could keep you out of this. But there's no one else I can trust."

"Don't you think you should tell me about it?" she traced his lips with her fingertips.

He shook his head. "Not yet. I don't think you would approve. I'm not even sure I have the courage to go through with it myself."

She frowned, "Go through with what?"

He shook his head again then kissed her gently and held her tight. "You'll know when the time comes."

Downstairs the lobby was in a state of uproar. Over half the hotel's clientele were foreigners, and not one of them wanted to be in Germany. The staff were beseiged by men and women yelling—some in English, some in German—but all waving fists of money, travelers' checks, even jewelry. Transport was what they were trying to buy. Anything that would move them the minimum fifty miles to the French border; preferably a lot farther.

But, he guessed, about one million foreigners and twice as many Germans had the same thing in mind. The airports would be in chaos, the highways to the west jammed, the gasoline stations untended as the fleeing drivers fought around the pumps. Even the trains pulling out of stations would be festooned with people clinging to the outside of the carriages and on the roofs.

Maxwell shouldered his way to the entrance and out into the street. Christ! It was beyond belief! Men and women fighting like crazed animals over the few taxis. A huge man broke from the crowd carrying a woman under one arm like a sack of straw. He was making for a taxi which had just turned the corner.

"Twenty thousand marks," the huge man yelled at the driver as his wife scrambled into the rear seat. "And the woman in the back's yours all the way to the French frontier. I'll drive."

David hastened on. If it was like this all over Germany, how the hell was anyone going to defend it, even if they wanted to! A car pulled up. "Herr Maxwell?" the driver said pointing a large and effective looking automatic at David's head. "Jump in." The driver eased the automatic back into his belly holster and U-turned the car.

The downtown area was empty. "Where is everyone?" David asked.

"Fighting on the Autobahn, at home glued to their televisions or praying," the driver replied with a dry laugh.

"How much farther?" David asked. He was not familiar with the route and he needed to know.

"About a kilometer," the driver replied.

Three minutes later they passed a narrow dead-end alley leading off the road. "Stop here, please," David said.

The driver glanced at him, puzzled. "Here?" he repeated.

"Yes. I want to walk."

The driver shrugged and stopped the car. Without moving his body weight, David reached for the door with his right hand. "Thanks," he said and crashed his left forearm across the driver's throat. He removed the driver's gun from its holster and struck him on the side of the head with the barrel.

He hauled the unconscious man into the passenger seat, then backed the car into the alley. On the right was a blank wall, on the left a series of unloading bays running down the side of a department store.

He dragged the driver out, tied, and gagged him with the strips of sheet, then hauled him into one of the unloading bays. Opening the hood of the car, he removed the rotor arm and slipped it into his pocket.

Maxwell now had the two things he needed—a car and a gun—neither of which Linke would give him without asking questions he was not prepared to answer.

"Sit down, Herr Maxwell," Wilfried Linke rose wearily and extended a hand over the desk. There was a genuine warmth in his handshake and his tired smile.

David did not return the smile. "The car?" he demanded.

"It was reported stolen at 5:05 this morning. By the baron himself."

A look of grim satisfaction crossed Maxwell's face. "Shortly after *I* stole it a hundred miles away, in other words."

"Precisely. But there's not the slightest doubt the baron's mistress will corroborate he was with her all night and support his claim that he discovered the car stolen from outside her apartment."

David snorted. "Is anyone seriously expected to believe that a sophisticate like Baron von Richter has to sneak out of his mistress's apartment in the early hours of the morning?"

"No, but the matter is academic. It would be your word against his—and he is one of the most respected men in Germany. Not that it will come to that. We have no evidence, not even enough to question him."

"Can I see the photographs?" David asked quietly.

Linke opened a drawer, took out a folder, and tossed it onto the desk. "It won't change anything even if you recognize him."

"It will for me," David answered opening the folder and examining the dozen or so photographs of Von Richter taken at state occasions and party rallies. He closed the folder slowly and looked up, eyes leveled with Linke. "It's him all right . . . the man who was directing the loading of the bombs onto the helicopters—I'd swear to it. But I'd like to keep the photographs."

"By all means," Linke waved a hand.

David looked at his watch: 7:30 P.M. "Where can I find the baron?"

"At his home."

"Has he guards . . . security men?"

"No more than a man of his wealth and position requires in these days of terrorism and kidnapping. A couple of men on the gate . . . three or four in the grounds, probably with dogs."

Linke stared at his hands, his eyes clouded with uncertainty, avoiding Maxwell's. Then he stroked his jowls, took a deep breath, and raised his eyes to meet David's. "Herr Maxwell, I do not know what your intentions are, but I do know you are a man of action. From this I assume that you propose attempting to intervene directly in events which are of a magnitude far beyond your understanding. Your efforts—whatever they may be—can be of no avail whatsoever and will very possibly have disastrous consequences for your own person."

"I'm the one to judge that," David snapped.

"Perhaps. However, you would be advised to hear what I have to say before you make that judgment. We are not merely dealing with one man, Baron von Richter, nor with a simple, if devastating, conspiracy between him and the Russians. We are *engulfed* in the tide of history. The commitment on the part of the Russians is self-evident: their ruthless operations in Zambu and their willingness to sacrifice thousands of their own troops in East German bases."

"Do you think I don't know what's going on?" David interjected.

"Not entirely, no. You are not familiar with the German side of all this. Some years ago Von Richter formulated the *Richterlehre*: a political and historical philosophy which asserts that world peace can only be obtained by a united Europe—including Russia. There are many in Germany who share this view. The activists among them are known to us as the *Weisse Kapelle*."

"The White Chapel?"

"Yes. A secret, though perfectly legal, society. . . . A drink, Herr Maxwell? I could do with one myself."

David waved his hand in a gesture of impatience. "No. Thank you."

Linke carried on speaking as he went to a cabinet and filled a glass. "As I told you, Von Richter is at his home. With him are many known and some *unknown* members of the *Weisse Kapelle*. Among them are politicians and members of the military who have already spoken out today against resisting the Russians and in favor of negotiating with them for a reunified Germany." Linke's eyes narrowed over his raised glass. "So, Herr Maxwell, we are not confronted by a spontaneous or panic reaction to a Russian threat. All too clearly it is a plot, meticulously planned and orchestrated by the *Weisse Kapelle* and the Russians. A cleverly designed coup for the *Weisse Kapelle* to take over Germany under cover of a trumped-up neo-Nazi threat and a so-called Russian police action."

"And the German people are going to stand by and let it happen? I don't believe it," David said.

"If you understood just how clever the plot is, you would not say that with such confidence," Linke replied, seating himself at his desk. "In their hearts most Germans have never accepted the division of their country into two parts. On both sides of the Iron Curtain millions of Germans are welcoming this as an opportunity—an *excuse*, if you will—to become one nation again. And to hell with the consequences for the rest of the world!"

"When we spoke on the phone, I said I had a question I wanted to ask you," David said quietly. "One only you could answer."

Linke nodded.

"If the German people knew that this was a plot. If they knew that they had been tricked . . . *betrayed* . . . what would they do?"

"If they *knew*!" Linke gave a short laugh "My God, they would hang the *Weisse Kapelle* in the streets, and the army would fight to the death."

"Thank you," David said. "That's all I wanted to know. Now, would you do a couple of things for me? I want a tape recorder."

"Of course, but—"

"Fine," David cut in. "The other thing. Contact the German Chancellor and ask him to keep the lines open to the President in Washington and the Prime Minister in London. Tell the Chancellor you expect to receive information that will dramatically affect the situation in Europe."

Linke stared open-mouthed. "Are you serious?" he gasped.

"So serious that if you fail to carry out my request, I will personally kill you," David said.

"But what can—what can *you* do? One man!" Linke spluttered still too astonished by the request to comprehend the threat.

"I can do . . . *one man* . . what no civilized nation in the world can do. Now get me that tape recorder."

For a moment Linke met Maxwell's stare, then lowered his eyes.

Maxwell walked out of the building, the tape recorder slung over his shoulders. Judy was waiting for him.

"Where are the guns?" he said.

"In a car down the street. They're not too keen on making this kind of transaction in front of BND headquarters."

"How many men?"

"Two."

"Okay. Let's go see them."

Judy fell in beside David as he headed rapidly down the street. "David, they want a lot of money! Six thousand marks for two guns and a hundred rounds of ammunition."

"It's a lot of money," David repeated.

"They think people who want guns at a time like this are good for blackmail prices."

"They don't get any brownie points for figuring that out."

"Did Linke give you money?"

"I didn't ask for any."

"David!"

"Linke would have got too curious if I had asked for that kind of money. I don't want anyone interfering. . . . Don't worry. I'll handle it"

"They're armed And *they're* curious."

"I said, I'll handle it."

Judy stopped abruptly. "David, *what is going on?*"

He turned and took hold of her shoulders. "Listen to me," he said, and there was a cold hardness in his eyes she had never seen before. "You have to trust me. I can't talk about it. Not now. Later. Understand?"

"Yes," she said. She didn't understand, but she *did* trust him.

They reached the car. A black BMW with two men sitting in front.

The driver's window glided open. "In the back," he said.

They climbed in. "The guns," David said. "I want to check them."

The man next to the driver surveyed David with expressionless, blue eyes. "Here? In the main street? Don't be stupid."

"There's a quiet alley a short way down. My car is parked there; so is my money."

The man sucked his teeth, scowled, then nodded to the driver. The car shot away from the curb.

"Just ahead on the right," David directed.

The car cruised very slowly past the alley, both driver and passenger scrutinizing it carefully. Satisfied, the driver reversed into the alley and backed to stop a few yards in front of the car David had left there.

The guns were handed to him. He checked them.

"Okay. I'll get the money." David got out and

crossed to the other car. He opened the door, and, leaning forward behind the front seat, he swiftly transferred the gun from his belly holster into the bright plastic bag he had used for the strips of sheet.

He returned to the car and climbed back in beside Judy. "Six thousand marks," he said.

"Six thousand," the man repeated, turning around in the seat to face David.

David reached into the bag and pulled the gun out.

"Get out—fast," David ordered.

They looked at David's gun, and they got out. Fast.

"Get in the other car," David said to Judy opening the door and getting out.

She obeyed. He covered the two men and climbed in beside her.

He swung the car onto the main street.

"Fit the silencers and load the magazines," he said. "We need the guns."

"David. For God's sake! You've got to tell me what's going on."

As he drove, he told her everything—almost. *The Iron Curtain moving to the Atlantic Coast and the total isolation of the United States!* The only way to stop the unthinkable—expose the conspiracy between the *Weisse Kapelle* and the Russians! The one chance: Von Richter. *But he must talk!*

Judy said, "Will Von Richter talk, even with a gun at his head?"

"He'll talk."

"Why should he? Admit to treason!"

"He'll talk," David repeated, the lines of his face grim.

Judy sat in silence. Something indefinable was

happening to David which she only vaguely understood. He was no longer an unwilling participant caught in a deadly world power struggle. Nor was he simply driven by a blinding compulsion to avenge his father and his sister. There was much more. Something deeper. A cold hatred within him. . . . *And she did not know its meaning.*

TWENTY-FIVE

Bonn, West Germany

As they approached the entrance to Von Richter's residence, David slowed down to let a speeding black Mercedes overtake them on the deserted, tree-lined street.

"You're ready?" he said with a quick glance at Judy as the Mercedes shot ahead of them.

"Yes," she answered, her hand under the slit in her long skirt and in her hand, between her thighs, the barrel of the gun with the silencer attached. She thumbed the safety off.

David, with his free hand reached for the door handle, opened it the half inch necessary to free the lug from its housing, then keeping his hand on the handle, held the door closed.

Wide iron gates stood open between the high walls. An ornate arch of wrought iron spanned the gap at the top rising to a centerpiece to which was affixed a heraldic coat of arms in red, black, and gold.

At the side of the gate stood two uniformed guards, submachine guns slung on their shoulders. As David turned into the entrance, one of them moved to block the way, his gun now in both hands, leveled at the windshield.

His companion, his gun also freed from his shoulder but angled downward in the crook of his right arm, advanced to the stationary car and addressed Maxwell through the lowered window. "Your name and identification, *mein Herr.*"

The suntanned guard at the front of the car smiled lasciviously at Judy, showing strong white teeth. Judy hunched her shoulders and lowered her head quickly, a gesture of displeasure at the unwarranted familiarity. Her free hand joined the one already on the butt of the pistol between her legs.

Maxwell turned around, put his right hand on the sill of the open window, and leaned out. He opened his mouth as if to speak, then flung the door open with all his strength. The guard staggered back, caught by the metal corner of the door with tremendous force on the side of his chest.

The suntanned guard took his eyes off Judy, the submachine gun swiveling to the point of danger. In that instant she raised the pistol, aimed, and fired.

There was a sound like a sharp whip of air. Immediately, a neat round hole appeared in the shatterproof windshield two inches above the dash. The heavy bullet shattered the guard's breastbone and tore through his heart. His body hurtled backward into the air, and he crashed to the ground on his back, arms and legs spread-eagled.

The guard by the door stood frozen in fear, clasping the side of his chest, his eyes wild, staring at the automatic in David's hand. He began to raise his hands, his eyes questioning, pleading. David fired. The man died.

Each taking a body, David and Judy dragged them

through and around the opened gates and lay them among the ferns which grew in the shade behind the high walls.

They drove slowly up the long winding sweep of the driveway which led through the grounds to the mansion. Climbing a grass-covered slope, a guard, with a German shepherd on a tight leash, turned to look idly at the car, then continued on his way.

Parked in the wide graveled bay in front of the imposing house, David counted nine cars. He took Judy's pistol, thrust it into his belt next to his own, and handed her the tape recorder. Then they walked to the entrance, side by side, Judy nearest to the house to conceal David's bulging jacket from the eyes of any perceptive observer.

They climbed the steps between the two fluted, black marble pillars which supported the porch.

David rang the bell. A tall, gray-haired butler in a black jacket and pinstriped trousers opened the door. He saw the gun in David's hand, and his mouth opened in a silent gasp. "Make a noise and I'll kill you," David hissed between clenched teeth. "Where is your master, the baron?"

The butler continued to stare. David reached out and, gripping his throat with fingers of steel, pushed him slowly backward into the hall. Judy closed the door behind them.

David's fingers tightened on the throat. "The baron —where is he?" He spoke quietly, but his voice carried a threat no less potent than the gun in his hand. He released the pressure on the butler who turned his head and nodded toward a door. "In there—the library," he answered hoarsely.

"And that room?" David nodded to a door on the far side of the hall.

"The dining room." The butler's eyes were fixed on the gun and the attachment he knew to be a silencer.

"Move in there," David ordered.

Once inside and the door safely shut, David handed Judy her gun. "How many people in the house? Apart from those in the library," he demanded.

"None," the butler answered quickly.

David's eyes narrowed, and his mouth tightened.

"I swear it, *mein Herr*!" the butler spoke quickly. "The baron's wife went to Brazil three days ago. Many members of his close family have gone as well. A family reunion. The baron was too busy to join them."

David grunted. *That* made sense. Von Richter *had* been too busy—far too goddamn busy. And he *would* want his family out of Germany—when so much remained unpredictable, events that might require instant and unhampered flight.

"The servants?" David snapped.

"None. This morning the baron told them to return to their homes. He said they should be at home with their families at a time like this."

That made sense too, David thought. *At a time like this* he would not want curious servants in the house.

"If I find one person in this house outside that library, you die," David said.

"I tell the truth. I *swear it*!" The butler's voice trembled.

"I hope so," David said. "Now take us to the library. Just open the door—without knocking—and walk in."

The butler led the way on unsteady legs with David

and Judy behind him. From years of ingrained habit, he raised his hand to knock, remembered, grasped the knob, opened the door, and entered.

Maxwell pushed him to one side and took in the scene with one glance. Nine men around a dark mahogany table. At the head, Baron von Richter. Four men on each side, papers in front of them, three in the uniforms of senior officers of the armed forces.

"Hands on the table and keep them there." Maxwell's command was harsh, not open to serious question.

Hands moved to the table—some quickly, others more slowly, but they all moved. Nine pairs of eyes stared in amazement at the man and woman holding pistols with silencers.

Maxwell spoke. "Von Richter, call the guards in the grounds. I want them in *here,* immediately. You will give them no explanation. Do I make myself clear?"

If the baron was perturbed, his watchful eyes gave no sign of it. "My dear fellow," he said with a faint smile. "I don't know what you want, but I would advise you to consider. There are nine of us—two of you. You may, if you are lucky, kill four of us. The other five—he raised his eyebrows and gave a slight shrug of his powerful shoulders—will kill you. I suggest you sit down and tell us what you want before you do anything foolish."

Maxwell did not know if Von Richter knew who he was. It did not matter. The baron was playing the only game open to him: with nine of them in the room and three or four guards on the grounds, time was his ally. Time for the two armed intruders to make a mistake; time for the guards to find their dead compatriots at the gate and know the house had been penetrated.

For this reason alone Maxwell must act swiftly. And there was another compelling reason for a quick and brutal response to the baron's calm composure. *It was imperative the baron understood—really understood—he was confronted by a man who would show no mercy. None!*

Maxwell moved the barrel of his pistol five degrees to his left and fired. A senior German officer at the end of the table hurtled backward in his chair, his neck arched in death as he slumped to the ground.

"Now there are eight of you, Baron. Every five seconds you delay there will be one less. Get the guards." His voice was vicious, almost a hissing sound. "One," he counted, and moved the direction of the gun toward the head of the table.

Eight pairs of eyes were turned to the baron. "For God's sake, do what the maniac says!" the man next to the baron urged hoarsely.

The baron hesitated, and Maxwell caught a fractional glimpse of fear in his eyes.

"Two . . . ," Maxwell said.

The baron rose to his feet, signaling his compliance with a curt nod of his head. He pressed a button on a console and spoke. "Schmidt, Keser, Gerlach—you hear me?" A short pause, then acknowledgments came through the speaker. "Report to me in the library immediately."

Von Richter turned to Maxwell. "Satisfied?"

"Yes," said Maxwell. But he wasn't. More extreme measures would be necessary before he could be confident that there *were* only three guards. And he would take *whatever* measures were necessary. *The freedom—maybe the lives of millions were at stake! Nothing—absolutely nothing—could be left to chance.*

The door opened, and the first guard entered. He stopped inside the door at the sight of the eight men sitting rigid, their eyes riveted on the wall behind him. He whipped around, grasping for the submachine gun on his shoulder.

"Don't do it!" Maxwell commanded from behind the door.

The guard froze.

"Against the wall," Maxwell ordered.

The man obeyed.

Maxwell closed the door.

In turn the other two guards appeared.

The three of them stood against the wall.

"Which of you is Schmidt?" Maxwell spoke.

"Me," one of them answered with a look of surprise.

"Schmidt," Maxwell said. "Are there any more guards in the grounds?"

Schmidt's eyes darted for an instant to Von Richter; then he looked Maxwell straight in the eye. "No, *mein Herr*. Only the three of us."

Maxwell fired. Schmidt's hand flew to his wounded shoulder.

"The next one's in the head," Maxwell said. "How many more guards?"

"Two . . . ," the terrified guard gasped.

"Get-them-in-here, Richter, before I start shooting around the table." Maxwell's face was tight with hatred as he spoke the words.

This time the baron hastened to obey.

The guards arrived. Maxwell disarmed them and ordered them against the wall with the others. He handed a submachine gun to Judy. "Keep them here," he said quietly. "I'm going to talk to the baron—alone. Only *his* words can expose the Russians. Time is running out. A few hours—that's all we have. Do you understand what I'm saying?"

Judy's eyes were wide. "No, David, You *can't*!"

Maxwell met her eyes. "I have no choice."

"Then in the name of heaven, let me do it! *Please,* David. I have seen more brutality than you have ever dreamed of. I can stand it. You won't be able to. And if you do. . . . Oh, David, it will kill *you*."

Maxwell shook his head. "It is my decision. I must do it. No one else can bear the consequences of such a decision."

Judy knew she had lost. But she made one last attempt. "*You* will never break the baron. He is a strong man. But there are things that I—a woman—can do to him that you could never do to another *man*."

"I-will-break-him." Maxwell hammered out the words. "The effect on myself is irrelevant."

Maxwell turned to face the table, looking at each of the men in turn.

The baron returned his gaze with cool, impassive eyes.

Maxwell looked at him for a long moment, then turned and left the room taking the tape recorder with him. He placed the machine on the table in the dining room. He switched it on and began to speak:

MY NAME IS DAVID MAXWELL. I AM SPEAKING FROM THE RESIDENCE OF BARON VON RICHTER IN BONN, GERMANY. THE TIME, 8:30 P.M. THREE AND A HALF HOURS BEFORE THE PLANNED OCCUPATION OF WEST GERMANY BY SOVIET FORCES.

Briefly Maxwell described all that had happened from the day his father had disappeared. He concluded:

IN SUMMARY, THREE BOMBS ONLY WERE MANUFACTURED IN ZAMBU. BARON VON RICHTER WAS INSTRUMENTAL IN THEIR DELIVERY. THE BOMBS EXPLODED IN EAST GERMANY WERE PART OF THE PLAN BY THE RUSSIANS TO OCCUPY WEST GERMANY UNDER THE PRETEXT OF ESTABLISHING PEACE AND ORDER. THE WEISSE KAPELLE, HEADED BY BARON VON RICHTER, HAS BEEN AN INTEGRAL PART OF THIS CONSPIRACY.

Maxwell depressed the "pause" button and rubbed his forehead in thought for a few minutes. Then he continued, choosing his words carefully:

TO PREVENT THE IMMINENT ENSLAVEMENT OF EUROPE AND THE CONSEQUENT DISASTROUS ISOLATION OF THE UNITED STATES OF AMERICA, NO ACTION CAN BE CONSIDERED TOO EXTREME. I INTEND TO PERSUADE BARON VON RICHTER TO EXPOSE THE SITUATION FOR WHAT IT IS—A RUSSIAN PLOT. THE METHOD OF PERSUASION WILL BE TORTURE. THERE IS NO ALTERNATIVE.

FROM HERE ON, THIS TAPE WILL COMPRISE A DIALOGUE BETWEEN MYSELF AND BARON VON RICHTER. ALL STATEMENTS MADE BY THE BARON WILL BE UNDER DURESS. BUT

A MAN CANNOT CONFESS TO WHAT HE DOES NOT KNOW. IT FOLLOWS THAT ANY INFORMATION HE MAY DIVULGE WHICH SUPPORTS THE EXISTENCE OF, AND HIS COMPLICITY IN, A RUSSIAN CONSPIRACY MAY BE ACCEPTED AS TRUTH.

THE DIALOGUE COMMENCES NOW—

Maxwell pressed the stop button, picked up the recorder, and left the dining room. At least a dozen doors led off from the hall. One would be the cellar. He opened the furthest door and felt the cool draught of air. He found the light switch and saw the stairs leading downward.

Rack after rack of dust-covered bottles stretched down the length of the cellar.

At the end face of the center rack, Maxwell grasped the steel struts which supported the wire structure laden with hundreds of bottles. It was rock firm, unmovable. Kneeling, he slipped the tape recorder under the five-inch clearance between the stone floor and the bottom layer of bottles. He pressed the start button then made his way up the stairs.

As he entered the library, the scene was like a tableau of wax figures: the men around the table motionless, the silence complete.

Maxwell went to the heavy velvet drapes at the window and ripped away the braided silk ties. "Richter!" he said with a quick turn of his head. "Move."

The baron rose and walked steadily to the door. He was ready. He had assessed the situation. Undoubtedly, this American and the woman with him were the two who had escaped from the Falcon. They had probably reported all they knew to the BND. No doubt they suspected his complicity in the atomic explosion. But they had no proof. They were powerless to act. So what did the American think *he* could do at the eleventh hour?

The baron could not answer this question.

But two things were clear. One: the American was under extreme stress, operating at the very limits of his self-control. Two: the American wanted him *alive.*

The American was vulnerable!

As they descended the stairs to the cellar, Maxwell noted that despite his size, the baron moved with the effortless ease of a man in the peak of condition—an athlete. Maxwell's grip on the pistol tightened.

Part way along the cellar between the racks, the baron's hand flew out to seize the neck of a bottle. He whipped around, the bottle directed with deadly accuracy to strike Maxwell's wrist. In his split second of surprise, David realized his mistake. He could not fire!

A violent pain shot up his arm, and the gun clattered to the stone floor. The baron was on him like a lion. His powerful arms circled Maxwell's body binding his arms, and the veins stuck out on his neck like rods of steel as he squeezed Maxwell in a bear hug of crushing power.

Desperately Maxwell struggled to gain purchase on the ground to break the baron's grip. But the baron, a good two inches taller, leaned back squeezing him with biceps of iron against his bull chest.

With one supreme effort, Maxwell forced his rib cage to expand and took a gasp of air. He arched his neck back and lunged forward with his forehead into the baron's face. Anticipating the blow, the baron jerked his head aside. But his concentration was momentarily broken. Maxwell flung his feet forward behind the baron's legs and brought his heels crashing down into the taut tendons of the baron's ankles.

The baron's legs buckled. With his feet firmly on the ground, Maxwell felt all the pent up fury in him explode in an immense near-berserk surge of strength, and he broke from the baron. He smashed the edge of his hand into the baron's neck, sending his heavy frame sprawling to the ground. Maxwell jumped to crash down with his knees onto the exposed stomach of the prostrate man. The baron's mouth flew open as the air shot out and his face twisted in pain.

Sitting astride the baron's chest, Maxwell seized his hair and started to bang his head against the stone floor with savage force. His mind became a vortex of blinding whiteness, the blood pounded behind his eyes. In his mind, only the image of his father's face at the moment of death swirled in and out of focus. Some sanity remained. *He must not kill this man!* He stopped, gasping for breath. The blood-covered face of the baron took form before his dazed eyes, and he was seized with panic. He *had* killed the man!

He grabbed the baron's wrist and groped for his pulse. He let out an audible sigh of relief as he felt the steady rhythm of the pulsating blood. The man had the body of an ox. Maxwell dragged the body and propped it in a sitting position against the end of the rack where the tape recorder was hidden. Rapidly he threaded one of the lengths of cord from the drapes through the wire framework and tied it tightly around the baron's neck. Similarly, he secured the baron's waist and hands to the solid structure. Then he squatted down in front of him and waited.

The baron's eyes slowly opened; he blinked, then grimaced as he moved his head and felt the chaffing of the cord binding his neck. His piercing blue eyes focused on Maxwell. "What is it you want with me?" he said hoarsely. His mouth was stiff; he licked his lips.

"Do you know who I am?" Maxwell said softly.

"A murdering savage." The baron's voice was heavy with contempt.

Maxwell kept his voice low, speaking slowly, seeking in this way to control the emotions which threatened to erupt within him. "No, Richter. It is men like you . . . politicians, statesmen. You pretend to act in the name of some political ideal. But underneath you are obsessed with power. Arrogant. You hold ordinary people in contempt. You manipulate the weakness that is in all men for your own ends. Your hands may not touch blood, but it is *you* who are the murderers, the savages."

"For a hired killer, your eloquence is most impressive," the baron replied. "However, I do not imagine you are here merely to lecture me with your adolescent sentimentality."

"No, Richter, I have come for the *truth*!" Maxwell's voice was a whisper. "My father and sister were killed by the men who made those atomic bombs. But the brutal sadists who did it were pawns. *You* gave them the licence to torture and kill. You have no sympathy with the neo-Nazis, yet you used Group 666 to make bombs. Why, Richter—why?"

Maxwell's eyes were locked with the baron's, but he saw nothing in their cold iciness.

"You're mad! I had nothing to do with those bombs."

The back of Maxwell's hand slammed down on the baron's face with vicious force . . . once, twice, and on and on, sending his imprisoned head jolting from side to side as, once again, the fury within Maxwell was unleashed.

The baron's face was smeared with blood and it covered the torn flesh of his cheeks and mouth.

"The truth, I said, the truth!" Maxwell said between clenched teeth. "I saw you unload the bombs!" He seized the pistol and crashed the barrel across the baron's mouth. The baron's jaw shattered. A sliver of bone protruded white and jagged from his cheek and the blood splattered from his mouth onto the floor.

OH GOD. LET HIM TALK. I CAN'T DO THIS. I CAN'T. The words screamed inside Maxwell's head.

The baron, broke into a paroxysm of coughing between his swollen, torn lips, and tried desperately to clear the blood and teeth from his throat. He gasped, "I know nothing about the bombs. Nothing."

"You are lying!" Maxwell stooped and raised the gun threatening to strike another blow.

The baron shook his head. "I speak the truth. I swear it," he said, meeting Maxwell's eyes. "But now . . . ," he swallowed blood, "now I act to save my people. Germany must make peace with Russia or be destroyed."

Maxwell's stomach churned, gripped by a chilling fear: the terrible realization that he had not done enough! *He must go on!* Somehow! He must act quickly, *ruthlessly*—beyond all civilized limits. Nothing less would break this man.

With shaking hands he unbound the baron's wrist, splayed the fingers on the stone ground and, kneeling on the wrist, held it there.

He gripped the pistol by the barrel and raised it above his head. He forced himself to see again the body of his father being torn apart by the storm of bullets from Kraske's gun—but his hand remained frozen in the air. *This he could not do!* Kill the baron, yes, but methodically crush the bones of a defenseless man . . . ?

Maxwell raised his stricken eyes from the exposed fingers. Through the swollen flesh of his battered face, he felt the baron's eyes were on him, and their eyes locked. In those eyes Maxwell saw the cold contempt and mocking of the victor for the vanquished—the arrogance of the ruthless and powerful toward the ordinary men of tolerance and decency.

The two men's eyes remained locked, each reading the other's thoughts. In those few moments Maxwell was filled with a determination even more powerful than the passion of his anger. He *must* find the strength of will to overcome every humane instinct within him. Failure would be an unforgivable act of cowardice.

His eyes returned to the baron's fingers, and, without hesitating, he slammed the butt of the gun down onto the baron's thumb with all of his strength. He felt the crunch and saw bare bone suddenly appear between the flesh and blood as the top of the thumb was severed at the joint.

The baron stifled a cry of pain and tried desperately to pull his hand from under Maxwell's knee.

Maxwell struck again and again. Then he stared, mesmerized with disgust, at the sight of the soggy mess in a pool of blood that seconds ago had been a man's hand. He raised his eyes to the baron's face. It was drained white, contorted with pain; but the eyes were still defiant, challenging.

Maxwell's stomach heaved. He felt the strength go from his limbs. When he spoke, his jaw was stiff, the words thick. "I'll give you one more chance, Richter. If you do not answer with the truth, I'm going to pulverize *every* inch of bone in your arms and legs. Even if you live, you will spend the rest of your life in a wheelchair—a head on a torso, no arms, no legs. Now, once again; why did you detonate those bombs?"

"I did not. . . ." Somehow the baron's smashed lips formed the words, the blood spewing from his mouth. He raised his arm as if in protest, and the hand hung there like a piece of raw meat, the blood dripping. He looked at it, then thrust it into Maxwell's face in an act of total defiance. Maxwell jerked back, wiping the gore and pieces of flesh from his face.

Seizing an empty wine crate, he grabbed the Baron's foot and slammed it on top of it. Straddling the outstretched leg, he held it steady, the knee gripped between his thighs. He bared the leg, then raised the gun and brought the butt down on the baron's shinbone with all his strength.

The bone snapped with a sickening crack, and the cellar was filled with the baron's roar of agony. He raised his free leg and kicked Maxwell's back with enormous force. Maxwell sprawled forward, knocking the baron's foot off the crate. As it hit the floor the leg bent into a grotesque angle, and the broken shinbone tore through the flesh of the leg. The baron screamed out in pain, and the blood oozed from around the protruding stump of bone.

Maxwell regained his feet, knowing he had to go on. He had to convince the baron there was no hope for him. That unless he spoke the truth, he *would* be pulverized into a physical cabbage.

He grabbed the baron's broken leg, placed the foot on the crate again and ripped the shoe off. For an instant he looked at the mutilated body of the baron —his shattered face, the bleeding splodge that was his hand, and the gleaming whiteness of the shinbone— and he was filled with a loathing of himself so intense the strength drained from him. *He* had done this! This obscenity!

Maxwell's body started to shake, the perspiration pouring from his ashen face. The cellar spun around him, and he began to sway.

Through the two slits that remained between the swollen flesh around his eyes, the baron saw all this. The reason for him being tortured no longer mattered to him. *But his will would not be broken.* Not by another man! And *this* man, he knew, had all but lost their gruesome battle.

Despite the agony of pain which wracked his body, the baron felt triumphant. He had won!

But, once again, Maxwell steeled himself to resist emotions.

He must not feel!

The fate of millions hung in the balance.

The choice was his.

Maxwell steadied himself, and the butt of the gun descended with a sickening crunch onto the baron's bare ankle.

Maxwell bludgeoned again and again, working methodically; first the ankle and foot and then the leg as far as the break.

At first the cellar echoed with the baron's screams; then there was silence save for the steady thudding of metal on flesh and bone. Sometimes a hard cracking sound, sometimes a dull squelching.

Maxwell stopped, and for an instant his eyes rested on the horrific remains of the baron's leg. His clothing soaked from the flying blood, splattered with flesh. And again the cellar began to swim before his eyes.

Dazed, Maxwell raised his eyes to look at the baron's face. His head was slumped forward, his eyes closed. He was unconscious.

Somehow Maxwell managed to rise to his feet. His legs were like water. He lurched from side to side against the racks, sending bottles cascading to shatter on the stone floor. He reached the cognac, pulled out a bottle, and returned to the baron. Forcing the baron's mouth open, he poured it down his gullet.

The baron's heavy shoulders heaved as he choked on the strong liquid, before bursting into a fit of coughing. His eyes opened to meet Maxwell's, and he took a deep breath.

"Talk, or do I start on the other leg?" Maxwell's voice was hollow.

"I have nothing to say. . . ." the baron forced the words out, his face twisted with pain. Maxwell's heart stopped. He could not go on! "Nothing that can help you . . . not now. Too late," the baron mumbled.

"Then for God's sake talk," Maxwell heard himself screaming.

The baron's swollen and broken face grimaced. Then he spoke slowly, forcing the words from his throat, his lips hardly moving. "The bombs, yes . . . Group 666 a cover."

"Why?"

"The Russians plan to invade Europe. . . . The attack . . . in two days."

Maxwell caught his breath, not certain he had fully understood. "You mean a military attack—nothing to do with the activities of Group 666?"

"Yes."

"How do you know this?"

"I know . . . from Moscow."

"You are a Communist." An accusation.

Again the bizarre grimace and a cough that might have been an attempt at a laugh. "No . . . a German . . . a European."

"Then why didn't you warn your government of this attack?"

"My country a battlefield? . . . Destroyed. . . . A hopeless war! The Russians fear only American missiles . . . devastation of their own country. They do not believe America will use those missiles—not to defend Europe. So. . . ."

The baron's voice trailed off, and his eyes closed, exhausted by the effort of speaking. The pools of blood around his shattered leg and hand were slowly spreading across the stone floor. He would soon lose consciousness.

Maxwell put the bottle to the baron's lips. Another bout of coughing, weaker this time. Slowly the baron's eyes opened.

"So . . . ?" Maxwell prompted.

Emptiness seeped into the baron's eyes. He stared vacantly at Maxwell. Then with a heave of his huge chest, he gulped for air, and recognition returned to his gaze. "I had to stop the devastation of my country," he said. "We used Group 666 as a pretext."

"We? Who're we?" It had to be on the tape!

"The Russians, the *Weisse Kapelle*—we worked together."

"And the atomic bombs in East Germany?" Maxwell held his breath; the one question to clinch it all—to expose beyond all doubt the depth of Russian complicity.

"Russian . . . deliberate sacrifice."

Maxwell felt the relief surge through him. *He had it!* All of it!

On hands and knees he moved forward to reach for the tape recorder under the rack. He pulled it out and pressed the stop button.

The baron was watching him. A slow, painful smile shaped his face. "You are wasting your time . . . my friend. It is too late."

But Maxwell wasn't listening. Suddenly he was overwhelmed with a numbing exhaustion, his psyche drained of all strength. Beyond caring. He knew only that somehow he must hold on to his sanity long enough to get the tape to Linke. . . .

He released the tape and, clutching it, reeled forward and up the stairs.

Judy faced him as he entered, and she saw in his vacant, glazed eyes the hell he had endured.

He walked stiffly like an old man to where one of the guard's submachine guns lay on the ground. Stooping, he picked it up, then turned to face the men around the table; their eyes riveted on this specter, his clothing stained with the baron's blood.

"If one of you tries to leave this room in the next five minutes, he dies," he said softly.

He led the way out of the library and into the hall. "They won't move," he said.

"I know," Judy answered.

Halfway across the hall he suddenly stopped. He handed the tape to Judy. "I'm staying here," he said. "Go to Linke. Tell him *everything* is on the tape."

"What is it, David?" Judy looked at him, her face fearful with anxiety.

For a long moment he looked at her in silence, agony in his eyes. When he opened his mouth, the words were like the groan of some wounded animal. *"In the name of God, I don't know what it is! Just go!"*

He turned on his heel and descended the stairs into the cellar and sat against the wall facing the baron.

Maybe it was his imagination, but for a moment he thought he saw the faintest of smiles come to the pallid face of the dying man. A smile of recognition, forgiveness, respect? He did not know. Any more than he knew why he had been drawn so inevitably to sit and watch the lifeblood drain from the mutilated body of his adversary.

How long he remained motionless, his eyes fixed on the baron's face as he slowly drifted into the coma that preceded death, he had no idea. But when the moment of death came, a rattle in the baron's throat as his lungs finally filled with his own blood, Maxwell stopped breathing.

TWENTY-SIX

Washington, D.C.

Five men sat in comfortable sofas at one end of the Oval Office. They were leaning forward intently, listening to the tape machine placed on the low table set between them.

As the last faint words of Baron von Richter came from the amplifier, the director of the CIA rose to stop the tape.

It had been relayed half an hour earlier on cleared lines from Bonn. It was the third time the men in the Oval Office had played it back, listening to every word, imagining what must have taken place in the silences punctuated by screams.

"Maxwell's identity has been authenticated beyond all doubt," the CIA director said, facing the President. "His voice has been identified positively by our chief operative in Bonn and by German and British intelligence."

"A confession extracted under extreme duress . . . ?" The secretary of state frowned in doubt as he spoke. "Can we act on evidence like that? No court of law—"

"For God's sake," the national security adviser interrupted impatiently. "Since when was diplomacy—war! —conducted in a court of law! Personally, Mr. President, I go along with it. Maxwell *did not* lead in his questions. In my opinion, once the baron was convinced Maxwell meant to go through with his threat, the baron decided to talk. Why not? He figured it was too late to stop the Russians, no matter what."

The President's mouth tightened. "Is it . . . too late?" He addressed the secretary of defense.

"With conventional weapons, yes, sir, Mr. President. Germany's in a hopeless mess. We've got only two options. One: we threaten an all-out nuclear strike against Russia if her troops move into West Germany. Or, two: we threaten to saturate her troop concentrations and communications all along the East German frontier with nuclear missiles. Stop them dead in their tracks."

The secretary of state ran his fingers nervously inside the collar of his shirt. "You realize either option could lead to a full-scale nuclear war?" He turned to the President. "You'd have to take the American people with you on that. I doubt—"

For an instant anger flashed in the President's eyes. "I think you underestimate our people," he cut in abruptly. "Maybe they wouldn't put the country on the line simply to save Europe. But when they know they have been double-crossed by the Russians, they'll go to hell and back to stop them. *Nobody* makes that kind of fool of our people. You can bet on it. We'll go for the second option."

"Sort of ironic, isn't it," said the national security adviser with a wry smile. "According to that tape the Russians were going to attack Western Europe anyway . . . calculated we would never use nuclear weapons to stop them. Now they've outsmarted themselves. Done the one thing to guarantee we *will.* There'll be no attack—not now. They don't want to get into a nuclear confrontation."

"It's more than ironic," the President answered grimly. "It's downright terrifying to think history has been changed by one man . . . this Maxwell. I want to meet him." The President turned to the secretary of defense. "And I want General Horton right on the mat in front of me the second he hits Washington. I'm the commander-in-chief of this army. Ordering the evacuation of our bases without my authority was at best gross dereliction of duty, at worst an act of downright panic. I'm going to discharge him . . . dishonorably . . . *personally*!"

The director of the CIA spoke. "Mr. President, sir, we've just heard from the military there's some doubt about the way General Buddenberg died. Seems his injuries are not totally consistent with a fall from a horse."

The President's mouth tightened. "Is that right?" he said slowly. He was silent in thought for a few minutes, then he slammed his fist on the desk. "That's it! It's all been too goddamn pat. The bombs, the *Weisse Kapelle,* the general's 'accident' . . . the evacuation. Panic? Hell! The Russians have got long arms. My guess is that one of them reached General Horton."

"It's possible," the director of the CIA said. "We'll find out."

"*After* I've seen him," the President said. "Now get Moscow on the hotline. Seems there's a lot of things they still don't know about Americans."

TWENTY-SEVEN

Washington, D.C.

David Maxwell felt the warm sun on his face as he advanced toward the President to receive the Presidential Medal of Freedom.

He walked steadily, erect, anxious that his bearing should not betray his inner anguish.

They had found him in the cellar sitting motionless, his eyes fixed on the face of the dead baron. The doctors later said he was in a state of shock.

Maxwell heard their words and wondered what they could know of the hell into which he had plunged himself, through a supreme effort of will—forged of necessity—and entered a world of moral twilight wherein there was no act of which he could say: *This I will not do.*

And he was filled with a profound sadness and a grieving for the lost innocence of the man he had once been.

Before the horrors of Zambu. The horrors of the cellar.

The President pinned the medal on Maxwell's chest.

For a moment the two men faced each other in silence. Then the President took Maxwell's hand and held it in both his hands. "A privilege, Mr. Maxwell," he said quietly.

David turned and descended the rostrum to return to Judy amid tumultuous applause.

Judy took his hand in hers and together they walked across the lawn, screened from the clamoring reporters by a solid phalanx of security people. The media wanted the story. The full story. They would never get it. Not from Maxwell and not from the handful of men in the world who knew at least some part of it.

Even an open society had to have its dark secrets—truths better left untold, deeds necessary to protect the freedom of decent men and women. Freedom, preserved by the brutal torture of a man, a general driven insane by the sacrifice of his son. The price of freedom: paid by a few, best kept from the many. A deceit, necessary until the world no longer lived in the shadow of evil.

The car driven by Judy came to a stop at the door of a small cottage in the Virginia countryside. David got out. He smelled the scent of summer air and saw the green leaves of the trees gently rustling in the soft breeze. At the bottom of the grassy meadow in front of the cottage, the sun glistened on the rippling waters of a small stream. From the distance he heard the happy laughter of children.

He took a deep breath of the soft air and felt hope. Hope that with time, with Judy's help, his mental agony would heal. . . . That they would find peace of mind. . . . Together.